Greater Trouble in the Lesser Antilles

Charles Locks

GREATER TROUBLE
IN THE
LESSER ANTILLES

Charles Locks

SCARLETTA PRESS
MINNEAPOLIS

Library of Congress PCN
2006934666

ISBN 13: 978-0-9765201-3-9
ISBN 10: 0-9765201-3-3

Book design by Mighty Media Inc., Minneapolis, MN
Cover: Anders Hanson
Interior: Chris Long

First edition | First printing

10 9 8 7 6 5 4 3 2 1

Manufactured in the United States of America
Distributed by Publishers Group West

A selection from **THE QUEUE**™

for friends in the islands
and friends in the high lands

St. Judas

no longer felt much like paradise. The island wore a steel-gray hemispheric skullcap, and an unusually cool breeze ruffled the leaden waters of the bay. I could barely make out my gray Zodiac inflatable tied to the concrete dock, not to mention its gray Yamaha outboard. The myriad grays prompted me to ponder the ambiguity of life in Flamingo Bay and reminded me of the dull eyes of dead men. I figured the sun would shine tomorrow, and the blue waters would sparkle again, but one thing wouldn't change: my friend Leif the Thief would remain dead.

Five days ago—the afternoon I returned from a voyage to South America—Leif's body was found in Doctor's cistern. I hadn't been here to see that he behaved himself, and I hadn't been here to learn if others behaved themselves. If I didn't know better, I'd have to concede that everyone in Flamingo Bay was absent along with me, for nobody seemed to know anything. Nobody even admitted knowing how he died. And the asshole cops weren't talking.

His death shocked and numbed us. Countenances grew quieter and grimmer. Suspicion, stifling. Custom, not spontaneity, sustained exuberance. We feared the killer could be one of us. Nobody wanted to believe it. Enough years had passed that only a few of us could recall the name of the last person murdered in Flamingo Bay.

Leif was a thief, but he was also a likable guy. As long as he didn't touch you for too much, you were inclined—after getting over the initial anger—to laugh and shrug your shoulders, but you couldn't just laugh and shrug your shoulders when his corpse turned up in Doctor's cistern.

The put-put of an ancient outboard caught my attention. I looked up to see Cherry Mary and Billie dinghy ashore from *Sappho*. Finally. I'd been waiting for Billie to help me transport the six-dozen T-shirts we'd silk-screened last night, the shirts she designed to commemorate Leif's funeral.

I got to know Billie several months ago when she and Wendy and I formed the Flamingo Bay Literary Society. Since then, we'd shared something of a topsy-turvy relationship, though probably not as chaotic as the relationship Billie shared with Mary. What Mary and I had in common: we both liked girls. The other thing we had in common: we both loved Billie.

Billie tied up at the dock and said, "What're you doing here?"

"Sitting on a dock on the bay, waiting on you."

"Don't tell me," she said, climbing out of the dinghy and holding the painter for Mary. "Your truck is missing."

I nodded, my eye drawn to the gold ring she wore on the second toe of her left foot, her only jewelry.

"Captain Brian, you okay?" Mary asked, stepping onto the dock.

"Pretty okay. You?"

"I don't know. It's the end of an era, isn't it?"

I nodded.

Mary, a lanky, freckled redhead pushing thirty, was an advertisement for a healthy meatless lifestyle. She stood a head taller than her lithe yellow-haired companion.

Billie said, "I'll get my jeep."

The two of them headed toward the Congo Club.

A growing din drifted across the bay from Easys, where folk assembled for Leif's last hurrah, downing Budweisers—the breakfast of choice—and getting rowdy, a fitting tribute to one of the rowdier members of the community. I closed my eyes against the hubbub, but my hearing remained fully acute. Then I retreated deeper into my mind and focused on my old friend.

Leif's juvenile years were decades past, but the influence of his street-corner apprenticeship propelled him toward a career in delinquency, and though he acted as wily and exasperating as a too-hip teenager, I learned to love the guy, especially his ability to snatch poise from perplexity. Whether caught with his hand in someone's till or up someone's skirt, Leif either deflected accusation or convincingly argued he perpetrated a great kindness—always with boyish innocence and a compelling smile, the squint in his blue eyes revealing distress that anyone would dare doubt his sincerity.

Leif didn't admit to being a career criminal, but he did declare— for whatever it was worth—that he robbed a Wells Fargo bank in California, under the guise of filming a movie. He maintained he got away clean and made it to Brazil. Feeling bigheaded over his success and untouchable in a country that didn't have an extradition treaty with the U.S., Leif mailed a video of the robbery to the FBI. Some months later, a federal agent, posing as a bounty hunter, abducted him. Hauled back to the States, Leif was tried and convicted. He spent eight years as the government's guest at Leavenworth.

In Flamingo Bay, Leif reinvented himself as the rebel persona of James Dean all grown-up (cool guy) with a dollop of Edward G. Robinson (tough guy). Leif might not have possessed the finest criminal mind—he was no Professor Moriarty—but he did possess the most thoroughly criminal mind I ever encountered. He tended to examine first all of the criminal solutions to a problem before he entertained solutions that wouldn't get him arrested. Maybe if he hadn't acted so quickly on his thoughts, he could've turned his life around. Still, he was the unluckiest of men.

Barely running on all cylinders when he acquired them, none of Leif's vehicles ran for long. He was a pedestrian the past several months and for most of the years he lived in Flamingo Bay. All his dogs died tragically—one shot, one poisoned, and one hacked apart with a machete. Both his boats sank—one during a hurricane, the other when electrolysis disintegrated the steel hull of his powerboat after the previous owner inadvertently removed the zincs. His only real girlfriend (a three-month relationship) had once been a man. Leif lived here and there, but he lived longest aboard an old wooden rowboat with only a tarp to keep himself dry.

I hadn't seen a visible sign that the police were even interested in investigating his death. It pissed me off, though it didn't surprise me: Leif relished spitting at authority. That didn't surprise me either: the veneer of civilization is merely epidermal in thickness, and the rumble and tumble of living forty years on society's fringe lacerated, contused, and abraded Leif's hide.

Billie touched my arm and said, "You haven't answered my question."

Lost in my own world, I hadn't heard her return.

"What question's that?"

She tugged at the bill of her faded-green baseball cap, fighting the breeze that whipped her yellow hair.

"What you're doing tomorrow?"

The question seemed simple enough—and the answer. Though my to-do list had grown to the length of a sumo wrestler's bill of fare, I figured I'd do tomorrow and the day after whatever Billie wanted me to. One thing about Billie: she glowed, as if each hair on her body was the terminus of an overheated fiber optic cable seconds away from meltdown. In her presence, everything became more vivid, more intense, more profound. Except me. I became stupid. Stupid because I loved her. Not a problem except that she was twenty-three years old. Not a problem except that nearly a generation separated us. Not a problem except that she didn't love me.

"What're my options?" I asked.

"I think we should team up to find Leif's killer."

"Why do you care? You never gave him the time of day."

"Only because he couldn't keep his hands off me. But I live here. And I like living here. And I don't want to think I'm sharing my energy with a murdering scumbag."

"What's stopping you from becoming Nancy Drew and finding the killer yourself?"

"Leif was your friend."

"But I can't bring him back, and I'm not sure that finding his killer will make me feel one bit better."

"It would make me feel better and plenty of others as well. You have the history here. People know and respect you."

"There's no shortage of people who share those qualifications with me, but I'm a sailor, not a detective."

She pulled off her baseball cap, loosened the adjustable band, and stuck it on my head backwards, tugging it to fit over my own cap.

"There. You look just like Sherlock Holmes wearing his deerstalker."

"Now I'm a detective?"

"If you want to be," Billie said. "You have to admit we make a good team."

I nearly choked on her words. From the earliest days of sea travel, any sailor worth his salt feared sirens. I feared sirens. No sailor wants to smash his boat against rocks, but more humiliating than crashing against rocks, more humiliating than being ignored, is being lured into the dreaded position of friendship with a beautiful woman.

"Team?" I asked, removing her cap and sticking it back on her head, pulling the visor down over her eyes with a sharp tug.

She stuck out her tongue and readjusted the cap's band.

"Sure. We already collaborate on designing T-shirts."

I got to my feet and walked a few steps to the end of the crumbling dock, lit a cigarette, and surveyed the harbor, protected on three sides by bulging hills—the overcast sky sharply delineating foliage in infinite hues of green. Clusters of modest buildings peeked shyly through dense vegetation. Red roofs capped the older cottages, and white roofs marked the newer dwellings. Elaborate structural frameworks, hidden by encroaching bush, anchored them to the steep hillsides—sometimes a concrete cistern and columns, other times crisscrossing lengths of dimension lumber that seemed as fragile as Popsicle sticks. A dozen fancy houses dotted the landscape as well. Ex-smugglers built some, but Statesiders built the greater number. Those folk stayed pretty close to home—the marine community tasted a bit salty to the discriminating palate.

Flamingo Bay—located on the east end of St. Judas—is roughly two miles wide, four miles long, and most days, eight miles high. The small harbor at the head of the bay didn't offer the bay's best anchorage, but it was convenient to the only dock and provided moorings for the marine community, a ragtag fleet of nearly sixty sailboats.

The fleet included sloops, ketches, yawls, and schooners. One boat was handmade, two were homemade, but most represented the modest offerings of shipyards—the Fords and Chevies of the yachting world. Diver Vaughn's boat, *Divertimento*, was the only boat that didn't rely on wind power.

Moored alone in deep water, about a hundred yards from the fleet,

Island Trader—my boat—slept like an island. A hundred-ton, steel-hulled Great Lakes pilot schooner, built in Thunder Bay in 1899, she boasted three masts, but I no longer owned even a yard of Dacron to hoist on them. I lost every inch of it when we encountered a tropical storm on the return voyage from Venezuela. I almost lost Big Gary as well, but he survived a collision with a wayward boom, suffering only a concussion.

Sailors thrive on superstition, and I was as superstitious as the next. When the disasters befell, I kept count. I relaxed after the sails set their own course in the direction of Antigua, thinking that bad news came in threes. I'd already put down a mutiny and been scammed out of five grand. Thinking I could enjoy a period of grace, I arrived home to learn about Leif. I no longer looked for a period of grace. I steeled myself for the two additional disasters just beyond the horizon—or the five or eight.

Billie sing-songed, "Yoo-hoo. I'm wait-ing."

"I'm think-ing," I accented each syllable, mimicking her.

I wasn't thinking. I was waiting for an epiphany. Sometimes it was like waiting for Godot.

I field-stripped my cigarette, dropped the filter in my pocket, and faced Billie.

"I've never been a team player," I said, "and I've been under the strong impression that you didn't want to play with me."

"Not when the game's like hide-the-weinie."

"What's the problem?"

"Men. All you think about is sex."

"Of course. Because men love sports, and sex comes closest to being the one pure sport—it can be participatory or not, there exist no allotted time-outs, no rigid conventions, it offers head-to-head competition and head-to-toe non-competition and everything in between, keeping score's optional and totally artificial. Everyone can play."

"Captain Brian, you're sick, and you're in love with your own mind. I like those things about you. But you've disproved your own point. Keeping score's important in sports. And sex will never work as a varsity sport. Hester Prynne is the only person I know who was awarded a letter for sex, and as I recall, things went downhill for her after that."

"The problem with women is they're too practical."

"They have to be—in a world where men aren't. But let's be serious. You know as well as I do the cops will never find Leif's killer."

"Probably because they won't look very hard."

The authorities didn't much care Leif was dead, but they'd probably come to miss him, too. There was now one fewer pre-packaged perpetrator to round up when the police needed an arrest. Though Leif was seldom charged and never convicted of any offense on St. Judas, the police did arrest him regularly. Whenever there was a crime on the island, he became the usual suspect.

We enjoyed watching the police take him into custody, and I suspected Leif enjoyed that bit of the routine as well. The cops never arrested Leif unless they had at least four armed officers—ridiculous because he'd didn't own a weapon and he'd never even been accused of more than simple theft. Three drew their guns, while the fourth handcuffed him. Because he seldom admitted to anything, except with a coy smile, Leif's adventures would never be fully chronicled in the Lore of Flamingo Bay.

"Captain Brian, I'm still waiting for an answer. Are you going to help me?"

"How am I supposed to find his killer? I can't even find my truck."

"Probably because you haven't looked very hard."

A mile away, from across the lifeless water on a Lady Jane day, Jimi Hendrix's distorted voice screamed from Easy's boombox: "You know you're a cute little heartbreaker...."

As I bent to pick up the box of T-shirts that Billie and I spent half the night silk-screening, Billie plunked her butt on it.

I picked up the second box and hauled it to her jeep, careful not to trip over the thick planks of greenheart stacked neatly on the beach adjacent to the dock, lumber I hauled up from Venezuela, lumber the contractor demanded we unload immediately upon our arrival five days ago, lumber that sat untouched since.

When I returned, I kicked the box she sat on and said, "We're going to be late for the funeral."

"I still think we need to solve the mystery."

"Some mysteries are unsolvable."

"Like what?" she asked.

"Why you're still a virgin—"

"I'm not a virgin."

"In the Virgin Islands, you are."

"That's no mystery."

It was to me. Discounting the improbable chance that a recent warp in the space-time continuum caused Billie to be spontaneously reincarnated as of one of St. Ursula's eleven thousand virgins—whose feast day Columbus celebrated when he named our archipelago—I hadn't a clue. Then again, Billie did claim that this wasn't her first go-round on planet Earth—in India, she'd tried on Eastern theology for size, and some of it fit.

"Enlighten me."

Billie pursed her lips. "Another time."

"Look, I don't see any conspiracy here. Leif did something to someone, and that someone retaliated. If somebody local killed Leif, it'll come out, and we'll take care of it."

Even as the words escaped my mouth, I doubted the veracity of my statement. If Leif had simply been engaged in his usual activities, why did someone wait until now to kill him?

"How?" she asked.

"Exile."

Billie had been around here long enough to know that criminals in Flamingo Bay usually got their comeuppance without benefit of constabulary. Sometimes a few well-chosen words sufficed. Sometimes the penalty required the infliction of minor contusions. Banishment—the extreme penalty—always worked.

"How about something more severe?"

"Exile worked for Napoleon."

"Not on Elba, it didn't," she countered

"It did on St. Helena."

"Because the Brits probably killed him."

"As Cicero said, 'The people's good is the highest law.' Getting the scum out of the community seems in line with that sentiment."

"I agree," Billie said. "I am one of three members of the Flamingo Bay Literary Society, and I have done my reading."

"Make that two members—"

"Wendy will be back."

I wasn't so sure Wendy would be back. Her new lover—the skipper of a sleek gaff-rigged schooner—possessed an enviable itinerary, and his sobriety marked him an immense improvement over her husband, Jason the Argonut. Still, Billie, like all of us, understood that the mystique of Flamingo Bay compelled people to return.

"If you agree with me, what's the problem?"

"As I recall, Cicero also said, 'Let the punishment match the offense.'"

I asked, "So what's your solution?"

"In a place where the only reason to call the cops is to tell them to like go fuck themselves, I don't have a solution."

Billie did have a solution—at least on the one occasion she needed it. Some months ago, Officer Richards stopped her for driving a vehicle without a windshield, not even a traffic violation. He asked her to hold his baton, while he wrote up the ticket. As he wrote, he compared his baton to his dick—long, black, thick. Billie whacked him in the nose with the baton. I didn't know if Richards felt embarrassed getting his nose broken by a woman or if he was still working on a plan, but he never arrested her, and he never came after her.

"Billie, we both have to live here. Snooping is going to make us no friends, and we may find ourselves as detested as the police."

"But wouldn't it be a better place to live if we didn't suspect there was like a fungus among us?"

It would, but snooping would likely lead nowhere and mark me as an outcast on the island. I didn't have many close friends left. While I straddled the equator, most of my friends had traveled north or south—selling out or giving up. The few that remained were dying. So many, it felt like an epidemic. Captain Lucky, Mad Max, Valerie, and Leif would all be missing Flamingo Bay's New Year's Eve party for the first time. I knew that medical examiners (had they been called in) could, in each case, point to specific causes that shut down the internal life support systems, but in my bones, I knew that all my friends died from immortality—the leading cause of death in Flamingo Bay.

"For argument's sake, suppose I agree to help. What's your plan? Do you intend to stop people on the street like the police do and ask if they're guilty?"

"Hardly." She folded her arms across her body and narrowed her green eyes. "I'm going to make a list of suspects first."

"Do you really think someone we know killed him?"

The five-day-old knot in my stomach—solid as a bowline—tightened a bit.

Billie replied, "In a place where you know nearly everyone, as often as not, the people you know do the damnable things."

"Okay, okay, let's hear your suspects."

She held up a single finger. "Diver Vaughn."

"No."

Two fingers. "Pirate Dan."

"No."

Three fingers. "Zeke."

"No."

Four fingers. "Jason the Argonut."

"Maybe."

"Maybe?"

"Ever hear about the fly-by-night dinghy deal?"

"I don't think so."

"Leif and Jason ingested large quantities of mushroom tea at a full-moon party on Tortola. Before heading back, they decided to stop in West End and steal the dinghies at one of the marina docks. They almost cleared the harbor before the authorities gave chase. They escaped, but they scattered dinghies all over the sea including their own."

"So?"

"Leif and Jason teamed up in the past to create mischief. They could've teamed up again on a more serious project that ended in greater misadventure. That's my only point. Billie, let's go. We're going to be late."

"I have more suspects. Don't you want to hear them?"

"Just tear out the three or four pages in the phone book that contain the listings for St. Judas, and you'll have the definitive list of suspects."

I watched as a glower transformed her face. Her green eyes widened, unblinking. Her lips puckered. I glowered back, but what I wanted to do was meet her puckered lips with my own.

Relaxing her facial muscles, she said, "I'm sitting here until you agree to help me."

"Name someone who's helped you more than I have."

"That's what friends are supposed to do for each other."

"If I were to become interested in investigating the murder, why shouldn't I do it on my own?"

"You do too much stuff on your own, and I want to help."

"What do you bring to the investigation?"

"Captain Brian, that's a mean thing to say. You know I bring more to the party than anyone."

Billie did bring more to the party than anyone. She brought so much to the party that I'd come to accept that without Billie there could never be another party—none I'd care to attend.

"Just now, the party is waiting on you. Are you going to get off your butt?"

"No!"

2

I LEFT BILLIE ON THE DOCK and trudged through the sand, dodging a few derelict boats and several badly rusted vehicles that looked abandoned but were not. Several vehicles that actually were abandoned—mostly stripped of usable parts—decayed in each other's company a short distance away at the rear of the fire station. Every summer a crew came over from St. Thomas to haul them to a scrap yard there, as part the government's annual clean-up campaign. When I reached the uneven turf between the fire station and the Congo Club, its run-down next-door neighbor, I stopped to empty the sand from my shoes. Closed today because of Leif's funeral, the Congo Club looked as abandoned as the vehicles on the beach.

The bar and dining area were situated on a large wooden deck. Old Dacron sails stitched together formed a canopy roof to protect patrons. An oversized beach shack, walls sided with recycled boards and plywood and topped by a corrugated-metal roof, housed the kitchen and toilet and provided lock-up storage. Every year, Pirate Dan flouted the authorities and quietly expanded the seating area. The pile of treated lumber stacked next to the railing on the bay side hinted at the imminence of this year's project.

The last time I patronized the joint—three months ago now—I took exception to Diver Vaughn providing cocaine to my former girlfriend, Sarah—once a woman of substance, now a slave to a controlled substance. Sarah behaved like a child enjoying an eternal Halloween—every night she played trick or treat.

For his complicity, I knocked Vaughn on his wallet. Pirate Dan took exception to the assault on his most influential customer and caught me in the knee with a Louisville Slugger. After I wrestled the bat away, I pulled an Elliot Ness—lots of broken bottles. Since then I had, understandably, not been welcome on the premises.

Dan ducked his head out of the shack and spotted me.

"Argh!" he growled. "Hold on."

Except for a long-billed baseball cap, he was every inch a pirate, but the missing inches were the most compelling. His left foot was shoeless, and his right leg was footless. Extending from the embroidered hem of his baggy high-water pants of faded blue a peg-shaped scrimshaw prosthesis provided mobility. Pegs are not the prosthesis of choice for most amputees, but then most recipients don't fancy themselves pirates.

I'd made no attempt to resolve our differences. Not a guy to go after a cripple, nor a guy to offer the other knee, I'd mostly ignored him these past months. Still, I met him halfway—Dan wasn't a brisk walker.

"I'm waiting for my three hundred bucks."

He maintained I owed him three hundred for his shelves of liquor I took out. I laughed at his chutzpah.

"I'm fucking serious."

"Everyone needs a purpose in life. Yours may be waiting for me to settle up. If that's the case, you could live to be a hundred. You may not thank me now or tomorrow or the next day, but someday you will."

Lost in the leathery creases of his neck, a rawhide thong held a gold doubloon. The T-shirt, designed by Billie and distinguished by its ripped-out neckband, displayed a line drawing of Dan's sloop under sail flying the Jolly Roger. On top of the emblematic circle that ringed the ship was printed: M.O.F.Y.C. The bottom of the emblem proclaimed: MY OWN FUCKING YACHT CLUB.

"Know anyone looking to wash dishes?"

Dan's gruff voice accessorized his persona, but he'd employed the device long enough that it no longer qualified as an affectation.

"You might have some difficulty finding a new dishwasher after the way you terminated your last one."

"Don't point your finger at me. Leif walked out of here at ten o'clock. Alone. Twenty people can verify it." The Pirate stuck a cigarette in his mouth from a pack rolled up in his T-shirt sleeve. "Nice move the other night, taking away half my customers."

The greenheart I hauled up from Venezuela was stowed beneath tons of mahogany, and the mahogany had to be unloaded first. Because I left half my crew, the mutineers, in Cumaná and half my remaining crew, Big Gary, in St. Thomas to get his head examined, I had to hire a small army—Dan's patrons—to unload the boat. It cost me nearly the entire profit I earned hauling it just to get the greenheart off the boat before dark.

"I simply hired them to unload my boat. It's true they all preferred to eat at your joint after we finished, but they were happy enough to eat a free meal at Easys. You really can't expect me to buy dinner for twelve in a joint where I can't get served."

I had no intention of telling the Pirate the meal ended up a disaster. It wasn't Easy's fault that his limited menu was less than satisfying after four days at sea, and it wasn't Easy's fault that just as he served our cheeseburgers, a participant in the procession of vehicles led by the police and paramedics down the road toward Pirate Cove returned to spread the word that Leif was dead.

He lit his cigarette. "How about a truce?"

I had to admit that my banishment from the Congo Club curtailed my social life. I also had to admit that Dan and I'd gotten on for five years—he'd even insisted on the appellation of "Captain"—demanding everyone use the formal term when addressing me. Yet, I was still miffed that he stuck his nose in my private business with Diver Vaughn.

"I've always stayed out of your business until you interfered with mine. You want to see my money again, better mind your own damn business. Those are my terms. Think about it."

I left him standing there. When I reached the road, I ran into a handsome West Indian with café-au-lait skin and close-cropped hair. His grandfather was a Scot—descended from the managers who once ran the estates for the Danes. He wore jeans and a carnival T-shirt adorned with moko jumbies, the characters on stilts that weave through local parades. Continentals see the dancing jumbies as figures of mirth. They don't know that West Indians once tied together the great toes of their dead so they couldn't dance, couldn't become jumbies. I wasn't sure it was a ritual many didn't still quietly perform.

"Pony Mon!"

He waved. "Captain Brian, mon!"

"You're showing up for Leif's funeral?"

He nodded. "I be catching up."

Agile and fit, he had an odd spring in his step I'd never noticed. Then I hadn't gotten used to seeing him on foot. He and his horse had been inseparable. Last summer he helped Billie out of a jam in Sugar Harbor—the only town on St. Judas—when Billie ran up against some local toughs. Astride Bongo Natty, Pony Mon swung Billie onto his saddle like a western hero. That was months ago—before Bongo Natty was shot dead.

A couple hundred feet farther down the road, sweat began pouring off me. One trick I regularly employed to put off perspiring as long as possible each morning was to brush my teeth before I showered. I figured it kept my shirt dry an extra ten minutes most days. All I could do to control perspiration while walking around the bay was slow my pace. Flamingo Bay doesn't offer much good terrain for the casual walker. The roads and trails should be posted with black diamonds.

Not much of a walker—that's why Ford builds trucks—I couldn't help reflect on my walk three weeks ago with Leif. We met up in Sugar Harbor. It was our last time together. Looking for a ride back to Flamingo Bay, Leif—dressed as usual in soiled jeans and T-shirt, in need of a shower, shave, and shampoo—headed with me to my truck. On the way, he managed to offend several people in as many minutes. Leif swiped a banana at the fruit stand in town, spit his gum onto the driver's seat of an unoccupied jeep idling at the curb, ate the banana, dropped the peel into the bag of a tourist walking by, helped another lady with her bag of groceries by grabbing her breast along with the bag, and finished by urinating in Pirate Dan's gas tank—all in only a hundred yards. Still, it was the best hundred yards I remember walking.

I stopped at the entrance to Valerie's driveway, massaged my aching knee, and glimpsed the red roof of her tiny cottage on the hillside. She'd been my best friend most of my years in Flamingo Bay, and we had some times there: sharing a number; taking turns leading one another through labyrinthine mind fields; finishing each other's sentences; just being damn silly. It didn't matter how many others were present; we were a society of two. Others didn't get that there was no initiation, just participation. You can't teach someone to laugh, though you can forget how to laugh yourself. I wiped my eyes and realized that you never forget how to cry.

At Valerie's funeral, I met her sister for the first time. She sketched for me the details of Valerie's life before she arrived in Flamingo Bay. The hellion in the family, Valerie went off to college and never returned home after she was expelled her freshman year. First, there were only men—Mike, Sean, Paul. And the places were generic—the mountains, the forests, the seashore. Later the men became generic—Tom, Dick, Harry. And the places became specific—Alaska, Colorado, the Florida Keys. When she arrived in Flamingo Bay about four years ago, all the disparate parts of Valerie's life came together. She blossomed. But the duration was about the same as that of a night-blooming cereus, a short-lived, white volleyball-sized flower of exquisite simplicity and complexity.

I visited Valerie the day before she died. Her long dance with death—one step forward, two steps back—left her all bones and tumors. Only her eyes remembered who she'd been. I twisted a number and held it to her lips. Slowly, she inhaled the smoke, and her lips formed a smile when she exhaled. She could barely speak, but she told me that she'd arranged to be buried in Flamingo Bay, and she admitted that she'd always wanted to have a child but the closest she could come to that now was to have a playground nearby where she would always be near children.

Then she confessed that she never believed any of that life-after-death shit and we both knew it, but why not cover all the bases. She directed me to an old metal canister, the kind that fancy cookies come in, the kind that rust in twenty minutes from salt air. The tin held nearly eight hundred dollars. She told me to take the money and build her a playground. I protested that I couldn't be counted on to return from the grocery store with the proper change. She didn't argue my point but responded that I was one of the few guys in Flamingo Bay who could be counted on to bring home the groceries.

Before I left, she told me that one day when I sailed way, way down island, I'd see the purple mountain rising out of the turquoise sea and she'd be waiting naked on the lavender sand. She'd have her breasts back, and we'd dance in the surf until it evaporated.

Life's whatever you make it; the afterlife's another deal altogether, and Valerie's words made me cry. I didn't know if I cried for her or I cried for myself. Our intimacy had been all about laughter and silliness, so I was unsure if the celebration she described on the lavender-sand beach was about exuberance or sexual desire—a fuzzy distinction, anyway.

Early on, Valerie and I discussed our mutual attraction, but she understood I'd made a commitment to Sarah. I stuck to that commitment until it became too ridiculous to go on. Sarah blamed my friendship with Valerie for causing every problem in our relationship, along with her cocaine addiction. I suggested to Sarah that I'd be more inclined to come home evenings if I didn't have to wait until morning before she showed up. I walked away from Sarah the last time on New Year's Eve, nearly eleven months ago, and I didn't mind admitting my loneliness since.

I took Valerie's money and invested all of it in mahogany, along with a few bucks of my own. That was in Cumaná, just after my tile deal with Lopez went south. I suspected that I bought the lumber from only one of its owners, the one planning to stiff his partners. In the States, it would be worth thirty, maybe forty thousand dollars. My plan was to run the mahogany up to Florida to get top dollar and use the money to build the playground. When the squall took the sails, I knew I wouldn't be sailing to Florida, so I mentally did to the lumber what Caesar did to Gaul—divided it into three parts. The first part would be the actual construction material. The second part would be sold locally to pay for the project's labor cost. The third part would be the elusive and often illusory profit—money to keep my old boat and my fragile business afloat.

I sailed for Cumaná with no idea where to build the playground, not sure there would be a playground. The voyage offered plenty of time to think, but even employing my favorite device—thinking about everything but the problem that cried out for a solution—provided no answers. The playground became a done deal, however, after a chance ten-minute conversation with Mister Aubrey, who offered me the only level parcel of real estate within miles, on the beach—and close to Valerie's grave.

Mister Rolly, the best carpenter on the island, agreed to accept lumber as partial payment for his labor, allowing the project to get started right away. Rolly was a fine craftsman and a fine man—the sort of man to chase you down the road just to greet you. The day after Hurricane Hugo—the day after I first arrived in Flamingo Bay—I spotted him cleaning fish on a flat rock by the beach, shirtless, his trousers rolled up past his knees. Squatting at his work beneath a leather-leafed sea grape, he wore a halo of hungry noisy gulls that circled and swooped for their lunch. Rolly still cleans his fish in the morning, and the circling gulls create a visible aura.

I turned and continued toward Easys. The old concrete road had been recently patched with asphalt. The irregular blue-black bumps seemed so foreign that I imagined the patches were tumors, and I sensed perhaps cancer grew beneath the surface of the island. I wondered if I was the only one who could see and feel the tumors.

When I reached the playground's site, I found Rolly and his helpers had sawed the lumber into full four-by-fours for the swing's tripod legs. The wider dimension of the top beam looked nearly five inches. Rolly hadn't installed the swings themselves because he didn't want kids playing at a construction site. The exquisite detailing of the structure impressed me. Not many people owned a piece of furniture built as solidly and carefully.

Monkey bars topped the day's agenda. One of Rolly's helpers turned dowels. Another steadied a board clamped to sawhorses, while Rolly planed it. Cinnamon-colored sawdust lay thick on the green lawn. The racket from the gas generator and lathe made talking impossible, but it didn't bother the three donkeys grazing on a thin line of weeds that marked the barrier between the playground's turf and water's edge. Rolly and I acknowledged each other's presence with a wave. The completion of the first piece of equipment put a smile on my face. I felt proud to participate in the playground's creation.

I watched for a minute all the dinghies buzzing back and forth from the moored boats in the bay, my clear view of the sea framed on either side by thick stands of mangroves. It struck me that not a single sailboat in the harbor belonged to anyone born in Flamingo Bay or even the Virgin Islands. People came from everywhere, but many followed

the Alaska-Colorado-Keys-Virgin Islands axis—a modern concep-
tion of the Oregon Trail. Some traveled back and forth—Easy used to
fish in Alaska in the summer and loaf here in the winter. Others—like
Mechanic Jim—stopped here for a breather before embarking on the
next legs of ambitious expeditions. A few had been successes in their
previous lives—Jason had done post-graduate work in science—but
most had not. I supposed all were looking for a new frontier.

Ferry service connects St. Judas to St. Thomas, and a crummy two-
lane road links Flamingo Bay to the ferry dock in Sugar Harbor. Hardly
any tourists disembarking at Cyril E. King Airport find their way to
St. Judas, and not many of those make it to Flamingo Bay. A few tourists do come to rent a private house for a week or two of sunshine, and
every so often one recognizes Flamingo Bay is pretty okay—and stays.

One thing is the insular nature of islands: each comes with its own
moat. J.M. Barrie stated that Neverland—a name used fondly by many
locals to label their community—is always more or less an island. The
other thing is more abstruse: islands are like truth, and the smaller they
are, the truer they are. It doesn't matter that Greenland is an island
and Australia is a continent. Both are too large. Truth—however profound—is tiny.

The Moravian church, the largest and oldest building in Flamingo
Bay, stands across the road and a hundred yards from the site of the
playground. The nineteenth-century masonry structure features
yellow stucco walls and a red corrugated-metal roof. The ten-foot-high
hedge of purple bougainvillea that rings it forms a suitable foundation
planting for the massive edifice. A small cemetery spills down the hillside next to it. For a Continental to be buried there is as unlikely as a
civilian being buried at Arlington, but it's now—six weeks into eternity—Valerie's home. Wilted flowers—oleander, hibiscus, and bougainvillea—decorated the simple concrete marker erected while I was
at sea. I walked only close enough to read the inscription. I didn't need
to do the math; Valerie was thirty-nine years old.

When I reached the road, I caught Officer Richards of the Virgin
Islands Police Department preying on tourists—his pickings were
slim when I wasn't behind the wheel providing him an opportunity to
practice his law enforcement skills. The emergency lights on his white

Blazer flashed and pulsed. I figured he stopped the tourists because of a bug splattered on their windshield or because it was Monday or they drove a green jeep. Richards was a relentless asshole. Just as homosexuals appropriated *gay* and pretty much restricted its definition, we did the same to *asshole*. In Flamingo Bay, you could be a lot of things, but unless you wore a badge, you couldn't be an asshole.

Elroy—squat and powerful, his head bouncing like a bobble-head doll despite his thick neck—stepped from behind a big clump of pink oleanders and stood by the side of the road. He stuffed his hands in his pockets and policed the policeman. When Elroy spotted me, he jerked his head in recognition and slouched toward me on bare feet. He wore a T-shirt and three pairs of tattered trousers, though he still showed some flesh where his trousers quit working.

Unlike people who hadn't a clue, Elroy, I'd always sensed, realized he'd been shortchanged. He never smiled. His grimace persisted whether he cut bush or kicked back. I knew he lived mostly in his head—fighting demons only death could exorcise—but I live enough in my own head that I can't help wondering what it's like not being able to get back out. I'm not afraid of much, but I'm terrified of that. I'd given Elroy hundreds of cigarettes and dozens of sodas, but he'd never spoken a word to me. He'd never spoken to anyone, as far as I knew.

Waving a traffic ticket, Richards stepped out of his vehicle, making several minor and unneeded adjustments to his Virgin Islands Police Department uniform (starched powder-blue shirt with an American flag on the sleeve; acutely creased royal-blue trousers with a gold stripe; highly buffed black shoes and leather belt that held handcuffs, pouches, and holster). The man's waist wasn't nearly large enough to comfortably carry all the accessories—he tugged at his belt to keep it up around his middle. If he ever ran after an outlaw, the belt would slip and he'd become a cop of the Keystone variety—he already wore a goofy mustache that looked even goofier with his crooked nose, bent out of shape by Billie.

While Richards delivered the traffic ticket to the tourists, I met Elroy in the middle of the road. He banged two fingers against his lips, and I fished out a cigarette from the pack, handed it over, and lit it. He

bobbed his head in thanks before wandering toward the tourist's jeep.
I walked over and leaned against the driver's door of Richards' white Blazer.

I watched what little I could see of the pre-funeral preparations and listened to Easy's favorite recording artist, Jimmy Buffet—just audible above the generator's din. Jimmy sang about Margaritaville, letting us know there was booze in the blender. Having listened to the tune innumerable times, I learned only that Margaritaville likely enjoyed a steadier supply of electricity than Flamingo Bay. There'd be far fewer drunks here if they needed electricity from the underwater cable to get juiced.

Easy did some schmoozing and laid out some cash for his temporary electric hook-up, and a three-stranded umbilical tethered his mustard-colored pop stand to a nearby utility pole. A permanent hook-up couldn't be made until his shack met the electrical code. Easy knew there would never be a permanent hook-up. What Easy had going for him was his West Indian landlord, Mister Aubrey, who liked Easy and the extra income Easy provided him each month, though I knew Easy was behind a bit on his rent. Aubrey especially enjoyed the deference served with his cocktails.

When Richards finished with the tourists, he shoved Elroy out of his way—almost knocking him down—and returned to his vehicle. His glare revealed he didn't appreciate that I didn't move out of his way when he tried to open the vehicle's door.

"Find Leif's killer yet?" I asked.

"Mind you own business."

Whenever I mentioned Leif in his presence, something in his attitude suggested Richards was more sinister than the buffoon I took him to be.

"It is my business, and you're my number-one suspect. If you did it, you can bet your ass I'm going to jam you up. Another thing. You're going to apologize to Elroy. I told you before not to push him around."

"I should arrest you for interfering with my duty."

I thrust my arms out, wrists together. "Go ahead."

He reached for his cuffs but changed his mind. I dropped my arms.

"Now, tell Elroy you're sorry."

Richards started to go for his cuffs again but adjusted his belt instead.

I called Elroy. He shuffled toward us so slowly that he seemed intent upon dissipating any sincerity Richards' apology might muster. Elroy—keeping his distance—stopped about five feet from Richards, stuffed his hands in his pockets, and glared at the cop.

"I be sorry," Richards spoke over Elroy's head, in words that barely exited his sneering lips.

"See, that wasn't so difficult," I said.

Richards smiled at me, as if in agreement, but in a contrary tone, he dismissed me by saying, "Get lost, you Yankeemuthascunt."

3

WITH HELP FROM HIS FRIENDS, Easy managed to pull together enough artifacts to create a nautical theme for his pop stand. Mechanic Jim donated an old oar nearly eight feet long, which leaned against the side of the shack near the hand-painted sign: EASYS. Fishnet, draped from the sign, held two antique bottle-green floats of hand-blown glass provided by Diver Vaughn. An ancient anchor that I found at the bottom of the bay enhanced the endeavor. About five feet tall, the anchor was so badly oxidized that it'd lost most of its mass. Six recycled wire spools served as tables, forming an imperfect semi-circle in the small clearing that butted against a grove of coconut palms. Past the palm grove, the hillside climbed quickly until it reached twelve hundred feet.

Four mismatched stools stood at the shack's counter. I grabbed the only empty one, plopping my butt down next to Nancy, just as she got to her feet.

"You'll keep an eye on her then?" she asked Pirate Dan, sitting on the other side of Nancy's ten-year-old daughter, Tanya. "The funeral committee demands my presence."

"Argh, no problem."

"Antsy Nancy," I greeted her.

She scowled.

"I'm sorry. Good morning, Nancy."

"Good morning, Captain Brian."

Nancy earned her nickname by becoming the second Nancy in Flamingo Bay. When her predecessor, Fancy Nancy, left to become a suburban housewife—two years ago now—the *Antsy* became redundant.

Easy brought me a beer as I watched the loading of coolers and the distribution of several hundred pounds of ice imported from Sugar Harbor for the occasion.

Tan skin and an abundance of ankle bracelets and hair—the unshaven split nearly evenly between the sexes—distinguished the assemblage, for the most part outfitted in sun-faded baseball caps and shorts, worn T-shirts, and boat shoes or flip-flops. The crowd numbered between sixty and seventy. I listened for information about Leif's death, hoping to learn for my personal edification whether Leif engaged in any anti-social exploits during my ten-day voyage that might have provoked someone to go after him—clearly, one person on the island hadn't been content to simply laugh and shrug his shoulders.

Of course, I assumed that Leif's death had something to do with his vocational bent. I couldn't see him doing anything else to seriously antagonize his killer. Leif had become such a pacifist in the last couple of years that he even quit eating meat. It wasn't for reasons of health. Anything with a face or a mother—his words—became off-limits.

Oddly, Leif's passing now seemed incidental to today's event. The upcoming lottery dominated conversation. I didn't hear a word of gossip about the murder. What I did learn would be helpful only to a food critic—the luncheon menus of the various participating boats. I also heard offhand comments about their stores of substances, controlled and uncontrolled—as if the event was too somber to be got through sober. I surveyed the crowd. I was willing to bet anything that no one present killed him—anything but my life.

The Pirate ordered a bottle of Grand Marnier, a can of orange juice, and two shot glasses from Easy. Dan instructed his prepubescent mate—a freckle-faced cutie, blue ribbons fastening her neat auburn braids—to fill her shot glass with orange juice. Tanya had a bit of trouble wielding the bulky can and poured about a jigger of juice into her shot glass. Dan filled his glass with Grand Marnier and wiped away the spilt juice with his hand.

"Argh," he growled, raising his glass. "Down the hatch!"

Tanya clicked his glass with her own. "Down the hatch!"

They tipped back their heads and swallowed, then slammed their glasses on the bar.

"Where's Billie?" Easy asked.

"Incubating the T-shirts," I answered.

"Huh?"

"She should be along soon."

Billie had pretty much convinced me she was serious about finding Leif's killer. Until her display of sincerity, I assumed she was merely looking for diversion; Billie showed a fondness for diversions. I liked diversions as well as the next person, but only the organic variety. If you had to plan it, it became something else entirely. I didn't moor my boat in Flamingo Bay because of any affection I harbored for artificiality.

Easy, keeping company with the other mourners present, didn't upgrade his attire for the event. He dressed in his usual lace-up brown boots, worn farmer-in-the-dell blue bib overalls, and T-shirt. Rubber bands controlled both his bushy black hair and beard. After handing me a soda, Easy turned over his bartending duties to Marsha, a recent hire and a recent infatuation. Marsha's boyfriend, Freddie Fellini, recorded the event on video from his perch in the crotch of an aged sea grape across the road. Easy desired to move his relationship with Marsha beyond its current professional status, but Freddie proved to be an obstacle.

Freddie, about Billie's age, showed up in Flamingo Bay two years ago. He settled in effortlessly and was able to find a niche and make a go of it when he hooked up with Diver Vaughn. Freddie derived most of his income videotaping divers Vaughn took down. He offered two souvenir packages. In the first, he would record the tourist's entire dive. In the second, he would record a portion of the tourist's dive and splice it into something of a highlight video—a compilation that included turtles, dolphins, rays, and nurse sharks, along with fish and coral. His relationship with Marsha likely worked because he was a voyeur and she was an exhibitionist.

Marsha's too-tight T-shirt accented her XXXL breasts purchased a few months ago on Tortola in what I perceived as a daring attempt to compete with Billie in the contest for fleshy allure, though the only thing large about Billie was her appetite for life. I admired Marsha's aspirations more than her breasts, and she fell as short in competing with Billie as my boat, *Island Trader*, would in competing for the America's Cup. Easy himself beat everyone in the flesh department. When he showed up here, he weighed a good fifty pounds more than I, and in the past couple of years, he'd added another fifty. If I hadn't been perceptive of Easy's sensitivity over his size, I'd have nicknamed him "Bunyon," but I figured I could resist that moniker until a blue ox ambled onto the scene.

Dan refilled his shot glass with Grand Marnier. Tanya refilled hers with orange juice. Nancy should've known better than to entrust baby-sitting duties to a pirate. Tanya lifted her glass.

"Skoal!"

"Skoal!" Dan answered, meeting her glass with his own.

Cute when it started, the Pirate's entertainment staled quickly, and the audience defected for more amusing fare. Freddie Fellini, who recorded the scene, grew as bored as the rest of us, and he swung his camcorder away from the bar to record the preparation for the sales and distribution of commemorative T-shirts.

A tongue-clicking rendition of the theme from *The Twilight Zone* by her chorus of fans alerted me to Billie's arrival.

Minor culinary miscues—cutting the eggs in half the wrong way while making deviled eggs, forgetting to add Dijon mustard when preparing shrimp Dijon, creating lasagna with pasta that was out-of-the-box crunchy—helped earn Billie the tag, "Space Cadet."

The thing I admired about space cadets was their ability to defy gravity, and Billie accomplished that regularly. But the stunt that made her reputation occurred at the Congo Club when, on a dare, Billie publicly demonstrated for the patrons her ability to achieve a real-deal no-hands orgasm—something she avowed to have learned in India. A few onlookers doubted the legitimacy of Billie's performance, but she assured me the orgasm—while not great—was real, and I believed her. The spectacle proved to me her infinite variety.

The other thing Billie accomplished in the seven months since she arrived in Flamingo Bay was the acquisition of half my T-shirt business. I usually silk-screened the shirts, for I possessed the equipment and the expertise, but Billie created many of the designs. I provided her a chance to earn some money until the tourists arrived in great numbers to purchase her art—the stuff was good. Billie also worked to promote our business—something for which I lacked time—achieving greater success than when I handled it solo, though most of the increased revenue ended up in her pocket.

Whether an officially sanctioned event in Flamingo Bay required a T-shirt or whether the existence of a T-shirt officially sanctioned the event remained ambiguous. I supposed the distinction lacked substance, simply because I'd never witnessed an event that didn't include a commemorative T-shirt. The shirt Billie designed for Leif's funeral celebration represented one of her finest efforts.

Apparently, Billie had been unable to handle the heft of the large carton of shirts, so in her inimitable manner, she transported all three-dozen on her body. It gave her the girth of the Pillsbury Doughboy.

An image of a Viking warrior decorated the shirt's front. The warrior—a good likeness of Leif—sported blond hair, a droopy mustache, and blue eyes. The horns on his hat resembled snorkels. A furry animal skin covered his body, and tiny flippers made his feet look webbed. He carried a yellow mesh bag that divers use to stow their gear, but loot—mostly portable electronic devices—filled this one. On the bottom was printed: LEIF THE THIEF and his date of birth. The rear view showed Leif in a dinghy lying on a funeral pyre, his loot scattered around him. Orange flames shot skyward. HE LIVED TILL HE DIED was printed just above the date of his death five days past. I realized that at forty-one, I was a year older than he'd ever be.

While Marsha sold shirts out of the box from behind the bar, Easy and Billie worked the crowd like carnies. Each carried a notebook, a pen, and a fistful of money.

"See a pair in paradise," she hollered. "Buy the shirt off my back. It's like getting hot in here. Twenty bucks gets you a shirt, and a shirt gets you an invitation to the funeral and the party afterwards."

She collected money as fast as her hands could move, and her male customers enjoyed helping her disrobe.

"You need a T-shirt to enter the lottery," Easy called. "Buy a shirt and help the little lady cool off. Put on a shirt and buy your lottery ticket. Ten little ones can get you five big ones. When they're gone, they're gone. Can't be a winner if you're not a player."

Easy sold tickets for ten bucks a pop. Numbered one through sixty, the chances represented the number of minutes in an hour, the number of minutes Leif's dinghy stayed afloat. The winner stood to gain five hundred bucks. Capitalism was okay in Flamingo Bay, as long as it wasn't flagrant, so I couldn't begrudge Easy the opportunity to make a few bucks on Leif's funeral. Easy stepped up when the authorities learned Leif left no surviving family, and Easy jumped through all the official hoops to get a permit to dispose of Leif's body outside the three-mile limit. I suspected Easy's request was so unusual that it would've taken the government years to make a decision. In the end, the government couldn't ignore it possessed the decomposing body, and turning over Leif's remains to Easy proved the simplest and cheapest course.

"Step right up," Billie shouted. "For twenty measly bucks you can witness the event of the season, party with your neighbors, and walk away with a souvenir T-shirt sure to be a collectors' item."

Big Gary, a stranger since I left him on St. Thomas to seek medical attention, wanted to be a player. It surprised me he showed so much initiative. Ironically, the only time on the run to and from Cumaná that Big Gary demonstrated any resourcefulness resulted in his losing consciousness when he improperly secured the boom that almost took him overboard.

"I want a sweaty shirt," he said.

"They're all a little sweaty," Billie said. "But if you want the last one, the really sweaty one, it's going to cost you forty bucks. You're going to have to wait though. The last shirt doesn't come off until I sell the others."

Easy whispered in her ear. Billie nodded.

"Change of plans," she said. "The last shirt's being auctioned to the highest bidder."

Billie wore about a dozen shirts and Easy still held a fistful of lottery tickets when a vocal group of mourners interrupted the proceedings. The group determined that Viking warriors were always sent to Valhalla with canine companionship. Leif didn't own a dog when he died. His last dog died of ciguatera after he fed it toxic reef fish. He doubted the old West Indian wives' advice that bad fish turned the cooking utensil black and used his dog as a guinea pig. Someone suggested we contact Mister Ralph, the king of roadkill, but no one took it seriously. The problem: dogs don't keep as well as pease porridge. Nancy's daughter, Tanya, hesitantly volunteered Snoopy. She carried the stuffed animal in her backpack.

Before sales resumed, Mechanic Jim, smelling less like petroleum and cleaner shaven than usual, spotted assholes aboard Diver Vaughn's boat. Jim warned Vaughn, and Vaughn alerted Freddie, who swung his camcorder around to document the boarding. I knew little jurisprudence, but I'd been led to believe that boarding a boat without permission of the skipper is illegal. It was why a flotilla of dinghies always headed to shore when the Coast Guard or other functionaries were spotted entering the harbor, but fleeing one's boat didn't always preclude it getting boarded.

Dissatisfied with his sightline, Freddie climbed out on a limb. The limb broke, and Freddie came crashing down with a shriek, falling ten feet onto the uneven ground. Freddie's scream alerted the assholes, and all four charged ashore. Freddie limped to his jeep and headed off down the road. The narcs came by boat, running their small craft onto the rocky beach. They climbed out and milled around until Officer Richards pulled up in his shiny Blazer. Three of the narcs—local assholes with BLUE LIGHTNING TASK FORCE emblazoned on the backs of their navy windbreakers—piled into the vehicle. Richards turned on his emergency lights and pursued Freddie.

Ever since the chief of police on St. Croix was caught on video looting in the aftermath of Hurricane Hugo, no one in law enforcement wanted to star in a home video, so the assholes were intent upon stopping Freddie. Freddie's big problem: only five miles of bumpy road lay ahead of him. The pavement ends just past Doctor's, and the road ends at Pirate Cove, offering Freddie no chance to escape.

I turned to look for Easy and learned I faced an unexpected problem: the asshole that confiscated my gun the other day at Customs—the one Fed in the bunch—confronted me. He sported the attire of a vacationing mobster—shades, Aloha shirt, unscuffed boat shoes, pistol bulge at the hip under his shirt. He was a couple of inches shorter than I—about six feet—lean, tough, swarthy. Ex-military, I figured—the rigidity of posture and discipline—but not the clerk-typist sort. He could thrive in the bush, lick lichen from rocks, drink his own urine—Force Recon or Special Forces. Could I whip him? I didn't feel comfortable making that decision without seeing his eyes, hidden behind gray lenses of aviator-style sunglasses. Because he represented for me everything I hated about the defenders of so-called morality, I wanted to go after him whether I could take him or not, punish him for being present and for simply being.

He didn't do a damn thing but stick his hands in his pockets and study me. I could play that game. I mean I could if his face wasn't as empty as my bank account. He exuded energy—both attractive and repellant—that even in its pre-kinetic state appeared more than casually dangerous. He broke the silence.

"I told you I wasn't done with you."

"Maybe you'll always be left with regret."

His predominantly red shirt revealed upon closer inspection the presence of most colors of the rainbow twisting and swirling in a hallucinogenic nightmare. The shirt itself assaulted my senses, but he compounded his affront to decorum by leaving the top three buttons undone. Around his neck he wore a heavy silver crucifix large enough to scare off a vampire at thirty paces but nearly invisible for the hair on his chest. The hair on his recently shaved head had grown to nearly a quarter-inch in length, and I suspected his five-o'clock shadow was permanent. Everywhere else his hair grew thick, black, and curly.

"We can do it the easy way or the hard way, but you're going to talk to me."

"I'm busy today with a funeral," I said.

"Then we'll talk tomorrow," he said. "Here, at ten o'clock. If you don't show, I'll put a warrant out for your arrest."

His fearsome expression alarmed me just enough that I couldn't come up with an appropriate rejoinder. Unsure at first whether it was the amount of hair on his body, the lack of hair on his head, or the menace of his five-o'clock shadow that intimidated me, I went with all three, blaming testosterone. Then I recalled testosterone caused baldness, not a precisely accurate description of his pate. Like a picnic at the beach when sand gets in your food, the conundrum tasted crunchy. When I substituted "Miracle-Gro" for "testosterone," it all made perfect sense, and I relaxed a bit.

"I might show, but if you don't bring the gun you confiscated from my boat, I guarantee I won't stick around long."

The more I thought about our initial meeting (which occurred five days ago when I cleared Customs on St. Thomas) the more certain I grew that the Shirt—a fitting appellation for the only man present who sported a shirt with a collar—hadn't shown up there by accident. He was waiting for me. He also knew I carried a forty-five aboard—a legal weapon.

"Then I'll arrest you."

The Shirt could arrest me for just about anything. If he played fair, it wouldn't stick, but I couldn't count on fair play. What I wanted to learn—and playing along might help—was who fingered me.

"Better bring a warrant and backup."

"I'd rather learn if you're as big a bad-ass fuck as you think you are."

He turned and walked away. Easy took his place.

"Cool shirt," Easy said.

Fascists love fashion. Hawaiians would absolutely blanch if they realized that a long sartorial tradition that began with Blackshirts and Brownshirts now culminated in Aloha shirts.

"Do these bozos all have a deal with a tailor in Honolulu?"

"Damned if I know," Easy answered.

"Seen him around before?"

"Few times."

"With Sarah?"

Easy squeezed closed his eyes and nodded. "Once." He opened his eyes and pointed. "Make that twice."

I hadn't seen Sarah arrive, but I suspected she'd driven my truck. I kept an eye on her, as I walked over to the road to look for my blue Ford. Sarah and the Shirt didn't appear to be strangers. I couldn't figure what she saw in him except as a potential source to feed her new addiction. I'd fed her old addiction—the sun and the sea. When she stepped off the dock in Florida and into my life—nearly seven years ago—she seemed the perfect boat chick. I was attracted to her long, tan legs, good heart, and toothpaste-commercial smile. She still possessed long, tan legs, but some combination of me and *Island Trader* released a cardiopathic agent into her blood, shrinking her heart. Sarah's teeth disappeared behind a persistent scowl, behind chapped lips once rose-petal soft and fourteen kinds of sweet like a bowl of Bing cherries. She no longer talked; she whined. Maybe in New York she'd fit in, but here—among melodious West Indian rhythms—her voice grated like sand in your swimsuit.

I spotted my truck about a hundred yards away, parked toward the end of a line of mostly beat-up vehicles. Eye contact revealed that Sarah had taken the truck. Eye contact also revealed that she knew I knew. I wondered how many ignition keys she had; I took what I thought was her only one when we parted. Sarah knew that associating with a Fed would make me nuts, but that likely provided some of her motivation. My long-term wish was Sarah would go back to the States to seek treatment and a life, but the one time she agreed to do it, she cashed in the ticket I bought her and the proceeds went up her nose. My immediate wish was someone would invite Sarah to sail on his boat, but nobody wants a whiner.

Heavy clouds massed over Tortola, promising to dampen more than spirits. It looked like one squall after another. Old wives offered no advice on funerals, but it didn't seem an auspicious day for any event at sea. I figured the Ides of March had proved a good time to die, and Easter, a good time to rise from the dead. My only opinion of funerals was that most of the guests of honor probably would've appreciated a little more attention along the way instead of getting it all on the back end.

Easy pulled two of his wire-spool tables closer together. He mounted one, and Billie mounted the other. I speculated that I'd probably be content for the rest of my life to walk around whatever pedestal on which Billie perched and gaze at her, for Billie possessed the gangly arms and legs of a child, the agility of a teenager, the torso of a woman, the face of a siren, and the aura of a deity. I'd be content just to look at her, but I doubted she'd stand still for that.

Then it struck me how myopic I'd become hanging out in Flamingo Bay. What the hell had I been thinking? Everything about Billie was first-class. The only thing first-class about me was my naiveté. I had a better chance of being struck by lightning than hooking up with Billie. I knew, too, that I couldn't stick around Flamingo Bay and watch her hook up with someone else.

Easy quieted the crowd. "Ladies and gentlemen, step right up. Buy the shirt off this girl's back—"

"Sweaty shirt," Billie interrupted, grabbing the front of the shirt between her thumb and forefinger, pulling it off her skin—away from her erect nipples—and shaking it.

"Buy this sweaty shirt off this girl's back. If you like, she'll even autograph it for you. We're starting the bidding at twenty dollars. Do I have twenty dollars?"

"Twenty d-dollars!" Big Gary responded.

"I have twenty dollars from G-Gary. Do I hear twenty-five?"

Pirate Dan, half loaded, pulled a bunch of bills from his pocket. "Thirty-eight!"

"Thirty-eight from the Pirate—"

"Make that thirty-eight-fifty."

"Thirty-eight-fifty from the Pirate."

"Forty!" Big Gary bid.

"Forty, from G-Gary. Do I hear fifty?"

Cherry Mary raised her right arm. "Fifty!"

Catcalls accompanied the bid of Mary, a woman who believed in angels and unicorns. She was Flamingo Bay's most prominent lesbian and Billie's roommate, though not her lover—an assessment vigorously supported by Billie and regrettably by Mary.

"I got fifty bucks from Mary. Do I hear sixty?"

A honking horn—three urgent bursts—caused Easy to pause. Stopped in the middle of the road in his idling jeep, Zeke, wearing his perpetual cetaceous smile, waved at the crowd, gold jewelry brilliant against his black skin.

"Zeke pay fifty-one for Blondie's shirt. He pay more if Blondie come with shirt." Zeke expressed a sentiment felt by most of the bidders. A ragamuffin cocaine dealer, Zeke could back up his offer with cash. "Zeke pay fifty-one hundred for Blondie."

When Billie smiled and shook her head, Zeke shrugged his shoulders and laughed. When people finished laughing with him, he drove off.

Easy regained control of the auction and shouted, "Do I hear sixty for the sweatiest T-shirt in Flamingo Bay?"

"No takers? Fifty dollars then. Going once. Going twice. Going—"

"One C-note!"

The Shirt's bid silenced the crowd.

"One hundred dollars. Going once. Going twice. Going three times." Easy paused. "Sold!"

Greater Trouble in the Lesser Antilles ⚓ Charles Locks

Easy stepped off the table to collect the hundred. Billie teased the crowd, lifting the hem in one-inch increments, again to the accompaniment of the tongue-clicking pirates and now Marsha's glower. Billie pulled the shirt over her head to a huge ovation.

Pirate Dan hollered, "Must be jelly. Jam don't shake like that."

Nobody quarreled with his observation or any of the competing comments offered by the vocal crowd. Not even Billie. She handed the narc her shirt, performed a pirouette, and caught the fresh shirt Easy tossed to her. She pulled it on and curtsied.

"That's all, folks."

The crowd demanded an encore performance, but Billie just waved, stepped off the table, and autographed the T-shirt.

Easy urged folk to load up their dinghies and start ferrying stuff to the boats, but he found it difficult to get the attention of the crowd, still vocal over the day's most exciting but fleeting moment. When the yelling and hissing diminished to a mumbled murmur of discontent, Easy found more success promoting his agenda to get the show on the water sooner rather than later. He sought rides for mourners without transportation and assigned about twenty people to *Island Trader:* Easy, the band, the chorus line, and the photographer, Freddie—if he ever returned—and Sarah.

I could get all the mourners aboard, if I had to. *Island Trader*'s beam was only about fifteen feet, but she measured eighty-six feet at the water line and well over a hundred feet from stern to bowsprit. Seventy or so passengers could crowd the deck without danger. I understood that Easy's choreography of the event required multiple boats, and that was fine with me.

The first wave of vehicles headed around the bay, and skippers of several dinghies carefully pushed off from the rock-strewn shore. I stayed behind waiting for Officer Richards to show up. Ten minutes, later he did. Freddie sat in the back seat, crunched between two narcs. They didn't immediately let Freddie go. I figured I'd be more hindrance than help, so I hung back.

When Freddie was finally released, the narcs—including the Shirt—piled into their runabout and Richards drove on toward the head of the bay. Freddie and I followed him on foot.

I asked, "What was that all about?"

"They wanted my camcorder and the cassette. I wasn't giving up the camcorder. My perseverance paid off. Now they have neither."

"What do you mean? I saw them take the cassette out of the camcorder."

"I switched cassettes before they caught up with me."

"Cool."

"It would be cooler if I'd given them something really boring, but unfortunately for Marsha, she's probably set to become the new idol at the cop house—all the footage is of her. There's lots of skin and only a red feather boa."

I appreciated that at least one man in Flamingo Bay was having more fun than I was.

"What happened to your vehicle?"

"Blew a tire out past Doctor's, went off the road, and into a tree. Minor damage only. I can live with that, especially since I fucked over those assholes."

The scene at the dinghy dock resembled a microscopic version of the chaos at Dunkirk, though I suspected Dunkirk's evacuees didn't much care on which boat they sailed or how much of their gear got left behind. They simply wanted to get the hell off the beach.

Freddie and I watched the dinghies being loaded. Jason and Vaughn went with Pirate Dan, giving him an even dozen. Mechanic Jim carried ten aboard his boat. The remaining two-dozen participants were split among the other four boats, all sloops.

Freddie asked, "What did you do to piss off the Fed?"

"Forgot to smile, maybe. Why?"

"Told me to tell you he's taking you down."

4

ONCE WE'D SECURED LEIF'S DINGHY with the stern lifeboat davits and the assigned contingent had climbed aboard, I fired up *Island Trader*'s diesel. It started with a growl and sent a shudder through the hull. The engine once powered a Greyhound bus, but it barely succeeded in its present job. Still, the price fit my wallet when I found it in a Florida junkyard. I shifted into gear and nudged the throttle to take the tension off the mooring chain. Easy released it, and I allowed the boat to drift clear of the buoy.

Easy headed aft, stood at the stern rail, and loaded a shell into his flare gun. He raised his meaty arm and fired. The projectile whistled into the sky on a trajectory that sent it toward the head of the bay and dozens of moored boats. Long before it reached the boats, the flare exploded with a pop. Even on a gray day, the flare's light seemed insignificant. The pop—saturated with significance—ricocheted off the hillsides.

Easy blew on the smoking barrel of his pistol before he hollered into his bullhorn, "Gentlemen, hoist your sails!"

Jolly Rogers quickly shinnied up the masts of five sloops and a ketch. Easy turned to see Pony Mon cleat the halyard to the mainmast of *Island Trader*. Easy's eyes ran up the mast, and his smile broadened as the skull and crossbones rippled in the breeze. His personalized commemorative T-shirt proclaimed in red just over his heart: PROUD SPONSOR.

I reached into a cooler, grabbed a soda, and popped the top as I made my way back to the helm, careful not to trip over the orange extension cord lying on the rusting steel deck. The cord powered the amplifiers of the band, Circle Jerk—four men who'd been around long enough to know their way around the nearby islands. My guess was each band member imitated his rock icon, at least in the hair department. I found a resemblance between the drummer and Ginger Baker, the bass guitarist and Paul McCartney, the keyboardist and Johnny Rivers. The lead guitarist was the odd man out; he'd shaved his head and face, leaving a few whiskers between his lower lip and chin. The tune was classic Jimmy Buffet—"A Pirate Looks at Forty." I ran the tachometer up to two thousand rpm. Slowly the engine generated forward momentum.

Today belonged to Leif, and I decided to think about his life and not his death, though I couldn't help thinking that I should've brought along a plank of the greenheart and invited the Shirt to walk it. Still, there was the problem of his gun. I wondered if he purposely disarmed me last week to give himself an edge. Speculating that he felt he needed an edge permitted me to puff out my chest a bit.

The six women in Billie's chorus line shared a joint and practiced coordinating with each other and with their palm frond pom-poms a few simple dance steps, but their giggles undermined all attempts at precision. Freddie—shaggy-haired and intense—mounted his camcorder on a tripod to record their missteps. As the camcorder captured the practice session, Freddie snapped a few photos with the Nikon he wore around his neck.

Freddie pivoted the camcorder and twisted his skinny bare torso to follow the progress of *Ketch 22* as she overtook *Island Trader*. Many eyes followed Freddie's lens and saw Mechanic Jim give a final yank to his headsail's halyard. Before he cleated it, he waved and grinned at the camera, doffing his baseball cap to allow his thick curly hair to decompress and grow luxuriant. Members of his crew bent over and dropped their pants.

Jim was a newcomer who'd arrived during the off-season, just after Billie. He asserted that he needed to work a few months to finance the next leg of his around-the-world excursion. An honest mechanic who grasped completely the complexity of an automotive drive train and the internal combustion engine, the community welcomed his arrival. Each time I figured Flamingo Bay had seduced him and he'd stick around, I recognized wanderlust in his eye.

On *Marauder*, Pirate Dan and his crew, running on a port tack, busied themselves trimming sails, too intent to clown for the camera. *Marauder* easily blew by *Island Trader* but fell farther behind *Ketch 22*. Dan shouted orders and raised his fist at Mechanic Jim, who flipped him the bird.

When the other boats, all sloops, left *Island Trader* in their wakes and the chorus line took a break, Freddie shut down his camcorder. He pushed his way through a throng gathered around one of several coolers and grabbed four beers. The band—working its way through a maudlin medley of teenage-death songs—finished a mocking rendition of "Teen Angel" and took a break when Freddie handed them the beers.

Glancing at my passengers, I spotted the parties within the party. Nonexclusive cliques sprawled against the bulwarks. The better equipped circled their lawn chairs. I likened the social dynamics of the event to a post-modern revision of the cocktail party, itself a modern adaptation of the tea party. Of course, each evolutionary adjustment of the function further compromised its civility and decorum. I suspected that with proper nourishment the final outcome of the event would be the orgy, but wasn't the orgy the uncivilized and indecorous forerunner to the tea party?

I often sailed out of Flamingo Bay with a boatload of partyers, white sails snapping in the breeze against a blue sky, warm sunshine feeding the exuberance. On this, Leif's last cruise, there were no sails and no sunshine, and only attitudes were blue. People weren't sure how to behave. It was as if some were afraid to have too much fun, while others worried they'd have too little. I recalled Robert Louis Stevenson's words: "Old and young, we are all on our last cruise." I didn't expect that any of us was heading for a lavender-sand beach. Still, in a world of infinite promise, all destinations offer hope—except the final one.

I wondered again whether it was time for me to leave Flamingo Bay in my wake for the last time. On the one hand, I accepted that leaving offered an opportunity to find greater misfortune. On the other, I knew I was running out of time and friends. I wasn't the young eager man that I once was. I didn't make friends easily, and I was old enough to be the father of the girls that incandesced, the girls who excited. I was old enough to have learned that I didn't belong with them, and they were smart enough to have figured that out. Still and always, the promise of the orgiastic future kept me dreaming, and my dreams kept me alive.

When I let my mind bounce the problem around, I found that it refused to fix on the overwhelming question: To leave or not to leave? That surprised me. Instead, I found the question that continuously presented itself to be even more overwhelming: Where do you go when you leave paradise?

I'd speculated about it for years, but I'd been able to ignore it because it'd always been merely rhetorical. Now it taunted and tormented, demanded an answer; but its immediate literal nature made the question no easier to answer. All I could conclude was that paradise was a place that you could leave and a place where you could go, but it wasn't a place you could live. Maybe Adam and Eve figured it right: paradise is a place you must leave before it destroys your soul.

I couldn't ignore, either, the niggling suspicion that my mind focused on flight because data, escaping from its pre-reflective state to its reflective state, recognized that Leif was likely killed by someone I knew, someone present in the funeral flotilla. The thing about denial: it works until it doesn't. I figured to nurse it along at least until tomorrow.

On the starboard beam, the wreckage of *Mango Mama* cluttered Rhymer's Reef. The thirty-six-foot ketch ran aground three months ago. Stripped by sea and pirates, nothing substantial remained except part of the collapsed hull, its beam no broader than a canoe's. Nobody knew what had happened. The incident occurred around midnight, and by dawn, Immigration rounded up about forty illegal Haitians who'd been aboard when the boat sank. The skipper, Mad Max, was still missing.

When we cleared the hillsides of Flamingo Bay, the wind increased and a squall roared down the Sir Francis Drake Channel to greet us. The musicians unplugged, and the drummer threw a tarp over their gear. Easy and Pony Mon helped him secure the tarp by weighting it around its perimeter with coolers. Freddie took his camcorder, and the musicians carried their instruments below deck.

Pony Mon, no particular friend to Leif, seemed glummer than the occasion called for. Always quick with a quip and prone to verbosity, he spoke little and said even less. It got me thinking about the validity of the rumor that he shot Bongo Natty, his own horse, so that the girl who jilted him would feel sorry for him and invite him back into her life. I hoped the rumor was untrue. I hadn't asked him about the incident—it was too personal; he'd tell me or not.

A big curtain of water danced toward us like a film noir version of the aurora borealis. The realization that the small canvas canopy covering the cockpit would keep no one dry sent everyone below deck. Alone at the helm I tugged on the visor of my baseball cap to keep it from flying away. Then I gripped the wheel with both hands to keep me from flying after it. Rain swept across the deck and poured out the scuppers. I was a bit nervous whether the ninety-five-year-old stern lifeboat davits would hold up in weather. In the seven years I'd owned the boat, I'd never used them—dumping Leif's body into the sea would spoil all Easy's planning.

After ten minutes, the wind—on its way west—left the precipitation behind, and the rain dropped steadily and vertically, soaking me to the skin. I didn't mind, really. The actual precipitation seemed insignificant. The Shirt had already rained on my parade.

When it rains on my parade—and it most often does—it pours. The anthem is quickly drowned. Its notes and the rainbow colors and the perfect symmetry and the high-stepping lissome girls with their chromium batons all dissolve into a muddy torrent sweeping along the gutter. Worst of all: there are no rain checks.

The squall passed, leaving the air thick and still. People gradually emerged from the companionway. The musicians plugged in their instruments and performed "Embryonic Journey," adding an improvisational coda to the short tune. *Island Trader*, a few hundred yards behind the rest of the flotilla, plowed through a dirty-dishwater sea.

"Oh, no!" Pony Mon alerted me. "Butcher, baker, candlestick maker, and cocaine whore."

Zeke's green runabout closed quickly from the stern with its contingent of mischief-makers. As the local Medicine Mon, Zeke had caused a great deal of mischief in Flamingo Bay all on his own. The Reverend Anal Richards—still recovering from four gunshot wounds inflicted by his brother the cop—sat up front with Zeke. Dressed in enough bandages to approximate a half-naked mummy, the self-appointed Reverend fingered his bullhorn. The tourist lady—last sighted dancing topless with Marsha a few nights ago at the Congo Club and now apparently estranged from her husband—was also aboard. Her deranged grin and Zeke's gargantuan smile strongly suggested that she'd sampled Zeke's medicine. Madison—the local rummy—reclined in the stern with the visor of his dirty white baseball cap pulled down over his eyes.

Zeke pulled alongside and cut back on the throttle. Easy warned him that he was crashing a private party, but Zeke simply grinned. The Reverend stood on his seat—grabbing the top of the windshield frame with his good hand—and raised the bullhorn to his lips with his injured arm, still bandaged and in a sling. Freddie—anticipating a video opportunity—rigged his camcorder and aimed it at Zeke's boat.

"This be God's sea," Reverend Richards announced over his bullhorn. "God make the sea, and He make the fishes, and He make me to be in charge of the sea and the fishes, and He make me to be in charge to lay Leif—slain by brother Cain...."

Passengers on *Island Trader* launched a barrage of beer bottles at Zeke's boat. Zeke jammed the throttle forward to escape the missiles, and the Reverend—uttering, "Yea, brothers"—lost his balance and splashed into the sea. We continued to celebrate the event even after Zeke dragged him back aboard.

Easy, standing next to me at the helm, rolled his eyes.

"Pony Mon nailed it precisely," I said. "What else can you expect from the rub-a-dub-dub club?"

"Good point," Easy conceded.

Pony Mon shook his head. "Least they not be you kin."

"Which one are you related to?" I asked.

"Every God one of them. First cousin to preacher. Second cousin to Zeke and Madison. I be kin to almost everybody born here."

It made sense that if your family had lived on St. Judas for nearly three hundred years—during which time the population never exceeded five thousand souls—you were everyone's kin.

"Pony Mon, why did the preacher get shot?"

It was common knowledge that Officer Richards pulled the trigger on his brother. He hadn't bothered to deny it. And there was no reason to deny it. No attempt was made to prosecute him.

"All grandchildren get land. Best land go to preacher because grandfather know he has jumbie in head. This blue vex policeman. He think he deserve best land though he be outside-son. When grandfather die, policeman want to swap land with preacher. Preacher say no. Policeman shoot he."

Some land disputes dragged on for generations, but I hadn't heard of shots being fired. Most of the fighting took place in court. Near as I could figure, West Indians loved courts, government, and bureaucracy. And why not? It seemed that about every other government employee received a white four-wheel-drive vehicle as part of the compensation package. How could you not like a place where the job of school-crossing guard provided fulltime employment, lifetime job security, and an attractive uniform?

"How about you? You have the best lot on the island, the Caribbean out your front window and the Atlantic out your back window. Why hasn't he come after you?"

He quietly uttered, "Bongo Natty." But he said nothing else before he walked away.

Pony Mon didn't throw accusations to the breeze. That he believed Richards shot Bongo Natty persuaded me of the falsity of the rumor he shot his own horse. I liked Pony Mon, and I wasn't the only one in Flamingo Bay disturbed by the rumor.

Muffled thunder snarled in the distance. Circle Jerk performed "I Fought the Law" at maximum amperage. Zeke kept his boat out of range of hand-fired objects but still within range of harassment, and Anal Richards preached and raved. The freshening breeze filled the armada's sails. *Island Trader* now lagged nearly a half-mile behind the armada.

Easy wandered toward the bow. He drifted past a scowling Sarah, who marched—arms cradling her breasts—in the direction of the helm. Neither slowed when they met, but each exchanged sharp words with the other. I wondered what Sarah had done to piss off Easy, though it was likely that Easy was pissed at what she hadn't done. As far as I knew, Easy was one of a handful of virgins in the Virgin Islands, and he'd been here permanently over two years. When a guy can't find success with a woman who's changed the luck of a dozen guys in as many months, it's difficult to be sanguine.

Most people assumed Easy hadn't earned his moniker because of his excitability, but I knew the opposite to be true. Last year, an old fishing buddy of Easy's came down from Alaska for a visit. He told me that in Homer, he knew the man as Easy Bill Engebritson, but "easy" meant "take it easy" or "whoa." Maybe it was the change in latitude, but Easy showed only occasional flashes of his former passion since his arrival.

Still beyond earshot, Sarah got in the last word, over her shoulder. When she turned and saw I was watching her, her sneer metamorphosed into a smile. She dropped her arms. Then she slowed her pace so her breasts wouldn't jiggle.

When I met Sarah, she wore her hair in a single braid that reached past her waist. She no longer braided her hair. There was nothing left to braid. It reached only to her chin, not much longer than my own. In the same manner in which *Island Trader* was more than just a boat to me, and Marsha's breasts were more than just breasts to her, Sarah's hair was more than just hair to her—it possessed a mystical quality. I couldn't fault her. It also meant something ineffable to me, particularly on those nights when she coaxed me to use her braid to tie her hands together behind her head. Last year, to prove some point I still didn't get, she lopped it off. It saddened me, but I guessed that she was sorrier about her decision than I was.

She averted her eyes, sipped her beer, and waited for me to greet her. Instead, I asked her what was going on between her and Easy. She told me to mind my own business. I did, but when I ignored her for nearly two minutes, she fumed.

"Why can't you be civil?" she asked.

An annoying human foible is when the guilty accuse the innocent of the very offense for which the guilty party is guilty and the innocent party is innocent. It'd become a trusty weapon in Sarah's arsenal.

"Because it's a social contract. Civility is lost on shrews—and traitors."

Smart enough to realize the conversation was going nowhere, but aggressive enough to keep it going, she sniffled and changed her tack.

"Sorry about the truck."

"Whatever," I said, as I watched her scratch at the label on her beer bottle. "But I'll take the key." She dug it out of her pocket and handed it over. "How many more do you have?"

"This is the only one."

"You're sure?"

"Positive," she said. "You don't have any cash you could loan me? I'm broke."

"Baroque? And I thought you were rococo."

"Don't be a smart ass. I'm serious."

"I'm even more broke than you are."

She tore off most of the label with a single motion.

"How come? You always have money when you get back from South America."

"Lopez ripped me off for five grand when the ceramic tile I bought for cash never showed up on the dock. I lost another five when I lost the sails."

She finally made eye contact. "Why didn't you call the police?"

"I did, but I was just another dumb Yankee. To make matters worse, it wasn't my money they stole but money that belonged to my erstwhile client, Mr. Outback, over on Water Island."

"The jerk who's been calling me at work?"

"News to me."

"Well, he has."

Sarah sniffled twice before she wiped her runny nose on the back of her hand. Her malaise was self-inflicted, caused by inhaling the white pollen.

"November colds can be such a bitch," I said.

"So you can't help me out?"

"Sorry."

"Figures. Everything here sucks."

I often wondered how the fresh and innocent face of youth turned unrecognizably sour and shrunken in maturity. I once thought it was simply part of the aging process, but I'd learned different. It was about traveling wrong paths and blazing dubious trails.

"I bought you a plane ticket home, remember?"

"All I get is a damn plane ticket?"

"I've given you every extra dollar I've had, so you could see the face of God. It would've been a lot cheaper if I'd just bought you a mirror."

"Don't give me any of that phony-baloney philosophy. If you'd sell this rusty piece-of-shit boat, I'd even consider getting back together."

"Seems like a good reason to keep her until I die."

"Prick."

"Sarah, why don't you just date Vaughn or Zeke or find someone else who has enough cocaine or cash to keep you flying for the rest of your life. That's all you're really looking for."

"Fuck you," she said before she stormed off, breasts jiggling. After a half-dozen steps, she stopped and turned. "Maybe I already have found someone."

"Good for you."

Island Trader slowly closed on the armada. Sails struck, the boats bobbed aimlessly in the six-foot seas, as neither the wind nor the current had yet straightened them out. I doubted that they were outside territorial waters, beyond the three-mile limit. Oh, well. It was my fault. An armada is only as fast as the slowest boat.

I loved being on my boat, and I loved being at sea—things generally moved at a pace that made Island Time seem frenetic, but I had books to read, stuff to think about, and dreams to build. Still, there existed one large drawback when I carried passengers: no place to hide. Billie was next up to try my patience. I watched, as she resolutely made her way to the helm. Unlike Sarah, it took Billie a while. Eyes focused on her. Arms reached out to touch her. She spoke an intimate word or two to each of her devotees, always making eye contact, always touching the hand, arm, or shoulder of her admirer.

She held up a joint. Cognizant of my responsibility as a designated driver, I shook my head.

"How about a cigarette then?"

Her green baseball cap was inadequate to control her shoulder-length hair. She held her hair away from her face with both hands, while I lit her cigarette.

"Pretty good turn out, wouldn't you say?"

I nodded.

In Flamingo Bay, you *did* need an excuse to party, and while almost any damn excuse would do, a legitimate one provided the sort of atmosphere in which excess could flourish.

"You're not wearing a commemorative shirt," Billie said.

"They're itchy when they're new."

"I would've washed one for you."

"When? We didn't finish printing them until after midnight."

It seemed to me that Easy was making a good profit on my buck by sponsoring the funeral as a moneymaking enterprise. I bought the shirts in Venezuela for a buck and a half less than they cost here, and I sold them to Easy at cost plus a buck for the silk-screening and art. No wonder my checking account was empty. Of course, I knew Easy was just barely hanging on to his business—part of the feast-or-famine cycle of tourism. The tourists would be here in force in another month. They'd keep him going until Easter. I wasn't sure what'd keep me going.

"Still angry?" Billie asked.

"I was never angry, just annoyed. Can't you at least let the man be put to rest before promoting your agenda?"

"Finding Leif's killer is everyone's agenda. Except yours. I thought you were a better man than this."

"Good enough to do your bidding, but not good enough to get in your pants?"

"I didn't mean it that way, but you can be so selfish."

"If you're going to continue to rag on me, please stand on my left. Sarah already filled my right ear."

"I could stand on my head, but it probably wouldn't change your mind."

"Try standing on my head."

"Very funny."

I gave her the cold-eyed, puckered-lip stare.

"Captain Brian, please don't do this to me again."

"Again?"

She cocked her head and gave me a stern look. "You know what I'm talking about. I've seen that look before. You've never really forgiven me for my Oscar-winning performance, have you?"

She nailed it. I hadn't forgiven her. I had to forget it first, but it stuck in my craw. Act one began with a picnic for two at a remote patch of beach accessible only by sea. She pranced around naked and behaved badly, alternately seducing and spurning me in a manner as playful and caring as the tides—always staying out of arm's reach. After lunch, I dozed in the sun and awakened when she straddled my legs to apply sunscreen to my back. She did it without using her hands, her erect nipples sending sparks to my spine. The day's climax occurred that evening when we motored to the Congo Club in darkness. After cocktails and dinner, she began singing in my ear a Maria Muldaur song. The specific line I misinterpreted—"Don't you feel my thigh"— was not an invitation to grope her. She slapped me hard across the face in front of thirty patrons. The denouement occurred some minutes later at the dinghy dock. She caught up with me, as I pushed off to motor to *Island Trader*. I told her that I loved her. She told me she didn't love me.

What can you do when lives and dreams refuse to merge? What can you do when they grind against each other like tectonic plates? I'd seen the green light in Billie's eyes. I hadn't realized I'd been looking for it my entire life until I saw it. If it wasn't for me, why did I recognize it?

I stayed away from her and didn't speak to her for days, assuming she'd get on with her life with someone else, preferably somewhere else. People came and went from Flamingo Bay, and beautiful young women quickly found the captain with a suitable itinerary and adequate resources to finance it, but that hadn't happened to Billie. She insisted I was her best friend. Ignoring my suggestion that if she wanted a friend, she should get a puppy, she dogged me for days. It became tedious to brush her off, but she didn't mistake my new civility for forgiveness, and she demanded to be a part of my life.

I figured that putting her to work would put her off. It didn't. If anything, it reinforced her resolve. We cleaned and painted below deck— about as much fun as latrine duty. Billie came back for more. She even helped me do a valve job on *Island Trader*'s diesel. Finally, when I ran out of chores, I surrendered. I didn't care to admit it, but late at night, I looked forward to seeing her in the morning, and gradually we became pals. At one meeting of our book club, we discussed *Heart of Darkness*— and as is often the case when reading Joseph Conrad—I digressed and let slip that I was trying to come up with a logo for the T-shirt I was designing for Easys. Billie's contribution stuck: A SUNNY PLACE FOR SHADY PEOPLE. It signaled the birth of our business partnership.

"And I always thought you earned at least three Oscars."

Her confidence disintegrated, and she mumbled, "Three?"

"The first for crushing my ego. The second for wrenching my soul. The third for breaking my heart."

Billie maintained her composure for about ten seconds before she turned and fled, sobbing. I thought about going after her but changed my mind. She didn't cry because she broke my heart; she cried because she was old enough to distinguish between real and make believe. I was, too, which was why I still punished her.

At three hundred yards, I idled the diesel and shifted into neutral. Momentum easily carried *Island Trader* to the staging area. Easy untied my inflatable dinghy and dragged it around to midship. He held the painter, while Pony Mon descended the ladder. The Yamaha gave Pony Mon a little trouble, but then it fired, and he motored around to the stern.

Easy cleared it with me and kept me up to speed with Leif's funeral arrangements, but I hadn't participated in the discussions and planning that went into the event—it was Easy's buck. When Easy's committee determined to cremate Leif's remains, Billie—a committee member—explained to me she'd witnessed a cremation on the banks of the Ganges two years before and how much the participants struggled to get the body to burn completely and how it seemed to take forever. I suggested she voice her concerns to Easy. She did, and Easy enlisted Jason's help to concoct an accelerant to make the fire burn hotter. Because of Jason's recent inattentiveness to detail, I wouldn't be surprised to learn that he'd just spit into a can of gas.

Easy and I carefully lowered Leif's aluminum dinghy—painted black for the occasion—using the stern lifeboat davits. Leif was in a body bag trussed up with a chain threaded through several concrete blocks, just in case Jason miscalculated how much heat the dinghy could take before its rivets started popping. Beneath Leif's body, Easy had placed a foil-wrapped, two-gallon plastic jug containing Jason's miracle accelerant. Leif lay on a sheet of corrugated roofing supported by the dinghy's seats. Scraps of lumber, some driftwood, a ton of homemade charcoal, and—compliments of Pony Mon—an unbaled bale of hay completed the list of visible combustibles. Leif's few worldly possessions—including Snoopy—were arranged around him.

Seeing Leif's remains made me see red. I'd bailed him out countless times. Leave him alone for a few days, and the son of a bitch goes and gets himself killed. Why couldn't he behave when his life depended on it?

The various boats were arranged in something that resembled a circle, though perhaps not to Euclid. Pony Mon towed Leif's dinghy halfway to *Marauder*. He doused the dinghy with diesel. The band played "Light My Fire." The archers—anyone equipped with bow and arrow—prepared their weapons. Pony Mon motored back to *Island Trader*. Tanya changed her mind about Snoopy, and Pony Mon made another trip in the Zodiac to fetch the stuffed animal and deliver it to *Ketch 22*.

"Captain Brian," Easy called from midship, "you'll say a few words?"

I left the helm to join Easy at midship. On the way, I scuffed a blister of rust loose from the deck with the toe of my shoe. Beneath it, the steel was black and lumpy from oxidation. It reminded me that I needed to come up with some cash soon to re-plate the deck, but my concern for the boat's maintenance was short-lived. Tears welled in my eyes before I became conscious that the lumpy black patch of steel resembled Valerie's tumors. I used my T-shirt to wipe my eyes and slowly dug through a cooler. I supposed it made sense to think of one dead friend while saying goodbye another. When the constriction in my throat relaxed, I was able to find a soda and my voice. Easy handed me the bullhorn. Off the top of my head, I started speaking.

"Bat Masterson—hired by Wyatt Earp as a deputy marshal in Dodge City—once remarked that most people figure things break about even in this world—"

My words came out garbled. Easy took the bullhorn and banged it a couple of times against the deck. While he applied his Stone Age technique to repair the electrical malfunction, I surveyed the scene— friends and neighbors and others, a pretty okay bunch. In the days leading up to Leif's funeral, I thought about modeling my eulogy on Pericles' funeral oration, but I lacked reference material. Antony's skillful filleting of Brutus could have worked as a pattern, but I had no one to point a finger at just yet. Last night I searched my poetry volumes for lines from *Lycidas*, planning to give Leif a send-off in the neoclassical tradition, as an alternative to the classical. Today Milton's obscure verbosity—"What hard mishap hath doomed this gentle swain"—became even more obscure and verbose in daylight. Dodge City. That was a reference folk in Flamingo Bay understood.

Easy handed me the repaired bullhorn. I started again and repeated Masterson's line, gaining the attention of many mourners.

"Masterson went on to say that he figured things broke even, also. He used ice—the stuff that's keeping your beer cold—to demonstrate his proposition. Most people get about the same amount, he argued—the difference being the rich get theirs in summer, while the poor get theirs in winter."

Mild applause encouraged me to continue.

"Leif was a reprobate of the first order, but he was our reprobate, and he didn't deserve to die. He had as much right as you or I to enjoy until old age the invincible summer of St. Judas, a place where the scarcity of ice is a year-round problem for rich and poor alike.

"As you know, Leif wasn't a religious guy, but he was a thoughtful guy. Leif didn't believe in God, and Leif didn't believe in life after death—not that I suspect adherents to that proposition are any more willing to go gentle into that good night. Leif argued it was simply a game. Leif figured that man created God, and man—always fearful that someone out there was having more fun than he—allowed God to create immorality. Saddled with a god grown omnipotent through institutionalization, man's only recourse was to rebel. So, in a brazen show of one-upmanship, man created immortality and stuck those words in God's mouth. Man and God have been courting ever since."

Realizing I'd lost my audience and annoyed that I'd wandered too far afield, I decided to wrap it up.

"I'm not the smartest guy in the world, but I've been around long enough to see that the world's exactly what one makes of it. I respect that there's no God in Leif's world. I respect that Leif didn't take his life too seriously. I respect, also, that Leif would like us to laugh when we remember him. I expect I always will."

I finished to the deafening racket of Anal Richards' preaching and the thunder that was gradually moving from the background to the foreground, but a few listeners applauded with enthusiasm.

"Thanks, man," Easy said and took the bullhorn. He lifted his arm and shouted into the device, "On my command, you may commence firing."

He dropped his arm, and seconds later a volley of flaming arrows soared toward the dinghy from the nearby boats. Most of the archers sported homemade weapons that looked like prehistoric versions of the longbow, and it didn't appear that anyone present would get an invitation to Nottingham for the finals.

Ten minutes passed before the archers ran out of ammo. The band did its best to drown Anal Richards and lift lagging spirits by offering a weak rendition of the last few minutes of the *William Tell* Overture. Spirits failed to soar, though I did hear someone exclaim: "Hi-ho Silver."

Pony Mon prepared to motor back to toss a match on Leif's dinghy, but over on *Marauder*, Pirate Dan pulled out a crossbow. He methodically wrapped the tip of the bolt with burlap and liberally applied fuel. Dan aimed and nodded to Diver Vaughn. The band picked up the cue. A drumroll. Vaughn lit the burlap. The Pirate pulled the trigger. Thunk—a direct hit.

Cheers shrank to groans and shriveled to an expectant silence when there was no immediate conflagration. Nothing much happened for nearly a minute. It was not spontaneous, but there was combustion. A dim blue flame grew orange and expanded rapidly, along with the applause.

Easy proclaimed, "Fire when you're ready, Gridley."

Kneeling in the bow, I took the cigarette from my mouth and held it to the fuse of my cannon. It was the real deal, a three-pounder—the fashionable instrument of choice of big-time yacht guys to greet fellow cruisers. I stepped away and plugged my ears.

Ka-boom!

Easy punched the button on his stopwatch. The band played "As Tears Go By." Waving palm frond pom-poms in a circular motion, the chorus of Valkyries arranged at the rail performed a little dance, kicking as they spread their arms. Then the Valkyries tossed their pom-poms overboard, grabbed the hems of their T-shirts, and flashed their breasts—first for Leif, then for Freddie's camcorder.

When Billie pulled her shirt down, I decided to reload my cannon.

I opened the locker where I stored the powder and wads I fired to greet fellow cruisers. After inserting the fuse, I dropped a load of powder down the barrel and tamped it. Then I loaded the paper wad and tamped it. I'd never actually fired a round—just the wads—though I possessed a single cannonball that came with the cannon's purchase. The cannon's seller suggested I find someone who could use the cannonball as a model to make more. Never finding a need for ammo and never finding anyone capable of manufacturing ammo, creating a store of ammunition felt a bit too extravagant—on a dull day you could salt the sea with a lot of iron. It wasn't nearly as cheap as buying a box of forty-five cartridges.

The incineration of the body bag and the presence of diesel created a great cloud of black smoke that danced over Leif's dingy like a spectral genie escaping from a lamp, reminding me that the other thing that upset Billie was that bowing to outdated West Indian tradition Leif's great toes had been tied together so he couldn't dance, couldn't become a jumbie.

Easy, joining me in the bow, nodded at the Valkyries and said, "Leif would've loved this."

"True, but if Leif were actually present, the women would most likely be wearing snowmobile suits."

"Also true," Easy said. "Except Marsha."

Easy and I watched as Marsha—still waving her shirt—deployed her store-bought breasts to challenge Flamingo Bay's negligible standard of decorum.

"Except Marsha," I agreed.

Across the way from *Island Trader*, Pirate Dan and Zeke exchanged words and gestures. Unsatisfied with the outcome, Dan fitted another bolt to his crossbow and let it fly. It pierced the fiberglass hull of Zeke's boat at the waterline. Zeke yanked on the preacher's good arm, dropping him into his seat. Then he jumped on the throttle and steered toward Flamingo Bay.

Pony Mon set up a makeshift kitchen in the bow of *Island Trader* with a charcoal grill and two card tables. He unloaded a cooler of chicken onto one table and brushed the pieces with his own barbecue sauce. Helpers filled the other table with potato salad, coleslaw,

and the usual picnic fare. When the charcoal was ready, Pony Mon
filled the Weber's grate with the first batch of chicken and covered the
kettle. While the chicken and Leif cooked, luncheon preparations also
took place on the other boats.

The oily cloud of black smoke that'd earlier wafted from Leif's
dinghy shrunk to a shadow of its former incarnation, as the fire burned
hotter. Suddenly Jason's homemade accelerant ignited like gasoline,
creating a huge ball of fire that exploded into the sky. The super-
charged conflagration fascinated the mourners. I could feel the heat
from fifty feet away.

When the massive flames subsided—almost as quickly as they
ignited—Pony Mon signaled lunch, and a line quickly formed in the
bow. A barbecue at a cremation—like a riddle wrapped in a mystery—
overloaded my senses, and I decided to delay lunch, though I assisted
Pony Mon by reloading the grill after he doled out chicken. He offered
one piece per customer, giving everyone an opportunity to get started.
People without lawn chairs lounged against the masts and bulwarks,
but most stood at the rail fumbling with plates, plastic forks, and beverages.

They watched Diver Vaughn and Jason the Argonut climb aboard
Pirate Dan's inflatable—not part of Easy's carefully choreographed
program. Jason operated the outboard, glumly taking orders from the
patrician Vaughn whose blond hair looked as though it'd been coiffed
at a Southern California surf shop. No one on St. Judas worked harder
than Vaughn to create, perfect, and maintain a personal image. At first,
he did it to promote his diving business—a tremendous success by Flamingo Bay standards. Later it became a habit or part of a conscious
program to make his personal life as successful as his business life.

When they reached the burning dinghy, Jason—the most visibly
injured guy in Flamingo Bay outside Reverend Richards—shut off the
motor and sipped beer through a straw. Flamingo Bay's token white
Rasta, Jason's waist-length blond dreadlocks had unraveled as thoroughly as his life. I learned upon returning from Venezuela that on suc-
cessive days Jason had engaged in altercations first with Vaughn and
then with Dan. Vaughn broke Jason's jaw with a single well-placed
punch, and Dan broke Jason's arm with his Louisville Slugger; how-

ever, Jason's most serious injury, the oozing sore above his upper lip, couldn't be blamed on anyone but himself. I once figured a slight cosmetic improvement to his appearance would suffice to allow Jason to hold his life together, but I'd come to realize that growing an Adolph Hitler mustache no longer provided a solution.

Neat in an untidy way, the relationship between Jason and Vaughn wagged a lot of tongues. Jason depended on Vaughn to supply him with cocaine. And Vaughn depended on Wendy, Jason's wife, to provide him with sexual satisfaction. Others depended on Wendy for sexual satisfaction, including Cherry Mary. I couldn't say for sure how many people Wendy disappointed when she sailed off with a young skipper three days ago. Billie and I were among them; Wendy was a pivotal member of our book club—sometimes three is a crowd, but not when you're discussing literature. It surprised me that Billie hadn't included Wendy among her suspects. Leaving Flamingo Bay after the killing was the most suspicious act I'd heard about.

Vaughn loaded up a very long stick with marshmallows and began to roast them over a fire that no longer sent ambitious flames skyward. The crowd seemed about evenly divided whether Vaughn's appropriation of Leif's pyre to cook food was sacrilegious or cool. I figured it was both, and it was a stunt Leif would've loved to pull himself. A few of those who thought it cool joined Vaughn to roast hot dogs and brats.

I considered for a moment about how in some tribal cultures the victors ate the vanquished, and I wondered if anyone present enjoyed a moment of quiet victory upon recognizing a perverse element of transubstantiation in the consumption of the victuals. I couldn't decide, but I didn't rule it out as a possibility down the road when the killer— if present—had time to reflect upon the occasion.

The heat melted the rivets or burned through the hull of Leif's boat, and the dinghy abruptly sizzled into the sea. Two hours and forty-seven minutes after the first shot, it was over. Little debris floated on the rolling waves. Easy gave me the command to fire the cannon to signal the end of the event; however, Nature—only rumbling until now—cooked up another conclusion.

At the instant the cannon fired, the air smelled funny and the hair on the back of my neck stood up. A flash of electricity shot out of the sky and split, striking both the mainmast of *Ketch 22* and the mast of *Marauder*. It sparked, as it always does in the laboratories of mad scientists in old horror movies. My skin tingled. The thunder that echoed the cannon shot cracked with the intensity you might expect to hear if Earth itself fractured like an egg. A blue haze hovered over the armada. We witnessed the real deal—the Mister Thor show.

Billie's "Oh-my-god!" rose above other mutterings and exclamations.

It took a few minutes before the electrons settled. People checked themselves out, then their boats, then their electronics. My radios escaped damage. Others weren't so lucky. The lightning scarred the masts and fried the radios on *Marauder* and *Ketch 22*. After skippers assessed the damage, Easy passed the word that Jason held the winning ticket. Unable to open his mouth, Jason's shipmates celebrated for him. I figured the whole five hundred would go up his nose.

Two boats bailed on the party, as the skippers blamed the lightning strike on the sacrilegious roasting of marshmallows and brats and saw it as a divine sign to get off the sea. Not me. I wished only that Leif could've been present for his own funeral. I suspected he might've adjusted some of his notions relating to the nature of the cosmos when he went out with a bang.

I thought first that T.S. Elliot had been wrong, at least in Leif's case, when he stated that the world ends in a whimper and not a bang. But the more I thought about it, I realized Elliot was probably right, and Leif did go out with a whimper. The bang occurred days after his death. Maybe the world always begins with a bang and ends with a whimper. Science seems to postulate that scenario for planet Earth. If bangs are beginnings, what was the cosmic significance to today's bang? Was there one? Was there any significance?

As I contemplated the difficulties that burdened a detective—eyes peeled, lips sealed, ear to the ground, nose to the grindstone, finger on the trigger, and foot in the door (all without getting one's ass in a sling)—I suspected that perhaps some significance did exist, even if it was only to focus my attention on Leif's murder.

Murder is the scariest crime, but murderers are not always the scariest criminals—simply making a victim of the antagonist often resolves the murderer's problem. I loved the logic, but I was smart enough to realize I was just setting myself up for failure, preparing myself for failure. I hated to fail.

Billie demanded I get involved in solving the mystery of Leif's death because he was my friend, and you're supposed to do something when your friend is murdered. She didn't know that I'd once saved Leif's life—it was how I met him. I don't know if that made him indebted to me or me indebted to him. Somehow, I thought the latter to be true. It was like saving *Island Trader* from the bone yard—I'd taken on the duty of keeping her afloat. If by saving Leif's life I'd taken on the duty of keeping him alive, I'd failed absolutely.

In a larger sense, Leif's murder was a crime against the community. Solving it couldn't help Leif and it wouldn't satisfy me, but it might satisfy the community. However you define it, justice, I suspect, is a lot like the victim's funeral: it's pretty much about the survivors.

5

On the trip back to Flamingo Bay, the sun made encouraging efforts to break through the cloud cover—as startling as when a frame of celluloid jams in a faulty projector and disintegrates under the lamp's intense heat. I expected the imminent exit of the tropical wave, but by the time *Island Trader* reached her mooring, the sky turned gray again and a gentle rain fell, forcing a change of location for the post-funeral party.

On my last ferry run, unloading people and gear from my boat, I dropped Easy at the dinghy dock. Pirate Dan, hands on hips and resting his weight on his good leg, greeted him. Easy needed an axe to complete his lumberjack image, and the Pirate needed a cutlass, but because both men were unarmed, negotiations between the two proceeded without bloodletting. After strong words from both parties and offer and counteroffer, Easy agreed to turn over to Dan four hundred dollars of the cash he collected from the T-shirt sales to provide refreshments for the party that would now take place at the Congo Club. I was still in my dinghy, engine idling, and about to head back to my boat when Dan stopped me.

"Where the fuck you going?"

I nodded toward *Island Trader*.

"I don't fucking think so."

"Now we're buddies?" I asked.

"Fuck off, but don't fuck off until midnight. Pretend you're Cinderella."

I didn't refuse his offer because I had nowhere else to go and the Congo Club was a pretty okay joint. When I grudgingly stepped into the place, I found the tables and chairs pushed away from the center of the deck to create space for dancing. Marsha, solo and uninspired, jiggled mechanically to the music. I walked by her and found an empty stool at the end of the bar. It felt good to get the weight off my knee.

About half of the funeral celebrants were present. I suspected those still absent would be along. Billie—whom I dropped at *Sappho* to change into dry clothes—numbered among those absent, and her missing energy diminished the level of excitement to that of a PTA meeting. Still, sex, drugs, rock and roll, and exuberant behavior existed in Flamingo Bay before Billie's arrival, and nobody ever complained about not having enough fun; but we'd become so used to Billie jump-starting an event that we tended to rely on her. Also, for however much Leif himself was ignored on the final day of his corporeal existence, a few people did have trouble recognizing the day as a celebratory occasion.

Many others who hadn't attended the event at sea joined the party. Word of free beer always insured a good turnout but also caused friction. The seventy-or-so mourners paid for the party, though they wouldn't be getting full value for their money. When Easy's four hundred bucks was drunk up—wholesale or retail, however Dan worked the numbers—beer would no longer be free, the cheapskates among the freeloaders would depart, and many of the partyers would be taxed a second time for their revelry.

The band set up in a protected corner against the wall of the shack. A Bob Marley tune, "Buffalo Soldier," played on the Pirate's tape deck. It occurred to me that Dickens was only technically correct when he stated that Marley was dead. While Jimmy Buffet's fans (Parrot Heads) elevated him to cult status, Marley's status among many of his followers reached loftier heights. To some, Marley was part of a Rasta triumvirate with God and Haile Selassie. To others, he'd already become like Julius and Augustus—the triumvirate's successor.

While I waited to get served, I studied Dan's collection of relics: the steering wheel to Fast Louie's Ferrari (Louie was last year's only casualty in Flamingo Bay), the barely recognizable front wheel of Pirate Dan's Harley after his final ride two years ago, the binnacle to *Mango Mama* (now piled up on Rhymer's Reef), the tiller to *Shamrock I*, the bowsprit to *Shamrock II*. Sadly, no memento existed of Captain Lucky's final command, *Shamrock III*, presumably lost with all hands—none local—during the first tropical storm of the season.

Leaning against *Mango Mama*'s binnacle, the charred transom board from Leif's dinghy awaited formal installation. Pirate Dan worked hard to become a custodian of the Lore, and I admired that about him.

The Lore—part history, part mythology, part bullshit—existed as Flamingo Bay's permanent record, a record that bore no resemblance to the archive stashed in the government's file cabinets. To be a candidate for inclusion, you needed simply to become a member of the community, which could be accomplished by surrendering your surname and perhaps adjusting your notion of privacy. No initiation or confirmation existed. The Lore embraced you as a lover, unless it didn't.

The Lore embraced Leif. No surprise there. The Lore existed for men like Leif who created adventure as easily as a magician produced rabbits and doves. When he showed up in Flamingo Bay, Leif was no stranger to another lore, the federal criminal justice system. Though I seasoned Leif's retelling of his exploits with grains of salt, I never doubted the criminal justice-system aspect of Leif's story.

Leif himself didn't have much to say about his anti-social activities in Flamingo Bay. But the accounts of his exploits witnessed by others filled the annals of the Lore; there was no way yet of telling how much space the Lore would dedicate to his murder.

In addition to the Congo Club's relics, dozens of photos commemorating regattas and parties decorated the limited wall space. An eight-by-ten color glossy pictured Neil Young's schooner, low and sleek with rust-colored sails. Bruce Springsteen's autograph hung next to it, tagged with the line he penned: BORN IN THE V.I. Paperbacks and periodicals that constituted Flamingo Bay's only lending library filled several cartons. Carved into the mahogany of the bar's countertop hundreds of names offered one- and two-word testimonials to Flamingo Bay's recent history.

The bartender served me the first beer of the day when Mary's dog nudged me with her nose, almost knocking me off my stool. A big mutt, Helga shared genes with the Newfoundland or Saint Bernard. I scratched and stroked her giant head with both hands. Salt encrusted her long hair—black, brown, and cream-colored. Helga rested on her belly when I tired of petting her, and she licked my toes through the holes in my shoes. Since the death of Sweetheart, a remarkable golden retriever and possibly the world's only coconut-fetching and -eating dog, Helga became my closest canine friend.

Behind the bar, next to a beat-up TV that was connected to a VCR—

because the Congo Club lacked a twelve hundred-foot antenna—hung a poster Billie created. HAITIAN VACATION it proclaimed from within its border of entwined hibiscus. It didn't offer escape *to* Haiti. It offered escape *from* Haiti. Bullet points highlighted the principal attractions under the all-inclusive AMERICAN PLAN: a four-day sail on a luxury yacht to the Virgin Islands; shopping in St. Thomas; culinary delights—including a detailed list of all the fast-food franchises—airfare to Cuba; two-weeks' relaxation at the U.S. government spa at Guantánamo Bay; airfare home.

Billie's comic vacation poster predated Max's voyage to Haiti. I found it incomprehensible that Max took Billie's jest seriously, but it could be argued that I took another of Billie's jests seriously enough that I believed she loved me. The evidence showed that Max transported forty illegal Haitians. Everybody proffered a theory about Max's disappearance. Too smart to bring them here and too experienced a sailor to run aground on Rhymer's Reef, I guessed that he never made it back to Flamingo Bay. I suspected the Haitians hijacked the boat and tossed Max overboard. I didn't expect we'd ever learn the truth.

Gossip surrounding the destruction of Max's boat in his home harbor would feed the grapevine a few months more, but Max's real legacy would focus on his lone crew, Billie, who hitched a ride with him here from Key West. Before Billie (who was without shame or inhibition) quit Flamingo Bay, I expected an entire volume of the Lore would be dedicated exclusively to her. I expected, also, she'd be canonized.

Max didn't mention a word to Billie about his plans. While Billie borrowed my truck to buy groceries in town, Max dumped her gear on the dinghy dock and just sailed off. Cherry Mary found Billie's gear and stowed it aboard *Sappho*. When Billie returned from shopping, she found Mary waiting for her on the dock. Mary told her of Max's departure and offered Billie a place to stay. The two came to some sort of understanding, and Billie still lived aboard *Sappho*. For a time, Billie's choice to live on *Sappho* branded her, like Mary, an anti-woman. When people learned Mary had been no more successful seducing Billie than all the men who'd tried, Billie again became a golden girl, a prize anyone could have if he or she could capture her heart.

Lights blinked on in the harbor and on the hillsides. The breeze, fresh and onshore, carried laughter and music up the hillside away from us. Sea grape branches swept the sky, and the clanking and rattling of the riggings on the moored boats could be heard during the pauses between songs.

Mister Aubrey came by with a couple of well-dressed West Indian men—dark slacks, white short-sleeved shirts, open collars—who were not locals. They took a nearby table, but when Aubrey spotted me he walked over to say hello, and I bought him a cocktail. With a full head of silver hair, Aubrey was a man of formidable strength and a man to be reckoned with—his biceps still stretched the sleeves of his baggy T-shirt. We'd always gotten on together. His wife was the unfriendly one, the keeper of books and purse strings; Aubrey did the living, while she kept score. Mildly concerned by rumors I heard that Aubrey did not have clear title to the playground's land, I asked him if they were true.

"Land by church belong to me and sister," he replied. "Government take some for the road, but they doesn't take it all. I doesn't get on with sister, so nothing come of the land. She live on St. Thomas. She not back here many years. She not coming back. She hate this place." He crushed his cigarette in the ashtray. "You build playground. I be watching you back. Don't worry."

The taller of Aubrey's West Indian associates, alternating nervous glances between his companion and his wristwatch, finally came over to drag Aubrey back to the table to discuss business. Aubrey excused himself with a broad smile and a further reminder not to worry.

Johnny Dollar, president of the Flamingo Bay Yacht Club, took Aubrey's stool. Trim, tan, handsome, rich, and forty, Johnny existed as a sharp reminder of what I lacked and what was lacking in me. His khaki shorts and polo shirt were faded to perfection but unfrayed. He wore three-hundred-dollar boat shoes, worn but not worn-out. Never too new, never too old, his clothes always presented a careless patina (as if he'd hired someone to wear them the first couple-dozen times to break them in). Johnny belonged to the previous generation—the generation of calypso and noblesse oblige. Unlike me, Johnny had enough money to support his habit. Maybe it was cheaper to belong to the previous generation than to the previous century where I seemed rooted, but I doubted it.

"Captain Brian, you okay?"

"Okay, Johnny."

Johnny lived in Sugar Harbor, and his annual presence in Flamingo Bay coincided with the Thanksgiving Regatta. Johnny ran the show, but tradition kept the race headquartered at the Congo Club. Though there'd been talk over the years of moving the regatta to Sugar Harbor, people understood the event wouldn't be nearly as much fun because— except for Officer Richards—no chaperones operated in Flamingo Bay.

"We've decided to go with two hundred T-shirts this year—give them to the sponsors as well as the participants."

"No problem."

"Also, we'd like *Island Trader* to be the committee boat for this year's regatta. Will you help us out? That's if you're not planning to enter the race. It can't be much fun to come in last every year."

Johnny knew nothing about coming in last. His ignorance of that particular subject compromised his conviviality. *Whisper*—the fastest boat I'd sailed on—composed a class all its own. Every year that he raced, Johnny won the event. The keel of the seventy-year-old schooner was the only identifiable original component still in place. Johnny's in-laws owned a shipyard in Mississippi, and Johnny had restored the boat there.

"I lost my sails to a squall."

"Bummer. But I can relate. Similar thing happened to me several years ago on the way to Bermuda. The storm took a big swipe at us. We lost all our sails *and* the foremast—snapped like a toothpick. Took a crew overboard. We were lucky to fish him out. Ran out of fuel. Day the Coast Guard found us we were seriously contemplating recycling our urine. Thank God for the Coast Guard. Must have towed us fifty miles."

He had a lot more to say, but an old salt standing next to me interrupted Johnny to tell his story about losing his boat to a hurricane in Montserrat. Another sailor spoke of fighting off Malay pirates. One thing about telling a tale of woe in Flamingo Bay: nearly everybody could counter with a story more humorous or horrific than your own.

While I listened to the adventures of those around me, Johnny, not a quick thinker, finally saw the obvious.

"If you don't have sails," he said, "you can't race." Johnny took a sip of his beer and awaited my response. When none was forthcoming, he added, "May as well be the committee boat."

Johnny didn't get that my financial situation threatened to make even the purchase of diesel a problem. The *QE2* got twenty-nine feet per gallon of fuel. *Island Trader* could beat that mark, but I didn't know by how much. I agreed to get back to him in a couple of days. He moved on to spread more cheer and enlist workers for his event. The band, all set up and plugged in, tuned its instruments.

Maybe it was murmurs from the crowd. Maybe it was the shriek of the lead guitar. Maybe it was the turning of heads. Maybe it was the way the keyboardist held the note. I wanted to believe I could feel the energy. All I knew was Billie had arrived; I didn't have to look.

I waited a second too long before looking for her. When I turned to seek her out, I found a squad of admiring volunteers—none of whom I recognized—clustered about her. I could only figure a tour guide with an entrepreneurial bent had included Billie among the island's tourist attractions—along with the beaches, ruined sugar mills, and petroglyphs—and bused sightseers in from town, locals as well as tourists; I understood the attraction better than anyone.

Billie's whim of the moment centered on three feral donkeys that shyly approached the building. She commandeered a head of lettuce from Pirate Dan, and her devotees watched as she broke the lettuce into three parts and proceeded to name and feed the animals that stuck their muzzles through the deck's rail.

"No! Ali Baba, you wait until I finish feeding Scheherazade. Okay, now it's your turn." She petted Ali Baba. "My you're a big boy." Ali Baba grabbed the entire chunk of lettuce in one bite. "And who do we have here? Frank— Little Frank. Little Frank, you remind me of a boy I knew in high school. I sure hope that when you like grow up you have more success with the ladies than your namesake."

When Billie tired of petting them, the donkeys wandered off. Her admirers weren't so easily discouraged. They stuck to her like tamarind seeds.

I couldn't figure why Billie required my help to find Leif's killer. She'd only have to ask, and she could mobilize every man in Flamingo

Bay to assist in her investigation. One thing I admired about Billie was that she didn't often behave like a princess. She seemed to have no interest in getting men to do her bidding, but her persistence in recruiting me to investigate Leif's murder left me wondering. Billie, enjoying the attention of her admirers, ignored me. It pissed me off, and it pissed me off even more that she showed absolutely no interest in any of her prime suspects, scattered throughout the crowd.

The band began its performance with a low-volume version of "Louie, Louie." I wasn't certain anyone knew the true words except its author, Richard Berry, but the band's version came off as a simple island love song with clearly enunciated G-rated vocals. When they finished the tune, the players turned up their amplifiers and performed it again with the wattage of a rock and roll anthem, redolent with obscene lyrics.

Billie's seeming lack of interest in her suspects got me thinking about them. When Billie presented her list to me, I pooh-poohed her choices—indicative of my contrary nature, as was my refusal to join her investigation. Of course, it was more than contrariness that scared me off; it was spending more time with Billie. I likened it to the discomfort of a recovering alcoholic tending bar.

I ordered the next beer from one of Pirate Dan's employees, and Zeke, who snuck up behind me, added a Heineken to the order.

"Captain Brian, mon. Zeke doesn't think he be seeing you here, but now that he is, he be saying hello."

"Cool earring."

He'd named his ear. The earring was gold and followed the curve of his earlobe. The letters spelled: ZEKE.

"Zeke buy you one, but ear not be big enough to hold all the letters, unless maybe you doesn't want to be 'captain' no more." He laughed, and he walked away on his bare feet. "Must deliver the medicine. Patients can't live without the medicine," he called over his shoulder.

It surprised me to see Zeke in such a genial mood after the earlier incident at sea, but he enjoyed carrying a grudge. He was happiest when he had an enemy, so happy, in fact, that when no real enemies confronted him, he created them. When he looked hard enough, Zeke could find disrespect in any man.

But Zeke wouldn't kill his target. He'd just keep pounding away at it. He behaved as violently as anyone in Flamingo Bay, but he measured his violence. He repaid people in kind for minor insults. For larger transgressions, he doled out punishment on the installment plan. That was the pattern, anyway. The last man to incur Zeke's wrath was Smiling Steve.

After the initial incident—whatever it was—Zeke hammered Steve. Afterwards, Steve made every attempt to avoid Zeke. About a month after the fracas, the two ran into each other again. Zeke behaved, and Steve thought his punishment was over. As time passed, Steve's boldness grew. Steve and everyone else thought Zeke had forgotten and forgiven, but as soon as Steve dropped his guard, Zeke hammered him again. Steve quickly relocated to St. Croix, forty miles away—St. Thomas, a twenty-minute ferry ride, was too close to trouble.

Pirate Dan stepped behind the bar to check his beer supply. A rubber band loosely gathered his gray ponytail that fell to the middle of his back. He consolidated the iced beers from two washtubs into one. In his billy goat-gruff voice, he ordered one of his employees to haul more from the storage area and fill the empty tub.

Dan worked the pirate thing to a fathom from absurdity: the swagger, the lingo, the dress. He fancied himself the ultimate pirate. I'd seen him around young boys. Their jaws hung open in awe when he recited how the great white shark took off his leg and how he killed it with a Swiss Army knife. He showed them the gold doubloon that hung around his neck, and he told them he knew where more of them were sunk in a Spanish galleon. All he needed was a crew to recover the booty. In five minutes, they were ready to ditch their parents, sign in blood on the dotted line, and run away to sea with him.

If I'd met someone like him when I was a boy, I wouldn't have waited until I was fifteen before I ran away to sea; I was ready to escape when I was half that age.

Dan carried a gun on his boat, as did every other skipper who sailed in foreign waters—except, at present, me—but it was common knowledge that the Pirate's weapon of choice was a Louisville Slugger, Mickey Mantle model. Dan and I—aside from the one incident—had always seen eye to eye.

Finding sunken treasure in the Bahamas financed Dan's purchase of the Congo Club (the Spanish galleon was no fiction), and the gold doubloon he wore around his neck wasn't the only one he owned. I figured that even if you had no interest in numismatics, collecting gold doubloons was a smart move. If Dan mixed it up with Leif, Leif would have a cast on one of his limbs, but he'd still be breathing.

"Don't blame me," Diver Vaughn hollered in my ear.

I turned. Vaughn wore his usual uniform: red baseball cap and red shorts, flip-flops, and white T-shirt with his logo in red: GO DOWN WITH DIVER VAUGHN. Perfect teeth dominated a face so well constructed that it lacked features. From his marshmallow-roasting escapade, he'd acquired the fragrance of an arsonist.

"For what?"

He jerked his head toward the dance floor. "She didn't get it from me. I just thought you ought to know."

Sarah, all tooted up, had joined Marsha on the dance floor. Both had taken off their shirts and twisted them into boa-like accessories, entertaining the crowd with their coordinated moves. They put on a pretty good show. I'd come to accept that if pointed at you, the two hardest things in life to ignore were bare breasts and a loaded gun.

"I appreciate that," I answered. "Know where she got it?"

Vaughn shook his head. "Look, if you need a short-term loan to buy sails, I'd be willing to help you out."

"Why?"

"Because you'd pay me back. And building karma is a good investment. Who knows, one day I could be in need of help."

I doubted Vaughn would ever need financial help. I doubted it as much as I doubted he was a suspect in Leif's murder. Vaughn and I were a lot alike. We worked hard, and for the most part, we minded our own business. The big thing that separated us was charisma. Vaughn had his own allotment plus what—in a fairer world—should have been mine. In the States, you had to be a follower to become a leader, and to be a follower you had to become a joiner. In Flamingo Bay, there were few joiners or followers. Everyone believed he was a leader. Vaughn was the most accurate in his belief.

"Thanks for the offer."

"What happened on your trip to Venezuela, anyway?"

"I didn't start with the best crew—"

"I heard that Rasta Bob's girlfriend had a baby girl."

"He bowed out at the last minute, so right away I was without my most experienced crew. Fernando, who's sailed with me on and off for the past couple of years, recruited Tim, a buddy of his from St. Thomas. Tim knew his way around a boat. I figured with two strong crew I could afford to hire the Garys, who'd been begging me for months to come along."

Vaughn rolled his eyes.

"I know, I know. But the Garys performed no worse than expected. Of course, I didn't expect to give them an opportunity to perform. As it happened, my two strongest crew proved to be the two weakest links in the chain of command. At times, I felt as paranoid as Captain Queeg."

"Carrying strawberries?" Vaughn laughed.

"Stolen strawberries, I could've handled. Contraband turned out to be a different program altogether. I've never allowed alcohol aboard, and since Uncle Sam began its Zero Tolerance program, I've banned ganja—"

"Makes sense," Vaughn said. "No point losing your boat because a crew's found carrying a joint in his pocket."

"My point, exactly. Fernando and Tim both ignored the rules. I confiscated Fernando's rum the first day out and tossed it overboard. The following night, I busted Tim. A few punches got thrown when he refused to turn over his stash. He made threats, so I carried my forty-five in my belt the rest of the way to Cumaná—the first time I've ever done that."

"So it was mutiny?"

"Worse. When we arrived in Cumaná, Tim and Fernando evidently determined to get even. They found Lopez, my tile guy, before I did, and the three conspired to scam me out of five grand. The tile I paid for never showed up on the dock. The police refused to go after Lopez because the bill of sale that Fernando translated was accurate. I bought nothing except 'Creamy Air,' which Fernando led me to believe was the name of the tile."

"Where *is* Fernando?"

"I left him in Cumaná along with Tim. After the tile incident, Tim disappeared on me, but I caught up with Fernando and hurt him bad enough that he would've been no help on the return voyage. Before leaving, I trashed Lopez's office looking for my money, and the police, uninterested in going after Lopez, came after me. I knew a storm was coming, but I figured I'd take my chances at sea."

As I took a swallow of my beer, I realized I hadn't really done much figuring except to get the hell away from Venezuela. Pumped full of adrenaline from my confrontation with Fernando, who pulled a knife on me, and angry over the loss of Mr. Outback's cash, my damn-the-torpedoes recklessness placed all the blame on me for the loss of the sails. Telling the tale also made me realize that I'd concentrated so much on the loss of *Island Trader*'s sails that I'd ignored another problem entirely: I could buy new sails, but I could never go back to Cumaná.

"With only the two Garys aboard and a fierce wind kicking up the sea, I decided to strike the sails. Then the comedy began. Big Gary didn't secure the boom properly. While he played with the halyard he'd fouled, the boom came loose and knocked him out. I gave the wheel to Little Gary, while I attended his partner, but he couldn't keep the heading. Squall hit us damn near broadside, and we lost every sail."

"Remind me never to let those goofballs aboard my boat." Vaughn lit a cigarette. "The offer still goes. Think about it."

I'd think about it later and only as a last resort. Instead, I thought about the gossip I heard that someone ripped off Vaughn the day before I returned from Venezuela. Because Leif was the obvious candidate, I asked Vaughn to confirm the rumor. He admitted to the loss of a kilo and four grand.

Stumbling upon a bale of cocaine—or, in the local vernacular, "square grouper"—turned out to be something of an annual event. Four had washed up during my years here, and another had been fished out of the sea near the mouth of Flamingo Bay. Like the Atlantic marlin and many trophy fish, the square grouper was a solitary swimmer, but in the exception that proved the rule, Diver Vaughn—a couple of miles out, on a night dive—came across an entire school. He could've lost a kilo a day for the better part of a year before he ran out of cocaine, so killing Leif for the loss of a single kilo seemed absurd to me.

"Any idea who did it?" I asked.

Vaughn paused and eyed Jason—sitting halfway down the bar next to Easy, celebrating his success in the lottery—before he shook his head and accepted an invitation from Nancy to dance.

Jason owned the prettiest boat in Flamingo Bay, a Cheoy Lee with a teak deck and mahogany cabin—the sort of boat I imagined Jack London would sail today—and he had the prettiest wife. Ten years older than Billie, Wendy possessed good bones and dewy skin, enhanced by divine distribution of body fat. What I liked best about Wendy was her mouth—as smart as anything designed by Intel—except on those occasions when she felt it necessary to verbally remind others of her genetic superiority and the subsequent privilege due her.

I used to be rather tight with Jason and Wendy. I not only hosted their wedding ceremony and reception on *Island Trader*, but I married them, a captain's prerogative outside the three-mile limit. As Wendy and Jason drifted apart, both drifted away from me, as if I somehow contributed to their unhappiness. We'd become so distant that it surprised me when Wendy agreed to join Billie and me to form a book club.

Jason, watching Billie taking turns dancing with one man after the other, didn't resemble the man Wendy married three years ago. Over the past months, I'd watched Jason's transformation from Argonaut to Argonut. Once a man of diurnal habit, Jason morphed into a man of nocturnal habit, then into a man with only a drug habit. With each shift in behavior, Jason became more and more scarce. He could be sighted here and there, but only for an instant. As soon as someone proffered an explanation of his activities, Jason was on to the next thing.

I found it difficult not to lament the loss of what was once a good man who possessed over-the-top style. Last year at the community Christmas party at Pirate Cove, Jason and Wendy, assigned to contribute a salad, brought a sticky rainbow-colored bowl of buds—a pound of primo ganja. He made other stylish gestures as well, but the fairy dust, which initially triggered in him a flash of luminous energy, gradually extinguished his flair.

My experience with cocaine users is that they become more like who they actually are, just pumped full of energy. Sarah didn't act much different when she was high than she did before she discovered cocaine—her highs simply lasted longer and crept up a notch or two in intensity. Cocaine hadn't given Sarah the confidence to dance without her shirt; she'd always exhibited a streak of exuberance, and in Flamingo Bay, women routinely took off their shirts.

Ironically, it was cocaine use that caused Sarah to cradle her breasts on *Island Trader* so they wouldn't jiggle. The drug caused her to act out of the ordinary when she wasn't high; it inhibited and depressed her. Consumed by depression on the slide down, she behaved as a mean-spirited, grasping, whining Fury.

As with any addiction, the need to keep scoring more and more drugs causes a bigger problem than ingestion. After all, it was Jason's two best friends—angered over his violent quest for drugs—who broke his jaw and his arm. Sarah's pursuit of drugs transformed her from a woman of reasonable moral values into a cocaine whore.

I turned to watch Sarah and Marsha. Seven years ago in the Florida Keys, I ran day-sails on my old Hinckley. Sarah and her boyfriend and another couple on holiday from Chicago hired me to take them out sailing and diving. Sarah's boyfriend, an argumentative blowhard, behaved the worst. He quarreled with everyone and everything. When I answered his query about the length of my boat, he immediately accused me of overstating that dimension. To avoid argument, I suggested that the boat might have shrunk from being in the water for so many years.

His hostility simmered all day. He drank, and he drank more than he should have. They didn't hire me for the following day. I figured I saw the last of them when they left me at the dock at sunset. About midnight Sarah appeared at the dock, dolled up and drunk. I replayed that scene in my head over and over for years. As near as I could figure, it had less to do with me than with her boyfriend and less to do with her boyfriend than with my boat. Sarah wanted to get laid on a boat, and her boyfriend, behaving badly, provoked her to thumb her nose at him.

I figured that I did them both a favor, and Sarah and I stayed pretty happy living on my boat and running day-sails. We had great fun for nearly a year until the adventures became workaday and Sarah tired of having strangers invade our home. I decided upon commerce as a new career—imports and exports. I sold the Hinckley, added my life's savings to the kitty and all I could borrow, and bought *Island Trader* and fixed her up. Then Sarah and I left Marathon and headed for the Caribbean.

Island Trader lacked amenities; Sarah never liked living aboard her. It took a few months to find a cottage here—hurricane damage and the subsequent shortage of building materials, labor, and electricity. She finally found a place, and we moved in. Sarah worked her ass off to make the cottage a home. It was as comfortable as any place I'd lived. But even after all our work, the cottage never met her expectations and neither did Flamingo Bay and neither did I.

Assaulted by the revelers' din of noisy desperation, I wasn't feeling happy myself. I was about out of business, out of money, out of friends, and stuck between Sarah, the woman I'd lost, and Billie, the woman I loved. I also had a gut feeling that tomorrow morning at ten, the Shirt would make my life a lot more difficult.

6

AN HOUR BEFORE DAWN I tumbled out of my hammock—my preferred sleeping venue. I dinghied to shore to find Pirate Dan's deflated inflatable lying on the beach. While I tried to assess the damage—nearly impossible equipped with only a cigarette lighter—I backed into the pile of greenheart I'd stacked on shore nearly a week earlier. I went down hard on my tailbone and gashed the calf of my right leg. Losing my temper and kicking out at the lumber—as if it was the lumber's owner—I inflicted on myself even greater pain.

The dinghy appeared to be punctured, not slashed. It would float again, and the vandal—most likely Zeke—dragged the dinghy onto the beach before stabbing it, saving the outboard from the sea. Dan miscalculated yesterday when he fired his crossbow at Zeke's boat. I suspected this conflict would escalate, for both participants could be hotheads, hardheads, and knuckleheads.

I climbed into my truck and rumbled through darkness past Easys, along the road to Pirate Cove. The Ford followed its headlights down the asphalt until the lights missed the curve and crashed into the hillside. Then they swept across the road, flashed over the bay for an instant, and stopped the seas in mid roll.

As the sky brightened, I pulled into Doctor's driveway. The newborn light—too immature to cast shadows—caressed land and sea with a golden soft affection like a lover bent on rendering pleasure.

Magnificently perched atop a knoll on the side of a mountain, Doctor's abandoned stone cottage offered a two-hundred-seventy-degree view of the Caribbean. A single shuttered window flanked each side of the centrally located entry door. A red corrugated-metal hip roof capped the symmetrical façade. In dire need of landscaping, the cratered front yard looked as inhospitable as a moonscape.

I'd seen enough movies and read enough books to know that the clever detectives always found something at the crime scene to help the investigation, though I couldn't be sure this was the scene of the crime. I couldn't even be sure there was a crime. I knew only what I'd heard, but none of what I'd heard came directly from anyone who I could be sure knew anything.

Why the cistern? That conundrum existed as my first obstacle in trying to make sense of it all.

Before climbing out of my truck, I checked for activity at Miss Lucinda's cottage, across the road about fifty yards away, the building half sunk in a hollow. Miss Lucinda's was the location of the only flamingo in Flamingo Bay. It was planted in her garden on crippled rusty legs and looked out at the Caribbean toward Norman Island. Once in the pink, it suffered now from both ultraviolet radiation and oxidation.

Miss Lucinda's cottage—built in the days before building codes—lacked a cistern. In the past, she collected water in large garbage pails, but since Doctor's death, she appropriated his water. The consensus of those present when the police interviewed Miss Lucinda was that in the course of fetching a bucket of water from the cistern, she found Leif's body.

Agriculture on St. Judas—a desert island—had been a risky business since the Danes clear-cut the timber and began planting sugar in the eighteenth century. Too small to influence the weather, St. Judas caught only the rain that happened by. After logging the precious hardwoods, the next error of great magnitude involved the introduction of the mongoose to kill the crop-eating rats. Because the rat is nocturnal and the mongoose, diurnal, both flourished.

Of course, none of these problems hindered the importance of agriculture on St. Judas—not even the fact that nobody grew anything. As a territory of the United States, the Virgin Islands rated an agricultural policy and subsidies just like everywhere else, and the goat became the agricultural commodity. The beneficiaries of the government's policy all seemed to be old ladies.

Miss Lucinda, armed with an old single-barreled twenty-gauge shotgun, benefited from the government's largesse along with a dozen-or-so other septuagenarians. Her herd roamed the roads and trails of Flamingo Bay along with many others. The herds looked alike to me, but the owners could easily tell them apart, and they could also discern the identity and ownership of the individual goats.

No natural predators stalked the goats on St. Judas. Many went missing just before holiday feasts, as some folk—wanting a traditional meal without paying for it—simply opened their car door, snatched a goat from the road, took it home, and butchered it. Most of the goat snatchers drove across the island from Sugar Harbor, though others journeyed from St. Thomas. A few dogs did go after the goats, which is why goat owners usually possessed a shotgun.

Near as I could tell, Miss Lucinda handled her shotgun with impunity, and she once put a few pellets into Leif's leg. She argued the incident was accidental. Leif—trespassing on her property—simply and stupidly stepped between her and her prey. In Leif's version, he was Miss Lucinda's prey. I didn't possess detailed knowledge of her hunting prowess, but I knew she'd shot Sweetheart, one of the best-loved members of the community. Sweetheart never bothered goats; she feasted on coconuts. The dog originally belonged to Doctor—a real physician—whose life was good until he found a square grouper, beached during a tropical storm.

Each man who captured a square grouper handled it differently. Vaughn reputedly stashed his in an underwater cave and doled out small quantities to friends and acquaintances. Zeke sold most of his—judiciously, a gram at a time—which kept him busy from the time he awakened until well into the evening. Doctor tried to inhale as much of the thirty-six kilos (according to his own count) as he could. His life got better over the next few months before it started getting worse.

Doctor convinced himself he was under satellite surveillance. Because his vehicle presented a bigger target than he did, he quit driving. Then, figuring the sophisticated eavesdropping equipment could monitor his movements on the roadways—even on foot—he and Sweetheart began to move cross-country, despite Jason's assurances that wearing an aluminum-foil beanie would thwart the government's space-based attempts to track him. Toward the end, weighing not much more than a hundred pounds and too weak to race through the bush, Doctor crawled.

Alerted by the wailing cry of Sweetheart, searchers found Doctor's body in the bush. The authorities were unable to determine how Doctor managed to seal all the doors and windows on the interior of his cottage with duct tape and still escape the building. After his death,

treasure hunters tore up his property with shovels and pickaxes looking for cash and cocaine—he'd begun selling large amounts cheaply to
would-be dealers who took advantage of his impaired judgment—but
no one confessed to finding anything.

The Congo Club and Pirate Dan adopted Sweetheart, but she still
returned here daily to wait for Doctor. When Miss Lucinda shot the
dog, Pirate Dan hired an obeah man through a West Indian intermediary. The obeah man worked alone and at night, so no one witnessed the
actual spell. All we saw were the physical results the following morning
when given an interpretative tour of the site by Dan's intermediary.

Our guide told us that to work the magic, the obeah man first killed
a chicken, and we found a chicken foot hanging by a thread over Miss
Lucinda's door. A cross was painted on the door in the chicken's blood.
Also, in the chicken's blood, a line was drawn along the length of the
doorway's threshold. We were told that a believer would never go
through that doorway.

Miss Lucinda removed the chicken foot and painted the door and
threshold that afternoon. I would've done the same if it'd happened to
me, so I was unable to judge the efficacy of the spell. Was it the obeah
or the vandalism that most captured Miss Lucinda's attention?

What captured my attention, as I sat in my truck waiting for inspi-
ration to investigate the premises, was how my mind promoted Miss
Lucinda—heretofore a seemingly minor character in the drama of
Leif's demise—to the rank of actual suspect. She'd already shot Leif
once. It may have been accidental, as she claimed, but there could've
been more to it, as Leif argued. Who could say for sure? She may have
believed Leif was poisoning her well, so to speak. If she believed he
had, she wouldn't have had a problem dumping him in the cistern and
really poisoning it.

Discerning no activity at Miss Lucinda's, I climbed out of my truck
and walked toward the cottage. The easiest way to get to the rear of
the cottage was through the front door, standing ajar. Upon entering, I noticed tiny shafts of light piercing the darkness from holes in
the roof, convincing evidence that Doctor *had* used a forty-five to kill
palmetto bugs and lizards that invaded his domicile. It also reminded
me that until last week I'd owned a forty-five. Despite my threat to

walk away from our meeting scheduled a few hours from now, I didn't expect the Shirt to return my gun.

The interior consisted of a single large room, which had been attacked by vandals. Debris, including dry foodstuffs, littered the white ceramic tile floor. All of the appliances and most of the furniture had been stolen. Termites feasted on the kitchen's oak cabinets, which had been installed by someone lacking knowledge of termites' fondness for oak. The place stank from dampness and neglect. A quick survey revealed a lack of hiding places and clues.

Despite my desire to escape the vandalism and neglect, I couldn't help being impressed with the building. Opposite the front door, an eight-foot patio door—not original to the building—faced the sea and allowed light into the space. The eighteen-inch-thick walls were built of local stone. Conch shells, coral, and wine bottles completed the materials used in construction. Only the dimpled foot of each of the brown or green bottles imbedded in the wall was exposed. Flat, finger-nail-sized red stones were spaced a couple of inches apart and centered in the mortar joints when the mason buttered the joints. It gave the effect of a necklace of beads dividing the cleaved faces of the large gray angular stones. I doubted many natives still did work of such quality.

I exited the cottage through a mahogany door that led to the bathroom addition. Another mahogany door separated the bathroom from the outdoor shower. The bath and shower walls were newer—probably the work of a mason from down island—but matched those of the cottage. When I exited the shower and passed through louvered saloon-type doors, also mahogany, the wind whipped my clothes. A few steps more and I found myself standing on the infamous cistern gazing at a priceless view of the British Virgins. Norman, Peter, Salt, and Cooper islands seemed like emeralds set in sapphire even in the ephemeral light of dawn.

Three dark shapes met the sea on the rock face of Norman Island. Knowing three caves existed there helped to persuade me that from my vantage I could distinguish them. The mythological part of the Lore alleged that the largest cave—miniscule as caves go—had yielded pirate treasure and inspired Robert Louis Stevenson to write *Treasure Island*.

My eyes traveled from Norman Island back to America. The hillside before me greeted the sea with a massive outcrop, which on its lee side protected a small but dense patch of mangroves. Several agave plants presented giant bouquets of rich green spikes on the mostly rocky and barren slope, which was untouched by treasure hunters, as it provided no real place to dig.

Fresh water is especially precious in Flamingo Bay. And while the building code dictated a cistern's capacity based on the square footage of the roof, the great size of Doctor's cistern—a cube with sides of approximately twelve feet, more suited to a multi-family building—suggested its builder possessed a bunker mentality. Constructed in recent years of poured concrete, the cistern projected about eighteen inches above grade on the uphill side to allow two four-inch PVC rain leaders to connect it to the cottage's gutters. Toward one corner, a steel-framed concrete trapdoor, hinged on one side, incorporated a hasp and staple on the opposite side to which a padlock could be fitted.

I walked around the site looking for something out of place. I dutifully zig-zagged nearly seventy-five yards down the hill to the sea. I found, tangled in some leggy tamarinds, a length of yellow police tape, but nothing else. I climbed back up to the cistern and yanked open its hatch. The cistern was about two-thirds full. The water smelled okay, though I speculated the germ of every disease I could think of probably incubated there. To make the whole concept more palatable I compared the cistern's contents to the primordial soup from which life emerged, and determined it contained just a thin broth.

Leif couldn't swim well, making him cautious around water. It would take the offer of a lifejacket to coax him into a bathtub. Leif either had help getting into the cistern, the cistern contained something more valuable than water, or his killer simply dumped the body there. I didn't expect to find anything, but I closed the hatch and headed back to my truck for a flashlight. Thinking of Leif's final resting place, all that made sense was that the cistern was dark as a tomb inside.

The flashlight, stuffed under the front seat, was tangled in a length of rope. One thing led to another, and I—curiously and reluctantly, after tying the rope to a nearby sapling—slipped feet first into the cistern. An inch of silt covered the bottom. I made several dives, stirring up the sediment with my left hand while holding the flashlight in my right.

I almost inhaled a snoot-full of water when I turned up a single gold coin. Finding it encouraged me to keep looking, until I reminded myself that I was as vulnerable as Leif—a fish in a barrel. The thought sent me shinnying up the rope. As I climbed out, I noticed a steel hook screwed into the concrete ceiling within arm's length of the hatch. Snagged on it were some threads and a bit of fabric. After I pulled myself out, I flopped on my belly, and reached back in to retrieve the fabric.

Luggage manufacturers use heavy-duty black nylon fabric like the bit I found. Its existence in the cistern suggested someone snagged a backpack or duffel on the hook. It offered one possible explanation for Leif's presence: he owned a black backpack, though others did also, including Billie. I slipped the bit of fabric into my right-hand pocket and pulled the coin I found in the cistern from my left-hand pocket. I'm no expert, but the gold doubloon looked like the one that hung from a rawhide thong around Pirate Dan's neck. The coin featured the Cross of Jerusalem with lions and castles alternating in the quarters created by the cross. It had to be worth several thousand dollars, though I suspected its value to a collector was greatly diminished because of the presence of a small hole drilled through it where a ring was attached so it could be worn as jewelry. I never realized diving for sunken treasure could be so easy. My success tempted me to check every cistern on the island.

I closed the cistern's hatch, untied the rope, and gathered my gear. Like a gambler on a roll, I inspected the cottage again, more thoroughly than the first time. Finding nothing, I climbed into the old Ford and followed the rutted dirt road to Pirate Cove. After a short level run, the road plunged to sea level. On the left lay a large chocolate-brown salt pond. Locals intent on harvesting salt stuck numerous twigs and small branches into the pond's muddy bottom to collect the mineral when the water evaporated.

Beyond the salt pond, the road climbed sharply and veered right. Then it switched left before it climbed to the top of another hill. I stopped at the crest and shifted into first gear. Carved from solid rock, the badly weathered road ahead needed grading to clean up the loose flakes of stone. I gingerly released the brake and moved at a crawl. The long steep descent ended in a mangrove swamp. Tangled roots as thick as saplings extended from the trunks into the mud, acting like stays and shrouds to stabilize the trees. Deep potholes held standing water. The Ford chugged through the muddy mangroves in first gear. The road disappeared into the swamp, but a rutted and dusty track rose from it attaining an elevation of several feet above sea level. A hundred yards farther, the track ended at a powder sugar beach that was empty most days, especially so early in the morning.

Apart from the narrow strip of powdery sand that sloped gently to the crystal sea, tortured cacti twisted precariously from creviced rock and struggled for survival. Long rocky arms, almost parallel to each other, extended into the sea to cradle and protect the cove. Near the farther arm, the jagged foundation of a Great House from the colonial period rose a foot or two above grade. Stunted trees, interspersed with sun-bleached succulents, wrapped the green hillside behind me, which reached an elevation of several hundred feet.

I stripped off my clothes, waded in, and scrubbed myself and my clothes with sand. I dove to rinse off the sand, swam back to shore, and repeated the scrubbing. When the saltwater burned my skin from head to toe until my entire body smarted like the gash on my calf, I figured I'd reached that state of godliness advocated by John Wesley. I swam to the center of the cove and treaded water for a few seconds before I dropped my arms to my side. The novelty of saltwater buoyancy never cloyed my midwestern freshwater sensibility. They'd positively shit if they knew I was born and raised in Kansas — I mean absolutely every-one in Flamingo Bay. They believed the sea flowed in my veins. They just worked it out, and I never bothered to deny it.

As I swam to shore, I noticed a small deciduous tree that grew on the verge of the bush. Barren and unremarkable when I arrived, it seemed yellow flowers now covered it completely and massively. I shook off the sand from my damp clothes drying on the beach and pulled them on. Then I slogged through the sand to investigate the tree. When I approached, the flowers took flight, turning into a zillion butterflies that scattered so successfully I couldn't spot a single one a minute later.

Nature provides all the clues to existence, not just on the elementary level (food chain and all that) but on a more sophisticated level as well. I knew that man had desecrated (and continued to desecrate) Eden, just as I had scattered the butterflies. The butterflies might return—though in five years I'd never seen them here before—or they might not. Of one thing, I was certain: Leif's murder had forever desecrated Flamingo Bay.

It worried me that Billie intended to rush headlong into an investigation that would result in greater damage to the community. Just as the presence of an observer affects what's observed, common knowledge of the presence of an investigator thwarts and muddles the search for answers—not a huge problem itself, though it can unleash blood lust. I thought I'd already dismissed the idea, but I couldn't help thinking, either, that for a woman who loved diversion, an investigation into the cause of Leif's death provided the sort of activity that would fascinate Billie. For all her energy and intelligence, she would have trouble concocting on her own such complete recreation.

I walked the beach until my clothes and I were dry. Then I sat down, removed my copy of *The Republic* from its Ziploc bag, and started where I'd left off. Our book club met twice a month, and we took turns choosing titles. Wendy favored the ancient texts, Billie loved poetry, and I liked novels. My problem with Plato: I preferred to read texts by Homer and those Plato labeled the "other liars." My other problem with Plato: I had to stop every few pages to figure out what he was saying. Today's immediate obstacle—"Everything that deceives may be said to enchant"—got me thinking. I lay back and closed my eyes. My problem with the concept was that the reverse seemed equally valid: Everything that enchants may be said to deceive. But my real problem wasn't the concept. My real problem rested in my own abridged definition of "everything": Billie.

Examining each sentence and finally each word of each sentence provided the sort of tedium that sent my mind wandering. One place it wandered was the South Pacific. I imagined two Polynesian princesses lounging in a hammock on the beach. They wore hibiscus in their hair, and garlands of purple and gold flowers entwined their limbs. Their voices sang of a paradise more languid than seemed imaginable, but I could imagine it. Not its essence. Just the sweetness that emanated from it. When I approached the hammock, they stopped singing and turned to look at me. Except for their glistening black hair, each was Billie.

A gust of wind kicked sand in my face. I opened my eyes. The princesses were gone. My hair had dried to the texture of brush, and my scalp itched from the freshly deposited salt. For too many years, I'd retreated into my mind to live. I could only conclude that my life had become so fragile that Billie intruded even into my fantasies.

I checked the shadows and the position of the sun to gauge how long I'd been asleep. Not more than an hour. I scanned the empty beach and the empty cove. It felt familiar. I'd always been alone. Even with Sarah, I was alone. It had everything to do with me—not my desire, but my character. I once believed in the temporary nature of that condition. But not any longer. It made no sense to hang around Flamingo Bay, dine on Billie's table scraps, and bury my friends. Of course, heading to another San Fernando and living the hermit's life like Alexander Selkirk made no sense either.

I looked up. High in the sky, the frigate birds soared effortlessly. Sleek and contemporary in design, they differed markedly from the low-flying brown pelicans. The pelicans—as obsolete as I—looked like pterodactyls. That I wasn't the only dinosaur in Flamingo Bay provided no consolation.

I might have been obsolete, but I wasn't stupid. Not yet, anyway.

I pulled the coin out of my pocket and examined it again. I'd failed to note the gold ring that passed through the hole drilled in the coin was still crimped so tightly in place that it couldn't have slipped off even the most delicate chain and certainly not Pirate Dan's rawhide thong. If there'd been such a chain in the cistern, I'd have found it. My big clue left me with more questions, the key question being: How did Pirate Dan's doubloon end up in Doctor's cistern?

As I climbed into my truck to head out, I heard the engines of a large boat. Curious, I lit a cigarette and waited to see who would show up. The cove was still empty when the boat's engines shut down. Then

I heard a splash and an anchor chain unreel. The sounds came from just on the other side of the cove's rocky arm to my left. Next, I heard the drone of an outboard motor. It seemed I was listening to the audio portion of a stage production while staring at an empty set. A minute later Vaughn appeared from stage right, alone in his wooden dinghy. I could've been mistaken about it being Vaughn, but I couldn't mistake the dinghy. He borrowed the Coast Guard's paint scheme, simply reversing the colors. A wide diagonal white stripe painted on the hull distinguished his red dinghy, the same design as *Divertimento*. He slowed the boat in an ever-tightening circle, but when he spotted me, he waved and goosed the throttle, disappearing in an instant.

Everyone in Flamingo Bay with larceny in mind speculated for months about the location of the underwater cave where Diver Vaughn kept his treasure stashed. I was certain that I had inadvertently stumbled upon it, and I was pretty sure Vaughn knew it.

When I turned the truck's ignition key, Vaughn popped back into the picture, skimming toward me at full speed. I killed the engine and walked down to the beach to meet him. About twenty feet from shore, he shut down his outboard, lifted the motor, and the nose of his dinghy slid onto the sand and came to a stop. He climbed out and waded ashore, blond hair plastered to his wet legs all the way to his knees.

"You're not going to fuck me up over this, are you?" he asked.

"Why would I do that?"

"Sorry. Look, I'm heading out tomorrow for a few days, and I don't have time to deal with that"—he pointed his thumb over his shoulder—"until I get back."

"Your timing's bad," I said.

"Why?"

"I'm meeting a narc today at ten. I can't believe he's really interested in me. What do you think?"

"That you're probably right. But I'd appreciate whatever help you can give me."

7

THE ROAD—SKINNY AND CRUMBLING—lacked shoulders, and I hugged the mountain in my Ford pickup. Officer Richards, pulling onto the road from a private drive, followed me like a trailer. He should've been out hunting for Leif's killer instead of wasting my time and his. To punish him, I ignored him. He stuck his left arm out the window, flapping it up and down as if trying to get his Blazer airborne. When I disregarded his gesture, he hit the switch to his emergency lights. Red and blue lights revolved in their Plexiglas canopies, amber lights flashed, and the white strobe pulsed. For added effect, he blinked his high beams. Though my rearview mirror buzzed from the rough road, I could clearly see his face. His Blazer was doing about twenty miles per hour, and his mouth was doing about sixty. Richards had plenty to say, but I didn't bother to read his lips.

I rounded a curve and spotted *Island Trader* moored about a mile and a half away. Her vertical prow split the two-foot blue seas. Her three masts stood steady as telephone poles. My heart pumped a little faster, then I shivered all the way to the ends of my fingers and toes. I feared the day when she wouldn't be there for me. She was more than a half-century older than I. Still, it was a toss-up as to which of us was more of an anachronism.

Tamarinds thrived on the deserted road's verge, intermingled with random puffs of wild cotton. To my left, vines twisted and climbed a wall of gray stone. Above that scar created by the road-builders, the mountain turned green. To my right, two hundred feet below, lapped the ultramarine waters of Flamingo Bay.

I figured I'd found a good spot for a confrontation with the police—no shoulders, no room for error—and I crushed the brake pedal. Tires on both vehicles screamed at the decaying asphalt. Richards swerved into the right lane—right is wrong in Flamingo Bay. No oncoming traffic presented itself, and Richards was fortunate not to go over the cliff, though I was startled that he trusted me not to nudge him over the edge. When the screeching ceased, we were stopped side-by-side blocking both lanes of traffic, bumpers toeing an imaginary mark.

I'd intended that my maneuver would cause him to leave the impression of his grille on my tailgate. I envisioned a buckled hood and fenders, steaming coolant spewing from the Blazer's crunched radiator, and a windshield crackling into an abstract mosaic. My miscalculation disappointed me. Richards and I had been engaged in combat for months, a gradually escalating contest that began when he insulted Billie.

Richards stepped out of his vehicle, baton in hand.

"Problem, orif—officer?"

He stuck out his jaw and stuck his arm in my window. "Driver license," he demanded, snapping his bony fingers.

I removed a sandwich-sized Ziploc bag from my pocket, my wallet from the bag, and my plastic Marathon Militia ID from the wallet. He'd seen it before. He shook his head and silently moved his lips to pronounce "Yankeemuthascunt."

"Driver license," he repeated. "Not that shit."

I pulled out my license—a limp scrap of paper with my picture on one side and my thumbprint on the other—and handed it to him.

"Brian Clancy, why doesn't you stop when I switch on lights?"

"Couldn't tell you were behind me. Too many lights. I thought maybe Martians were trying to abduct me."

Referring to the mirror with my eyes, I watched a blue jeep pull to a stop behind me. Zeke, smiling broadly, tapped both thumbs on the steering wheel. Then Mechanic Jim, one of the steadiest men in Flamingo Bay—the first stop on his round-the-world itinerary—pulled up behind Zeke and tested his horn. In the States, the plumber was man's best friend; in Flamingo Bay, the mechanic. There was a strong reason mechanics were revered here—good physics. The second law of thermodynamics asserts things move from a state of order to a state of disorder, a circumstance that seems more apparent in paradise. Mechanics attempted to restore order.

"Registration," Richards demanded, his wrinkled fingers wiggling.

I reached over and dug the truck's registration from the glove box, separating it from several traffic tickets.

He glanced at the tickets. "Why does you always break the rules?"

I didn't break the rules. I broke the law. Richards didn't get the distinction I'd devised. Laws are created in legislatures, but you create your own rules. That makes rules voluntary, but to comply with them is obligatory, and it makes laws obligatory, but to comply with them is voluntary.

Physical laws—those codified by men in laboratories—are another program altogether and are difficult to transgress. Not for lack of trying and not lately, I'd been able to violate the law of gravity only a few times in my life, and I'd never approached the speed of light except in my mind.

I handed him my registration, and he took it with him when he strutted toward the rear of my old Ford, examining the blue sheet metal. He probably considered ticketing me for driving a dirty truck, just one in a comprehensive list of offenses included in the legislative code under a special addendum printed in invisible ink: DWW—Driving While White.

Dirty sheet metal was all I could come up with. I'd just gotten everything squared away for the annual inspection—except the horn, which worked intermittently and only by jiggling the steering wheel. After my third unsuccessful try, the inspector took pity on himself and gave me the shiny new sticker for my windshield.

Richards kicked my loose rear bumper. It screeched like a hull scraping a reef. It was a hell of a wake-up call. It bothered Zeke, too. He responded by blasting his horn, and Richards got his own rude awakening. He spun, grabbed his baton, and slammed it against the hood of Zeke's jeep. The concussion was huge, but no one could mistake it for a steel drum—too tinny. Still, it aroused Zeke. He erased his smile and hopped out of his jeep.

Barefoot and wearing half-zipped dirty jeans, torn T-shirt, and several thousand dollars' worth of jewelry, Zeke didn't attempt to conceal he was a ragamuffin cocaine dealer. A diamond that could be mistaken for the rock of ages sparkled from his pinkie ring; the gold on his neck and wrists glittered in the sunlight. The jewelry's large and numerous links gave him the air of a prosperous one-man chain gang—practice, perhaps, for a head start on his next career. Zeke, a head taller and about seventy pounds heavier than Richards, jabbed his finger at the cop's face.

"Zeke think maybe he whomp you ass for denting his hood. What does you think?"

"Where is you shoes?"

"Shoes be in jeep. Get dirty walking on road."

Richards shook his head and stepped toward Zeke. Zeke scowled and met the cop halfway until they were in each other's faces. Each spoke to the other, though too quietly for me to hear. Their dialogue broke down when they each stopped listening and simultaneously delivered a noisy but unintelligible verbal monologue to the other. Zeke clenched his fists and struck a John L. Sullivan pose, breaking the verbal clinch.

"Zeke be thinking about whomping the Mon," he shouted.

The blockade stopped a few more vehicles, and the several spectators present shouted words of encouragement to Zeke.

Zeke unclenched his fists, held up his hands as if to protect his face, then cringed and whimpered, "But the Mon doesn't want to fight. The Mon want to know where is Zeke's shoes."

The audience responded with boos and raspberries.

Zeke continued his harangue. "Maybe the Mon fight only with Blondie."

Reminded of Billie's assault, the small group of bystanders, who'd exited their vehicles, doubled over in laughter.

Richards grabbed Zeke's arm, but Zeke didn't budge when Richards attempted to lead him back to his jeep. Mechanic Jim clapped to applaud Zeke's resolve. Others quickly joined the applause.

Possibly because Zeke had nothing else to prove, he returned to his jeep when Richards released his arm. Richards finished his circumnavigation of my truck and stuck his face in my window.

"Truck be a hazard! Mon could be cut on sharp edges of sheet metal."

"It passed inspection last month."

"Rust more since then." Richards glanced over his shoulder at the two vehicles he'd blocked in the oncoming lane of traffic. He seemed proud of the traffic jam he'd created, pleased by the honking.

"How do you know that?"

He scrawled in his ticket book, then looked up, "Not pass inspection otherwise."

"What do you suggest?"

"Get new vehicle or get duct tape." He handed me a ticket, the registration, and my license. "Have a nice day."

As he walked away, I shouted, "Hey! You guys find out yet what happened to Leif?"

"Mind you own business," he answered, climbing into his Blazer.

"I told you yesterday that it is my business. Nothing changed overnight, especially my promise to jam you up if you were involved."

"I could arrest you," he said.

"And I could throw you off the cliff if you tried."

He pulled his door closed.

After returning my wallet to its waterproof bag and adding the ticket to my collection, I casually saluted Richards before I drove slowly away, unjamming the traffic. He turned off his emergency lights and barely nosed out Zeke to fall in behind me. After all the fuss, I was still ahead of him and he was still dogging my ass. Oh, well.

Elroy suddenly and quietly appeared thirty feet away, trudging toward me on bare feet. I couldn't figure what delayed him. Elroy's only job was to be present. He was, after all, Flamingo Bay's official bystander. I felt certain that the details of most of the locals' comings and goings slumbered fitfully in Elroy's brain. How to tap into that trove eluded me for five years.

Elroy jerked his head in recognition and banged two fingers against his lips. I braked to hand him a cigarette. Richards honked, so I pulled out my Bic and lit the cigarette. Elroy bobbed his head in thanks, and I saluted him before releasing the clutch. Richard's honked again, and I tapped the brake. We weren't traveling fast, but he almost rear-ended me. I waved my finger at him in warning before I released the clutch a second time.

Keeping an eye on Richards in my rearview mirror, I watched him spit at Elroy, seriously pissing me off and foolishly escalating our conflict. I aimed the truck down the middle of the road. When I reached a straight stretch, I ducked my head and reached under the dash to pull the plug from the brake light switch. I corrected my course, built up some speed on a downhill run, and stood on the brake pedal. I caught Richards unaware, and he banged into me, knocking my bumper off. I plugged the wires back into the brake light switch before climbing out.

Apparently, Richards had had his fill of me. He didn't say a word and refused to leave his vehicle. I'd had my fill of him, also. Except for the bumper, neither vehicle sustained damage. I picked up the bumper and banged it against his headlight—shattering the glass—before I dropped it into the bed of the truck. He still refused to speak, so I climbed back in and headed out. Richards followed at a safe distance.

From my vantage, the bay looked empty of boats except for *Island Trader*. Not for the first time, I grasped how out of place she looked in Flamingo Bay. Always a workboat, she was never stylish. Often I wished I could go back in time to learn *Island Trader*'s history. I did some research, but I didn't learn much. I did discover that she spent twenty years at the bottom of Lake Superior. Though I never articulated it, I suppose I made a pact with myself that as long as I was alive she was going to stay afloat.

As I approached the head of the bay the number of buildings increased and the environment became less arid. While there were still plenty of agave plants and other succulents, tamarind, mango, key lime, flamboyant, and dozens of other tree varieties matured under harsh conditions. Except for the coconut palms and the mangroves, the trees didn't flourish so much as survive. I spotted a single manchineel tree. Its apple-like fruit was rumored to have killed one of Columbus' sailors. Besides bearing poisonous fruit, old wives maintained that if you stood beneath the branches when it was raining, you'd be burned by acid from its leaves. It might be dumb gossip, but somehow it seemed dumber to challenge it.

The green hillsides that meet the bay are not a jungle—there's no real jungle on the island. A pretty good imitation of a jungle can be found on the other side of the mountain. That's where clouds dump rain; that's where green comes in infinite hues. The trees in Flamingo Bay are specimens, just like the individuals who live in the community.

The road skirted the bay and bobbed and weaved between old stone buildings with red roofs, sturdy doors, and unglazed windows. Brightly colored pennants of laundry waved on clotheslines. Chickens scratched and goats idled in the morning sun. Rusting hulks of abandoned vehicles—transformed by the bush into a permanent part of the landscape—decayed slowly and quietly like the old men who owned them.

I checked my mirror. The parade I'd been leading caught up, as I slowed the truck to allow a young boy and girl to cross the road to join their parents and siblings in the sea. I waved to the kids, and they waved back. When I braked at Easys and pulled to the side of the road, Richards led the vehicles along the bay before swerving left to follow the road over the mountain. The asshole was probably going to drive twenty miles per hour—the limit—all the way to town. If he really had a hard-on, he'd drive fifteen.

When I learned that Easy hadn't shown up at his pop stand, I continued around the bay. A hundred feet down the road I stopped for Madison. Hitchhikers used their index finger to solicit a ride, not their thumb. Usually everyone just pointed in the direction he or she was heading. Madison waved his finger as if it was a wand.

He tugged on the door and said, "You okay?"

"Okay." I helped him get the door open, but he still had trouble climbing in with his machete and gunnysack.

"My name is Madison, but they calls me the cool cat. I be a big shot in the islands, mon. It be okay to talk with me. I been to New York. I been to Washington. I be a big shot—"

"Madison, it's me."

I waved to Rolly, who was swinging the monkey bars into position at the playground, while Madison studied my face trying his damnedest to recognize me.

"Captain Brian?"

"Bingo."

Pretty proud of himself, Madison relaxed for the final few hundred yards of his ride hanging his right elbow out of the window, draping his left arm across the top of the seatback, and smiling with the pomp of a chauffeured dignitary. Madison's most significant contribution to the Lore occurred last New Year's Eve. He and his brother, both driving drunk, crashed into each other head-on near the Paradise Club. Madison was arriving, and Hamilton was leaving. Since then, both have been begging rides and the roads are now safer. Madison would've been happy driving around with me for the rest of the day, but to his disappointment, I dropped him at the fire station, though not until I asked him what he remembered about finding Leif's body (doing chores for Miss Lucinda, he'd accompanied her to the cistern).

I knew before asking that I picked a bad day for the question. Madison's memory was usually sharpest in the morning, but last night he must have engaged in an overly dulling binge, and today his memory was no sharper than cheddar. He looked at me blankly before I dismissed him. As he turned to leave, I noticed a bulge in his front pocket.

"Hey, Madison," I called, and he turned to face me. "Can I borrow a buck?"

Again, I got the blank stare, but it may have been because I'd never asked him for money before. He'd always done the asking, and I'd bought him more shots of rum than I cared to think about. Still, his hand dove into his pocket, and he pulled out a wad of cash that totaled in the hundreds.

"Rob a bank?" I asked.

He had no answer, but he peeled off a dollar for me. I didn't want his money, but I took it, and he was happy to give it to me. Maybe the transaction made us blood brothers or something. Then it occurred to me that a dollar wouldn't do me much good, but two would get me a beer at Easys. I indicated that I needed more money, and Madison forked over another dollar.

After digging several quarters from the truck's ashtray, I headed around back to use the public telephone. When Sarah and I first arrived, we ordered telephone service. Two years later when the telephone company got ready to install it, the fire station's public phone had become as familiar to me as any of my personal possessions, so we canceled the order.

I called everyone I could think of who might be interested in owning quality mahogany. I started with Mr. Outback, the man from Water Island, to see if he was amenable to trading "Creamy Air" floor tile for mahogany. He wasn't, but he was pleased I called, and he wanted to know when he could expect to receive the five grand I owed him. "Soon," I told him. Then I called the lumberyards on St. Thomas. I was unable to generate a sale. When my most promising prospects failed to show interest, I called, with little enthusiasm, a few contractors I'd supplied with building material in the past. My luck was no better.

I phoned for a second time the owner of the lumberyard in Sugar Harbor, dropping the price by a few thousand from what I'd quoted him the previous week. He would've loved to own the lumber, and he carried enough cash with him that my modest asking price wouldn't substantially reduce the bulk of his wallet. He was, however, willing to forego making an obscene profit because he was annoyed that I brought only an occasional load up from South America. He'd spent years fleecing his customers, and he'd just built himself the largest house on the whole damn island of St. Judas. I found it rather intriguing that he possessed even one principle. He refused to bite even after I told him I'd burn the mahogany before I sold it to him for a penny less than the price I quoted. His only response was to laugh.

8

Easy lined his four mismatched stools in front of his shack and crooned along with Jimmy Buffet. Elroy, collecting empty beer bottles and plastic cups from yesterday's social event and depositing them in a plastic trash bag he dragged along behind him, nicked me for a cigarette even before I was able to get out of my truck. Madison lay sleeping beneath the palms.

"Captain Brian."

"Easy." I saluted. "Give me the first one."

"Jeeze, you're limping like a cripple."

"No worse than I feel."

I dropped the two dollars I borrowed from Madison on the bar, and Easy stepped inside his shack and reached deep into his beer cooler. For a big guy his movements were elegant. I'd never seen him perspire despite his year-round, summer-in-Alaska, lumberjack attire.

"One Budski." He twisted off the cap and set the beer on the bar. "What're you doing here so early?"

"Meeting the Shirt, the asshole I was talking to yesterday. Beats going to St. Thomas. Figure I let him waste a half-day travel time and pay the tariff to get here."

"I can dig it, man. St. Thomas gives paradise a bad name." Easy paused. "This about Leif?"

"I think it's about *Island Trader*. I think they want to make me drug trafficker, a cocaine cowboy."

"Need spurs for that."

Behind me, I heard a dull thud and a squealing chicken. Easy grinned. I spun on my stool. All I saw were two chickens—one brown, one white—flapping their wings, simulating flight.

"Close call," Easy said. "Falling coconut nearly nailed the white one."

"Could be the start of something big if Henny Penny and Ducky Lucky get wind of it."

"Don't forget Goosey Lucy."

Nobody who'd been here two years ago was likely to forget her. Goosey Lucy was the woman Easy hired to run his business that first summer when he went back to Alaska to go after halibut. While it isn't necessary to graduate from business school to run a pop stand, Lucy ignored every principle of business including the most basic— just showing up—and when she did show, she based her business hours on whimsy as much as custom. She abandoned the business midway through the summer after she met a captain and after they removed the pop stand's inventory to his boat.

"Easy, your job is to keep the beers coming. If I go for the Shirt's throat, you have my permission to pull me off. If you get there too late, you'll have to help me bury him."

"Cool. Don't own a shovel, but it's not a bad day for a burial at sea. After Leif, I'd say we got this burial-at-sea shit down to a science."

"I was thinking of something quieter—cement overshoes, overcast night, sharks."

"Oh, man. What, no rock band, no cannon, no flaming arrows, no bare tits?"

"That sort of pageantry might prove to be rather dangerous."

Easy looked over my shoulder.

"Here's your Shirt—flashy dude."

The flashy dude in the shiny black jeep overshot his destination and whipped a U-turn before pulling half off the road and parking.

"Uh-oh!"

"What?" I asked

"You got trouble. Looks like Mister Ralph nailed his ass."

Ralph was a proponent of the proposition that critters other than cats deserved nine lives—particularly dogs. He operated from the bush near the top of the mountain. His kids scouted the road for him, keeping watch for the telltale bumper sticker identifying the vehicle as a rental. Just as the target vehicle reached him, he tossed a dead dog in its path. Ralph made certain the collision was sudden and belly churning.

I focused on the Shirt's jeep. The left headlight was dirty. The rest of the vehicle was spotless, so it wasn't mud. Easy probably guessed right, and it was blood smeared on the headlight.

A single donkey ambled down the road. He stopped in the middle of the asphalt near the Shirt's jeep, looking at neither the harbor of moored boats on his right nor the Shirt exiting the vehicle on his left. Donkeys are smart; they are not curious.

None of the Shirt's clothes looked older than twenty minutes. He wore *the* shirt—a Molokai cocktail of color—outside his off-white trousers. It obscured but didn't hide the pistol in his belt. His black socks nicely complemented his brown leather boat shoes and their pristine white soles and laces. Opaque Ray-Bans still hid his eyes. To yesterday's ensemble, he'd added a black baseball cap emblazoned with the logo of a Florida sport-fishing club. I didn't think he wore the black cap and socks because he was mourning Leif, and his outfit told me he didn't know shit. He hadn't been around—*here*, anyway.

I figured that gave me the home-field advantage. It could be huge, especially in Flamingo Bay, but only if the skirmishes stopped short of war. In war, the home field becomes a distinct disadvantage—your own stuff gets messed up. I led the Shirt to the table farthest from Easy. I took the chair with the view of the harbor and *Island Trader*. I didn't trust the asshole not to have his stooges all over it, while he interrogated me. It was the correct decision—he acted uncomfortable with his back to the bar.

He asked, "What do you know about this character, Mister Ralph?"

"Good morning," I said.

"Mister Ralph?"

"Good morning."

"Morning," he mumbled.

"Easy," I said, holding up my bottle, "bring me the next one when you get the chance."

The Shirt agreed to a beer, and I added it to the order.

Easy replied, "Aye, aye, Admiral."

The Shirt looked puzzled. "Admiral?"

"There's dozens of boats in the harbor, but mine's the biggest," I said, proud of my battlefield promotion.

The Shirt didn't reply, but a toothy smile dominated his mildly weathered face, and isobars—tight and faint—radiated from the corners of his mouth.

A minute later Easy set two beers on the table. As the Shirt fumbled for his wallet, he studied my T-shirt and frowned. All the lettering on the shirt was done in Braille, and apparently, the Braille alphabet was not on the syllabus at the University of Narcotics.

"I'll buy the beer—you'll talk."

I almost declared that I could afford to buy my own beer. It was a lie, and I didn't mind lying, but a mental audit of my finances slowed me down enough that I missed the opportunity.

Instead, I countered, "You'll buy the beer, and I'll tell if you tell. By the way, where's my gun?"

"Always this hot?"

"It's more comfortable on top of the mountain, but this is about the coolest spot by the sea." It was, and it was cool that only the interrogator sweated. "Wind funnels up the bay. Christmas, when the trades really get cranked, you'll have to hold onto your Budweiser with two hands."

The Shirt dropped both hands from his beer bottle. I thought he'd been using the chilled bottle in an attempt to lower his body temperature, but he didn't seem the sort of guy who'd waste much time on futile projects.

"Mister Ralph?"

"You didn't hit his hundred-dollar dog on your way down the mountain?"

"Didn't think I was the first."

"You're probably not even the first today. You didn't pay?"

"Do I look stupid?"

It wasn't a question I was ready to answer, but I guessed Ralph exacted some part of his toll. Especially convincing were the crying children mourning the loss of their pet: *Mistah Toto, he dead.*

"Just one of the cottage industries."

The Shirt's left elbow rested on the table, and he rubbed his chin between his thumb and forefinger. I wondered if he could feel his whiskers growing.

"How was the funeral yesterday?"

"Copacetic until the occurrence."

"The occurrence?"

"Got struck by lightning."

"Seriously."

"Seriously," I said.

He was curious, so I gave him my version, though I expected there were about seventy versions among actual witnesses. Throw in the versions of those who didn't bother to attend but wished they had and those who weren't actually witnesses but felt they had an intuitive understanding of how such things ought to happen, and it was easy to see how subsequent attempts to recap the occurrence would prove unsuccessful. As time stretched between the event and its recounting, the capsule that was the occurrence would be breached by a hundred intrusions that ranged from the cosmic to the comic—entrusting veracity to pirates is like entrusting virgins to satyrs. I expected it would take time before it all got sorted out in the Lore.

"Tell me about Leif the Thief."

I relaxed a bit when I learned the Feds were concerned with Leif and not me. I thought it was great the Feds were investigating Leif's death. Still, I was surprised they cared about him, though I wouldn't have been surprised if the Shirt was starting with Leif but working his way to Vaughn and the square grouper. Evidently, I relaxed too much, and the Shirt rapped his fist twice on the table as a wake-up call.

"Who's there?" I asked.

"You think I spent two hours getting to this backwater to tell knock-knock jokes?"

"If it suited your purpose," I answered.

"Just tell me about Leif."

I noted the Shirt studying my T-shirt again.

"Helen Keller," I responded to his unasked question about the face on my shirt.

"What does it say?"

"Above her image it says, 'Helen Keller Regatta.' Below her image it says, 'Was this the face that launched a thousand ships—'"

"'And burnt the topless towers of Ilium'—Christopher Marlowe. But he was referring to Helen of Troy."

While Braille wasn't offered at the University of Narcotics, it stunned me to learn Elizabethan literature was.

"Troy, Keller—they were both Helens," I answered. "The real point, of course—Helen Keller's face wouldn't launch a thousand ships, except maybe for an evacuation exercise. Leif came up with the idea." I

stood and turned showing him the back of the shirt. "'A Leif the Thief
Production.'"

"Clever. Now that you've finally managed to focus your attention on the subject, tell me about him."

"I knew Leif for over five years. Met him the day I arrived, the day Hugo raped the Virgins."

"Hurricane Hugo?"

"Yeah," I nodded. "What a stupid name for a hurricane."

Naming storms after both sexes represented the sort of errant sensitivity that made living in America ponderous. The other thing: Why not name them afterwards? Barbie is a whole different story from Bertha.

"Be careful, my father's name was Hugo."

"My point, exactly."

The Shirt looked like he was ready to assault me. Instead, he played with his whiskers. I decided to get back to my story. As it was only midmorning, I figured he'd give me plenty more opportunities to insult him.

"I found a good anchorage near the mangroves in Hurricane Hole. I set four anchors and tied two lines to shore. Then I waited. When it started raining in the middle of the afternoon, Leif sailed over from the harbor to anchor next to me. It wasn't much of a boat." I looked across the bay to point out what was left of Leif's boat, but the stove-in blue hull rotting in the mangroves was just outside my field of vision. "Damn thing was a toy compared with mine. Leif wasn't concerned about being crushed by *Island Trader*. As it turned out, he had no reason to be. He possessed only one anchor and no seamanship. Storm started for real after midnight. Didn't take an hour before Leif's boat ended up in the mangroves. I rescued his ass—at considerable risk. If it'd been you I rescued, the President would've probably given me a citation."

"Medal of Honor?" The Shirt smirked.

"More along the line of a Lead Star. Maybe with a dingleberry cluster. Maybe two dingleberry clusters."

He shook his head. "Another comedian. You also supply dogs to Mister Ralph?"

"I used to, but I couldn't keep up with the demand."

"Get back to the hurricane."

"Big-time storm. Blew until midmorning. Stuff got moved around—roofs, buildings, trees, cars. Two-dozen boats no longer had water beneath their hulls. Half of them never sailed again. The wrecks provided opportunities for the pirates."

"Aren't piracy and comedy on everyone's résumé?"

"One thing that's changed over the centuries is you no longer need a boat to be a pirate—you don't even have to be a sailor. A rule of thumb: pirates and would-be pirates wear long pants and sailors and would-be sailors wear short pants. It's a rule of thumb, but really there are no rules."

"Which are you—sailor or pirate?"

"Island trader."

The Shirt crossed his legs. His foot dangled and danced, showing off his new boat shoes and black socks. I should've kept my mouth shut, but I couldn't resist the opportunity to pimp him.

"Also, unlike sailors, pirates prefer to wear socks—black, especially. Matches their flag. Like school colors. You know, 'Attack, attack, for the old white and black.'"

The Shirt's lips pursed, and his foot froze in mid-shuffle.

Habitués had straggled in. A few locals sat at tables as far away from us as they could get. Others drank quietly at the bar. Nobody wanted to get too close to the Shirt, and nobody wanted to make eye contact with me.

"Your turn to talk," I said.

"My turn?"

"I tell and you tell—remember?"

"Tell what?" he asked.

"During the hurricane Leif regaled me with tales of his criminal career, short but meteoric—before Leavenworth, anyway. Did he do what he claimed?"

"What did he claim?"

"If you're going to be coy, I expect our conversation will be brief."

"Spent eight years in Leavenworth for robbery."

"Did he or did he not dress a dozen guys precisely alike in cowboy hats and dusters and rob a Wells Fargo bank in Los Angeles under the guise of filming a movie?"

The Shirt thought it over and replied, "Something like that."

"Did he send a video of the robbery to the FBI?"

"Rumored."

"Did he escape to Brazil where he was abducted by a Fed posing as a bounty hunter?"

The Shirt stopped fingering his whiskers and stiffened. "Where did you hear that tale?"

"From the abductee."

"All that goes back to when Christ was a corporal, and Hugo was years ago." Leaving his elbow in place, the Shirt raised his arm from the table and stroked his chin with his index finger and thumb. "What's Leif been up to since?"

Confirmation of Leif's activities by the Shirt would solidify Leif's place in the Lore—Leif wasn't the most reliable and credible eyewitness, particularly to the events in his own life.

"Leif pulled one brilliant scam. Nothing he did after was more than penny-ante. He ripped people off. Sometimes he sold the stuff. Sometimes he held it hostage, returning it to the owners for a finder's fee. He washed dishes and cut bush. He was a lowlife looking for the high life. He had *no* shortage of enemies."

"If people were killed over penny-ante rip-offs, Leif would've been dead years ago." The Shirt folded his hands and rested them on the table, and he hunched forward in his chair. "We know for a fact cocaine was involved, bales of cocaine."

"What killed him?" I asked.

"I haven't seen the medical examiner's report. I did hear something about a single shot to the chest—shotgun."

I'd seen men shot in the chest—men I knew. It wasn't pretty. It didn't take much imagination to picture Leif's life oozing out of him. It made me want to cry.

I downed my beer and stood. "Be right back."

"Going somewhere?"

"To relieve myself."

While I waited to use the space-age facility, I thought of Thomas Hobbes. I remembered he said that men fear most a violent death. Me, I've never gotten beyond the basic universal fear of death—how it came never seemed to matter much. When staying alive isn't an option, is the manner in which you die—beyond the final test of personal courage—really significant?

What was important for me was the enormity of the crime—one thing about murder: there's no real justice, no real vengeance. While it can be argued that *an eye for an eye* works, a *life for a life* doesn't.

When I returned to the table I found Madison sitting in my chair entertaining the Shirt. Diver Vaughn—Madison's sometime employer—always called him Eddie, as if all rummies should be named Eddie. Madison had never seen *To Have and Have Not*, and the nickname Vaughn gave him could hardly be more uncomplimentary than the T-shirt that accompanied it:

I DO NOT HAVE A DRINKING PROBLEM!

I DRINK

I GET DRUNK

I FALL DOWN

NO PROBLEM!

Madison was a likable and entertaining guy, especially in the morning before he started drinking seriously, though lately, he seemed to be drinking more than usual. I suspected it had everything to do with the wad of bills in his pocket.

I'd had enough experience with drunks to know they weren't all likable and entertaining. Even if they started that way, they often ended up becoming mean. The man my mother married was mean. He told me when I was four years old that he wasn't really my father. I never forgot what he said—I don't forget much—though I had no idea then what he was talking about.

"They calls me the cool cat," Madison told the Shirt, his broad smile revealing a missing incisor in his upper jaw that marred his good looks. "I be a big shot in the islands. It be okay to talk with me, mon. I been to New York. I been to Washington. You dig? I live in the big white house in Turtle Bay—swimming pool, hot tub. You know the place?"

The Shirt didn't answer. I figured he'd done the math, and it didn't add up. Madison adjusted the bill of his dirty white baseball cap until it was appropriately aligned with his face, but the cap sat far enough back on his head that the bill pointed skyward.

"Today, I be walking. Car break down. Big Mercedes, mon. Buy it in

Mercedes-*Benz*."

"Madison, we're having a meeting here."

"Captain Brian, you tell this mon that it be okay to talk with me. Tell him I be a big shot."

"Madison's a big shot," I told the Shirt.

The Shirt didn't say anything. I saw that Madison had pissed in his pants—so much for his credibility. He needed to learn to control his fluids.

"Madison, you're interrupting us. We have important business."

He nodded, picked up his machete and his gunnysack that held three or four coconuts, and wandered to the bar.

The table had been cleared of empties. Easy usually left the empty bottles so I could count them, an important component in my quest to develop a theory of equilibrium. Not profound or even innovative, my theory simply advocates the control of fluids—a proposition that continues to inform and define the construction of roofs, pottery, ships, plumbing, and raingear. Because my theory includes bodily fluids— blood, bile, semen, adrenaline, et cetera, as well as external fluids, it borders on the Strangelovian, and I wonder sometimes if I haven't experienced too much sun. Though I don't expect anyone will ever read about it in a scientific journal, my theory is devilishly tenacious.

I dragged Madison's chair away from the table and exchanged it for a dry one. It appeared the Shirt didn't smoke, so I lit a cigarette.

He answered by popping a corona into his mouth and lighting it in such a way as if to say: "Mine's bigger than yours." He attempted to blow smoke rings, but the trade wind seldom allows smoke ring days in Flamingo Bay.

The white chicken took a sudden liking to the Shirt's shoes. It pecked at the stitching around the toes. The Shirt pushed the bird away with his foot, but the bird came back for more.

"You've found at least one friend on the island."

"Don't be so sure," he said, launching the chicken with his foot.

The chicken squawked and fled, wings flapping, head jerking. Pirates loafing at the bar seemed to wince in sympathy with the aggrieved fowl. I asked the Shirt if he was investigating Leif's murder.

"VIPD is handling the murder investigation."

"You mean his murder's not being investigated."

"No control over the VIPD and its procedures—"

"Procedures? They stop people on the street and ask them if they're guilty."

"Police here aren't sophisticated," the Shirt conceded. "But neither are most of the crimes. You know the drill. All the guilty party has to do is leave the island, and the law enforcement process effectively stops. Even if the police were more aggressive, only American Airlines would profit."

"Lack of sophistication's only part of it," I argued. "The other part's how they spell *justice*—j-u-s-t u-s. Us and them. If you're not sure whom *us* signifies, you're *them*." The Shirt looked bored and began toying again with his whiskers. "So you don't much care that Leif was murdered. That investigation's being conducted by the VIPD. You don't care *who*—you're just trying to determine *why*."

The Shirt smiled and nodded. "Catching on." He paused. "Now that we've exchanged pleasantries, let's get down to business."

"What business?"

"Cocaine," he said. "Ready to begin the beguine?"

"I don't dance."

"For me you will."

I got to my feet. "I don't think so."

"Sit," he commanded.

"I'm out of here."

"Not so fast." He was on his feet. "Two choices. Sit and talk, or I take you into custody, and we have this interview on St. Thomas."

"There are plenty of people here to talk to—why me?"

"Word on the street is I'd like you so much, I'd offer you the shirt off my back. You could certainly use it."

"Who told you that?"

"Word's out. You're a celebrity. Word is you know everybody. Word is you know everything."

"I don't know if I'd wear your shirt. All my friends would have to buy dark glasses like you wear."

"Suit yourself," the Shirt chuckled. "Walk around looking like an indigent slob. Or is it about *machismo?* Your way of telling me you're a bad-ass fuck?"

"Who *are* you?"

"Maybe your best friend," the Shirt replied.

"Unlikely."

"Going to talk?"

"If I don't?"

"You can scrap your rusty scow and find work at Mimosa Cafe with Sarah. No business license, no business. Be a shame if it wasn't renewed next month."

I already suspected Sarah had sold me out to the Shirt. Still, I was stunned and speechless. Cement overshoes seemed the ideal solution for both of them.

I downed my beer and turned.

"Going somewhere?"

"I need another beer. Either that, or I need to know for sure whether I can kick your ass."

The Shirt laughed. "Go ahead. Get another bottle of courage. I'm going to the head."

"Sputnik."

"What?"

"It's a satellite toilet."

"And when I get back, you're going to tell me everything you know about Diver Vaughn and the bales of cocaine he fished out of the Sir Francis Drake Channel."

I needed an actuarial table to determine if the Shirt would live long enough to hear all I knew. I needed my head examined that I was even thinking of considering telling him anything. It would mean war—loose lips sink ships. I didn't want to get into it with Vaughn or any of the locals—everybody's stuff gets messed up during a civil war. And I didn't want to get into it with the Shirt and lose my home-field advantage. I decided to stretch my legs and take a hike. My knee ached. Sitting, standing, walking—after a while, the pain was about the same. Stretching my legs would also provide an opportunity to learn how serious the Shirt was in recruiting me as an informer, though I suspected he was quite serious in his pursuit of Vaughn's cocaine.

When I reached the road, I heard Easy's throaty laugh, shrill as a large bird of prey. "I told you he wouldn't get shit out of Captain Brian."

9

As I walked toward the head of the bay, I glanced over my shoulder several times to see if the Shirt followed me. He didn't, and his failure to pursue me was more intimidating than if he just gave chase. He wasn't going to let me off so easily. I could only conclude our interview was not simply a one-time thing but part of a larger plan. Beyond learning the location of Vaughn's bales, I hadn't a clue of his intent.

I stepped under the mangrove canopy. The humidity grew thick and a trace of sulfur permeated the chilly air. Black on yellow, a road sign announced DIP where the road dropped below surrounding grade to provide drainage. Someone had scratched CLAM onto the sign.

Mister Aubrey, piloting his front-end loader, headed in my direction. Since his pickup broke down, he used the yellow monster to get around Flamingo Bay. I wasn't sure who owned the piece of machinery. I wasn't sure Aubrey knew. Few people in Flamingo Bay possessed clear title to anything except their lives.

As he bounced toward me, engine roaring, black smoke spewing, I spotted four hoofed legs sticking straight into the air from the machine's scoop. I remembered the day Bongo Natty's carcass filled the same scoop, a horrible and sickening sight the magnitude of which I could only equate to losing *Island Trader*—Bongo Natty meant everything to Pony Mon. Aubrey pulled alongside and stopped. I couldn't even look at his cargo. He shut off the machine and dismounted with agility, a feat for a man nearly twice my age.

"Good afternoon." I extended my hand.

He grabbed it with a solid grip. "Captain Brian, you okay?"

"Okay. You?"

"I be suffering."

"Come on."

"Here am I with this dead donkey when I could be liming, but what's a poor mon to do?" He shrugged. "Damn neighbor boy get drunk last night at Paradise Club. Boy doesn't want to walk, so he catch this donkey. I doesn't know how. Hard for donkey to be dumber than this boy—born behind God's back. Boy so drunk he think maybe he will keep donkey. That be all the thinking he does. He tie this animal to a tree and go to sleep. Poor animal stumble and choke in the night. 'Mister Aubrey,' boy's mama whine at my door. 'What we gonna do?'"

"What are you going to do? Dump it into the sea?"

He nodded.

"How many dead donkeys have you dumped into the sea?"

"Poor mon like me can't count that high."

I just laughed. Though he lived as modestly as his neighbors, Aubrey's real estate holdings were reputedly worth over thirty million. I pulled out my cigarettes and offered him one.

"Mister Aubrey, people say the playground's site is worth a million dollars to a developer."

"Land worth nothing to me. Playground worth million dollars. Playground maybe keep kids out of trouble. Maybe keep them young. They grow up too fast." He shook his head. "Money. No happiness in getting. No happiness in spending. Just make folks jealous—he build house too big, she wear too much gold. I doesn't know—maybe I be just another old man who piss into the wind."

Aubrey's eyes glistened, as he reminisced about growing up in Flamingo Bay: fishing for yellowtails, hunting crab and whelk, shinnying up palms for coconuts, raiding the guinep trees and gorging on the fruit until his belly ached. No adventure was bigger than traveling to Sugar Harbor. It took nearly an entire day to climb the mountain and walk the eight-or-so miles to town, goods and possessions strapped to a donkey. They'd do business on the second day and return on the third, the donkey loaded with supplies. For the first thirty years of his life, Flamingo Bay had no electricity, no real roads, no telephones. Tears welled in his eyes when he spoke of playing the ukulele and wooing his wife when the young folk gathered on the lawn of the Moravian church in the evening.

He closed his eyes, and his reminiscence became private, though in a sense, he shared his thoughts. Like a guide, he laid out the scene, leading me into the past, urging me to open my eyes to a lost world of ackee and salt fish. I was certainly a willing candidate. It was precisely the world of ackee and salt fish I hoped to find in the West Indies. Even though the new millennium loomed on the horizon, I seemed firmly rooted in the last century.

"I give land for children and Valerie. I liked that woman. If you say, let's build playground for Leif, I spit."

I hurriedly caught up with Aubrey and the present and realized I'd momentarily omitted Valerie from my thoughts by focusing so much on the playground. I knew I had only this chance to get it built. I felt failure dogging me.

"What about a building permit?" I asked. "Is that going to be a problem for us?"

"Only a problem if we apply. It take easy one year to get permit. Everybody with grudge try to stop process, including sister. You build. I watch you back. Enemies can stop me building, but they can't stop me when it be finished."

"You didn't like Leif?"

"He never steal from me or neighbors, but I hear he steal from own friends. I doesn't understand. He show no respect."

Leif was hardly alone in failing to show proper respect to West Indians, but I didn't know anyone who considered that particular transgression a capital offense.

While I dug a couple more cigarettes out of the pack, I looked up and thought I spotted Officer Richards' Blazer parked at the head of the bay near the Moravian church. To get a better view I walked into the mangroves to water's edge. Aubrey followed me. From my new vantage, eyes following the shoreline, I could clearly make out his vehicle. I didn't see Richards, but it was rumored that his outside-woman lived in one of the cottages near the church. In most places, common knowledge of a police officer's girlfriend would be a liability for the cop and spending working hours with her would be even dicier, but here none of it was a problem, not even outside-children.

"How about if I get rid of it for you?" I asked, nodding toward the carcass.

"Where?"

I pointed to Richards' Blazer. "I think it will look good on the roof."

"He be kin."

"You're related to everybody on the island."

Aubrey bobbed his head. "True."

"Just because he's family doesn't mean he isn't an asshole."

"Also true."

"Pony Mon suspects he shot Bongo Natty."

"He have a temper, that one." Aubrey dropped his cigarette in the mud and stepped on it.

"What's the problem?"

"He just pay me three thousand dollars he owe for two years."

"This could be the interest."

Aubrey tapped at the cigarette butt with his toe, looked up at me, and said, "Know how to drive this behemoth?"

"I'm a quick learner."

He smiled. "Okay, then, if you have the bowels for it."

We walked back out to the road, and I climbed into the single seat. Aubrey, standing on the ladder's lowest rung, offered a two-minute tutorial on the machine's operation. I forgot most of it the second the monster diesel roared to life, jarring my brain cells, disconnecting the synapses.

I got the thing turned around and bounced down the road at a noisy five miles per hour, my vision screened by the scoop and swarming flies, my lungs filled with unburned hydrocarbons and decaying flesh. I could've used a little stealth technology, but I would've been satisfied with a decent muffler.

Field Marshall Montgomery—never one of my icons but a keen observer of armed conflict—once stated that there are two principles of war: never march on Moscow and never fight a land war in Asia. I felt I violated both principles simultaneously. I also felt I moved at a ridiculously slow pace.

When I reached the Blazer I pulled as close to the front of it as I dared. After a little trial and error, I sorted out the controls and lifted the scoop high into the air. I put the machine in gear and nudged closer to the Blazer, hitting the brake when I bumped it. It took forever for the scoop to rotate, and then I wasn't so careful. The carcass slipped from the scoop, brushed the light bar, and hit the roof near the windshield. The windshield popped out and landed on the hood, and the dead animal landed on top of it, its rear legs resting against the roof on the driver's side, its head dangling over the right front fender.

Certain a smirk as prominent as a small atoll covered my face and certain my smirk was self-satisfied—at least until I realized I hadn't an idea in hell where to find reverse gear—I banged the front-end loader into the Blazer a half-dozen times before I got it right. A quick survey of the Blazer showed I did some serious damage, much more than I contemplated doing on the road earlier in the day.

I couldn't believe I didn't alarm the neighborhood, though I did get the attention of Mister Rolly's crew, which interrupted its assembly of the monkey bars to watch. Still, no one ran out of any of the few cottages scattered low along the hillside screened by bougainvillea and oleander. West Indian men like their women built for comfort—I could only figure she was on top.

I got the monster turned around and headed back around the bay, pedal to the floor. It occurred to me the machine was not unlike *Island Trader*—it pitched and rolled and yawed. I was sure there was a certain speed below which "hightailing" became antithetical. I didn't approach that mark, but I drove as fast as I could. Each time I glanced back and didn't see Richards, I got another jolt of confidence.

Building confidence can be overrated, especially when it's derived mostly from escaping the authorities. Of course, a bit of confidence is required to attempt escape, but in the end, it's the authorities that are going to win—not much of a confidence booster. I didn't like to think about it, but I recognized that my luck couldn't hold out forever and I was too old a dog to learn new tricks, particularly the "Sit!" and "Roll over!" bits.

When I reached the mangroves where Aubrey had taken refuge from the sun, he waved and directed me into the dense trees—a good alley had been cleared out a few weeks ago when a ready-mix driver missed the turn and parked in the bay. Camouflage paint or netting would've helped, but I suspected the mangroves did a pretty okay job of concealing the bright yellow machine.

I jumped off the front-end loader, and Aubrey and I celebrated our success with laughter and a short version of the local hand jive. From our vantage—seeing but unseen—Aubrey and I waited for Richards to discover the prank.

As we waited, a brown pelican swooped toward us, low across the bay between the masts of the moored boats. I watched it light on the shiny black outboard of Zeke's powerboat anchored about forty feet from shore. Everyone else used the dinghy dock across the bay. Zeke must have used the cleared-out alley where the front-end loader now sat to park his jeep. I figured he did it out of a misplaced notion of secrecy—everyone knew what he was up to—but I appreciated his showmanship. Then I noticed that very little of the green fiberglass hull of the boat was visible. The control of fluids is important in any undertaking, but it's especially important in a naval enterprise.

Anchored bow-to-shore—always a risky business—a line fixed the boat to a mangrove tree. An anchor secured the stern. Confident that Zeke had repaid Dan in kind—a puncture for a puncture—I couldn't be certain if Zeke repaired the wound to his hull, if Dan punctured it a second time, or if an errant swell simply washed over the transom.

It didn't much matter why Zeke's boat was sinking. Boats sink in Flamingo Bay. Most boats go quietly and gently under the waves like Zeke's would, though the last boat to sink exploded. The schooner's owners set off a bug bomb to rid the vessel of pests—a necessary bit of maintenance if you're stupid enough to bring corrugated cardboard aboard. Unfortunately, they neglected to turn off the pilot light to the propane stove. They were lucky to have been on deck when it blew.

I pointed out to Aubrey the likely drowning of Zeke's boat.

"You doesn't want to help Zeke," he said. "Bad boy."

Zeke equipped his twenty-two-foot boat with a new two-hundred-horsepower Mercury motor. Like the guy or not—and I did—I couldn't let this piece of machinery go under.

"The motor will be ruined," I pleaded.

Aubrey acquiesced and agreed to lend a hand. I untied the line from the mangrove and retied it to the arm that attached to the front-end loader's scoop. Before I could kick off my shoes to go in after the anchor, a swell swept over the transom, and Zeke's boat started going down—neutral buoyancy, anyway. Everything but the windshield and outboard motor slipped below the surface. Extruded polystyrene, installed by the manufacturer, kept the boat suspended with zero free-board. Lifejackets, Heineken bottles, and bumpers floated free. Even the pelican abandoned its perch.

As a retro guy, I liked wooden boats—wooden sailboats, especially.

I disliked plastic, and I disliked powerboats, and I especially disliked plastic powerboats, but as I examined the precarious condition of Zeke's boat—not quite afloat and not quite sunk—I found it difficult to deny the efficacy of plastic.

A shiny writhing slick of cockroaches twice as large as the boat covered the surface of the water. It surprised me there were so many roaches and so much polystyrene—I couldn't figure what else they'd be eating. The brown monster undulated on the waves and glittered in the sun. I waded in and made a big detour, not wanting to invade the roaches' territory. Then I swam to the stern and managed to pry the anchor loose from the silt-covered bottom.

Aubrey started the machine and shifted into reverse. He released the clutch too quickly. The eyelet pulled out of the hull, and the whipping rope sent it into the front-end loader's scoop with the impact of a bullet. The boat barely moved. Aubrey tossed the rope to me, and I mixed it up with the roaches before I could tie it to a deck cleat. Aubrey gave the boat another yank, and it swam closer to shore. When the green hull made contact with the muddy bottom, the deck cleat popped out. Zeke would need to perform some minor repairs to the fiberglass hull and deck, but we saved the motor. I tied off a line from the one remaining deck cleat to a mangrove tree and piled on the beach the gear that floated loose from the boat.

Aubrey helped me pick off the roaches that hitched a ride ashore. He worked on my back and I worked on my front.

"Enough here for a meal," he laughed.

"No thanks."

When he finished, he had me bend over so he could comb his fingers through my hair.

"Damn things will inherit the earth, I swear. This be the last God one of them on you head." He flicked it off his finger. "You has to find the rest. I doesn't want to get reputation as anti-mon."

Aubrey headed to our lookout spot, and I dropped my shorts and finished the job. Officer Richard's curses skipped across the water. I pulled up my shorts and joined Aubrey.

Throwing a tantrum, Richards circled his vehicle several times, kicking the doors and ranting. Aubrey and I smoked cigarettes and

chuckled. Then Richards climbed into his Blazer and started the
engine. He squealed the tires in reverse, but he couldn't shake the
donkey. After two more attempts, he discovered how physics worked.
He shifted into forward gear, built up some speed, and slammed on
the brakes. Smelling victory, he tried the maneuver again at higher
speed. He hit the brakes, and the donkey and the windshield slid off
the Blazer's hood onto the road. The only problem: he neglected to
stop completely, and he gently rolled over the donkey and the windshield, trapping both under the vehicle. He climbed out of the Blazer
and got on his hands and knees for a look.

After assessing the situation, Richards climbed back into the Blazer
for round two. I figured the four-wheel-drive feature of his vehicle
gave him an advantage over the donkey—a benefit General Motors
never capitalized on in the company's advertisements—and he broke
his Blazer free.

Richards stopped again and climbed out to examine the mess on
the road. He dragged the windshield to the shoulder, but—both hands
grasping one of the donkey's hind legs—he wasn't able to budge the
dead animal. Richards let the dead donkey lie, climbed into his vehicle, and drove off.

When not contriving their own entertainment, folk on St. Judas
satisfied themselves with videos. The donkey incident would probably find its way into the Lore, but the full extent of its humor wouldn't
be realized because Freddie Fellini, custodian of Flamingo Bay's video
library, hadn't been present to record the event; it didn't, however, stop
Aubrey and I from enjoying it live.

Screeching tires warned us of Richards' arrival. Evidently, the front-
end loader was not as well hidden as I believed. It was hard not to
laugh when I saw his Blazer. It would take a magician to install a new
windshield—I'd messed up the roof pretty good. Richards climbed
out, pulled off the loose windshield gasket, and tossed it onto the front
seat. Then he rubbed the handle of his pistol with the palm of his hand
and eyed me.

Before Richards could open his mouth, Aubrey stepped into the line
of fire and walked out to the road to look at the Blazer. From all the
pointing and head shaking, I gathered that Aubrey denied any knowl-

edge of the donkey incident. At the end of the discussion—unintelligible bursts of words and energy—Aubrey, with a big grin on his face, climbed aboard the front-end loader.

"Good afternoon," he said. "Police need this old mon's help to clean up road. Poor mon must make a dollar when he can."

He fired up the machine and backed out to the road where Richards waited to lead him around the bay. I jumped aboard taking advantage of the shuttle service. I preferred my Ford as a daily driver, but a front-end loader offered advantages the average vehicle didn't. Richards pulled off the road, and Aubrey came to a stop. The road and the donkey looked rather gruesome—like an animal sacrifice gone bad. I hopped off and kept going, waving to Aubrey over my shoulder.

At the playground, I inspected the newly completed monkey bars and watched two young would-be Tarzans traverse the span. It worked for them, so it worked for me. Three other children played on the swings. Rolly acknowledged that he couldn't keep the kids away from the site, so he decided to hang the swings to keep the kids away from the jungle gym where he worked with his crew.

I'd pretty much given Rolly control of the project. He wanted to be in charge of the construction, and I didn't want to be noticeably involved—too many opportunities to inadvertently disrespect the West Indian community, a huge liability if you were actually trying to accomplish something. Left unsaid but understood by the two of us was the fact that I didn't possess the woodworking skill of even Rolly's most inexperienced helper. I could fix almost anything, but all I could accomplish with lumber was to make toothpicks of it.

I discussed with Rolly what I thought was the best location for the playground's sign—near the road next to a clump of purple-red bougainvillea. I don't know if it was because I needed to make a contribution to the project or if I was beginning to feel useless physically, but I worked to dig a three-foot hole in which to anchor the playground's sign, a four-by-twenty-inch slab of mahogany seven feet long. I fought every inch of the way. The pickax, as often as not, just bounced off the compacted earth. As Rolly hadn't yet cut the inscription with his router, I took my time.

I studied the bougainvillea as I worked. One thing I've noticed about bougainvillea: the leaves and flowers seem to operate on two distinct cycles. Sometimes the flowers are brilliant, and the leaves sparse and drab. Other times the leaves are lush and the flowers only so-so. There's only a few-month period every year where both the flowers and the leaves are at their peak; any time of year, however, I can cut a bare eight-inch woody branch and stick it halfway into the ground, and in two weeks, it'll be blooming and the leaves will be lush. It's as if it has to grow up before it gets weird and obstinate—just like people, just like cells that mutate and kill. It's curious, but the second law of thermodynamics explains it.

When I hit the blue bitch—a rock that has perplexed diggers on the island since human habitation—I was drenched in sweat and about ready to succumb to what I figured was a combination of sunstroke and heat exhaustion. Though suffering from both afflictions simultaneously may be a medical impossibility, the contradictory symptoms fit nicely with my contradictory state of mind, as I didn't know if I was coming or going.

Rolly's crew laughed at me, but Rolly hauled me over to the Congo Club, ordered lots of ice and water, and got me cooled down. When I felt and behaved like a human, except for a massive headache, Rolly— after instructing me to stay away from the construction site—headed back to work.

I realized I hadn't eaten, and ordered lunch. Figuring out how to pay for the meal didn't occur to me until Madison joined me. I endured for the hundredth time his spiel about his status as a big shot. Finding an attentive listener who wasn't a tourist was evidently worth the price of a meal to Madison.

I raided the Congo Club's aspirin supply before I headed back to the playground. Rolly wasn't happy to see me, but I insisted on finishing the job. The hard work was made easier when I learned the blue bitch was just a large chunk of loose bedrock, no longer actual bedrock. Removing it necessitated digging a hole much larger than I intended, but I managed.

I finished about the time the sun dropped behind the mountain. Rolly and the crew loaded their tools and equipment into their truck. I emptied the last of their water jug, but it didn't really quench my thirst—the water seemed to vaporize when it hit my tongue, as if I was pouring it onto a hot frying pan. When the work party drove off, leaving me alone at the site, I tried one of the three swings and watched the glowing clouds scurrying to catch the sun. The clouds all seemed to be illuminated from within, just like Billie, but I knew they were stealing the sun's rays, thieves just like Leif. I viewed the show until the lights went out.

The swing was a bit tame compared to some of the rides I'd taken as an adult, but I remembered the freedom I experienced as a child, pumping my legs, climbing toward the sky, and trying to fly. A lifetime later, I knew that the freedom I experienced as a child at the playground was both real and an illusion, like the freedom of a dog on a chain. The exuberance, however, was genuine and worth duplicating. I quit pumping, released my hands from the chains, and hurtled about ten feet before landing awkwardly on my bum knee and losing my footing. I got to my feet slowly and checked my limbs for damage. I hurt all over, so it was difficult to assign specific aches to either work or play. Still, I was thankful that Freddie Fellini had taken the day off.

10

IN WHAT FELT LIKE THE MIDDLE OF THE NIGHT, I awoke from a sound sleep and tumbled out of my hammock when Billie banged on the hull of *Island Trader* and called, "Yoo-hoo, anybody home?"

I dragged my aching body to the starboard rail, reluctantly admitting to myself that while ditch-digging hadn't changed much over the past couple decades, I had. I chalked it up to another simple activity that became a challenge with age, like reading the fine print.

Cherry Mary, providing shuttle service to Billie, steadied her dinghy by grabbing *Island Trader*'s rope ladder. Life without meat and men agreed with Mary, though tonight she seemed a bit testy.

Billie called, "Permission to come aboard, skipper?"

"Sorry," I answered. "No one can be piped aboard, while the bosun's on strike."

Billie imitated the sound of a bosun's pipe—authentic except for the giggle that accompanied it—dropped her backpack over the bulwarks onto the deck, handed me a Styrofoam bucket containing a six-pack on ice, and climbed aboard. Mary waved goodnight with her flashlight and motored toward *Sappho*.

"What time is it?" I asked the barely visible Billie who smelled of bay rum and bristled with energy.

"About ten."

"Shouldn't you be in bed?"

"I'm not tired." She lit cigarettes for both of us. "What happened to you yesterday? I was saving the last dance for you."

"I'm tired of coming in last."

"You know I didn't mean it that way."

At Easys, Jimmy Buffet was living and dying in three-quarter time. At the Congo Club, Eric Clapton was mooning over Layla. I turned my head until I heard mostly Clapton in my right ear and Buffet in my left.

"What?" Billie questioned my noggin nodding.

"Buffet, Clapton," I said, pointing with my thumbs.

"Cool," she said, imitating me. "But I worry that maybe you don't get out enough and mingle."

"If you think I'm any goofier than anyone else in Flamingo Bay, maybe *you* don't get out enough."

A comeback seemed to form on her lips, but she closed her mouth. She left me wondering about her exact words but not their gist. I realized I should've tempered my statement. Because we all get goofier with age, I should've added that qualifier.

"For this evening's entertainment you have your choice." Billie smiled and pulled a copy of *The Republic* from her backpack. "We can discuss Plato. I agree with him that the unexamined life's like not worth living. I think, too, the over-examined life presents its own life-diminishing consequences. What do you think?"

"I'll second that, but my biggest problem with Plato is that he successfully promoted the dualism of mind and body that's become imbedded so deeply in Western thought that I don't see it going away. Ever."

Billie said, "I think he's a toga Nazi. Can you like imagine anyone having fun in Flamingo Bay if Plato were running things."

I laughed, and Billie's cigarette glowed brightly as she inhaled.

"Billie, if you're so sure Wendy's coming back, maybe we should wait on her. After all, discussing Plato was her idea."

Billie dug into her backpack again and pulled out the artwork for the Easy Rider Rally T-shirts. "Another option. We could silkscreen shirts."

"It's a little dark."

I almost laughed at my understatement. Depending on the status of the moon—and it was a brand-spanking-new moon—it was either dark or darker. Darker was when you couldn't see your fingers if you extended your arm.

"You could turn on the generator."

"Diesel is a problem."

After potable water, fuel is the most important fluid the sailor needs, and I was running low on both.

Billie stepped closer and put her arm around me.

"We could put our heads together and figure out what happened to Leif."

I stepped away from her.

"You never give up, do you?"

"Never, and that's one of the things you like about me."

I wasn't sure her tenacity was what I liked about her, but after all these months, I was still trying to find a defect somewhere—the deal breaker—but I always found just a bit of perfection in Billie's imperfections.

"It might also be one of the things I'm liking less about you."

"Only because in this instance, you know I'm right. Down the road you'll thank me."

"I'm already working on the problem of Leif's demise," I said. "Quietly."

"But I want to work with you."

"Every time I walk around the problem, I fail to see how joining forces will move the project forward. First off, you're a lot smarter than I am. Second, you have a whole coterie of admirers that are willing to do whatever you ask, so you don't really need me. Also, you can be as subtle as falling masonry. It could become more of a circus than an investigation—one reason I don't need you. Given all that, you have to convince me why we should join forces."

"Simple," she said. "Everyone respects you, West Indians included, even the few people who don't much like you."

"Old territory. You'll have to do better."

"You're smart in all the ways I'm not. We complement each other. Working together we can do anything."

"Anything?" I asked.

She cocked her head and raised her eyebrows. "We can conquer the world."

Every man knows in his heart he's got a bit of Napoleon in him, and every man is flattered when a beautiful woman recognizes it. I figured I had maybe more of Napoleon in me than the next man, and Billie's compliment swayed me.

"Consider me browbeaten," I said. "But you have to understand up-front that I'm not making a career of this, and if our investigation becomes common knowledge, I'm walking away from it."

"I can keep a secret."

I screwed my mouth shut so I wouldn't laugh. Maybe she could keep a secret, but entrusting sensitive information to Billie wasn't my first choice. On the other hand, no one was more adept at gathering information than Billie. She could squeeze every drop of juice from a key lime without bruising the pulp.

"Okay," I said. "Tomorrow we'll come up with a plan. I'm too tired to think."

She kissed me, a full-frontal smooch with body english. Even my good knee buckled, but not my willpower. She'd fooled me once and shamed me; I wasn't going to allow it again.

When she removed her tongue from my mouth, I asked, "What's that about?"

"Just checking."

"Checking what?"

"To see if I could reach your lips," she answered. "Otherwise I'd have to wear platform flip-flops, and I'd like probably tip over."

"What *are* you talking about?"

When she didn't answer, I used the awkward moment to shore up my defenses. When my heart quieted, I felt the flush blanch from my face and neck.

"Like I said, I'm not making a career of investigating Leif's death. I have other problems."

"Such as?" she asked.

"I need to sell my lumber to settle up with Mr. Outback and buy sails. I need to figure out how I'm going to earn my next dollar—I can't go back to Cumaná—and I need to deal with the Shirt."

"Who *is* he?"

"Good question. As soon as I come up with an answer, I'll let you know."

"What else?" she asked.

"I'll tell you about it next week."

Billie momentarily frowned, but then she cocked her head and flashed a smile. "There's now one other item under consideration for this evening's amusement."

"And that is?"

"You could boink my brains out."

I didn't know for sure I could boink her brains out. Inability to perform had never been an issue, but lately, I'd been feeling pretty useless. My ditch-digging endeavor did nothing to increase my self-worth.

"Careful, you could get your ass thrown overboard."

"Oh, well. I suppose we could like just stand here all night, or we could crawl into your hammock and smoke this." She pulled a joint from behind her ear. "And drink the beer I brought."

It took a bit of maneuvering to get us both in the hammock and comfortable. While we burned the number, we shared a beer. Stars loomed in the black sky. Connecting the constellations' dots proved to be child's play.

"This isn't working," Billie said, as she slithered out of the hammock to the deck. "Too cramped."

"Just take my dinghy," I said without looking at her. "Come get me in the morning. "

"I'm not going anywhere. There. This is much better."

I turned my head, and she was standing naked.

"Snatch to match. Isn't that what guys call it?"

I didn't reply. I closed my eyes and enjoyed the boat's slight rhythmic movement and the soft breeze. Easy shut down his pop stand, but from the Congo Club Buffalo Springfield sang "Nowadays Clancy Can't Even Sing."

"You may as well be comfortable, too," she said, grabbing at my T-shirt.

"I'm perfectly comfortable." I fought her for my shirt. "And you're going to freeze your ass."

"Good point."

Billie returned from below deck with a camouflage poncho liner—a souvenir from Vietnam—and climbed back into the hammock. She covered us with the blanket, then squirmed and snuggled until she got settled and I got unsettled. Her hand slid down my belly. I grabbed it just south of the navel base.

"I don't think so."

"Why?" she asked. "It's the woman's job to have a headache."

Too exhausted from my bout with physical labor and too stoned to get my mind around Billie's new maneuvers, I answered, "I've embraced celibacy. It's not at all sticky like embracing flesh."

"Don't make me laugh."

"Then plug your ears."

While I believed I was aware of almost everything that was lacking in me, I knew I possessed determination equal to Billie's. For seven months, I tried to get her interested. But nothing had changed since the day of her Oscar-winning performance—the day she said that she didn't love me. Until I knew what was going on in her head, I wasn't going to allow her to seriously pierce my defense, and if required, I intended to extend the skirmish line infinitely.

"I guess that means goodnight," she said.

"Goodnight."

Billie's breath was warm on my cheek. As I dropped off to sleep, I was thinking that I could've lived a hundred years more, but I'd never get closer to paradise. Though, as I started thinking about it, I concluded that all you could ever do was get close to paradise. I wondered if maybe paradise wasn't like the black hole at the center of the galaxy: it just swallowed you up if you got too close.

I swirled along in the star field, backstroke, sidestroke. I sipped from the big dipper, rode a fiery-tailed comet. I butted heads with the Ram. I punched Orion in the belly and pinched the butts of the Pleiades. Then Billie nudged me awake, and my mind exchanged my kaleidoscopic dreams for the fleshiness of my somewhat-out-of-focus kaleidoscopic dream.

"Go to sleep," I mumbled.

"Poor Leif."

"What?" I asked.

"I was just thinking that he'll never get laid again."

"I doubt that was the last thing on his mind."

"You mean the first thing on his mind."

"I mean at the end of his life he was probably more concerned about staying alive than he was about not ever getting laid again."

She kissed my cheek.

"You know, if you'd really wanted me, you could've had me five minutes after we met."

"Go to sleep."

"I'm serious."

"What was I supposed to do, walk up and say, 'Wanna fuck?'"

"Not the smoothest line I've heard, but it would've worked, if you'd handled the words properly."

Someday when I was fully alert, I planned to ask her just how upon meeting a nubile woman one handled those particular words properly. Of course, just thinking about her revelation brought my brain to a higher level of awareness.

"How long was that particular window of opportunity open? Just curious."

"Not long."

"Then what?"

"Then I realized you didn't really want me because you wanted me too much."

I said, "Makes perfect sense to me."

She reached down and grabbed another beer from the Styrofoam bucket. She held the bottle; I twisted off the cap for her. She took a swallow and offered it to me. I declined and she took another swig before returning it to the bucket.

"What I'm trying to say is I need for sex to be physical and for you, sex needs to be spiritual," she said. "You didn't think I'd figured that out, did you?"

"For someone who needs sex to be physical, you've managed to intellectualize it."

"But I'm right, aren't I?" she asked.

"I'm not a God-fearing man. God ranks dead last among the things I fear, right after space junk falling out of orbit and landing on me. The only religious experiences I've had were with women, though not with most of them and not most of the time."

"And that's been like a problem. You're looking for a deity, and I know you think I'm like ever so much more, but I'm just a girl."

"All you had to do was show up."

"I know that now."

"Got a cigarette handy?"

She fished around in her pile of clothes and produced two cigarettes and a lighter. She stuck both in her mouth and lit them. I took one from her.

"Explain the day you won the Oscars," I said.

"By then I'd reconciled my fears. I'd concluded that sex could be spiritual for you and physical for me. It didn't have to be a problem. I wanted you to take me at the beach, but you behaved like a gentleman. Then at the Congo Club you behaved like a jerk."

"Women. Treat them like people and they want to be treated as sex objects. Treat them as sex objects and they want to be treated as people. But that was months ago."

Billie said, "Then you became my best friend in the world, and I was afraid to ruin our friendship."

"What's changed?"

"I'm getting like really horny."

"It's taken you long enough," I laughed. "But you can get off with no hands."

"If doing it alone worked so well, everybody would stay home and do themselves."

"What can I say?"

"How about the truth?"

"Which truth do you want?" I asked.

"There's more than one?"

"All things are true, and all things are not true—it's relative."

"Start wherever you want and run down the list," Billie said.

"I presume you're aboard for the long voyage?"

"You're asking if I'm a day-tripper?"

"It crossed my mind."

"I haven't slept with anyone because I've been waiting for you or for someone to come around. I have to admit that I don't want to walk into the Congo Club and find—like most of the other women who've been in Flamingo Bay awhile—that I've like boinked half the men in the place and they're sitting there comparing notes. Dating in Flamingo Bay's like playing musical chairs."

"Always odd men out?"

"That, and the stakes are higher."

"Maybe if you loved me, things would be different, but I'm leaving Flamingo Bay."

"Oh-my-god!"

Even as I lied to her about the seriousness of my intent, my brain tried to grasp the nature of obsessions. Why does a fifteen-year-old boy from Kansas, who's never seen the ocean, run away to sea? How does a man on the downhill side of the meridian, a man of reasonable intellect and experience, suppose that he can just throw out a sea anchor and a blonde nymph riding a crimson shell will simply catch up to him and not torpedo him and leave him foundering in her wake?

"I'm just trying to be fair here."

"Why're you leaving?"

I couldn't admit that one big reason I was thinking of leaving was because of her. Maybe if I hadn't planned such a voluptuous future with Billie, I'd be more inclined toward peaceful coexistence. Who was I kidding? How can you peacefully coexist with a woman who rips your guts apart every time you see her? Certainly not by admitting it to her. The words of our last book club author came to mind.

"You know," I said, "John Donne was wrong when he proclaimed that no man is an island, because that's precisely what a man is. He's not alone unto himself, but part of an archipelago. He's influenced by the same tides and winds, ill or otherwise, and he in turn influences those forces. Each island, separated by currents and undercurrents, has an effect upon the others—sometimes too subtle to notice, other times too profound to ignore. Donne was wrong when he proclaimed that no man is an island, but he was right about how a man is diminished by another's death. Each of the deaths in Flamingo Bay has diminished me. All of them—Mad Max, Captain Lucky, Doctor, Valerie, Leif—were my friends. And all died after flaunting their immortality."

As I pronounced the final syllable of my speech, I finished convincing myself of the validity of every word. I hadn't a clue whether my discourse convinced Billie.

"People die. It's part of the great circle."

"Except for you and Easy, my friends are gone. You're young, beautiful, and bright, the most adorable creature I've known. I can't expect that you'll be hanging around here much longer whether you're my friend or lover. You can do what you want and be what you want—"

"Being alive and living works well enough for me," Billie said. "You could use maybe some help on the living part."

"I've already done enough living for two men."

"I'd guess three or four—or ten. But you've like lost the fun."

"At best, I'd become an anchor and hate myself for it. At worst, you'd hate me as well."

"So are you afraid of hurting me or you?"

"Me."

"That's selfish."

"Yes and no. If I hurt you, I hurt myself. You don't think I'm sick over what's happened to Sarah?"

The music died at the Congo Club, and for the next several minutes the only sounds came from *Island Trader*'s rigging, jingle-jangling in the breeze, and the waves lapping against the hull.

I took a sip of the beer she offered, and she said, "By noon tomorrow, everyone in Flamingo Bay will know that we slept together tonight."

"Noon?" I asked. "I never figured you for a girl who'd kiss and tell. You said you could keep a secret."

"Well, maybe one o'clock. Mary knows what we're up to."

"Is that going to be a problem for you?"

All along, I assumed that Mary would continue to allow Billie to live aboard *Sappho* if Billie didn't get sexually involved with anyone. I also assumed that when Billie did find a man, Mary would likely give her the heave-ho.

Billie said, "We'll see, though tonight may like be a bigger problem for you than for me."

"How do you figure?"

"My manhood's not on the line."

"Because you're a girl."

"Ha, ha. If you're okay being branded a no-show in bed, we can go to sleep. If you want a chance to perform, you have my permission to go for it. Look at it this way, you may find I'm a lousy lay, and your obsession will go away. I could like really be doing you a favor."

"I don't want any favors. Go to sleep."

11

THE SUN'S HEAT AWAKENED ME about seven o'clock. Billie was gone. I reached for the pack of cigarettes lying on the deck and smoked one before climbing out of the hammock. Short of fresh water but groggy, I dived off the boat, clutching a bar of Ivory soap in my hand. I'd lost enough bars of soap in the sea to appreciate that Ivory floated. As a boy, I carved boats and ships from the air-infused soap bars to create bathtub armadas, a risky business that usually resulted in my getting slapped around for extravagance by the man who was married to my mother.

Success in life isn't just knuckles and know-how, but knuckles and know-how started me on the road to independence. Around age ten, I practiced punching an old cottonwood. Smaller targets—closer to my own size—grew in the weedy lot, but I was ambitious. Wearing home-made boxing gloves held together with friction tape, my fists pounded the tree until my knuckles bled and the tree sported a ring of pulverized bark. At fifteen, I was ready to fight back.

I blocked the punch with my left forearm, and with my right fist, I sent the man who was married to my mother to the carpet for the full count and then some. I packed my stuff in a gym bag and was out the door before he gained consciousness. I never went back, and I seldom looked back. I'd been in a few skirmishes before and many since, but that punch was still the most satisfying.

I scrubbed my scalp with both hands, while the soap bar bobbed nearby. After I rinsed and opened my eyes, I spotted a new boat in the harbor. Anchored near the moored boats toward Easys' side of the bay, the blue-hulled sloop looked like a Little Harbor, a boat worth a half-million dollars. From time to time, a sleek yacht belonging to one of the rich and famous did anchor in the harbor, but it didn't stick around long—rich and famous or not, if you didn't live in Flamingo Bay, you didn't really live.

Bathing in the sea wasn't my first choice, but I'd done it enough to know that if you towel off briskly, your skin's less sticky afterward, a lesson I learned from Leif who regularly bathed in the sea because he'd had limited access to plumbing pretty much all his years in Flamingo Bay. Lack of regularity in Leif's bathing habits was just an additional social handicap he endured.

I toweled off, dressed, and climbed into my Zodiac.

When I tied up at the dock, I learned that my truck was missing. I also learned that making myself available to the Shirt wasn't optional. He sat in the passenger seat of his jeep with his legs crossed, heels resting on top of the windshield frame, drinking a Red Stripe.

Robert McNamara—the alleged architect of my generation's war—and his cronies almost cured me of fighting, though I still had a few good punches left in me. Unless one or both of them eased up on their harassment, I figured my next punch would be to the jaw of either Officer Richards or the Shirt.

"Jamaicans know how to brew beer," the Shirt said. "I'd offer you one, but I'm fresh out." When I didn't reply, he added, "You're not taking our interview seriously."

"Way I see it, there's gravity and there's levity. I strive for balance."

The Shirt removed his sunglasses. He lifted his left arm and wiped his face and forehead on the sleeve of his mostly green Hawaiian shirt. After he repeated the procedure, finishing the job with his right arm, I looked into his eyes, but I couldn't see a damn thing. They were cold and metallic, almost as if the formula for their crystalline lenses contained too much lead oxide. I took a deep breath, while he fiddled with his shades. If eyes were really windows to the soul, the Shirt's needed a quick wipe with a squeegee. That, or the view afforded me was of oblivion.

"I have an errand to run, but before I leave, I guarantee you'll have the proper perspective." He put on his shades and sipped his beer. "Tell me about your boat."

I glanced at the high, round fat-ass stern of *Island Trader*. She looked pretty good now, but she was a sorry sight when I'd found her abandoned in St. Augustine, Florida—no engine, no masts, no nothing. I spent almost five years getting her squared away. Reworked the diesel I salvaged. Found three masts. Had new plates welded to the hull last year in Venezuela and repainted the hull. The deck still needed some work—my next project. I tried not to think of the pride and the anguish of ownership and the romantic dreams from another century that marked me as chronologically incorrect.

"Fifty-seven thousand tons, *Iowa* class, nine sixteen-inch guns—"

"Get serious."

"*Serious* is a hundred-ton Great Lakes pilot schooner with one three-pound gun. Always a motor-sailer, she ran on steam, and four stubby masts carried sails. During both World War I and World War II, she was a fireboat. She sank after World War II—these particular boats have an unfortunate tendency, under certain extreme conditions, to keep sailing right to the bottom. Twenty years later, she was refloated. After that I found no history until the late 1970s when she was operated by missionaries—"

"Only because missionaries like to keep records of their good deeds. Tons of contraband have been smuggled aboard that boat, but pirates don't keep records. We nabbed the last crew of pirates. When we nab the next crew, we grab the boat, too—zero tolerance."

Zero was the tolerance I had for the Shirt's threats, and zero was the tolerance I had for the ridiculous ZERO TOLERANCE signs the Feds made me plaster to *Island Trader*. The signage was optional, of course, but if you refused to post it, you were automatically assumed to be guilty of transporting controlled substances—so much for presumption of innocence.

The Shirt held up his beer bottle, aimed it at the sky, and gazed into its mouth like he was peering into a telescope. "I see a slight but very real possibility of the navy getting its hands on an ancient silver-hulled schooner and using it for torpedo practice."

"You're wasting your time. You'll never get my boat. Only narcolepsy could cause me to be that asleep at the wheel."

"Don't be so sure," the Shirt said.

"The boat's all I have. I'm not going to risk losing it over contraband. More drugs are transported on the St. Thomas ferry every month than I could haul in a year. Getting boarded's become a weekly ritual. You're the only federal face of my acquaintance that I don't remember seeing aboard—we talking deep cover here?"

"How much did you earn on your last trip to Venezuela?"

"You could probably tell me."

"Lost five thou' when the sails went."

I downplayed the extent of my financial calamity by telling Sarah the sails were worth only five grand—not a number the Shirt could guess. Just as he couldn't guess when I'd be arriving in St. Thomas with a load of lumber. Just as he couldn't guess I knew as much as anybody about what went on in Flamingo Bay. For the dissemination of that intelligence, I had Sarah to thank. I didn't even want to think what else she told the Shirt about me.

"That was after you lost five thou' when the ceramic tile you bought never showed up at the dock."

"What do you know about the tile not showing up?"

"What we know about it we learned from the police there," he said. "You *did* file a report with them. And you left two of your crew behind, after assaulting one of them."

"I simply fired them. With his cut of the five grand he helped to rip off from me, Fernando could afford to pay medical expenses. The only reason Tim's still alive is because he found a better place to hide."

"You'd kill someone over 'five thou'?"

"I once smoked marijuana—it made me want to kill. What is it *you* want?"

"Among other things, I want to get your attention."

"You have it, but don't bend over, or I'll sail *Island Trader* right up your ass."

"I'll forget I heard that," he said, as he slid his legs from the windshield, stood on the passenger seat, stepped onto the driver's seat, and slid down into it.

"Let's have lunch." He smiled. "Easys at noon."

He fired up the engine, tossed me the empty bottle, and roared off.

After kicking the pile of greenheart with my heel (my toe still smarted from the last assault), I headed on foot to look for my truck.

I slowed my pace when I reached the playground. No fear that the equipment would go unused: three kids played on the swings; several formed a queue behind a boy having difficulty traversing the monkey bars. The first level of the wedding-cake design of the jungle gym looked complete, and Rolly and his crew were assembling the second tier. Each of his crew seemed to hold either a plumb line or level. It gave me a kick to see grown men perched all over such a diminutive structure, like Titans building a skyscraper.

Zeke blew by me before stopping fifty feet down the road. He shifted into reverse and covered the distance between us at nearly the same speed. I climbed in, and he grinned.

"Zeke be thinking Captain Brian should wear bigger smile." He laughed. "For sure Zeke be smiling more, if he jook Blondie last night."

I couldn't help wondering if Billie was out selling T-shirts to commemorate an event that hadn't occurred.

"Captain Brian, mon, you okay?"

"Okay."

"It vex Zeke that Sarah be jooking a narc. But now you is jooking Blondie, Zeke be not so vexed."

"What happened to the tourist lady?" I asked.

"Oh, Captain Brian like Zeke's little girl? Don't bother. She not worth it. Off jooking someone else. She like Zeke's medicine more than she like Zeke."

"Some of them can be pretty mercenary."

"Captain Brian, Zeke hear you be the one to save boat. He not be forgetting."

"Sorry about the hardware, but it was full of water. Aubrey and I didn't have time to do anything."

"Zeke doesn't worry about that. He worry about his new outboard motor."

"Never got wet, so you're okay." I noticed that he winced with each shift of the gear lever. "What happened to your hand?"

"Zeke have unhappy patient. But patient more unhappy after Zeke kick his butt. He be so bandaged, nowhere to hit he, so Zeke kick his butt."

"Jason?"

"That mon doesn't sit for a week."

"So how did you hurt your hand?"

"Kicked that butt so hard, Zeke fall and hurt hand."

Zeke slowed at Easys.

"I'm heading out to Hard Labor," I said.

The Danes divided most of the island into estates and gave most of the estates the names of girls — Caroline, Catherine, Charlotte. Located on the beach, Sarah's cottage is sited on land that defeated all attempts at agriculture — hence the name. I presume bad neighborhoods have existed forever.

Zeke put his foot into the accelerator. I held on. The ride offered amusement park thrills. If Zeke ever could afford a Ferrari, I suspected his life expectancy would be no greater than Fast Louie's. He smoked the tires coming to a stop at the cottage I used to share with Sarah, and I climbed out.

"Zeke, I heard a rumor that Vaughn lost a kilo of cocaine last week. You don't have any new competitors?"

"Zeke be wondering the same thing already today when two patients doesn't want medicine."

"Any idea where they're getting it?"

"They say they doesn't have money, but if they be buying from someone, Zeke find out. Must go now. Patients can't live without medicine. Zeke can't live without patients."

I laughed and waved goodbye, but my spirits dropped when I turned the bend in Sarah's driveway and found the Shirt's jeep but no truck. I knocked on the door. No answer. I checked the jeep for keys, but the Shirt hadn't left them in the ignition. I rummaged through the cottage. No keys.

Frustration kicked in, and I used the vehicle's tire iron to pop the ignition switch to hot-wire the ignition. Not exactly brain surgery, I thought, when I started the job. But the more I got into it, the more it seemed like brain surgery. Replace anesthesia with a hammer and surgical instruments with a hatchet, and you get a pretty good idea of how badly I botched the job. Still, I got the vehicle started and the steering unlocked. All I really wanted was a ride back to the head of the bay, but now I was too embarrassed to drive it. I didn't want anyone to see my handiwork — humiliation is a great motivator. I'd gone to a lot of trouble to get the jeep started, enough trouble that I reexamined the situation and decided to park the thing in the Caribbean instead of driving it.

One part of my mind began composing a country song, while I 131

analyzed the possible outcomes of destroying the Shirt's rental vehicle. Never a big success at accomplishing much with a divided mind, I came up with no bad outcomes and only a couple of lines to the song:

YOU CAN BANG MY BROAD; GAWD SHE'S A FRAUD,
BUT IF YOU TOUCH MY TRUCK, YOU'RE SHIT OUT OF LUCK.

Even if I introduced liquor and a dog to the mix, it proved to me that I'd made a better vocational choice going to sea, rather than Nashville.

Scrubby vegetation covered the rocky hillside, and enough vines tied the shrubs and scrubby trees together that I couldn't be assured of my plan's success. Still, it seemed a good idea. I popped the hood and adjusted the idle to about fifteen hundred rpm. After backing up the jeep, I made a trial run releasing the clutch without touching the gas. It chugged along at a pretty good pace. I backed it up again and performed the same maneuver except that I jumped out when it approached the hillside.

For the first fifteen feet or so it bounced down the hill as true as an arrow. Then the right front tire hit a rock and the jeep started to turn right. The farther it traveled the more it veered off course until it ran almost ninety degrees away from the slope. When the jeep began running slightly uphill, I kicked myself in the ass for failing to tie the steering wheel. The right front tire climbed a good-sized slab of rock, and the vehicle began to jerk for lack of acceleration. The engine died, and the vehicle halted for an instant before it rolled over on its back, then onto its wheels. Momentum carried it into the sea where it splashed belly up, the tires poking a few inches out of the water.

I dashed to the road where I caught Zeke on the flip-flop, and he gave me a ride to Easys.

Easy staked me for a beer, while I watched him fill his cash register with money. Then he attempted to get some answers from me about my night with Billie.

"Look, Billie slept aboard *Island Trader* last night, but she didn't sleep with me."

Visibly relieved, Easy said, "Got to take a shit. Don't let anyone walk off with my pop stand."

"I'll guard it with my life."

Easy laughed. "Things get that serious, shotgun's behind the bar."

A tourist jeep stopped. The woman climbed out, leaving her man in the vehicle. I climbed off my stool and dug out two beers.

"This is legal, right?"

"Buying beer?" I asked.

"Drinking and driving?"

"Long as you don't fall out of your jeep," I answered, taking her money.

"God, what a great island."

"Just remember, left is right," I called after her. "Don't crash into the locals."

Before I returned to my barstool, I noticed Easy's twelve-gauge shotgun behind the bar. Easy was the only Continental in Flamingo Bay I knew who owned a shotgun. I jokingly asked him when he returned if Leif had borrowed the shotgun to kill himself. Easy wasn't amused, but we were both saved from a confrontation when Aubrey interrupted our conversation.

After the usual greetings, Easy mixed a Cutty Sark and orange juice for his landlord. Then he produced a sealed envelope that he handed to Aubrey.

"If I could sponsor a funeral every month," Easy said, "I could pay my rent on time and keep this joint going in perpetuity."

The breeze in the flamboyant tree scattered the skittish sunshine along with Easy's lazy laughter, but the breeze didn't scatter my thoughts. Easy was probably right that he could pay his rent on time if he sponsored a funeral every month, but he'd have to be up to speed on his accounts payable to accomplish it, and he wasn't. When I did the math, the net income from yesterday's event barely covered his monthly rent, despite my under-wholesale charge for the T-shirts. Of course, the four hundred he paid to Pirate Dan to support the party probably cost Easy another hundred and fifty to two hundred—the difference between the wholesale cost and the retail sale price of beer.

From what I knew of Easy's business practices (and I knew a lot),

Easy first paid his utilities. The Water and Power Authority took perverse pleasure in shutting off the juice to its Continental business customers promptly on the day after the due date for payment—it'd already happened to Easy—and the propane guy demanded cash for gas. Rent had always been Easy's next priority. Suppliers, counting on continued business, often allowed Easy to slide a bit, especially now that tourist season was approaching. That Easy hadn't paid his rent until today—two weeks late—suggested he hadn't paid his suppliers in a while and his financial position was bleaker than he'd let on.

Depending on how far behind he was, the arrival of tourists would carry him until summer, but that income might not give him enough of a cushion to make it through the off-season, as last year's off-season consumed the remainder of his savings earned in Alaska. I still liked the Shirt and Officer Richards as primary suspects, but the shotgun connection and Easy's financial situation warranted his inclusion in any list of suspects.

Patrons began to stroll in, including the Garys—two men who weren't on anyone's list of suspects, except as pretenders. Survivors of my last Venezuela expedition, the Garys grabbed beers at the bar and sat at a table. Big Gary—known in Flamingo Bay as G-Gary because of his speech impediment—wasn't large, but he was tall and skinny as a jumbie. He wore his unkempt carrot-colored hair at shoulder length, like an escaped clown from one of the carnivals I'd attended as a boy in the Midwest. Little Gary stood in black high-top sneakers, wearing legs that belonged to a shorter man and a trunk that belonged to a taller man. Despite the anatomical confusion, he reached about average height. He was also an indolent son of a bitch. Though Big Gary could never be accused of being industrious, Little Gary was the only crew I ever hired that was probably too lazy to masturbate.

It was the first time I'd seen them together since I left Big Gary on St. Thomas to get checked out by a doctor. Neither acknowledged me. I figured both Garys had already had their fill of me and the sea. I also figured that in a few months or a few years, the voyage would become profound and meaningful, something to tell their children about—it was one hell of a storm we experienced.

I never should've given the wheel to Little Gary after his partner was knocked unconscious—steering a boat to a compass heading is counter-intuitive, much like backing a vehicle with a trailer. Of course, neither Gary would've had an opportunity to touch anything important if it hadn't been for the mutineers. A package deal, the Garys were broke and looking for adventure—getting laid in a third-world country, mostly. Love isn't free in Venezuela, but it is a bargain.

Last night, Billie railed against the Platonic concept of a just society, and I had to agree with her that it was bit too buttoned-down to appeal to me. I didn't agree with Plato's formula to determine the citizens' vocations, but I couldn't find anything wrong with a man finding a suitable occupation, whatever it was, and simply doing his job—it had even worked for Judas Iscariot. If the Garys had done their job, I'd still be in business. If Officer Richards did his job, Leif's killer would be unmasked. If the Shirt did his job, he'd go after lawbreakers and get off my back. Of course, the one man in Flamingo Bay who couldn't be accused of not doing his job was Leif, and it had likely gotten him killed.

As Easy delivered beers to the Garys, I saw what I was waiting to see: the Shirt at the wheel of my truck and Sarah at his side. It appeared they were on their way back from town, and the truck was loaded with enough provisions to feed and quench the thirst of a small army. Both kept their eyes on the road, and the Shirt didn't slow the vehicle as he barreled down the road toward Sarah's.

The Shirt had balls, I had to admit. I had to admit also that my highest priority now should be to bust them. It should take precedence over finding Leif's killer. Precedence over selling my lumber. Precedence over my mating dance with Billie. But I couldn't say for sure that it did.

As I finished my beer and prepared to leave, Billie's jeep screeched to a halt in a cloud of blue smoke. She climbed out sporting a T-shirt of recent design that advertised Flamingo Bay:

PIRATES

FAIRY DUST

LITTLE BOYS WHO NEVER GROW UP

"Hi guys," Billie said. "What's shaking?"

"Your tits," Big Gary answered.

I'm pretty sure Big Gary could've gotten away with his comment if he'd smiled when he said it. Billie would pick her moment, but in the end, she'd skewer him. For the moment, Billie contented herself with a lighthearted retort.

"Hey, let's keep sexual harassment in the workplace where it belongs."

Hoots and guffaws followed her pronouncement. Billie performed a slight curtsy. She was upstaged for a minute by Mary's dog, Helga, soaking wet after her morning swim. Helga stood in the midst of the throng at the bar before shaking and dispersing hydrophobic patrons. Billie retreated in the direction of the Garys' table.

"Oh-my-god! G-Gary! You've come up for air. How was your date last night?"

Gary scowled.

Billie cocked her head, and she placed her hand—fingers together like a salute—alongside her mouth, as if she was going to whisper, but she never did. If anything, she raised her voice by a few decibels. It was one of her most intriguing mannerisms, and what was most intriguing was the way in which her golden eyebrows arched and her green eyes widened to register and convey her own shock and disbelief to her forthcoming words. Billie, always animated, further accentuated her stance by remaining perfectly still until she grabbed the attention of every patron.

"Did you boink her?" Billie asked, moving only her lips.

Billie's question caused patrons to laugh so hard that many had tears running down their cheeks, including me. Big Gary, who missed the opportunity to reply when the audience was caught up in mirth, waited patiently—like one-half of a comedy team—before answering with minimum thought and maximum effect.

"No, I d-didn't b-boink her."

Billie was the only person I knew who could seriously ask the pope if he was Catholic and get a serious reply. Big Gary had set himself up, and Billie wasn't finished with him.

"That's too bad. *I* got boinked last night."

Her statement elicited another round of applause from the patrons.

"Good for you," Big Gary replied.

"Did she suck your wienie?"

"D-don't I wish."

"So did you like play with her titties?"

"I never touched the b-bitch."

"Why not? I can't believe you didn't at least stick your tongue down her throat."

"I hate women. All of them. I hate my mother. I hate my ex-wife. I even hate my d-daughter. I hate them all," Big Gary declared. "They c-can eat shit and d-die for all I c-care."

"Eat *caca?* Evidently your evening was not a success."

"A success? Only from her p-perspective. She d-didn't p-put out. But I know why Mother Teresa b-became a nun."

"No! Why?" Billie asked.

"So she wouldn't have to b-boink," he answered. "Same reason my ex married me. Same reason all women g-get married. Too hot, too c-cold, too tired. I've heard all the excuses."

"Well, you know what the women say about the men in Flamingo Bay."

"What's that?" Big Gary asked.

"The odds are good, but the goods are odd."

Again, the patrons cheered, and the dizzy expression on Big Gary's face resembled the one I'd seen at sea after he regained consciousness from his dispute with the wayward boom.

Billie waved me over to an empty table. She opened her backpack and pulled out the art for the Easy Rider Rally T-shirts. I fingered the bit of black nylon in my pocket that I retrieved from Doctor's cistern and looked for damage to Billie's backpack. I found no fraying.

"Here's the front."

"Good morning, Billie."

She flashed a coy smile and answered, "Good morning, Brian."

"So you got boinked last night? Was this before you came aboard or after you left?"

"I exaggerated a little." She shrugged. "What do you think of the design?"

The undersized jeep—cartoon-like—featured smiley faces for headlights and wheels way out of alignment. Two big guys rode in it, caricatures of Dennis Hopper and Peter Fonda. Joints hung out of their mouths, and they flashed peace signs. Below the jeep was printed: EASY RIDER RALLY.

"And here's the back," she said. "One color, black on white. Sixty shirts should do it."

It showed the rear view of the jeep with Jack Nicholson stretched out—legs hanging out the rear, ankles crossed, feet forming a peace sign. He wore oversized shades and a maniacal grin. A series of smoke rings blew out the tailpipe. A Jolly Roger waved from the antenna. Below the jeep was the rally's motto: DOWNHILL ALL THE WAY.

I gave her the thumbs up. "Looks good."

"If you've got some time, we could start right now. I'm available to help. Oh, look! Bananaquits!"

Two plump little birds with gray and gold feathers flitted in the branches of the flamboyant tree. Billie pulled a plastic canister from her backpack. She opened it, dug her hand into it, and extracted several ounces of sugar. She held up her cupped hands to the birds. They lighted on her thumbs and fingers and eagerly attacked the treat. More and more birds joined the party. Soon two-dozen birds engaged in a full-scale feeding frenzy. One swooped and dove into her hands.

"Ouch!" she said. "Come on you guys. Be nice."

Billie seemed a child and just as precious. I'm not a religious guy, but as I watched her feed the birds, she became sacred.

"When did you start carrying sugar?" I asked.

"A couple months ago when I decided there's never sugar around when you need it."

"You don't by any chance have the philosopher's stone stashed away in your backpack?"

"Sorry, no."

Sugar spilled from her cupped hands, and a few birds pecked it from the table and from her feet. When the sugar was history, Billie rubbed her hands together over the table to brush off the granules. The birds attacked the table.

"That's all for today, guys," she said. "Go get some exercise."

"*Go get some exercise?*"

"Sure, I don't want them to become diabetic."

"I wasn't aware that birds suffered from diabetes."

She said, "They might. Does anyone really know?"

"Are we going to silk-screen shirts?"

"Right now."

Billie packed up her sugar and her artwork and I followed her to her jeep.

"Oh, guess what."

"What?" I asked.

"Valerie's sister, Alice, is back. She and Vaughn motored out of Flamingo Bay early this morning."

"Vaughn told me he was heading out for a few days, but he neglected to mention the identity of his companion. But I'm not surprised." And I wasn't. Alice and Vaughn hooked up when she came down for her sister's funeral. "The only question's whether she's here permanently or on vacation."

Billie started the engine.

"Guess what else."

"I give."

"*Golden Parachute*, the fancy yacht, belongs to the Shirt."

I couldn't think of anything the Shirt could possibly be, do, or have done that could piss me off more.

How does a civil servant skipper a half-million-dollar boat?

"That's probably good. It means he likely isn't planning to sail out of Flamingo Bay on *Island Trader*, though the thought never crossed my mind before now."

Then I told Billie about seeing the Shirt and Sarah in my truck and about all the provisions they carried. I didn't mention that I figured the Shirt must have thought he was pretty close to getting me to roll over on Vaughn—I couldn't believe he was going to leave Flamingo Bay without Vaughn's cocaine.

"I have more news," she said.

"What?"

"I'll tell you for a cigarette."

Billie was so eager to tell me, she blew out my Bic twice before she could get her cigarette going.

"I visited Miss Lucinda this morning and brought her a watercolor I did of a goat. She said that after she found Leif's body and called the police, she and Madison waited at the cistern. When the police arrived, one cop questioned her and the other cop questioned Madison. Then the police pulled Leif's body and his backpack from the cistern. When they opened the backpack, the police found a big bag of coke but no money."

I wondered who in Flamingo Bay, besides Madison, Officer Richards, and maybe Easy, had more money than he or she should.

"Guess what else."

"Leif was killed by a shotgun blast?"

"Miss Lucinda didn't say anything about that, but she did say Leif wore handcuffs when they pulled him out of the cistern. You may be right that Officer Richards is the culprit, or the Shirt."

"You and Mary don't use handcuffs when you get it on?"

I smiled when I said it, but Billie slugged me in the arm.

"There's one more thing. Miss Lucinda said that when she went to Doctor's at noon for water, Leif's body wasn't in the cistern, but it was there at five when she returned. That would set the parameters for time of death unless he was like killed somewhere else."

"That's too bad."

"Why?"

"It gives the Shirt an alibi."

Billie asked, "Where was he?"

"He was with me at Customs over on St. Thomas, searching my boat and confiscating my forty-five. It was the day I returned from Venezuela."

"No way he could have done it?"

"I don't see how."

Billie jammed the shifter into first gear, and we started around the bay to the dinghy dock, while I contemplated the day's most distressing revelation. I hadn't realized how badly I wanted the Shirt to be Leif's killer.

12

Billie and I printed one side of the Easy Rider Rally T-shirts before breaking and allowing them to dry, and I arrived at Easys unfashionably late for lunch, figuring it would do the Shirt good to stew for a while. I'd understood for years that cops and crooks are cut from the same canvas, and I believed the Shirt worked both sides of the law—he displayed tenacity beyond that which the civil service instilled. I suspected that if he were to get his hands on Vaughn's cocaine, he'd tender his resignation to Uncle Sam and go into business for himself.

The Shirt barely acknowledged my presence when I took the chair across from him. In an odd sort of deference, he sat with his back to the bar—in the very spot he'd been uncomfortable sitting yesterday—allowing me the chair with the view of the harbor.

Sacked out in the palm grove was Madison, head resting on a gunnysack, machete at his side. I suspected that he dreamed of a sleek white yacht to match his house and Mercedes.

About a dozen patrons ate and drank. Jason the Argonut—probably not suffering from an inner ear infection—lost his balance and tumbled from his bar stool. The resulting laughter seemed to piss him off more than the fall. He stood and finished his beer, set the empty on the bar, and ordered three more. He dropped a twenty on the bar, and while Easy made change, Jason stuffed one beer in each of the pockets of his shorts and opened the third. He sipped the beer and headed down the road toward Pirate Cove, on foot and looking unstrung—his waist-length blond dreadlocks half unraveled and swinging to his gait.

I expected the Shirt to accuse me of parking his jeep in the sea, but he remained silent. I recognized all the vehicles parked on both sides of the road, so he'd evidently gotten a ride to Easys from Sarah in my truck.

I waved to Marsha for a beer.

It was still weird to see her with hooters. Marsha had always had big hair, and now she had breasts to match—tits from Tortola. She was wearing and falling out of a red tank top. The Shirt wore green. Together they looked like an advertisement for a Honolulu Yule.

She set our beers on the table, bending slower and lower than necessary. The Shirt dropped his head and stared over the top of his sunglasses. Marsha caught him looking. She straightened up, put her hands on her hips, and scowled. The Shirt seemed resigned to serious verbal abuse, but Marsha faked him out. She lifted her shirt and slapped each of his cheeks—bam, bam—with her bare breasts.

It was as quick as the lightning bolt, but unlike the lightning strike, the incident ended almost before patrons realized it had occurred, though one pirate at a nearby table told Marsha he wanted to order from the Shirt's menu. Seconds passed before the Shirt regained control of his senses and the dozen-or-so patrons resumed their conversations. I lit a cigarette and waited. The Shirt didn't know if he should be insulted or ecstatic.

"What was that about?" he asked.

"Getting your face slapped. It was also about nudity being one of the highest forms of personal expression."

"How do you figure?"

"Nudity spits in the face of society—you're society. Think about it. If tomorrow the human brain got rewired so anyone with a gun, for instance, had to be naked—instead of dressed in a Hawaiian shirt—to commit a violent act, Congress would pass gun control laws so quickly, they'd melt the circuitry of the vote tabulator."

The Shirt sipped his beer. "You're still not taking this interview seriously."

"I'm here."

"But not in spirit. I thought my vision this morning of a sunken schooner would instill that spirit of cooperation and sharpen your focus."

"It did. It reminded me that I'm getting sick over the amount of my time you're wasting. I return from Venezuela, and you spend hours going through my boat at Customs. When I get back to Flamingo Bay, you're waiting for me here to do it all over again. What time are your boys coming over today?"

The Shirt looked at his watch, a giant silver Rolex about the size of a travel alarm. He could barely find the damn thing through the hair on his arm; the guy needed to shave his wrist just to tell time. The Shirt pulled out his wallet and handed me a pristine business card.

"Just a small incentive to help your concentration."

MEYER J. LOFGRIN it said, and there was a seven-digit phone number. That was all. The card had been printed recently. It was only three weeks ago that I saw the announcement in the *Daily News* that in the coming months everyone's five-digit phone number was being increased to seven digits.

The man didn't look like Meyer J. Lofgrin—too many vowels. While it wasn't a name I recognized, I couldn't help feeling I'd heard the name before. I searched my memory. All I could conclude was that I hadn't heard it from him; he'd never formally introduced himself to me. From someone else then. But who?

"Turn it over," he said.

I did. Scrawled on the back was: GET OUT OF JAIL FREE.

I thought for a moment. When I looked at the Shirt, his grin was nearly as large as my own. He grinned because he thought he'd seduced me. I grinned because he hadn't. Years of chasing women gave me keen insight into the mixed signals of seduction. I removed my own wallet from its Ziploc bag, produced my plastic Marathon Militia ID, and handed it to him. On the front in the upper left-hand corner was a small photo featuring full frontal nudity. Across the top in raised letters was the motto: ALL FOR ONE, ONE FOR ALL. Below that was printed, also in raised letters, all the natural and unnatural acts the bearer was entitled to perform.

"Flip it over," I said.

GET OUT OF JAIL FREE was printed on the back.

I grinned and said, "You see—I already have one."

"Fancier than mine," the Shirt chuckled. "But I think you'll find mine has more standing in the law enforcement community. If I overlook the fact that you disappeared yesterday, you've been cooperative enough that I think your business license could be renewed. You're working now toward the reward."

"There's a reward?"

"Not officially, but I've been authorized to provide compensation for certain specific information."

He rubbed his chin and the front of his neck and pondered for a moment. "I don't think so."

"That's one thing we're in agreement on. How large is the unofficial reward? I presume it's in U.S. dollars and not pesos or pork bellies."

"Federal Reserve notes. To remain in contention, just keep talking. I'll let you know if you're getting warm."

"I'd be more inclined if I were getting paid by the word."

"There's not enough money on this island to pay you by the word."

He nailed it precisely, and I laughed.

I asked, "So how much am I looking at?"

"How does fifty thou' sound?"

"Every man has his price, and you're getting awfully close to mine."

He slid his hand from his chin. "Good. I thought it would get your attention."

I wondered if he kept checking his whiskers because he suffered from werewolfism or some other such hirsute syndrome. It was as if something lunar or stellar or some event of more obscure origin occurred to trigger immediate massive hair growth. But it wasn't as if a bell went off in his brain telling him his hair was growing, so he had to keep checking. It could've been like a variation of incontinence.

"So what is it that you want?" I asked.

"The bales of cocaine that were picked up in the Sir Francis Drake Channel about four months ago."

"These the bales stamped by Customs, or are we talking about different bales?"

"Customs does not stamp bales of cocaine," he said.

"The only cocaine I know about has 'U.S. Customs' stamped all over it. Wrong cocaine, I guess. Sorry I can't help."

"Let's talk about the cocaine you *do* know about."

"I don't have it."

"We understand that. Diver Vaughn has it. But you know where it is."

"Makes sense to me to ask him."

"Vaughn's gone. I don't expect he'll be showing his face in Flamingo Bay again."

"I'll bet boat titles you're wrong."

"If he does show, here's the scenario. We'll meet his boat when he arrives, confiscate it, and drag his ass over to the jail on St. Thomas. Then we'll determine that a gram of his cocaine made it to— Oh, how about Texas? Then we'll drag his ass to some hick town there and put him on trial. The prosecutor will ask for life, the jury will ask for death, and the judge will be accused of leniency when he sentences him to fifty years. You'd be just saving us some time, and you'd be doing Diver Vaughn a big favor. We've no interest in prosecuting him. Awkward position having a ton of nose candy fall like manna from heaven. Heavy responsibility protecting it. Probably already wishing he hadn't found it. We just want the cocaine. If he were here, I'm sure Diver Vaughn would agree to give up the cocaine to avoid prosecution and confiscation of his boat. But he's not here, and it's not his decision. However, you can make it for him, and he'll thank you."

Motes of truth floated in and out of the Shirt's lies. Vaughn didn't even use the stuff. He sold small quantities and gave away larger quantities. He didn't need the money. He *did* seem to enjoy the Come-to-Jesus ritual of the supplicants. But not enough to lose his boat. And not enough to go to jail. His diving business was a tremendous success. Vaughn would sooner lose the cocaine than his boat. Question: What would the Shirt tell me to appeal to any sense of loyalty I had toward Vaughn? Answer: Whatever I wanted to hear.

Still, the intensity of the Shirt's words persuaded me that he planned to take Vaughn down. As a diver, Vaughn went down regularly, but the Shirt's threat was another deal altogether. No risk of nitrogen narcosis faced Vaughn at the Shirt's proposed destination.

"The concept I'm having trouble with is you guys actually waiting for Vaughn to show up somewhere before nailing him. The Coast Guard thinks the Caribbean's their private pond. The U.S. has already intimidated the nations washed by its waves into abrogating their territorial sovereignty. The exception is El Caballo in La Habana—the only leader with integrity in the Caribbean."

"Christ. A cop-hating commie anarchist. Is it the alcohol or the sunshine?"

"Another matter of principle's the war on drugs. Some believe this. Some believe that. I believe that Republicans pose a greater threat to the Republic than drugs do. If we're going to have zero tolerance for controlled substances, then we should have it across the board for all illegal acts. It would be great for tourism in Washington. No public buildings crowded with lawmakers and their entourages. Daily executions on the Capitol mall—"

"So you *do* think you're a bad-ass fuck." He shook his head and checked his watch. "Going off on my favorite uncle isn't going to be remunerative."

Marsha brought us burgers and beers. The Shirt didn't know where to look. I think he wanted to get slapped in the face again, but he wasn't sure how to make it happen.

"You may as well peek," Marsha told the Shirt, "because you're not going to see them again otherwise." She bent low over his plate, and he fixed his eyes on her breasts. "Fourteen dollars," she said.

The Shirt pushed a twenty in her direction.

She smiled and pocketed the bill. "Thanks for the tip."

The Shirt turned to me and said, "You do know where it is, don't you?"

"Where what is?"

"Diver Vaughn's cocaine."

"Of course I know where it is."

Persistent horn honking caused both the Shirt and I to glance toward the road. The Reverend Richards stood barefoot in the middle of the road, blocking traffic. He was dressed in an old sheet, impersonating a prophet. It looked as though he'd been double-teamed by a pair of front-end loaders. A bandaged wrapped his head. A sling held his left arm immobile, but he was still able to clutch a bullhorn in his fist. A single crutch supported him, though a flying buttress would've provided better support.

"The day of judgment is at hand!" His amplified voice rattled my brain and beer bottle. "A serpent lurks in the garden! He wear Joseph's coat of many colors."

"Who the hell is this?" the Shirt shouted. "And what the hell happened to him?"

"Reverend Richards. He was shot four times by his brother, the cop, over a disputed inheritance. Flew him over to San Juan to have the bullets removed. Not a big deal, at least not a big enough deal to make the *Daily News.*"

Easys patrons repaid Anal Richards with raspberries and expletives. Conversation was impossible; it was precisely what had happened at Leif's funeral—the same confrontation at nearly the same volume. The Shirt's jaw worked overtime, but I couldn't hear a word he said. I shrugged my shoulders, feigned chagrin, and squirted ketchup on my burger.

While reassembling my burger, I watched the two chickens dodging furniture and scattered coconuts. The white one did its neck thing, while the brown one pecked at withered palm fronds, cigarette butts, and the hard, dry earth. I know chickens aren't particularly bright, but the white one seemed to catch my eye and bob its head, as if it recognized me. Almost like a trusty dog whose master is being threatened, the chicken approached the table with purpose and attacked the Shirt, going for his shoes.

The Shirt gave it a swift kick, and the chicken fled. The Shirt was smart enough to appreciate his dilemma: big tough guy with gun intimidated by a cripple and a chicken. He could take out the chicken with one shot, but he'd most likely have to reload—bad form—to take out Reverend Richards, a man nearly immune to lead.

The Shirt and I worked on our burgers, while the aggrieved chicken—running in circles—echoed the Reverend's squawking. The Shirt took even larger bites from his burger and chewed even faster. Though he remained seated, the Shirt's feathers seemed as ruffled as the fowl's. When he stuffed the last bit of burger into his mouth, the Shirt suddenly pounded his fist on the table, almost upsetting our beers. He jumped out of his chair and strode over to the road where Anal Richards preached about a kaleidoscopic serpent defiling the garden.

The Shirt ignored the sermon's message (or maybe he didn't—there was only one man in Flamingo Bay who dressed like Joseph), and the Reverend disregarded the Shirt's anger. The Shirt grabbed the Reverend's bullhorn and slammed it on the road. Single-minded in his purpose to enlighten the masses, the Reverend seemed unable to focus his attention on the pending threat he faced. Instead of capitulating, the

Reverend stooped on one leg to pick up his bullhorn, positioning the crutch to his flank to maintain balance.

Once in possession of the bullhorn, the Reverend stuck it in the Shirt's face and screamed, "Fuck you! Amen!"

The Shirt seemed as startled as everyone present, but his response was quick and decisive. He drew his pistol, cocked the hammer, and pressed the barrel against the Reverend's jaw.

"And you, you pathetic piece of shit. Where's your Savior now?"

The Reverend turned toward the bay and raised his arms, but the sea didn't part. After a single admonishing glance at the heavens, he stumbled down the road in search of a new pulpit.

Patrons cheered the Shirt; he holstered his gun and nodded to the applause.

"Let's talk about the cocaine," the Shirt said, taking his chair. "Specifically, where it is."

I wondered again who the Shirt was. It was a bit late, but I wouldn't have minded seeing some sort of official identification. Then again, witnessing his temper tantrum rather dampened my enthusiasm for that sort of inquiry.

When I looked up, I saw assholes illegally boarding *Island Trader*.

"Who's on my boat?"

The Shirt shrugged.

I left him at the table and raced to the road. As the barracuda swims, I was only a bit more than a mile from *Island Trader*, but I couldn't swim as fast as a barracuda, so I continued on foot to the dinghy dock, a good mile-and-a-half away. I reached the mangroves—only a quarter of the way there and out of breath—when Mechanic Jim came by. I hopped into his jeep and told him my problem. He pushed the accelerator to the floor.

"Want help?" he asked.

I waited until I could see the port side of *Island Trader* before answering.

"Thanks, but we're too late." I pointed to a runabout off in the distance, heading toward the mouth of the bay. "That's probably them. They've searched my boat regularly for five years looking for cocaine. I suspect they've decided to make the job of finding it easier. If they bring it aboard, they know it's there, and they know exactly where to look. Assholes!"

"Good luck," he said when he dropped me just past the fire station.

I climbed into my Zodiac, started the Yamaha, and skimmed across the water. Sure enough, when I reached my boat nobody was aboard. I first searched the obvious places and found what I was looking for in a locker in the galley—a clear plastic bag that contained a whole kilo.

The question that plagued me: Was there more, the odd gram or two cleverly hidden?

A thorough search of the boat turned up no more cocaine. The local narcs would never be so generous to use so much cocaine to set up a bust; it would be needed for evidence and temporarily taken out of circulation. They were really for re-circulating it. It had to be the Shirt's doing. He apparently liked to play games. I was unsure how serious this game was. Finding this much cocaine aboard, the Feds could not only grab my boat, but send me on a long vacation to Leif's alma mater. I had a hundred and fifty grand tied up in the boat, and my freedom was worth a whole lot more. I sure wasn't going to risk losing either over drugs.

I took the kilo with me in the dinghy and headed back to the dock, wondering if the planted cocaine was the warning shot across the bow or something else. I prepared to dump it overboard if the Shirt just happened to be waiting for me on shore. He wasn't, but Zeke—barefoot and unkempt as usual—was.

"Captain Brian, mon, Zeke has long memory, longer than elephant. He not be forgetting that you save boat. Must go now. Must deliver the medicine. Patients need the medicine. And Zeke need the patients." He laughed a booming laugh that began somewhere below his belt and fairly erupted from his smiling mouth.

A thought grabbed me. I wrestled with it a few moments before surrendering. "Zeke, Merry Christmas." I threw him the kilo.

"Zeke see Captain Brian be having himself one fine day."

The "ho, ho, ho" that followed was enormous. I laughed with him.

"Does you find the square white grouper?"

"No such luck," I answered.

Nearly two years ago Zeke found a square grouper of his own. It occasioned a career change. He switched from cutting bush to delivering medicine.

"One favor I want in return."

"Captain Brian doesn't want Zeke to sell medicine to Sarah?"

"And Jason."

"You doesn't have to worry about that. Okay?"

"Okay. But you be careful. There's a new sheriff in town."

"He doesn't catch Zeke. It take whole posse. Zeke be too slippery. Tomorrow, Zeke be looking for you. Don't be sailing away. Don't be making Zeke chase you across the sea in his poor boat."

He hurried to his jeep and waved goodbye.

13

WHEN MY DINGHY CLEARED THE HARBOR'S MOORED BOATS, I spotted Billie standing alone at the end of the dock, barefoot and holding a flip-flop in each hand. She wore a dress. I'd never seen her in a dress before. I agreed to have dinner with her, but this was looking like a date. I'd cleaned up for the occasion—laundered T-shirt and shorts. I would've returned to my boat to upgrade my attire, if I wasn't already wearing my most presentable clothes. I goosed my outboard's throttle a bit, perhaps fearing she'd be gone when I tied up.

Fashion doesn't exist as a priority for most Continentals in Flamingo Bay, including the women. Clothes cost nearly as much to launder as they do to buy—water's scarce and electricity erratic. And if your clothes aren't especially attractive, what's the point of cosmetics? Members of both sexes powder their noses, but there's no Mary Kay here. There is an Avon lady, but her success is closely tied to Skin-So-Soft's reputed protective barrier against no-see-ums.

I figured clothes may make the man, but it's lack of clothes that make the woman—the more severe the deficit, the better. I didn't recall ever making that observation to Billie, but if she'd asked me to dress her, I'd have come up with the same outfit she wore, a simple cotton sundress in pale green that ended a mile short of her knees. Still, it surprised me to see her for the first time in a dress and without her usual accessories: baseball cap and backpack.

I nosed my dinghy to the dock, tied it off, and greeted her. "Who are you waiting for?"

"You."

"Then do you mind just standing on the end of the dock all evening, maybe turning slowly every hour or so?" I asked. "I'll just sit here and watch."

"Maybe if I weren't so hungry."

I climbed onto the dock and gave her one of those intense cocked-head stares she always gave me. "Ready to run off down island with me?"

"Oh-my-god! You're serious."

"I haven't much money, but I think I could afford to keep you in underwear."

We walked together in the direction of Billie's jeep.

"It's that noticeable, huh?"

"It'll be dark in five minutes."

Billie informed me earlier in the day that dinner—not a meal at Easys or the Congo Club—would be the proper gesture to cement our agreement to work together to find Leif's killer. It seemed a reasonable request, and I had a credit card on which I'd be able to squeeze dinner. I hadn't a clue what I'd do if more meals were required.

Billie's twenty-three-year-old jeep—a true island vehicle—was born the same year she was. It had no top, no windshield, and its frame— bent and twisted from a long-ago collision—caused the vehicle to lead with its left front wheel. It sported plywood quarter panels, and a wood bench replaced the original front seats. Enough blue smoke poured from the tailpipe to considerably reduce the chances of contracting dengue fever, as long as the engine was running. It started right up, and we headed across the island toward Sugar Harbor.

"Didn't I tell you about my first trip to New York?" Billie asked.

"Not that I recall."

"I was a little scared. Everyone had warned me about *something*. I wasn't supposed to do *this*, and I wasn't supposed to do *that*. 'Don't slow down.' 'Walk fast.' 'Never make eye contact.' I was like really nervous. I was in the Port Authority, and people were staring at me. I did what everyone said. I kept walking. I didn't make eye contact. I thought I must be looking really good. I walked the entire length of the building with my dress tucked into my panties. But I learned a lesson."

"What's that?" I asked.

"I learned never to wear panties."

I had a good laugh. I hoped this evening would be one of those times that my face would hurt from an overdose of mirth.

"I had a really good time in New York. Know what I did?"

"What?"

"I bought a pencil from a blind man on Fifth Avenue. "

"Okay."

"The blind man liked me so much he gave me a New York Yankees' baseball cap, but it was stolen from me in Morocco."

Billie had gotten around. She once told me that her mother blamed it on *National Geographic*. Her mother's decision to cancel the family's subscription to the magazine only increased Billie's desire to leave home. The day after she graduated from high school in Nebraska, Billie bought a bus ticket to New York. A month later, she caught a plane to London and began to travel the world. I wasn't sure if she was still traveling.

"It's a good thing for him you didn't buy two pencils," I teased.

"Why's that?"

"He probably would've given you his Social Security check."

"That's not fair," Billie replied, before she joined my laughter.

She stopped near the top of the mountain for a herd of goats. A half-dozen or so separated from the others and attacked a hibiscus, deflowering and defoliating it in sixty seconds, leaving the canes trampled. Goats wouldn't generally let a person within six feet of them before they scampered into the bush, but if they had a quorum, like now, they were fearless when it came to blocking traffic. Billie asked them politely to allow her to pass, and seconds later, they did.

"Billie, I'm surprised they didn't give you the key to the city when you arrived in New York."

"Whoever handles those things probably didn't even know I was in town. I wonder if there's a number you call for something like that."

"Of course there is—1-800-BLONDIE."

Billie suggested that we stop for cocktails at the Green Parrot— named after a bird that might've been only slightly less rare locally than the flamingo. We found a cozy table with a view of the harbor and ordered drinks and conch fritters. The lights on St. Thomas fluttered in a breeze that was lush with the scent of flowering plants and the sea.

Leaving the stemmed glass on the table, Billie sipped her frozen daiquiri through a straw, tilting her head, holding her cigarette in one hand, holding her yellow hair out of the way with her other. I wasn't the only one watching her, though only about half the patrons gave the impression of trying not to stare. I couldn't blame them. There's no substitute for good protoplasm. I didn't know if Billie was oblivious or simply used to the attention.

Beautiful people live by a different set of circumstances and a different set of rules. Still, like everyone, they're on their last cruise. I'd often contemplated whether the birthright that provided for automatic upgrade from steerage to first-class accounted for all the difference, but the evidence proved inconclusive. All I knew was that I admired those like Billie who handled their good fortune with grace and disliked those who didn't. At that moment, my displeasure focused on the people at two nearby tables—ten tourists in all.

All were nearly knee-deep in bags acquired during profound and meaningful duty-free experiences in the scores of shops that sold nothing one couldn't live without. Of the men nursing their drinks—dressed in polyester by the women in their lives—none seemed to be more than an arm's length away from a camcorder, and at least two had the gadgets resting on their laps. The women—wearing large-sized versions of slim, magazine styles—alternately adjusted their outfits and fiddled with their hair.

The tourists' tentative chatter and forced laughter made it seem like they were waiting to be released from boredom. Perhaps they should've stayed home and watched the Travel Channel. Then again, maybe they'd lucked out and come to the right place after all. It all depended on Billie. I suspected her presence could turn the performance of a Wagnerian opera into a hootenanny.

I'd been so focused on Billie and those watching her that I noticed for the first time that Billie had painted several of the artworks decorating the room. One of my favorites was a watercolor that depicted a small cottage on a beach where goats wandered among palms and sea grapes. The image of a conch shell informed the entire picture. The lip of the shell created the beach in front of the cottage, and the tapering spine formed the sloping hillside behind the cottage.

An oil painting of a group of donkeys foraging on a hillside appeared lifelike except for the donkeys themselves. One was pink. Another lavender. Others were yellow, orange, and blue. On the opposite wall hung several gouaches of fish. Most were not recognizable species, but the oceans would've been richer had they actually existed. In the process of creating the fantastical fish, it seemed Billie had discovered several new colors not found in nature.

"Congratulations."

Billie let the straw slide from her lips. "It took you long enough."

"It wouldn't have taken so long if you hadn't dressed so provocatively. I haven't been able to make up my mind whether to look down your dress, up your dress, or through your dress."

"Seems to me you've been doing all three." Billie cocked her head and placed her hand—fingers together in a salute—alongside her mouth. "If you'd ask me to, I'd strip off my dress right here in front of like God and everybody."

I suggested that she wait until later in the evening, but I was the only man within earshot who felt that way. The half of the room that hadn't wanted to be caught staring earlier quickly lost their shyness. One tourist even began fondling his camcorder.

"After that pronouncement, I doubt you'll be able to escape with your flip-flops. They'll be mobbing you if you try to get out the door with more than your skin."

Under the pretense of filming the restaurant's interior, the tourist directed his camcorder at Billie. After she made a face and stuck out her tongue, I learned that she'd sold two of her pictures in the two weeks they'd been on display. When throngs of tourists started showing up next month, I figured she'd have difficulty meeting the demand.

"Want to get down to business?" I asked.

"You mean take off my dress?"

"No, the murder business."

"Oh-my-god!" She raised her voice and pretended surprise. "Murder?"

"Murder."

"Well," she said in a normal voice, causing nearby patrons to crane to hear her words, "don't count on me to help you murder your wife." She rubbed her hand on her belly. "What I want to know is what you're going to do for me and our baby."

"I was thinking of trading it to Columbians for cocaine."

"No way! If we're selling the baby, I want heroin!"

I held up my end of the dialogue for a few more rounds, while I sneaked glances at the restaurant manager. He kept his eye on Billie, waiting for his opportunity to come by and look down the front of her dress. When Billie's charade collapsed under the weight of our laughter, the manager saw his opening. He pretended to just spot her and made his move. After introductions, I excused myself to visit the restroom. I wasn't gone long, but when I returned, the manager was introducing Billie to the patrons. The program was only slightly more sophisticated than the T-shirt auction at Easys, but the effect was the same. People couldn't get out their wallets fast enough.

By the time we were able to leave, Billie had sold nearly every picture and had been filmed and photographed by a half-dozen patrons. On our way out the door, she promised the manager she'd return tomorrow with more pictures. I stuffed her wad of cash—over three grand—in the pocket of my shorts. She looped her arm around mine, and we sashayed our way down the street to the Agave Grill.

Billie turned pensive during our walk, and she wasn't interested in grandstanding after we were seated outdoors at another table with a view of the lights on St. Thomas. Billie had some trouble keeping the lime honey sauce on her shrimp from running down her chin, but I refused her invitation to use my tongue. My prime rib was medium-rare, just as I'd ordered it. It was a good meal, and Billie's presence lent an elemental quality to it like feasting at the periodic table.

When the waitress cleared away our dishes, Billie asked if I wanted to get down to business.

"What business?"

"What business do you think?"

"I don't know," I said. "I've never done business with a twenty-three-year-old conglomerate before."

"It's only fair. I'm doing business with an aging hermit curmudgeon. Curmudgeon. Conglomerate. We're not that far apart."

"Maybe in the dictionary."

"Okay," she said. "Murder."

"What do you know about the demise of our mutual friend?"

"I don't know if I've learned anything helpful, but while you were in Venezuela chasing señoritas—"

"I didn't chase any señoritas. I left that activity to the Garys, though I'm not sure how successful they were. I, on the other hand, cut quite a swath through Cumaná."

"You're now Captain Cowboy?"

"My tile guy, Lopez, cooked up a phony bill of sale. Instead of buying ceramic tile, I bought 'Creamy Air'—the police got a real chuckle. I thought it was the tile's color. When I called Fernando on it, he pulled a knife on me—"

"Oh-my-god!"

"I broke his arm getting the knife out of his hand—"

"No! He came after you with a knife?"

"The real deal—sharp and shiny."

"Weren't you scared?" Billie asked.

"I didn't have time to think about it."

"Did he hurt you?"

"Minor. All healed."

"Did you turn him over to the police?"

"What was the point?" I answered. "They'd already proved their lack of sympathy. By then, I didn't think about Fernando. I went looking for Lopez to get my money back. He'd evidently taken a holiday. I rifled his office looking for my cash. By the time I determined there was no money, the place was something of a mess, so I turned it into a real mess before I left. That's when the police decided to get involved, and that's when I decided to leave Venezuela."

"Wow! You have all the fun."

"Right."

"Okay," Billie said. "While you weren't chasing señoritas in South America, there was a theft in Flamingo Bay. I told you about it the other day. Someone ripped off nearly a kilo of coke and some cash from Diver Vaughn—"

"Four grand," I interjected.

"Word on the street is that Jason the Argonut set Vaughn up for the police by leaving a gram of coke in Vaughn's truck. I don't know if that's what happened. I do know that Jason was on St. Thomas with Mechanic Jim getting car parts when Vaughn was arrested. The police kept Vaughn in jail overnight, but they let him go in the morning. Vaughn thinks it's because he wasn't in his truck when they found the cocaine and his truck wasn't locked. Speculation is that Jason intended to rip Vaughn off, but somebody else got there first."

"How do you know that?"

"Because when Vaughn got out of jail the next day, he cut off Jason's supply. If Jason had a kilo of coke, he wouldn't have risked going after Vaughn and getting his jaw broken. Also, Miss Lucinda said the police found coke in Leif's backpack. I think the police have all the coke. I don't know what happened to the money."

"So you're thinking that maybe Leif ripped off Vaughn before Jason had an opportunity and someone other than Jason ripped off Leif and killed him?"

"One scenario."

It worked for me. Leif could've used the cistern to hide the cocaine he stole, hanging his backpack on the steel hook. Of course, I'd never know for sure. His backpack went up in flames along with his other possessions.

Billie asked, "Have you learned anything?"

"An interesting fact I did learn that may be neither here nor there is that Pony Mon is first cousin to the preacher and the cop—not all that surprising since nearly everyone's related. But what is interesting is that Pony Mon blames Officer Richards for shooting Bongo Natty. Here's a guy who's shot his own brother and perhaps his cousin's horse. Doesn't seem to me that Leif would have to get too far out of line to get Richards' attention."

"The flip side of that coin," Billie said, "is why Richards would bother to hide Leif's body. It seems like he can get away with whatever he wants."

"An excellent point, but who would've handcuffed Leif before killing him?"

"Someone who had access to handcuffs."

"Like Richards."

"Or someone wanting to frame Richards," Billie added.

"Ever hear the name Meyer J. Lofgrin?"

"Should I have?"

"I don't know. It's the Shirt's name. I feel like I've heard it before, but I don't know where."

Billie said, "All I know about him is he wears his souvenir T-shirt from Leif's funeral to bed every night. Oh, and he promised me, he'd never wash it."

"Really?"

"Really."

Billie stubbed out her cigarette, and I lit one. We ordered another round of cocktails.

"What's the plan?" she asked. "Do we have a plan?"

"Why don't you just wear the outfit you have on? I'd be surprised if any man would refuse to be interrogated."

Billie laughed and said, "I think we need to stir the pot."

"Don't you mean smoke it?"

"They're not mutually exclusive, you know."

I looked at the slender arm propped on the table across from me and at the opalescent nails at the tips of the long fingers and determined that there wasn't a better arm than Billie's to stir any pot. Still, she'd have to wait her turn.

"I already have," I said. "At least I've stirred the Shirt's pot."

"You said he had an alibi."

"He does. And I'm it."

"Then why're you wasting time on him?"

There was no way to explain to Billie why I redoubled my efforts to go after the Shirt when I concluded he couldn't have killed Leif. Hell, I couldn't explain it to myself. It was just a feeling that he was involved. Maybe because I wanted him to be involved.

"The Shirt scares me," Billie said. "Doesn't he scare you?"

"Only when I think about it."

"Always so cavalier! Promise me you won't like do anything foolish to piss him off."

"Any more than I already have, you mean?"

"What're you saying?"

"I committed vehicular homicide this morning."

"Get serious."

"I am. I killed the Shirt's vehicle."

"You're becoming like Leif," Billie said. "Taking on the authorities."

"Somebody has to do it."

And somebody did. I could build a playground for Valerie, but all

I could do to keep Leif's memory alive was to shoulder part of the burden he carried in life.

"Are you aiming for his arrest record, too?"

"No, I'm not planning to ever be arrested."

"You will if you push too hard."

"How about if I pull, instead?"

"You're incorrigible." She shook her head. "What should I do to move things forward?"

"I suppose one important focus of inquiry is Leif's last hours. Pirate Dan told me Leif left the Congo Club alone on the night before he was killed. Somebody must have seen him after ten o'clock in the evening and before the following afternoon. Another thing is to keep your eyes and ears open to learn who might be four grand richer. Officer Richards and Madison have more money than they ought to, perhaps Easy, too."

"I'll see what I can do."

"Here's the deal: no commemorative T-shirt, no business card, no announcing we're investigating anything. Can you handle that?"

"Of course. You make it sound like I can't keep a secret, when in fact, I'm keeping one this moment. A very big secret."

"Anything to do with me?" I asked.

"Sort of. I can't wait to see your reaction when I tell you."

The thing about a secret is that as soon as you know it exists, you want to be let in on it. After my lecturing, I resisted the temptation to ask.

"I'm good, too," Billie said, "at finding out others' secrets. I know one of your secrets, for instance."

"And that is?"

"You're building a playground in Flamingo Bay."

"How do you know?"

"It's a secret."

Billie would have to start wearing underwear and clean up her act a bit, but she knew how to get people to open their wallets, and she was bright and facile enough to become the first woman president of the U.S. She'd have to wait a dozen years to qualify to run, but if she started her campaign immediately, Congress would probably set the wheels in motion to amend the Constitution to lower the age requirement to allow her to run.

"Are we done?" she asked, slurping the last of her cocktail.

"Almost. The important thing is to stop by the Congo Club tomorrow and chat with Pirate Dan about the weather."

"You've lost me."

"When you stop by, you should be wearing this around your neck." I handed her the gold doubloon.

"Oh-my-god! Where did you find it?"

"I'll tell you after you give me the report on his reaction. Do you have a chain you can hang this on?"

The only jewelry Billie wore was that gold ring on her toe.

"I can find something," she said, handing me the doubloon. "But keep this until we get back."

"On second thought, let's visit Dan together tomorrow evening."

Billie—now flush with cash—paid for dinner. We walked back to the jeep. I drove because Billie brought along a frozen daiquiri in a go-cup. She wanted to take the scenic route, so I headed out along the island's north shore. From up on the hillside, we could see the lights on several islands and cays, and three mast lights waved in a dark bay below us. Farther along, when the road dipped to sea level, we heard the ground swells rolling to shore.

"Pull over," she said. "Here."

She climbed out and dug a blanket and a canvas bag with towels out of the back of the jeep.

"What's the program?" I asked.

"Skinny-dipping."

A moderate disturbance in the Atlantic created ground swells that I guessed were about twice their normal size, though I couldn't actually see them. I couldn't actually see the fruit bats either, but I could feel their presence. The magnitude of the surf worried me a bit, but it energized Billie. She desired to flirt with danger; she desired to flirt with me.

"Help me with my dress."

"What exactly do you want me to do?"

"Just grab the hem and pull it over my head."

"What will you be doing?"

"I'm going to be holding my arms over my head in surrender. If you were to take advantage of my vulnerability, I wouldn't mind."

"Billie, I think you need to find yourself a young stud."

"Now you're too old? You have more excuses than a virgin. I'm beginning to suspect you're impotent."

I pulled her dress over her head and hung it on the branch of a sea grape.

"My turn," she said, pulling off my T-shirt, then my shorts. "No, I can feel you're not impotent."

"Let's swim."

"Not yet." She wrapped her arms around my neck and locked her legs around mine. "We'll do it your way—no penetration—but I will have my way with you."

Billie clung to me like we were joined by static electricity. With my shorts down around my ankles—acting like leg irons—I couldn't move. She sensed my dilemma.

"Don't lose your balance. You might hurt yourself."

"If I fall over, you might hurt yourself."

"No," she said, "I'm drunk. Drunks never get hurt."

I mustered every bit of willpower to not engage in her program, but Billie still eked out an orgasm. She rated my performance—on a scale of one to one million—a one. I almost told her that I generally had about as much fun watching paint dry, but that was a lie. Having her climax in my arms rated as one of life's more erotic experiences.

I scuttled like a crab into the sea, figuring to dump her into the water, give her a big shock. The first breaker sent us tumbling. No big shock: the water was as warm as the air.

Swimming proved difficult in the surf, so we splashed around and body surfed. We tried for nearly an hour to perfect the art of tandem body surfing, but all we accomplished was multiple major irrigations of our sinus cavities, though we experienced several thrilling moments. Getting picked up and tossed around by big-time breakers may be the poor man's best shot at defying gravity.

Then we lay on the blanket and watched the sky.

"Since the day I got here," Billie said, "you've been like insisting the best snorkeling in the Lesser Antilles was between my legs. Last night when I did the open-sesame bit, you backed off. Tonight I wore my sexiest dress, and here I am—defrocked—offering you a religious experience. Nothing. What gives?"

What Billie didn't get was that I'd reached the point in life where how you got what you wanted was just as important as getting it—sometimes more important. Also, I had nothing to offer. I didn't have to more than glance in the mirror to grasp that I was a tired, broken-down old sea dog facing slim prospects. Could she actually see in me something that I couldn't recognize in myself?

"What gives is each of us makes his or her own rules. One of my rules is to never have sex with a woman who doesn't share with me a similar emotional involvement. A one-night stand is fine if that's the agenda, but it's not fine if upon waking up you learn you're expected to meet the family for brunch. It doesn't work either if one player is in love with the other but it's not reciprocated, and you've made it clear you're not in love with me—'Open Sesame' is not the magic word."

"You're a man," she said. "What's love got to do with it?"

"With you, love has everything to do with it."

"Maybe I am in love with you."

"Maybe I could hold my breath until the Second Coming."

Billie took my hand, and we listened, as the arrhythmic pattern of waves breaking on the beach drowned out the chirping tree frogs and the rustling sea grapes. We shared the daiquiri and smoked.

"If you could live anywhere on this island, where would it be?" she asked.

"Probably Doctor's."

"Most people would choose the north shore. Why Doctor's?"

"Lots here go for a million or more. You get some breeze off the water, but you don't get the trade wind, unless you're at the very top of the mountain. It's also wetter and buggier, and the nearby beaches are crammed with tourists in season and locals off-season. Doctor's is small and simple, but it's built like a fortress, and the stonework is top-notch. You maybe can't see the farthest, but it's one of the best views. It's remote, and it's close to my favorite beach. How about you?"

"I like Doctor's," she answered. "I walked around there today after

I visited Miss Lucinda. And despite what happened to Doctor and
Leif, the building has good energy. I think Miss Lucinda likes me. She
invited me back. She likes you too. Did you know that?"

"Never thought about it. After she shot Sweetheart, I pretty much
ignored her."

"What surprised me," Billie said, "is that Miss Lucinda owns Doctor's cottage. Evidently, she sold it to him on a contract-for-deed. He
put in the cistern and the bathroom addition and some other improve-
ments, but when he died, he defaulted, and she took possession. I don't
understand why she wouldn't live at Doctor's. It's so much nicer than
her place."

"West Indians don't like to live in buildings that aren't protected
from hurricanes. Oceanfront land is not desirable. Her cottage is sited
almost in a hollow. There's enough of a rise in the land between her
place and the sea that she feels safer across the road with no view."

We dressed and shook out the blanket and headed back to Flamingo Bay. At the top of the mountain, I stopped the jeep and shifted
into neutral. The brightest light shone from the top of the mountain
on Peter Island. It represented another skirmish won in the conquest
of Eden. Many small lights sparkled in the distance on Tortola, but
only a few lights still burned in Flamingo Bay. The heavens were a different story altogether: all the lights had been left on.

"What are you doing?" Billie asked.

I shut off the ignition, released the brake, and let the jeep roll.
"Tuning up for the Easy Rider Rally. Hold on."

"I think you should give someone else a chance to win."

I asked, "Why would I do that?"

"You've won it both years it's been run."

I hunkered down to find the right lines through the curves but
found rhythm elusive. I chased it down the road; our butts slid back
and forth on the wooden bench.

"The old bump and grind," Billie said. "You really know how to turn
a girl on."

My fingers gripped the steering wheel like clamps. Unable to
become one with Billie's machine, I might as well have been piloting
Aubrey's front-end loader for how smooth I was. Of course, the jeep's

suspension was probably inferior to the suspension of Aubrey's front-end loader. The tires squealed in protest at the first hairpin curve; Billie squealed louder.

I understood I was trying too hard. Thinking is the most important issue in turning in a good performance: if you can't visualize winning, you're going to lose. Once the performance starts, however, thinking becomes the greatest obstacle: you can't choke unless you think about it.

"Are you trying to get us killed?"

Coming out of the corner, we lost so much momentum that simultaneously driving and talking presented no problem.

"That would be too easy. Not getting us killed is the program. Death precludes the orgiastic future I'm planning. Now let me concentrate."

"One more question. Where do I fit into this orgiastic future?"

"That's for you to decide."

To turn off my mind, I counted utility poles. I entered the second hairpin on the perfect line, but I struggled coming out of it when I had to dodge a donkey standing statue-still in the middle of the road. Again, Billie squealed along with the tires, and I lost momentum. I entered and exited the third hairpin on the ideal line, and I started to pick up some real speed for the first time, but not enough.

The jeep rolled to a stop a hundred feet short of my winning mark from last year, and I wasn't even close to my winning mark from the year before. I wanted to blame my poor performance on Billie's vehicle, and clearly that was part of it—poorly aligned wheels can frustrate gravity. Still, I couldn't help thinking that I was slowing down, inching toward the rag and bone shop.

I shifted into gear and continued on to Sarah's to steal my truck back.

14

THE STEADY BREEZE TOOK THE EDGE OFF THE MORNING SUN, but the nearly eighty-five-degree heat began to drive folk from their boats. Outboards propelled the small inflatables to and from the dinghy dock. Nobody had anywhere to go, but everyone seemed in a desperate hurry to get there—more desperate than I, certainly. Jason the Argonaut seemed in the biggest hurry. Racing at full throttle, he randomly looped his dinghy amongst the moored boats and almost collided with me. After encountering him a second time, and after recalling the words of an ancient Greek sage who remarked that an accident at sea can ruin your day, I steered toward land and followed the shoreline to the dinghy dock.

Even before I tied up, I saw that my truck was missing again—so much for last night's effort to reclaim it. In its place stood Elroy. He wore only one pair of clean trousers today and his T-shirt proclaimed:

IF IT'S TOURIST SEASON
WHY CAN'T WE SHOOT THEM?

When I climbed out of my dinghy, Elroy jerked his head to greet me, and he banged two fingers against his lips. I dug out a cigarette and lit it for him.

"She take you truck," Elroy said. "Sarah."

Staggered by Elroy's sudden attempt at oral communication, I stood in silence and watched, as he turned and tramped through the sand on bare feet.

I'm not much on miracles, and as miracles go, Elroy's first public utterance didn't rank with the more celebrated phenomena documented by witnesses from ancient times to the present day. Still, I saw no reason why a holiday shouldn't commemorate the occasion. A few holiday-less weeks still existed in the Virgin Islands. The governor could proclaim November 16, Verbal Day, a time to celebrate the spoken word. At the very least a T-shirt should mark the occasion.

A glance at the larger picture changed my perspective. It confirmed that government employees didn't deserve another day off work, and Flamingo Bay didn't require any proclaimed holidays. Each day existed solely to celebrate freedom in as noisy a fashion as you desired. Every day masqueraded as the Fourth of July.

A T-shirt then. I'd talk to Billie.

I walked along the bay to the playground where workers fit pieces of lumber with mortise and tenon joints to the top tier of the nearly finished jungle gym. Rolly interrupted his lettering of the playground's sign and took a minute to walk around the site with me. He pointed out that he'd used stainless steel hardware to hang the swings, and he used stainless fasteners in the construction of all the equipment. No ferrous material is resistant to salt-air corrosion over the long haul, but the playground equipment stood a chance of outliving me, and it provided a measure of immortality to Valerie for those who'd never know her.

When Rolly returned to work, I wandered around the area and spotted an empty cloth tobacco pouch lying on the ground. I picked it up and began to toy with it. Tossed away fairly recently, it remained in good condition. A yellow drawstring still functioned to close it. The pouch gave me an idea. Just as Emily Post recommended sending a thank-you note to a gift-giver or party hostess, I believed that proper etiquette demanded responding to less benevolent favors as well. The Shirt needed acknowledgement that I received the kilo, so I embarked on a scavenger hunt for small trinkets to fill the bag. I found a button, a twenty-two shell casing, a seashell, a bay leaf, a piece of string, and a chunk of donkey dung.

While Rolly changed the bit in his router, I tried to learn what he knew about obeah. He became increasingly reticent even as I explained I wasn't looking for the real deal, just a cheap imitation. It didn't matter. He denied any knowledge. I didn't press him because I knew starting out that he wasn't likely to say a word. It wasn't something West Indians talked about to Continentals.

Before I left, I picked up a few more items, including a small chunk of mahogany I intended to fashion into a juju. I headed around the bay and compiled in my head everything I knew about the mumbo jumbo.

I knew that voodoo was a combination of Catholic and African religions, and I guessed that obeah—less flashy—was the Protestant version. I supposed it was more like sorcery than religion. Practitioners shook bones and chanted and did things with plants and animals and potions; medicinal herbs played a big role.

Back in Africa, back in the old days ("backtime," as the West Indians called it) people were regularly poisoned. It presented a dilemma of sorts—no Food and Drug Administration—as many of the tribes from Guinea (a major source of slaves transported to the area) practiced cannibalism as well as obeah. Obeah was outlawed in the Virgin Islands during the slavery era, and West Indians were no more eager than Rolly to talk about it. I had no idea how much it was practiced, and I had no idea how much of the stuff that passed for obeah was legitimate. I'd heard plenty of rumors, but the only conspicuous example that I'd seen was at Miss Lucinda's, after she shot Sweetheart.

Over the years, I'd talked to three different people who believed in obeah enough to pay a practitioner to work the sorcery for them. Each paid an obeah man five hundred dollars, and each maintained the obeah men were successful in carrying out the missions—something that didn't surprise me at all. It was covered in the first law of thermodynamics, the principal of the conservation of energy. All the obeah man did was tap into the universal energy—with genuine intent. Of course, it wasn't quite that simple. You needed two believers. You couldn't work the magic against someone who didn't believe. Most societies figured this out in prehistoric times. I'd heard somewhere that Australian Aboriginals still guilt wrongdoers into dying, simply because the wrongdoers believe that once sentenced, they will die.

I'd also done a bit of reading. My favorite story concerned a woman on St. Judas who, back in the nineteenth century, paid a man for a love potion. He buried a small pouch of trinkets at a crossroads where the object of the woman's affection passed daily. The story didn't list any of the items, but I assumed most came from the obeah man's oanga bag, his toolbox. Influenced by the magic, the man should've fallen in love with her. When he didn't, the woman took the obeah man to court to get her money refunded. I recalled that the judge ruled against her.

Blacksmiths constructing Samurai swords recited a specific prayer while tempering the blades. A researcher discovered that the duration of the prayer was precisely the period of time required to temper the blade properly. I had no idea what rituals the practitioners of obeah followed, but I had a feeling that the individual—to create the preferred outcome—designed a ritual best suited to his own temperament. Many rituals became codified, though an adherent probably adjusted the ritual to suit his own needs. I suspected that with training and regularity of activity, the ritual lost some of its importance, for when you have experience and do something with regularity, it doesn't take long to get into the proper state of mind or zone—hell, as soon as I drop the line from my mooring buoy, I'm a sailor. That isn't to say that individual sailors don't each have a specific program for getting their boats underway. Much like a baseball pitcher, there is a rhythm to his work. Jog that rhythm, and the pitcher can go into the tank—mostly because he believes he will.

Rattling the Shirt with an imitation of obeah was, I realized, no different from practicing obeah. I just needed to focus my intent, and I needed to convince the Shirt he believed in mumbo jumbo—two big obstacles, admittedly. Mulling it over in my mind, I determined that the key to success in obeah—just like the key to success in any endeavor—is determination. While I believed that I possessed the intent of an obeah man, I was uncertain of my ability to focus that intent for the required duration, because I had no idea of the time required. I once saw a man reputed to possess the power of obeah stand in the bush in a trance-like state for two days. I didn't continuously watch him, but I passed by him a half-dozen times and never even glimpsed him flinch.

When I reached the mangroves where Aubrey and I hid the front-end loader yesterday, Zeke called to me. I found him in his jeep parked nearly at the water's edge. I suspected that his hideout might be infested with cockroaches, but I didn't spot a single one. Zeke climbed out, flashed a huge smile, and handed me a formidable roll of cash that must have weighed a pound.

"Keep it," I said. "I didn't agree to sell it to you."

"Business be business."

"I'm serious."

"Zeke be serious too."

"I gave it to you because you're the most responsible person I know with cocaine. Nearly everyone else wants to inhale it in large quantities."

"Zeke appreciate Captain Brian trust he. Now take Zeke's money or Zeke be tempted to whomp you ass."

Flat-ass broke, mindful of my financial obligations, and a bit giddy at such a windfall—I quit protesting and took the cash. I split the money and stuffed half into each pocket. To make room, I took out the tobacco pouch.

"Zeke, you haven't got a pinch of fairy dust on you?"

"Zeke doesn't think he see the day when Captain Brian sniff the medicine."

"Just a pinch here in this pouch. It's not for me."

"Zeke doesn't think he see the day when Captain Brian does the magic. Next thing Zeke know, Captain Brian be shaking them bones."

His laugh—rich and genuine—erupted, and I opened the pouch; he added a pinch of medicine.

"Zeke, what do you know about obeah?"

"Zeke know nothing. They doesn't tell he." He laughed. "You hasn't heard?"

"What?"

"Zeke be bad boy."

"So how many West Indians in Flamingo Bay believe in obeah?"

"Every God one of them. You doesn't see the chicken foot hanging from the trees? Come Sunday, they all be in church singing to Jesus, except Zeke. He be delivering medicine."

"Thank you," I said. "I'll spend the money wisely."

"Zeke hope not," he laughed. "Go find Blondie, buy her something pretty, and jook her brains out."

"Sounds like a plan." I waved and continued on my way.

Under normal circumstances, the windfall I received from Zeke would have my mind skipping like a stone across the waves until it met the horizon; instead, the dilemma it presented allowed the stone to skip only a couple of times until it slowly began its descent to the bottom of the Puerto Rico Trench.

I could pay Mr. Outback, or I could buy sails. Buying sails could put me back in business, allow me to earn the money to pay him. Of course, there also existed the possibility that my next entrepreneurial endeavor could be even more disastrous than my last—anything can happen in the Caribbean.

If I paid Mr. Outback, I'd retain my reputation as a fair business-man and hold onto whatever modicum of honor I still possessed. What scared me was that another opportunity to buy sails and get back in business might not occur—you survive in this world until you don't. I'd always considered myself a strong man, but I couldn't think about the humiliation of losing *Island Trader* at a fire-sale price. Then I remem-bered Vaughn's offer of short-term loan and realized I didn't have to think of the worst-case scenario just yet.

At Easys, I grabbed a beer and took a seat at one of the tables. I knew if I sat at the bar, I'd be tempted to grill Easy about Leif. I had a lot of questions, but the question I itched to ask concerned the where-abouts of Easy's shotgun when Leif was killed. As Easy was about my last close friend on the island, I didn't want to get into it with him. Billie could handle that. The other thing—and there's always the other thing—I wanted to borrow Easy's truck.

I pulled the small block of mahogany from my pocket and began to whittle. It didn't take but a few minutes before the reflective part of my mind focused on my juju, only occasionally interrupted by the eth-ical consideration fomented by my debt to Mr. Outback. I decided to let my pre-reflective mind take care of Mr. Outback, and I carved furi-ously, interrupting my work every half-hour or so to buy a fresh beer.

A week ago I would've been disturbed a half-dozen times by acquaintances asking my opinion about this or that or just stopping by to chat. Since the Shirt showed up and began monopolizing my time, I'd become a pariah. No one wanted to speak to me, though patrons' oblique glances and subdued conversations suggested my present activ-ity didn't pass unremarked.

Four empty bottles stood at attention in a ragged formation when Elroy snuck up on me. I couldn't say how long he watched me work the piece of mahogany before he moved closer to the table to get my atten-tion. I set the juju on the table and dug out my cigarettes. Elroy picked up the juju and bobbed his head in approval. I was unsure whether he approved of its small penis and big ears, its overall design, or just the concept that I was carving it. Elroy indicated by pulling the hair on his head that authenticity required the inclusion of hair. Since the Shirt didn't have any hair on his head, I accepted Elroy's criticism as a compliment. I took one cigarette from the pack, stuck it in my mouth, and handed the rest of the pack to Elroy. He fished one out, and I lit both.

"Elroy, who shot Leif?"

If there were a witness to the event, Elroy was the likely bystander—it was his job. His head—in a slight and sharp motion—bobbed up and down, as he exhaled smoke and chose his words.

He answered, "Nobody shoot he." Then he turned and wandered away.

I made a note to buy lots of cigarettes. At the rate in which he divulged information, it would take several packs to learn all Elroy knew, and it seemed he did know something. Even employing bribery, detective work took patience.

At Elroy's silent suggestion, I roughed the fetish's chest to give the impression of body hair. When my favorite Fed arrived in a shiny red jeep, I added the juju to the tobacco pouch, scattered the wood shavings with my foot, and waited to learn what was on his mind. He didn't stop at the bar for a beer but walked directly to my table and took a chair.

"Now that you've had a chance to sleep on it, come to any conclusion about my offer yesterday?"

"I've taken it under advisement, and I'm seeking direction from my spiritual counselor."

"Always the comedian. But now who's being cagey?" He picked up an empty beer bottle, pointed it skyward, and peered into it like it was a telescope. "What's this I see in your pockets? Federal Reserve notes. Looks like ten thou' from here." He set my bottle down. "Probably never earned ten thou' a week in your life. Who helped you earn it? Think I don't know what's going on around here? I didn't come after you the other day when you rescued Zeke's boat. I didn't come after you because how is Zeke going to pick up medicine for his patients without a boat?"

It was a good question and an even better answer. The Shirt's words gave me plenty to think about, but mostly I thought about how time was running out on my delaying tactics. If Vaughn didn't get back soon, I'd be forced into a decision—one I wasn't looking forward to making.

"I told you I could be your best friend, just like I'm Zeke's best friend. You have a short memory. What you need to do is spend some time thinking. The offer won't be on the table long." He set his jaw and hunkered like a millstone. "I'll catch up with you later today. If I were you, I'd have an affirmative answer on the tip of my tongue."

I thought about Zeke, and I thought about my next meeting with the Shirt, but mostly I thought the Shirt had caught up to me—I was barely a step ahead. Some things are worth waiting for; waiting for the other shoe to drop isn't one of them.

The Shirt got to his feet and headed to the sputnik. When he closed the door behind him, I walked over to his new jeep and tossed my little pouch of tricks onto the passenger-side floor then returned to the table.

On his way to his jeep, the Shirt stopped at the table to reemphasize his threat. I told him I was close to making a decision revealing the whereabouts of Vaughn's cocaine.

"Before the sun sets today," he called over his shoulder while walking away.

It occurred to me that the Shirt's next move might be to chase after Billie; he'd already chased after Sarah—successfully. I pondered for a moment whether that possibility should influence my behavior. I decided it shouldn't. Billie was a big girl; she could take care of herself.

I approached the bar. I could tell something was up with Easy. Instead of twisting off the cap to a Bud, he acted like I was a stranger.

"If this interviewing process goes on much longer, I'll have to find a new home."

"You hit that nail on the head." Easy spoke very, very slowly—the way I suspected old people screwed. I noticed I thought for the first time how red his lips and mouth were. I knew it had to do with his pasty skin and black beard, but still I was surprised. The sanguinary effect was off-putting, and I checked the toes sticking out of my leather topsiders.

"In theory, it was a cool idea to meet the Shirt here. It's mellow and out in the open, all very groovy. But why're you still talking to him? Nobody in Flamingo Bay has that much to say to a narc. You have to be telling him something, and that makes people nervous. Real nervous."

"I haven't told him shit," I shrugged.

"The appearance, man. It appears you're telling him shit."

"That's one way of looking at it, but if I were telling him shit, he'd be talking to somebody else by now. The whiners should realize that if I wasn't wasting my time to deal with him, they'd be wasting theirs."

"All I'm saying is people're concerned. You've never been this broke before. People honestly fear you'll do whatever it takes to land on top. Makes them nervous. What makes me nervous is the Shirt just might take you down. Watch your step, man."

I had a lot more to say, but I surrendered. I borrowed Easy's green pickup and headed back to *Island Trader* to count my cash, though I was pretty sure I had exactly ten grand. Before I dinghied to the boat, I stopped at the fire station to call my erstwhile client, Mr. Outback, a man obsessed with the Down Under and getting the biggest bang for his buck. I told him I'd be in town in about an hour with five grand in my pocket. He said he would catch a boat and meet me there. I was certain it was one boat he wouldn't miss.

15

AFTER I CONFIRMED THE SHIRT'S ACCURACY in estimating the value of the roll of cash I carried, I separated five grand to pay Mr. Outback, three grand to pay Rolly, and headed to shore. After I tied up, I disconnected the fuel line to my outboard and carried the gas tank to Easy's truck. At the playground, I stopped to give Rolly cash to pay his crew. Workers expected to be paid at the end of each day. That Rolly kept them showing up every morning without pay proved to me the respect he'd earned.

At the fork in the road, I met Anal Richards, preaching to an invisible congregation. Standing in the middle of the intersection propped up by a single crutch and looking like a renegade from a toga party, he persisted enough in his vocation that I imagined he'd one day get sponsors and his own TV show.

Handled the right way, one good miracle could produce a lot of goodwill. If the Reverend were able to equip *Island Trader* with sails, heal the sore above Jason's lip, help Pirate Dan grow a new leg, or raise Leif from the dead, he could probably count on me to tithe.

Despite Reverend Richards' mostly successful effort to impersonate a prophet, his main competition in winning the souls of Flamingo Bay's denizens was Diver Vaughn. Masquerading as the messiah in his favorite game—Come to Jesus—Vaughn wasn't as visually convincing as the Reverend Richards, he didn't have any special connection to the deity, and he hadn't performed any miracles. What he did was regularly respond to specific prayers of intercession, helping those in need, especially those in need of cocaine or cash—a man doesn't need the philosopher's stone to turn $C_{17}H_{21}NO_4$ into Au, turn white powder into gold.

The Reverend didn't attempt to block my lane, so I didn't stop, but as I passed, he shouted: "Devil in Joseph's coat be on you tail."

A few days ago, the profundity of his observation would have startled me; now it was old news. One thing about prophecy: timing is everything.

On my way up the mountain, I encountered what could've been the thousandth episode of the Ralph and Toto Show. I stopped for the finale. The brindled dog, which hadn't taken a breath in days, was lying on the road half under the tourist jeep. Four children clutched each other at the side of the road and sobbed convincingly.

I climbed out, examined the dog, and walked over to Ralph.

"Captain Brian, mon," he said. "These folks kill children's dog."

The middle-aged, red-faced driver—still in his seat, knuckles white from choking the steering wheel—demanded Mister Ralph fetch the police.

"No, Mister," Ralph said. "You doesn't understand. You hit a hundred-dollar dog."

It was Mister Ralph who didn't understand. He seemed to think the tourist wanted to report the accident to the police; I didn't doubt that the tourist wanted to report Ralph to the police. Also clear to me: the substantial fleshiness of the driver's companion clouded Ralph's judgment—West Indian men like their women built for comfort, and comfort swelled from the top of her one-piece swimsuit.

The woman knelt by the side of the road, trying to console the children. She asked them the dog's name.

"Hundred-dollar dog," the youngest piped up.

"You poor baby," the woman said, hugging the child, burying his head between her breasts.

If the dipstick behind the wheel only allowed his wife to hug Mister Ralph in a similar manner, they could've maybe resumed their vacation, no poorer. Instead, the man got what he wished. Officer Richards, on his way from town to harass the folk in Flamingo Bay, pulled up behind the tourist jeep and climbed out.

"What be happening here?"

The man in the jeep pled his case, arguing that Ralph attempted to shake him down for a hundred dollars for running over a dead dog.

"How does you know dog dead when you hit it?"

"It was stone cold."

Richards motioned the man out of his jeep, walked him down the road several yards, and asked him to touch the sun-baked rock wall, jagged from the road builders' dynamite blasting. "Feel cold to you?"

The man admitted it didn't.

"You own up you be wrong when you say dog stone cold. Maybe you just want to believe you doesn't kill this poor animal. You business be with family who lose pet. Police not get involved unless you doesn't want to pay for you carelessness."

"But a hundred dollars?" the man protested.

"It be his dog. You has to pay he what he asks."

The man glumly returned to his jeep. I rather enjoyed not being the object of Richards' attention for once—at least until he decided to ticket me for parking on the wrong side of the road.

"I stopped only because of the accident. If I'd stopped on the other side of the road, I'd block traffic."

"Accident none of you business. Let me see you driver license."

"Come on, you remember me. I'm the man who promised to jam you up for killing Leif."

"Shut you mouth."

"How much did the Fed pay you? Three grand? Four? Five?"

"Want to go to jail?"

"What I can't figure is why you left your handcuffs on Leif after you killed him. Because you're chicken shit?"

"One more word, I put cuffs on you."

I thought he might be serious, so I shut my mouth and handed over my driver's license. I had rattled him, though. When he finished dotting the *i*'s on the parking ticket, he didn't even bother to check on the negotiations between Ralph and the tourists. He climbed into his Blazer, squeaked the tires, and raced off down the road.

The tourists' lack of cash resulted in a standoff with Ralph. They had only sixty bucks and change. Ralph didn't take checks or credit cards. I studied the dog and then joined Ralph.

"Mister Ralph," I said, "it looks more like a fifty-dollar dog to me."

Ralph walked around to the other side of the jeep to take another look at the animal. It took him long enough that I thought he might be performing an autopsy. He returned, nodding his head.

"Captain Brian, you be right. It be a fifty-dollar dog."

I suggested to the man that he pay Ralph and get on with his vacation. He took my advice. The woman returned to the car, and the couple drove off.

"You're about out of business," I said.

Ralph nodded. "Not much life in the old fellow."

We shared a laugh, and I climbed back into Easy's truck. Just as I prepared to pull away, Jason the Argonut, heading toward Sugar Harbor, blew by me as if pursued by Cerberus.

Once over the mountain, I met all the folk coming back from town—Zeke, Mary, Marsha, the Garys. I kept a finger near the horn to answer them. It was quicker to drive to town when everyone was going your direction. You could use both lanes, no problem dodging rocks that had tumbled onto the road or the many potholes. I braked often to soften blows to the suspension and to avoid the odd mongoose or cow and the many pigs. The road was crummy enough that I'd never gotten more than three thousand miles to a set of tires.

Vegetation encroached upon the roadway. In some areas, I drove through a leafy tunnel. The speed limit was twenty, but people often drove as fast as they could go. In eight miles, the road only straightened once. That hundred-yard stretch offered the only opportunity to safely pass another vehicle. Head-on crashes were common on the other sections of the road, especially during tourist season—left is right on St. Judas, and right is wrong. The straightway ended with a sharp curve to the left, marked by a black-green dumpster. The dumpster still displayed red paint and adjacent trees bore scars from the Ferrari incident.

The Ferrari made its brief appearance on the island a couple of months after Fast Louie returned from the States after his mother's funeral. When Louie missed the curve, he'd been driving the car for less than a month. Neither Louie nor the Ferrari survived the collision. It was better for everyone that Louie was no longer driving. Still, a big chasm existed between revocation of your license and your life.

As I approached the end of the straightway, I discovered that Jason, like Fast Louie, had met the dumpster head-on. I stopped and climbed out. Steam still escaped from under the crumpled hood, and the totaled jeep leaked its fluids on the decaying asphalt. I called to Jason and searched the roadside bush. The vehicle's windshield revealed no damage. The Argonut apparently walked away from the crash. Either that, or he fell out of his vehicle before the crash—not the first time he parted company with his vehicle when it was in motion. His practice came from falling off bar stools.

I drove the short distance to town in second gear, keeping an eye out for Jason. I didn't spot him. He'd either made it to town on foot or gotten a ride, no doubt continuing his quest for the Golden Fleece.

As the road began its descent into Sugar Harbor, I met a water tanker grinding up the hill. Water tankers are almost as common on St. Judas as heating-oil tankers are in the great frozen North. Tankers and ready-mix trucks offered the only competition—size counted— for safari buses that hauled tourists to and from the beaches.

I coasted down the hill, and the time zone abruptly changed from Atlantic Time, where everything seemed a struggle, to Island Time, where nothing seemed a struggle. I didn't reset my watch, just my attitude. I arrived at the Caribbean touted in tourist brochures. Here local color collided with four-color printing. Here human flesh—thanks to genetics and sunshine—came in all shades. The hues, vibrant and sticky, always reminded me of melting ice cream cones.

"Island Time" is a subtle concept, an attitude, really, that takes months to develop. It's mostly about going with the flow, learning not to be frustrated with the existing rhythm of life—at least not exhibiting frustration openly and publicly. Continentals, especially, expect that the experience should be an event, as swift and fulfilling as an orgasm. When they find that it isn't—and a week or two of sun and water isn't nearly long enough to grasp the experience—they often increase their ingestion of drugs and alcohol, so Island Time for them is really about substance abuse. I suspected that was what happened to the Continental contractor who purchased the greenheart from me. His lumber still sat untouched at the dinghy dock, and I hadn't seen him since the day I returned from Venezuela.

I stopped at the island's only gas station to fill Easy's truck and the tank to my dinghy's outboard. A small shack housed the office. The hoist and the tire machine and the air compressor and tank that operated them were bolted to a concrete slab adjacent to the shack. On the other side of the shack, next to the rank of fifty-five-gallon oil drums— some fitted with hand cranks—sat an oil-saturated pile of discarded engines, transmissions, and differentials. In front of the shack stood a soda machine and a bench.

When I shut off the engine and climbed out, I received a half-hearted ovation from the two employees and the several habitués headquartered there. Apparently, word of my night with Blondie had already traveled across the island. Another slow-news day on St. Judas. I attributed my supporters' lack of zeal to jealousy—like extending congratulations to the lottery winner, all the while convinced you're more deserving than he.

While I pumped gas, I concluded that, unlike my night with Billie, my association with the Shirt hadn't yet traveled across the island. Eventually, it would, but until then, I wouldn't have to leave St. Judas to enjoy social intercourse.

I started the engine to leave when the owner of the only lumberyard on St. Judas pulled up on the other side of the pumps.

"Still got that mahogany?" the Continental shouted.

"You can't afford it."

He climbed out of his new pickup and flashed a wad of cash at me.

I flashed my own wad of cash and answered, "In my league, you get only two strikes before you're out. I'd rather burn it than sell it to you."

As I drove off, he shouted for me to wait. I gave him the finger and kept going. It took ten minutes to drive two blocks to the waterfront. I didn't get to town much in the middle of the day, and there were people to greet—most of the West Indians, including many pals, lived and worked in town.

Government House—a two-story white masonry building crowned with a red tile roof—occupied a small promontory marking the town's northern border. Once the private residence of a wealthy family, the government maintained the building as if it still was, and a fulltime gardener kept its grounds manicured. The building housed a few ancillary services, but most governmental offices operated out of St. Thomas.

Trapped in a line of traffic, I inched along toward the pier. In my rearview mirror, I caught a glimpse of the senator and island administrator turn and walk together up the long winding driveway to Government House. I seldom saw the two of them together—probably because the senator's business took place mostly on St. Thomas. The two stopped and faced each other. Both were fit and energetic men. The senator—the only man on the island to dress in a suit and tie— wagged his finger to press home a point.

While Zeke invested thousands of dollars in gold to glitter when he walked, the senator achieved the same effect with only a simple wedding band. When I reflected upon the tiny gold ring that Billie wore on her toe, I felt I'd compiled all the proof I needed to confirm that less is more.

Almida, the island administrator, shrugged his shoulders in what could've been deference to the senator's movie-star charisma—the man could've found employment as Sydney Poitier's stunt double. The intensity of their conversation alerted me that something was up. I wouldn't have minded watching the scene play out, but a safari bus pulled up behind me, blocking my view.

Just past Government House, a small park lay near the waterfront. It offered several benches and a bandstand—unfinished, no roof or railing, but already deteriorated. It looked more than anything like a square shallow box turned upside down and connected to a short flight of squishy stairs. Taxi drivers filled the folding chairs grouped around four rickety card tables. Slapping dominoes clashed with the calypso strains from a nearby boombox. Harry Belafonte sang: "Down the way where the nights are gay...."

Cobbled-together buildings and shacks surrounded the park on three sides. Proprietors sold cold drinks, conch fritters, T-shirts, and tourist accessories. The road bordered the park, following the shoreline of the bay. It consisted of two lanes but was one-way—a recent innovation to keep traffic flowing, while passengers and luggage were picked up and dropped off at the ferry. Coconut palms lined the road on the bay side, along with several ancient sea grapes that filled the spaces between the trunks of the palms. A rank of safari buses parked along the waterfront, backed up against the beach, filling in most of the spaces left unblocked by the trees and hiding from view the narrow strip of powdery sand that separated the road from the bay.

The park offered the only bit of vacant land. A hundred mostly modest buildings—many of them painted in pastels—filled the hillside, bumping against one another, as if fighting for a place in the breeze. Traditional red roofs still capped a dozen-or-so structures, but many older roofs had been lost in hurricanes, and newer white metal roofs now topped most of the buildings.

Sea breezes cooled the sun's strong rays. Beautiful people—seeing and being seen—clutched mimosas, coladas, daiquiris, beers, and sodas. Melodic West Indian cadences rose to scattered crescendos. Dogs and adults sought shade. Children frolicked and chased bewildered chickens and each other. Day-trippers, fried in oil at the end of a hard morning at the beach, waited to be transported back to St. Thomas. They stuck out like their blotchy skin, lousing up the photographers' images of paradise. I watched, also, a few Martian-complected tourists disembark after a rough ride from St. Thomas.

The harbor provided moorings for about fifty boats. Unlike Flamingo Bay—where there was no fuel—about half were motorboats. A concrete pier jutted from the shore. Five passenger ferries docked there. The blue hulls of three ferries were trimmed in white. The competing company favored white hulls trimmed in red.

Trying to break out of the herd of luggage-laden tourists, the sartorially splendid Mr. Outback frantically searched for me. He wore a short-sleeved khaki safari jacket and shorts, knee-high forest-green stockings, and low-cut desert boots, trying unsuccessfully for the Ernest Hemingway look. A remarkably pristine bush hat with the brim snapped up on one side represented his homage to New South Wales, though he hailed from New Jersey.

I honked and waved. The look on his face approached ecstasy when he spotted me. He saluted and waddled toward my truck on bowlegs. It took him a minute, as his gait incorporated a lot of lateral motion.

He'd found a new source for his ceramic tile—a retailer on St. Thomas. I believed that he originally gave me the contract because of a romantic notion. He could point to his floors and tell his guests how he commissioned a boat to sail to South America to fetch the tile for him. He hadn't lost much—only the difference between retail and wholesale—and he still had a story to tell. I wouldn't be surprised if during his narration the boat and its cargo went down in a storm.

When my tile deal with Lopez went south, I phoned Outback from Cumaná to persuade him to wire me more money. I'd already lost his five grand, but if he'd wired me more money, I'd have had an opportunity to cut my loss. I supposed that I couldn't really blame him, but it would've been easier not to blame him if I didn't dislike him.

He stuck his head in the window. "Captain Brian, great to see you."

"Especially with cash. Sorry about all the trouble."

"I'm the one who is sorry. The substitute tile isn't working out as well as I'd hoped."

I pulled the wad from my pocket and handed it to him. He didn't take the money. Instead, he looked nervously around and motioned me to keep it out of sight. Then he walked around the truck, opened the door, and climbed in. He closed the door, took the wad of cash, unrolled it, and flipped through it.

"How's the house coming?" I asked.

"Slowly. We're at least six weeks behind schedule."

I wanted to laugh. Hell, I knew people who were six years behind schedule.

"It's all here?"

"Count it."

"Hey, I didn't mean anything by that." He stuffed the cash in his jacket pocket and buttoned the flap. "Everyone's aware of your reputation. Your word will always be good enough for me. I'm just nervous walking around with this kind of money. One of the natives might try to relieve the white man of his burden."

He was as big a racist as Officer Richards, and like Richards, Outback was so clueless that I could see no point in even calling him on his prejudice. All my smart retorts sailed over his head. Still, I couldn't resist one last try.

"Don't worry. The *white man* is the natives' burden."

An air horn shrieked, signaling the imminent departure of the Charlotte Amalie ferry.

"We all have our burdens," he said. "My boat. Thank you, and good luck."

He fled the truck and dissolved into a group of tourists.

I found an illegal parking space and headed on foot to the clinic, expecting to find Jason. Housed in an old storefront as a temporary measure after Hurricane Hugo, the government still hadn't figured out how to get the six-year-old state-of-the-art clinic up and running five years after the hurricane damaged it. I didn't find Jason sitting in the crowded waiting room, and according to the sullen West Indian girl at the desk, he hadn't been there.

I decided to grab a sandwich and celebrate my first step toward financial freedom—owing nothing to anyone, though it would take more cash or a bit of luck to put me back in business. I found an empty table at a burger joint bordering the park.

A week ago I might have thought of scamming the Shirt out of his reward money by promising to deliver Vaughn's cocaine and taking my chances when the Shirt learned that I'd stiffed him. I hadn't much to lose. I'd already pretty much lost everything but my boat. With Billie creeping into my life, I knew I couldn't take a chance on making a big mistake. The other side of that coin was I knew Billie wouldn't stick around long if I didn't make her life comfortable. Then there was the promise I'd made her not to upset the Shirt. The coin I'd created was unique. It had three sides: obverse, reverse, and perverse. While I tried to concoct a new metaphor, I caught a snippet of conversation from the next table and realized the sailors spoke of Leif.

Leif became something of a folk hero in the Caribbean, mostly for the exploit that sent him to Leavenworth. The man talking, a lean and weathered skipper with a glittering eye, told his cohorts that he first heard of Leif a few years ago when anchored on Culebra, which I thought was interesting because Leif had never been to Culebra, a small island off the east coast of Puerto Rico.

"The guy had balls, I'll say that," his drinking partner chimed in. "I'm over at the Wooden Boat Race on Jost Van Dyke two years ago. First time I met Leif. Along with everyone else, I spent the evening drinking at Foxy's. Leave to return to my boat and my dinghy's missing. Next morning Leif comes by and says he thinks he can get it back for a hundred bucks. I'm smart enough not to fork over the hundred until I see my dinghy. He and I agree to let a third party hold the C-note until noon. Quarter to twelve, Leif shows up with my dinghy. I felt pretty lucky until I learned that he made about a grand that day returning stolen dinghies. By the time we realized he stole the dinghies himself and we started looking for him, we learned he'd left the island."

I missed that regatta two years ago, and I hadn't heard that particular story before, but listening to it put a smile on my face. Remembering the misadventure of Leif's fly-by-night dinghy deal, in which he and Jason not only lost all the dinghies they stole on Tortola but Leif's own dinghy, I was heartened that he was able to bounce back and score a big hit with his dinghy-held-for-ransom scam. It put a smile on my face, at least until it struck home that the Lore would receive no new contributions from Leif.

Leif's noisy and blazing send-off had been a longtime coming, sort of like the final gurgle when the last of the water funnels down an unvented drain. His arrest after the bank robbery dislodged the stopper that'd kept Leif and his world afloat. Ever since, he'd swirled in a maelstrom, his head barely above water, his life and options diminishing with each revolution of the accelerating spiral that carried him downward to his death. Opportunities to pull himself out presented themselves, but Leif couldn't hold onto them any more than he could hold onto his possessions. Everything he had owned wouldn't even fill his backpack.

The only suspect with a perfect alibi was the Shirt—my suspect. Still, I believed the Shirt knew more than he let on. I had a simple plan that promised a measure of success, depending upon what the Shirt actually knew, but acting on the plan might force me to leave Flamingo Bay—something that no longer excited me as much as it did before Billie began her recent mating dance.

I paid my check, and walked to the post office to pick up my mail. While waiting in line, I spoke with Mister Hector who invited me to a pig roast a week from Saturday—an all-day affair that offered the best of local West Indian haute cuisine. The usual program was to bring your own knife and cut off the chunks that interested you—the eating started hours before the pig finished roasting. I promised him I'd be there.

I caught a glimpse of Sergeant March—a gazelle of a man, still as fit as an eighteen-year-old—patrolling the streets. Elder in his church, pillar of the community, and a genuinely honorable man, March proved the exception to the rule; he was the only cop I'd met who wasn't an asshole.

Every time I saw him, I was reminded of the sole survivor of one group of slaves that committed suicide rather than risk capture after a slave rebellion in 1733. The single survivor was a little boy named March. The policeman was his direct descendent.

I had a few bills and one package from a stateside bookseller. It was the Albert Camus book I'd ordered; although, now that Wendy was gone, I hadn't a clue to whom I'd give the third copy of *The Stranger*.

I hiked back to where I had parked Easy's truck. Before he saw me, Sergeant March—pen in hand and foot on the rear bumper—pulled out his pad of tickets.

"Somebody must have moved it," I called from twenty feet away. "I'm positive I parked legally. Did you check with that Rasta down the street? I think he's been working the obeah on me."

He turned and laughed. "Captain Brian, this be your truck?"

"For the afternoon. Mine was stolen by some Fed. Steals my truck and steals Sarah to ride around with him. Should I contact the governor—auto theft, kidnapping?"

"Why not the President? Go right to the top. Right to Washington."

"Good idea." I laughed and stepped under the slippery shade of a small lignum vitae tree. "You okay?"

"Okay." He stuck the pad into his pocket. "For best excuse to park illegally I hear all week, I let you off with warning."

"Thank you."

"You still limping on that knee?"

"I think it's getting better. I just need to spend more time in my hammock."

Sergeant March and I served in Vietnam, though we didn't know each other then. I was at Camp Carroll and he was with the artillery at the Rockpile, just down the road. Having the Marine Corps in common triggered our friendship.

I said, "If there's ever a big updraft to heaven, you'll be platoon leader."

"That be something. Get Medal of Honor from Jesus."

We both laughed.

"You know," I said, "I don't think this tree has grown more than an inch in height during the five years I've been here."

"I don't think you have either," he laughed. "But you already know about lignum vitae. Maybe you want to know about something else?"

"I do. The Fed who stole my truck told me Leif was killed by a shotgun blast. Another man declared Leif wasn't shot at all. I know the police aren't going to spend a lot of time figuring out what happened. Leif wasn't a model citizen. But he was the first person I met when I anchored in Flamingo Bay. We had some history. If it's not top secret, can you tell me how he died?"

"No shotgun. Head injury. Maybe he fall. Maybe he pushed."

The Shirt lied about how Leif died. What else had he lied about?

"You're sure Leif didn't drown?"

"Put in cistern after he die."

While it was theoretically possible that Miss Lucinda clubbed Leif in the head, Sergeant March's information removed Miss Lucinda from the list of suspects, at least for me—not that a list actually existed. That Easy's shotgun was obviously not the murder weapon clearly weakened the case against him, though the money angle still existed— somebody likely walked away from the cistern four grand richer.

Neither of my two key questions—why the cistern, and why now— had been answered, though the importance of the cistern seemed to have lessened.

"You hear about handcuffs?" March asked.

"I heard. Makes it all very untidy, doesn't it?"

"Messy as police vehicle come in yesterday from Flamingo Bay."

I said, "I can't imagine who would commit such a brazen act of vandalism."

He looked me hard in the eye before smiling and shaking his head.

"What you be up to, anyway? Senator and island administrator be talking all morning about you and Aubrey. You planning revolution for Flamingo Bay?"

"Nothing that serious. Just building a playground."

Aubrey's plan to get the playground built before it became public knowledge seemed to have failed. I could accept the playground as it now existed. I just hoped that I wouldn't have to watch it get dismantled by the government.

"Even the governor be talking about you. Be careful."

"Thanks for the info," I said. "Ever need a favor, let me know."

"About that Medal of Honor."

"Look, I don't carry that much weight, but a Navy Cross isn't out of the question."

It wasn't out of the question. I had one stashed away on the boat with my personal stuff. It'd long since lost its luster for me, and I'd give it away in a minute, but I knew I couldn't give it to Sergeant March. It would disrespect him. Besides, he already had a Silver Star of his own.

We laughed and banged fists. Sergeant March went back to work, and I headed back to Flamingo Bay. I passed by the waterfront again on my way out of town, and I recognized the man at the end of the queue for ferry tickets. It was the tourist lady's husband, solo and struggling with his bags. I hadn't seen her since Leif's funeral and hadn't a clue what she was up to since she walked away from Zeke, though it didn't appear she was up to returning to the States with her husband.

It seems that paradise—where beginnings are limitless with prom-ise—offers few happy endings.

16

AFTER I UNLOADED MY DINGHY'S GAS TANK, I returned Easy's truck, surprised that the Shirt wasn't waiting for me at the bar. I drank a beer with Easy and in an oblique fashion, attempted to patch things up. I didn't know if I needed to, and I didn't know if I succeeded. Before I left, I asked him if he'd ever heard of Meyer J. Lofgrin. Easy hadn't.

On my way back to the dinghy dock on foot, I stopped at the playground. It impressed me as much as any sculpture garden I remembered. Each new piece of equipment enhanced the composition. Everything was square and plumb, temporarily, at least, defying the second law of thermodynamics. The rich red of the mahogany contrasted nicely with the green lawn and the blue sea. If it'd been up to me, I'd consider putting a fence topped with barbed wire around it and spend my days polishing the wood.

While Rolly's helpers completed the details on the seesaw, I helped Rolly carry the finished signpost. He dropped his end into the hole I'd dug earlier. He and Aubrey took up positions on either side of the sign, and one of the workers took a position in front. They directed me to get it plumb. When everyone was satisfied, two men with shovels packed rocks and dirt around it. When they finished, Aubrey produced a camera and took a picture of Rolly, his crew, and me. I then took a picture of Aubrey, Rolly, and the men standing alongside the sign, which read:

VALERIE

MEMORIAL

PLAYGROUND

The completed equipment included swings, monkey bars, jungle gym, tetherball, and seesaw. The slide was to be the last piece of equipment, but Rolly hadn't rounded up all the materials. After building the slide, Rolly planned to add a couple of benches. Benches fit into the budget, and I gave him the go-ahead.

A couple of small kids weren't strong enough to play on the monkey bars, so I held them and walked them the length of the apparatus, while they grabbed the bars with their hands. Tony, Rolly's five-year-old son, hopped off a swing and asked me to help him across the monkey bars. I hoisted him up, and he grabbed the first bar.

"My dad build this," Tony said.

"He did a great job."

"He be best carpenter on island. Best fisherman, too."

I assured him his dad was the best carpenter and the best fisherman. Tony and his buddies dared me to traverse the monkey bars. When I didn't accept their challenge, they rounded up their older siblings to taunt me. I had to bend my knees ninety degrees to keep from dragging my feet on the ground. They cheered when I finished. They then dared me to do it backwards. I did it, but it damn near killed me.

Ready to leave, I glanced toward the fork in the road and spotted a public works vehicle parked there. I wouldn't have given it a second thought, except for its flashing emergency lights. A moment later, another public works vehicle pulled up behind the first, lights also flashing. It appeared the cavalry was assembling. I figured they were coming after us. I expected them, but I didn't expect them until tomorrow. I hadn't said a word to my partners about Sergeant March's warning. Why spoil the moment?

It was quitting time for Rolly. In ten minutes, he'd be on his way home. It was also quitting time for public works, but like the Shirt, public works displayed tenacity beyond which the civil service instilled. Something else must be going on. I figured it could be anything—a long-running feud, personal or political, even a social snub, and its agent could exist anywhere in the hierarchy of the government. I also figured that unless someone in the know explained it to me, I'd never comprehend it.

In most third-world countries citizens feared the army—certainly because the army had guns, but also because it had political power. The Virgin Islands has no army, but it has public works. A couple of years ago, Asphalt Mike was almost shot when the governor sent him to pave the road by the ferry dock to spruce things up for a visiting dignitary from the States. The governor evidently hadn't obtained a permit.

Public works caught up with Mike in the middle of the job and threat-ened to shoot him if he didn't climb down from his paving machine. One shot was actually fired. The gunshot got everybody's attention. The confrontation continued until the island administrator ordered the police to arrest the public works contingent and escort it to the ferry. When the ferry accelerated out of the harbor for St. Thomas, Mike finished the job but admitted he'd pissed in his pants when the public works guy pulled the trigger.

I watched Officer Richards join the cavalry, pulling in front of the first vehicle. I alerted Rolly. He sent one of his men to fetch Aubrey who'd walked over to Easys for his afternoon cocktail. When the second cop car joined the formation, the parade proceeded toward us with the solemnity of a funeral procession, emergency lights flashing and pulsing. The vehicles turned off the road and fanned out on the lawn surrounding us. Six armed men—two cops and four public works employees—exited the vehicles and converged on Rolly and me. Rolly nodded his head, and another of his workers fired up the gas generator, making conversation impossible.

Richards motioned for the generator to be shut down. Rolly cupped his hand around his ear and hollered, "What? I can't hear you!"

The standoff lasted nearly ten minutes, providing time for the audi-ence to gather. Easys' patrons received word of the event from Rol-ly's worker. I suspected the mass exodus there alerted patrons at the Congo Club. Some came on foot and others in vehicles. It wasn't as dramatic as when the word of free beer got out—no stampede—but spectators quickly outnumbered the players, and they kept coming. Madison carried his gunnysack and machete. Freddie brought along his camcorder and set it on a tripod. Easy—not one to miss an entre-preneurial opportunity—sold cold beer from a cooler in the back of his pickup. Billie plunked her backpack on the lawn and dug out her sketchpad.

All we needed was a moko jumbie or two, steel drums, and barbe-cued chicken to turn the event into a carnival. All we needed to turn the event into a disaster was a trigger-happy asshole.

Seeing the official vehicles spread across the lawn pissed me off. I was ready to blame it on Aubrey for his refusal to get a build-ing permit, until I remembered a story that Asphalt Mike confirmed shortly after I heard it. About fifteen years ago, his company—located on St. Thomas—determined that the efficiency of its operation would increase if it had its own dock. Equipment could be directly loaded onto a barge without hauling it across the island on trucks and unloading it at the ferry dock. Somebody at the company screwed up the procedure of its permit application, reversing the order of two of the many required steps. Because of that error, which disrespected the senate, the company was told that it would never get its dock. Fifteen years later, it still didn't have a dock. I supposed Aubrey was right: get it built and then deal with the flak.

Richards and his cohort—after a short consultation—advanced toward the generator, guns drawn. Rolly's worker submitted to being handcuffed and led away to one of the cop cars. I picked up a club-sized piece of lumber and stood guard at the generator—still roaring—waiting for the cops to return. Freddie moved his camcorder closer to the action.

As the cops approached, I lifted the board and rested it on my shoulder, holding it like a baseball bat. The cops stopped about fifteen feet from me and conferred. I suspected they were deciding whether to shoot me. I was deciding whether I should try to take off Richards' head before his pal could pull the trigger.

Aubrey returned, and Rolly signaled me to shut down the generator. It took a few moments before my hearing returned to normal, but when it did, I heard two or three hammers driving nails. The cadence of the hammers—like a tattoo performed by an epileptic drummer—echoed, as it bounced off the hillsides, signaling the start of Pirate Dan's construction project. Only a pirate starts a construction project at four P.M. in a place where the sun sets at six. I figured that as soon as public works finished with us, they'd be looking for the source of the pounding and paying the Congo Club a visit.

I joined Aubrey and Rolly, just as Aubrey ordered public works off his property. One thing: Aubrey—in the island scheme of things—had legitimate social standing. The other thing: he was the only one present who had. Public works seemed to seriously consider Aubrey's request, but I guessed they were only being respectful, because a couple of minutes later, the honcho demanded that the playground be disassembled immediately or everyone was going to jail.

Aubrey, without a word, climbed aboard his front-end loader, hit the ignition, and pumped the machine's accelerator. He rumbled forward to line up his machine behind one of the public works vehicles. He dropped the scoop, made contact with the rear bumper, and began pushing the vehicle toward the bay, the Blazer's locked-up rear wheel tearing at the grass. I couldn't help laughing. No wonder Aubrey and I got on so well together.

As the two cops ran toward the front-end loader, the island administrator, barreling down the road, swerved his white Blazer off the concrete and bumped across the lawn to become a player. He whipped around Aubrey and stopped his Blazer in Aubrey's path. When Aubrey switched off the ignition to the front-end loader and dismounted, the island administrator, Rupert Almida, climbed out of his vehicle.

Earlier in the afternoon, I couldn't help notice how Almida compared unfavorably with the senator in stature and charisma. On his own, Almida was handsome and forceful, though he always seemed a bit uncomfortable.

As Aubrey pled our case, all of us on the home team gathered around. I was privy to the exchange, but Almida slipped into the local patois as quickly as Rolly and Aubrey. Half the time I hadn't a clue what was said until Aubrey brought me up to speed with a translation. After the translation, the conversation resumed in English until passions erupted.

When he finished with us, Almida went over and talked to public works. While that conversation dragged on, we migrated toward Easy's truck, and Aubrey bought beers for all of us. Freddie continued to videotape the proceedings. I figured that Billie, pencil still in hand, worked on a sketch that would find its way onto a T-shirt to commemorate the event. I scanned the crowd. No Elroy. I couldn't figure where he was: it was his job to be present.

After a final salvo from Almida, the police and public works released their prisoner, climbed into their vehicles, and killed the emergency lights. Defeated, at least temporarily, they seemed in a big hurry to head back to town, but vehicles belonging to jeering bystanders trapped them on the field. Richards exited his Blazer, ticket pad in hand. The first two drivers he approached refused to move, so he tagged them. Bystanders cheered. The third driver, Cherry Mary, reluctantly moved her vehicle, allowing access to the road.

Almida, accepting a beer from Aubrey, admitted that everyone on the island would like to see the playground built. Even the governor, who showed up in Flamingo Bay only once or twice a year, favored the project. Almida agreed that public works was behaving in a petty manner, and its demand that the playground be dismantled was silly. Just when we started feeling pretty good and a little vindicated, Almida pointed out that we were the ones breaking the law. Public works was simply doing its job.

I grudgingly admitted to myself that I was the strongest proponent of a man doing his job. Still, it annoyed me that Almida nailed it: public works was right, and we were wrong.

A young boy appeared and tugged at Almida's pant's leg. "You isn't going to let those men take our playground?"

Almida knelt. "You like the playground?"

"Yes."

"Well, then, I suppose we can't let those men take it. Don't worry. Go have fun."

The boy thanked him and ran off to join his friends. Almida stood.

Aubrey asked what was next.

Almida promised to lobby the senator to lobby the judge to buy us the weekend. He also promised to protect what was standing, if we promised to do no more work after public works obtained a court order—a certainty. Left unsaid but acknowledged by everyone was that once the court order was issued, construction would probably not start up again in our lifetimes.

I knew that land disputes remained tied up in the courts for years, but for the first time, I wondered if maybe it was because nobody really pressed hard for a resolution, preferring the status quo to possibly losing. Like me, West Indians are resistant to change.

My favorite anecdote concerned William Hastie, appointed by President Truman, in 1946, to be the first African-American governor of the Virgin Islands. Hastie wasn't a Virgin Islander, so his motives were suspect from day one, but before being appointed governor, he spent time in the islands as a circuit judge. During his term in office, the islands switched electrical current from DC to AC. Citizens should've been thrilled at the modernization, but the opposition was tremendous. Hastie couldn't understand why. Nobody was happy, but nobody was talking. Finally, a West Indian on his staff took pity on him and admitted the people preferred DC, Danish Current, to AC, American Current.

Almida invited me to walk with him back to his vehicle. "Thank you for playground," he said.

"You're welcome."

"Now, thank me."

"Thank you."

"You welcome, but next time you screw up—jail. I call in all favors to keep you out this time."

"What did I do?"

"Police car. You remember?"

"Oh, that."

"Captain Brian, whose side is you on?"

"My own."

"Ah, spoken like a true, er ... honorary West Indian." Almida set his beer on the car's hood, took a pack of cigarettes from his shirt and stuck one in his mouth. "You responsible for building this playground. I take senator to see it earlier. He want to give you civic award. Then I tell him about police car. He want you in jail."

"It's my duty as a citizen to go after Richards. He shows no respect to anyone. Nobody in authority wants to tell the people in Flamingo Bay how my friend died and who put the handcuffs on him. I have no proof, but I know Richards was involved. Until he admits it, I will hound him."

"He not going to jail, I guarantee you, whatever he do."

"Why?"

"You doesn't know his wife?"

"No."

"She be sister of Governor's wife."

"I get it. But let me ask you this. What would happen if Richards murdered your brother?"

"Just between the two of us," Almida smiled. "Take he fishing."

We finished our beers and crushed our cigarettes underfoot.

"Captain Brian, ever think of leaving St. Judas?"

"Every day."

"Island maybe not be big enough for you and Richards."

"Maybe not," I agreed.

He climbed into his vehicle and drove slowly across the lawn, the remnants of the crowd cheering him for his earlier performance. Easy was the next to pack up and leave, ending the event.

Billie added the finishing touch to her sketch before she showed it to me. It showed a gang of kids, reduced to the size of Lilliputians, tackling a Gulliver-sized public works official. Below the drawing was a quote from Jim Morrison:

THEY GOT THE GUNS

BUT WE GOT THE NUMBERS

"Cool," I said.

Billie retreated a couple of steps, put her hands on her hips, and looked me in the eye.

"Brian, you can like make me so angry."

"What did I do now?"

"Stuff on your own. You saw all the people here supporting you. They would've helped build the playground. You know that."

"Time was a problem."

"We could have done it like an old-fashioned barn-raising."

"There was only a small window of opportunity that's now swung closed. It's Aubrey's project, and Rolly's doing work of a quality that may never be equaled. You have to appreciate that he has a passion for working with rare and beautiful lumber."

We walked toward the road, passing by Aubrey and Rolly who were throwing construction debris into the scoop of the front-end loader.

"Who paid for all this equipment?" Billie demanded.

"Valerie did."

"She didn't have any money."

"She had enough to get it started."

"How about if we hold a fundraiser?"

"Sounds good to me, but that's Aubrey's deal. My promise to Valerie was to get it built. Decisions that affect it will be up to Aubrey and the community."

"You can be such a stubborn cuss."

"Me?"

"I don't want you to take this the wrong way, and I still think you're not much of a team player, but I do think you've turned the corner on your life."

"Does that mean I'm now headed for the rag and bone shop?"

Billie relaxed her arms—set in motion to drive home her previous point—and gave me her cock-headed stare, her eyes widening until the expanse of green seemed larger than the lawn we stood on.

"It means that while I know you'll never be a pussy cat, you're not the alley cat you pretend. It also means that I think I'm like madly, passionately, lustfully in love with you."

"Because I'm fulfilling Valerie's wish?"

"Partly, and partly because of the style you're doing it in—though I've always liked your style. Also, because I saw you helping the children earlier." Then she stuck her fingers inside the waistband of my shorts and pulled me close to her. "But it's mostly because you make me wet whenever I see you or think about you."

"Maybe it's the humidity."

She removed her hand from my shorts and placed it on her hip. "That's what I used to think."

"If today's revelations are so mind-boggling, I don't even want to know what you thought of me yesterday."

"You're right. You don't want to know."

Of course, her response only piqued my curiosity, but I refrained from asking. When we reached the road, her vehicle was the only one still parked. Everyone else had moved on to recap the recent diversion or to seek another. We confirmed our dinner date at the Congo Club, and Billie climbed into her jeep. The cloud of oily smoke from her exhaust chased her around the bay.

Aubrey and Rolly were still cleaning up the site when I returned to have a few words with them. I suggested we forget the slide and just build the two benches. Rolly figured that he could get everything built by Monday. I left the decision to him.

Aubrey and Rolly looked past me and chuckled. I turned to see Pony Mon astride a donkey—no saddle or bridle—his arms wrapped around the animal's neck. Pony Mon always used to gallop, but now he trotted. He was a thirty-mile-per-hour guy on a five-mile-per-hour ride. To become a knight-errant again and rescue damsels, Pony Mon needed horsepower, but since the death of Bongo Natty, the horse became extinct on St. Judas.

He waved. "Captain Brian, mon, how does you like my new ride?"

I gave him a smile and thumbs-up. "Looking good."

He trotted off in the direction of the Congo Club, almost trampling Elroy who shuffled along gingerly, head down, as if he walked on a field of loose marbles. Elroy stopped to take a sip from the soda he carried and watched Pony Mon ride away.

I had another question for Elroy and an extra pack of cigarettes in my pocket, so I said goodbye to Aubrey and Rolly and walked across the field. Elroy jerked his head to greet me, and I dug out the fresh pack and handed it over. He accepted it with a head bob, set his Ting—the Caribbean's answer to 7-Up—on the ground, and tore off the cellophane. He pulled a cigarette out of the pack, stuck it in his mouth, and I lit it.

Figuring I'd get only one question answered, I went straight to the heart of the matter. "Elroy, who killed Leif?"

Elroy took a drag off the cigarette and pursed his lips to exhale the smoke through his nostrils like a dragon low on fuel. He jerked his head to look me in the eye.

"He already dead when Madison take his money and put he in cistern."

Damn! The perfect witness—my own Baker Street irregular—had been tardy for his most important assignment. Even for a whole pack of cigarettes and self-acknowledgment of his failure, Elroy allowed no follow-up question. He picked up his soda and trudged toward the road on bare feet, soda bottle dangling from his fingers, cigarette dangling from his mouth.

As unsatisfying as the answer was, what I once considered the biggest obstacle to the investigation had now been overcome. The body in the cistern was no longer a mystery, simply a curiosity. Unfortunately, the problem's explanation moved me no closer to a solution to Leif's murder. Nor did it make me especially confident that Billie and I would find a solution that perfectly satisfied us.

What the hell was going on in Madison's head?

Stealing from the dead made some sense—the corpse had no use for cash. But dumping Leif's body in the cistern made none. No matter how many times I walked around the problem, I couldn't find an angle where I could glimpse an explanation. Of course, I could ask Madison, but lately, the simple act of comprehension befuddled him. His brain seemed to operate only on a binary system: rum—no rum.

With the scoop of his front-end loader filled with construction debris, Aubrey pulled onto the road. Rolly and his helpers loaded the generator and power tools into their pickup and drove off in the opposite direction. I needed a beer and figured I'd stop at the Congo Club on the way to my dinghy.

I felt good about the playground. Before I waved goodbye to the dozen-or-so kids and headed out, I communicated to Valerie that feeling. I don't have any special connection to the cosmos, but I can easily visualize a purple mountain rising out of a turquoise sea, lapping onto a lavender-sand beach.

When I reached the road, a medium-sized flatbed truck braked alongside me.

A sleek Continental—wearing a businessman's haircut—hollered from the passenger seat, "You Captain Brian?"

I nodded.

"A blond girl at Easys said I might find you here. I'm Schmitty— Mike Schmidt—and I'm building a house on the north shore. I'm looking for some mahogany—kitchen cabinets, interior trim. I hear you're the man."

"Owner of the lumberyard send you looking for me?" I asked.

"Said he couldn't make a deal with you."

I hopped onto the back of the beat-up truck and directed the dour Rasta behind the wheel to turn the vehicle around and guided him to Rolly's place, a mile past Easys.

I knocked on Rolly's door and called to let him know we were looking at the mahogany. He joined us. Rolly and I conferred about the amount of lumber I owed him for his services, while the two men looked it over and determined how much of it they needed for their project. They decided they'd take half, and the Continental offered me ten grand. We shook hands. And he pulled out his checkbook.

"Can I take it with me?" he asked.

"No problem."

"Personal check okay?"

I nodded.

"Nobody takes checks here," he said, acting surprised.

"It's changing, and there's really little risk. One thing—if you can afford a lot on the north shore, I'm sure you're good for it. The other thing—it's illegal to write a bad check in the V.I. I go to the bank and there's not enough money in the account, I go to the police station. They call you or visit you, and they give you a half-hour to bring them the cash. You don't show. They throw you in jail."

"Let's say, this check bounces, I refuse to make good on it, and I get thrown in jail—we're talking hypothetically here—how do you get your money?"

I liked the guy, and I liked the manner in which he framed his question. He seemed like a man not afraid to step on toes, but smart enough not to try to crush them underfoot. He was someone I could do business with, especially since he was the one putting me back in business. In the half-hour I'd known him, he hadn't uttered a single racial epithet, unlike Outback, who could keep his less enlightened thoughts to himself for no longer than five minutes.

"I could hire a lawyer—just like in the States—but I mistrust lawyers, so while you're in jail, I borrow my friend's front-end loader and just push your house down the hillside."

"I believe you would."

"I don't get my money. You don't get your house. See how it works? In many ways, the V.I. is a tough place to do business, but for simple financial transactions, I've never been anywhere that's fairer."

"It simplifies dealing with deadbeats."

"Moving on from the hypothetical, if you need more lumber— South American hardwoods, particularly—or ceramic tile, I can beat anyone's price."

"We're building with concrete, and we're thinking about tiling the floors. If we go ahead, I'll give you a call."

I gave him my business card—with Easy's phone number—and we shook hands. The four of us loaded up the truck with lumber, and I hitched a ride back to the intersection. Heading out on foot for the dinghy dock, I wished I'd learned to whistle—there's no better feeling on earth than to have serious money in your pocket, money you haven't already spent.

My feeling of well-being lasted about a hundred yards, until the Shirt caught up with me. He pulled up in his jeep from behind me on the wrong side of the road, nudging me with his bumper, nearly knocking my legs out from underneath me and then laughing at my alarm. He climbed out and dropped the tobacco pouch on the hood.

"What's this? I found it in my jeep this morning."

"Whoa!" I took a step back. "You must have pissed off someone big time."

"It's what I do for a living."

"I'd think about getting into a different line of work."

"You'd like that." He paused. "What's this about?"

"Looks like mumbo jumbo to me."

"Mumbo jumbo?"

"Obeah, man." I picked up the pouch, loosened the string, and dumped the contents on the hood. "Your life insurance paid up?"

"You think I believe this silly shit?"

I separated the contents of the pouch with my finger.

"Let's see. For starters, this is serious."

He stepped closer. "How can you tell?"

"Donkey shit. That immediately puts it into category five."

"Category five?"

"Same as hurricanes. The most serious category."

"What else?"

"As you can see, everything's covered with cocaine. Cocaine is going to kill you. Not ingesting it. The pursuit of it." I pointed to the juju I'd carved. "This is you."

"How can you be sure?"

"The button." I laid the juju on its back and set the black button on it. "You have the only shirt with a collar in Flamingo Bay."

"What else?" he asked, boredom giving way to curiosity.

"Well, this person obviously wants you dead. The bay leaf and string suggest hanging as one possible method of meeting your maker. The shell casing suggests another method. The nail could be a knife, or it could be a nail—crucifixion. The seashell suggests drowning."

"What's the stone for?"

"You notice it isn't just any stone. It's a white one. It signifies a head-stone, and the few blades of grass represent a cemetery."

"That's all?"

"That's it."

"What do I do?"

"Well, you can do nothing and learn how powerful the magic is."

"Or?"

"You can find a practitioner and pay him—I think the going rate is five hundred dollars—and he can flip the whole thing around on the person who's working against you, your enemy. Your fate will become his fate."

The set of his jaw convinced me that he listened to my words. Then I saw my face reflected in the Shirt's Ray-Bans and studied for several seconds the image of the man who could become the object of a real obeah man's magic if the Shirt decided to get professional help.

The Shirt asked, "What if my enemy hires someone?"

"That's really the problem. These things can escalate. Remember the Hatfields and McCoys? You're like me. You don't seem the sort of guy who believes any of this shit. Of course, you *can* disarm it. Just like a bomb. Soak it in seawater for five minutes every evening at sunset—no less, no more. It'll take a while, but as soon as the shit dissolves, it's disarmed."

"I don't have to sacrifice a virgin?"

"You could. I mean sacrificial virgins cure almost everything."

I looked up and saw Pony Mon heading toward us on foot. He no longer had a spring in his step. He limped. A jagged line of dried blood stained his cheek.

"Captain Brian, mon."

"Pony Mon, you okay?"

"Just when I think that animal like me enough to come home with me, he dump me overboard."

I motioned him to join the Shirt and me.

"Someone left this in my friend's jeep. I explained how serious it is, that someone wants him dead. I told him he could disarm it by soak-ing it in saltwater for five minutes every evening at sunset until the shit dissolves."

"That would work, but to be safe, then he must burn it on the night of a full moon, and blow the ash at the sky."

"That's right, I forgot that part."

"You're in this together."

"Not a chance, " I said. "Pony Mon, how much do you have to pay the man to fix it?"

"Five hundred dollars," he answered, before he turned to walk away.

The Shirt carefully returned each of the items to the pouch before he stuffed it in his pocket.

"Ready to deal?" he asked.

"Ready."

"Fifty thou' for Diver Vaughn's cocaine?"

"It was fifty until I learned you lied to me about the shotgun. Now it's sixty. Sixty and Leif's murderer."

"That wasn't the deal," he said.

"You mean that wasn't your offer. We're making the deal right now."

"I don't know who killed Leif," he said.

"And I don't know where Vaughn's cocaine is. Ta, ta."

I started walking, and the Shirt paced me in his jeep, driving half off the road in the wrong lane, protesting his ignorance. This went on for another hundred yards until I stopped.

"Look at it this way. The fifty grand belongs to Vaughn—it's his cocaine. What we're negotiating now is my incentive to help you. So far, I have none. Also, you've wasted a lot of my time, and I happen to concur with Benjamin Franklin that time is money."

I lit a cigarette, while the Shirt fumbled for a response that didn't have to do with measuring his eternal five o'clock shadow. When he wasn't forthcoming, I continued to walk. In his attempt to keep up with me, he released the clutch too quickly and killed the engine. Then he flooded it. I listened to the starter motor's continual drone until I broke through the sound barrier. One last glance revealed the Shirt still behind the wheel of his stationary vehicle.

It felt good to finally leave somebody in my dust.

17

BILLIE MET ME AT THE DINGHY DOCK at dusk. She wore an ankle-length pink sundress cut low enough that her breasts were accented as much as the rare coin that hung from her neck on a gold chain. Her damp hair and impish smile lent her a just-laid look. I caught a faint scent of bay rum on her skin and a strong odor of alcohol on her breath.

"Felicitations upon your effulgence," I said.

She smiled and clumsily tied off the painter, and I climbed out of my dinghy.

"Still playing dress-up?"

"I've never worn jewelry, and nothing this valuable," she said, slightly slurring her words. "My mother refused to let me pierce my ears. I was angry about it for a long time. All my friends had theirs pierced. Then it became one of the things that like separated me from them. When I left home, I thought about piercing my ears and doing the cosmetics bit—lipstick was another thing that was forbidden—but I was happy with who I was. Life's for living, not primping."

"You're drunk."

"I know," she giggled. "The things I do to promote our success."

"Specifically?"

"I shared a bottle of rum with Madison at Easys. By the way, what's the deal with Easy? He was sure unfriendly today. And yesterday, come to think of it."

"You've noticed that, too."

Billie asked, "Is it just us, or is it everybody?"

"I think it's just us. And it's all your fault."

"What did I do?"

"Led him to believe we're sleeping together."

"Aren't we?"

"Depends on how you define *sleep*."

"You're saying it's because I'm with you and not with him?"

"Just now, the thought crosses my mind."

"Ho-hum."

"So tell me about your chat with Madison. I'd think that rum would be just the thing to shut him up."

"Depends on what you want to talk about," Billie said.

"What *did* you talk about?"

"The body in the cistern."

"And?"

"Madison told me that he found Leif's body lying next to the cistern, and he dumped it into the water."

"After he took Leif's money?"

She asked, "How did you know?"

"A lucky guess."

"By the time we got to that part of the story, Madison was pretty far gone."

"Did he say why he dumped Leif's body into the cistern?"

"I asked him several times, but we never quite connected on that point. It was like I asked him the color of the trade wind."

"And what color is it?"

"Depends on the day and the time of day and lots of other things. Today at dusk, it was the color of the inside of a conch shell."

"Is that why you're wearing a pink dress?" I asked.

"And you claim you're not a detective."

"Getting back to Madison."

"When I pressed him, Madison rambled about the local practice of dumping the carcasses of dead animals into the sea—I confess that by the time we got that far, I'd over-medicated him. He was passed out when I left."

"He didn't give you a clue what was going on in his head?"

"I think that to him Leif's body was just another animal carcass," Billie said. "And I gathered that the one thing the sea and cistern have in common is water."

"You're saying that Madison didn't seem able to sort out either the distinction between a cistern and the sea or the distinction between human and animal remains."

"Exactly."

"I suppose they're tough distinctions when you're a big shot in the islands, mon."

"Have you learned anything new?" Billie asked.

"I learned that Leif was killed by a blow to the head, no shotgun. Maybe he was hit in the head, or maybe he fell and hit his head. Sounds to me like that's about as definitive an answer we'll get from the police."

"So the Shirt lied to you."

Billie put her arm around me, hooking her thumb into an empty belt loop on my shorts. I held onto her shoulder. We walked through the sand listening to Cream, with Jack Bruce on vocals, weave a story about brave Ulysees, though only snatches of the song—"Tiny purple fishes run laughing through your fingers ..."—escaped the din created by drinkers and diners at the Congo Club.

"Let's have a drink before finding a table and ordering dinner," I said. "We don't want Dan to have to look too hard to spot his doubloon."

Billie nodded. "Dinner should be good. Freddie's on tonight. I heard he's serving pot roast."

Pirate Dan developed an interesting arrangement to provide food to his customers. The cooks were independent contractors—culinary conquistadors. Each had his or her own shelf in one of the refrigerators and another in one of the freezers and was responsible for ordering his or her own groceries from a supplier on St. Thomas that delivered twice a week. Each paid Dan a fee to use the kitchen. The food was good and the price fair; it seemed to work for everybody. The Congo Club hadn't yet obtained its first Michelin star, but it boasted running water, a kitchen, and eating utensils. Easy, who served only hot dogs and hamburgers on paper plates, offered grease, but he hadn't yet introduced the spoon to his establishment.

I followed Billie up the few steps to the deck. Before she dropped her hand from the rail, the music died and she arrived to a standing ovation. The chorus that regularly piped her aboard with its tongue-clicking rendition of *The Twilight Zone* theme joined in the applause, simultaneously clicking and clapping. Billie grabbed at her dress and performed a small curtsy. I wasn't sure the acclaim was because we were this week's celebrity couple—love *is* a lot like musical chairs in Flamingo Bay—or if it was acknowledgment of Billie's outfit.

Pirate Dan stood behind the bar, and Billie headed straight for the one empty stool. Dan, who didn't acknowledge me but enthusiastically greeted Billie with his eyes, wore a doubloon on what could've been the same old rawhide thong. Billie ordered a dry martini straight up, and I ordered a beer. Dan saw the coin Billie wore but didn't react, at least not until he slammed my beer on the bar and excused himself.

I hadn't a clue what he was up to. You could never tell with Dan. Some years ago, Walter Cronkite showed up at the Congo Club for the Thanksgiving Regatta. I first learned of Cronkite's love for sailing when I heard a quip from his wife to the effect that Erroll Flynn died aboard a seventy-foot yacht in the company of a seventeen-year-old girl and that Walter entertained a similar dream. Unfortunately, for Walter—she made it perfectly clear—he was destined to die on a seventeen-footer with a seventy-year-old.

The first time Cronkite came in, Wendy, who tended bar in those days, instantly recognized him. The party wanted piña coladas, so she made piña coladas. It was the Pirate's day off, and everything was cool. The next day the same party came in and ordered piña coladas again. The Pirate, who hated making frozen drinks, tended bar. He told Cronkite his blender was broken. Cronkite replied that it had worked the day before. Dan muttered to himself and made a big production of getting the blender assembled and plugged in.

Dan made the drinks, all the while cursing the men who drank scotch and bourbon in the States and came down to the Caribbean and ordered prissy drinks. When the Cronkite party attempted to leave, Dan growled at them to sit down, telling Cronkite that he'd listened to his ass for twenty fucking years so Cronkite could listen to him for twenty fucking minutes.

When he finished his drink, Cronkite looked at his watch and told Dan his time was up, that he only got nineteen minutes because Cronkite anchored the news only nineteen years. Then, in a complete turnabout, the Pirate behaved like he and Cronkite were old friends, laughing, joking, and refusing payment for the drinks.

Helga came by and head-butted me in the thigh. I set my beer on the bar and petted her.

"Mary thinks Helga likes you more than she likes her," Billie said.

"A dog knows a good man when it sees one."

Even as the words escaped my lips, I feared I'd never be the man Billie wanted me to be. Shit, I knew I'd never be the man *I* wanted to be. I stopped petting Helga, and she went to work on my toes with her tongue.

Dan, apparently in a good mood, returned with a stemmed cocktail glass. No baseball bat. Everyone else drank from plastic cups. Billie oozed star power, and Dan respected her as a drinker. A few months ago, she drank him under the table. The bet was a hundred dollars, the odds, five to one. I fronted Billie the ante, and we split the five hundred.

When Dan polished the glass to his satisfaction, he asked Billie, "How dry?"

"Kalahari dry."

Dan poured dry vermouth into a stainless steel cocktail shaker, swirled it around, and emptied it into the sink. He next filled the shaker with ice before pouring a liberal amount of gin over the ice.

"Shaken or stirred?"

"Shake, rattle, and roll."

Dan shook the cocktail, covered the shaker with a strainer, and poured Billie's drink into the stemmed glass.

"Olive?" he asked.

She nodded, and he opened a jar, stabbed an olive with a toothpick, and dropped it into the glass.

Losing the battle for control of her yellow hair to the strong breeze, Billie pushed it from her face with her fingers, turned into the wind, grasped the glass's stem, and sipped.

"Excellent!" she said.

Several patrons, monitoring the drink's creation, applauded Billie's pronouncement. Billie nodded her appreciation, and she and I smoked cigarettes and chatted with each other, while Dan caught up with the backlog of drink orders. But even after he caught up, Dan kept his distance—so much for my intent to shake him.

I dug Billie's copy of *The Stranger* from my pocket and handed it to her.

"Our next book club selection?" she asked, paging through it.

I nodded.

"Why did you pick it?"

"For a lot of reasons. Camus did win the Nobel Prize for literature. Also, it has one of my three favorite opening lines: 'Mother died today. Or maybe yesterday; I can't be sure.'"

"And the other two'"

"'Call me Ishmael.'"

"*Moby Dick.*"

"'It was a bright cold day in April, and the clocks were striking thirteen.'"

Billie thought for a minute then shook her head. "You've stumped me."

"George Orwell ring a bell?"

"*Animal Farm?*"

"Close. *1984.*"

"Maybe we should recruit another member for our book club."

"Any prospects?" I asked.

"Mary would sign on if we limited the selections to New Age stuff."

"No thanks."

Billie downed the last of her martini and ate the olive. Then she cocked her head and did her hand-alongside-the-mouth bit—the prelude to a whispering aside, always delivered with wide eyes and over-the-top amplitude. "Brian, I need wood."

"Wood?"

"You know, lumber."

"Building an ark?"

"Sort of. You haven't sold the mahogany yet?"

"I sold half of it a couple hours ago, but there's still a lot left."

"Can I have some?"

"Why not. Talk to Rolly. It's stored at his place."

She kissed my cheek. "Thank you."

When a table opened up, we left the bar and ordered dinner. Billie, who confessed that martinis tasted a lot like pine trees and that she ordered one only to see how Dan would handle it, asked the waitress for a beer. I asked Billie if when her ark was finished we'd be running off down island together on the new boat.

"Why do you like keep pushing me to leave Flamingo Bay?"

"You can't feel it?"

"Feel what?"

"The tumors," I said, explaining about the cancer that I suspected was growing just beneath the surface of the island.

"I've seen something of the world. I've seen real disease. I'm not sure that what you're describing is even malignant."

She actually understood what I was talking about. That sort of connection couldn't be bought with pockets full of cash. I figured Billie's yellow hair could turn white, her clear green eyes could cloud over, her supple limbs could wither and knot, but—like Valerie—she'd just reserved a place in my heart and head forever, even if she walked away from me tomorrow.

"I think you have to like consider two important things," she continued.

"They are?"

"I'm not going anywhere, and our relationship can succeed in this place at this time for who we presently are. Change any of those pieces and the composition may no longer work. Think of the *Mona Lisa* painted against the backdrop of the Duomo. It would still be the *Mona Lisa*, but it wouldn't be the same *Mona Lisa*."

"Good point," I countered. "But a contrary view is you'd get the best of both Brunelleschi and Leonardo."

"Gilding the lily and diminishing the value of each."

"Or to be accurate:

To gild refined gold, to paint the lily,
To throw a perfume on the violet,
To smooth the ice, or add another hue
Unto the rainbow, or with tapered light
To seek the beauteous eye of heaven to garnish,
To garland Billie round in a sundress
Is wasteful and ridiculous excess."

"Brian, you always surprise me."

"I have to surprise someone. I no longer surprise myself."

Billie glanced over my shoulder and exclaimed, "Oh-my-god!"

I turned to see the donkeys—Ali Baba, Scheherazade, and Little Frank—standing at the rail, peering into the restaurant.

"They look hungry, don't you think?"

"Billie, they're fat and sassy."

"You're wrong. Only Scheherazade looks fat, and that's because she's preggers. She needs to eat for two. Look at Little Frank. He's not getting enough nourishment. Neither is Ali Baba."

Billie jumped up and headed toward the kitchen. She returned a minute later breaking a head of iceberg lettuce into sections. She made her way to the railing and offered the first section to Little Frank.

"Ali Baba," she said sternly, "Little Frank is first today. You wait your turn."

Ali Baba backed off, and Billie fed the donkeys in turn. While the donkeys munched on the lettuce, Billie petted and chattered at them.

Except for Helga, curled up and dozing at my feet, I had no real connection to animals. I lived my life and allowed them to live their lives. With Billie, it was different. She had to get involved with every living thing. At first, I thought she was a little goofy. Later, I figured I was the goofy one. Part of it was me, and part of it was my gender.

On the gridiron of life, men generally operate between the thirty-yard lines, while women use the entire field. Billie included the sidelines, stadium, and parking lot in her area of operation. It exhausted me to even think about a domain of such gigantic proportion. Still, she managed it effortlessly, and she was the richer for it, and I was the richer for knowing her.

Half the people in the joint watched Billie feed the donkeys. When I realized the other half watched me, I wiped the look of love from my face and took a swig from my beer. After she sent the donkeys away with the admonition to behave themselves, Billie returned to the table.

"What are you up to tomorrow?" she asked.

"Nothing to write home about."

"When *was* the last time you wrote home?"

"When I was about your age."

"Brian, I remember your line about families being unhappy in their own way, but I think you're awfully mean-spirited not keeping in contact. It's like you're half aesthete and half Neanderthal."

"You're wrong on both counts. I suspect that Neanderthals enjoyed a rich family life and were probably superior to me in any measurement you could devise. As far as being an aesthete, you have to've developed along the way a critical eye. I haven't, and I never will. The bottom line—I'm much farther down the food chain than you'd like to believe, though I may have a more vivid fantasy life than anyone else you know."

"All I'm trying to communicate is my birthday's tomorrow, and I'd like to celebrate it with you."

"What do you have in mind?" I asked, studying the tan line she revealed on each of her lips.

"I'm thinking of snorkeling at Norman Island, lunch at the *William Thornton*—I'm hungry for a chicken roti—then a naked weekend at a swanky hotel over on St. Thomas."

"You're so indecisive. The Easy Rider Rally?"

"We could go to St. Thomas Saturday evening after the rally." She cocked her head. "If you don't know what you want, you won't enjoy it nearly as much when you get it." She adjusted the skinny straps on her dress. "Are my areolae exposed?"

"You still have a long way to go—about a thirty-second of an inch."

"Good. Modesty is the best policy, I always say."

The only suitable response was to laugh. Billie joined me. Before we finished, the waitress interrupted us with our dinners—pot roast drowning in gravy, boiled potatoes and carrots. The food heaped on the plates would keep an impoverished family going for a week.

"I learned something interesting today," Billie said, her mouth still full. "Mmm, this is good." She swallowed. "Mary thinks that Diver Vaughn and Alice are getting married."

"Really?"

"What's wrong?"

"I'm just hoping that Vaughn's not counting on supporting his new wife with the cocaine he has stashed."

"Why?"

"I'm thinking of selling it to the Shirt for fifty grand. I'm giving the money to Vaughn, but he might not be happy with the fire-sale price."

"But you don't know where it is."

"Don't I?"

"Oh-my-god! Where?"

"In a certain underwater cave at a certain cove."

"That's illuminating, but you're seriously thinking of telling the Shirt?"

"I'm considering it."

"Why?"

"One, because he's threatened to nail Vaughn, send him to Texas for trial, get him locked up for life. Two, because I'm sure as a quid pro quo, the Shirt can come up with some valuable information about Leif's murder, though this afternoon, he denied he knew anything. Three, because I'm getting sick over the amount of my time the Shirt's wasting, and I'm annoyed he's alienated me from a bunch of people who're convinced I'm a snitch. Also, a few grand—my fee—would give me a small financial cushion, put me back in business. I'm smart enough to know beautiful women have expectations that are significantly higher than those of their plain sisters."

"Leave me out of this. I don't want to sound immodest, but I've had opportunities to chase the dollars, whether it was from pirates, trust-funders, or middle-aged businessmen, even a certain man with a fondness for Hawaiian shirts."

"You're kidding."

Even as I spoke, I knew she wasn't kidding. The Shirt—no matter what he accomplished in Flamingo Bay—could find no greater success than seducing Billie.

"I told you he sleeps in the shirt I autographed for him. Well, he's offered to take me anywhere I want to go and all the money I care to spend."

"You're awfully picky."

I had a lot more to say on the subject, but I decided silence was best. Billie would always attract men. The question: Could I remain silent forever?

"I don't care for him, and I don't need money from a man. You must've figured out by now that I'm not hanging out with you because I think you'll like provide me with a luxurious life."

"No?"

"I'm hanging out with you because you're the best man in Flamingo Bay, the best man I know, and you know … I told you earlier."

"The humidity?"

"Exactly."

The waitress carried away our plates, still heaped high enough that if we hadn't put big dents in the food, she could serve our leftovers to another couple and they'd think they were getting full portions. She returned with another round of beers. Dan followed her and took a chair. He unrolled his T-shirt sleeve to get at his pack of cigarettes and lit one.

I broke the silence by telling Dan about the brouhaha at the playground and suggested that he'd picked a bad time to extend his deck. The Pirate figured one time was as good as another. I figured public works would have the project shut down in twenty-four hours. But Dan wasn't interested in discussing building projects.

He growled, "Argh! Billie, looks like you need to design new shirts for me."

"I thought you liked the ones you have."

"I do, but how can it be 'My Own Fucking Yacht Club' now that you're a member?"

Puzzlement swept across Billie's face like a shadow. It passed, and she smiled.

"Oh-my-god! I didn't know that becoming a member of the Doubloon Society qualified me to join your yacht club. I don't even have a boat." She fingered the coin. "Brian gave this to me. I thought it was like a reward for my performance last night. I rocked the boat." She cocked her head. "Ask him."

Some people are naturally equipped with the ability to put others at ease. Some can boil another's blood with a glance. Billie rendered the loquacious speechless. Dan hadn't a clue how to respond. Instead, he looked at me.

"Been diving for sunken treasure?" he asked.

"Actually, I have."

"I didn't think you found it lying on the road."

"I didn't," I answered. "I found it in Doctor's cistern."

"It's yours?" Billie asked Dan.

Dan nodded, and Billie worked to unclasp the chain from behind her neck.

"Keep it. It looks better on you. It'll help you remember me when your present lover's no longer able to get it up." Billie covered her giggle with the back of her hand, and the Pirate lost his gruff voice and spoke softly. Not that he needed to. The music was loud enough to keep every conversation private. "Just for the record, I didn't lose the doubloon. It was stolen off me by a woman we all know, who shall remain nameless—at least until I have an opportunity to talk to her."

"That would be Sarah," I said after the Pirate limped back behind the bar.

"No!"

"There are only a few men here who can afford to support her habit. Zeke—at my request—won't sell to her, and Vaughn cut her off. That left the Pirate the most likely candidate until the Shirt showed up."

"Now what?" she asked.

"My speculation is the Shirt's into it up to his eyeballs, but he didn't do the deed. My problem is I don't have a mind that works obliquely."

"What's that supposed to mean?"

"Ever hear the one about the little kid who goes to the brothel?"

"I don't think so."

"The madam asks him what he wants, and he says he wants to catch syphilis. She asks him why, and he says he wants to give it to his sister. The madam, still not grasping the situation, continues to question him. The kid gradually unwraps his scenario. His sister will give the disease to his father, who will give it to his mother, who will give it to the milkman. The kid admits that the milkman is the one he's really after—the milkman stepped on his pet frog."

"The point?"

"Incest is fine, as long as you keep it the family."

Billie frowned. "The real point?"

"I view murders as train wrecks, not the collision of bumper cars."

"You're saying that the collisions have to be full-speed. They don't. And they don't have to be on tracks."

"Casey Jones might disagree with you."

"He wasn't much of a detective."

I wasn't much of a detective either, but for the first time since embarking on this investigation, I seriously considered the possibility that Leif wasn't killed for being a thief. Perhaps his vocation had nothing to do with his death. Perhaps he was killed because he washed up in Flamingo Bay. Perhaps he'd inadvertently picked the wrong port in a stormy life.

"What now?" Billie asked.

"I suppose your next move is to interview Sarah and learn what she has to say about the doubloon. No way she'll talk to me. Which reminds me, I need a lift to Sarah's to get my truck."

"I can handle Sarah. What are you going to do?"

"Wait for an epiphany."

"Detection by epiphany?"

"Exactly. Otherwise I'll start working like the cops—stop people on the street and ask if they're guilty."

Billie dropped me at Sarah's. I took my truck and followed Billie back to the dinghy dock. She held the flashlight for me, while I cut the primary ignition wire under the dash and installed a toggle switch. Confident the truck would be there in the morning, we motored to *Island Trader* in my dinghy.

Billie didn't rock the boat—it weighed a hundred tons—but she did rock me, a world-class performance worthy of a varsity letter.

18

Billie and I awoke pretty pleased—with ourselves and with each other. We spent the early morning on *Island Trader* touching and talking. Still, I couldn't deny that we behaved awkwardly toward one another. Something bothered her. I supposed she wrestled with the same question I did: What do we do now? Because we needed to finish up the T-shirts for tomorrow's Easy Rider Rally, little time existed for either navel gazing or decision-making.

Billie reminded me she needed to deliver more pictures to the Green Parrot before we left for Norman Island. We left the sixty shirts—draped all over the boat—to dry, and I ferried her to *Sappho*. Seeing the name in gold script on the stern always gave me a chuckle. I couldn't understand why lesbians, generally, didn't know that Sappho killed herself over a man. On the other hand, I also couldn't understand why more women weren't lesbians.

We loaded my dinghy with her art and threw a blanket over it. Then we transferred the cargo to her jeep, using the blanket to pack it. While she was in town, Billie planned to stop at the bank to deposit the cash from her picture-selling adventure. I gave her my ten-grand check to deposit.

Once Billie's jeep was loaded and she set off for town, I figured I had time to kill, so I walked over to the playground to see how Rolly was coming along. He worked alone, cutting lumber for the benches. He turned off the table saw and shut down the gas generator when he spotted me.

"Good morning, Mister Rolly. Where's your crew? Out spending money?"

Because laborers needed to be paid at the end of each day, it was hell getting them back to work the following day. Yesterday they'd been given several days' wages—a windfall.

"I just be building benches. No slide. Public works find judge before senator does. Public works doesn't wait to return to St. Thomas. They call from Sugar Harbor. By time Almida return to office, deal already done. Almida say he sorry for screwing up. Aubrey call to say we be getting court order today to stop work."

"We're probably better off without a slide. I can see some kid getting hurt and lawyers making our lives miserable."

"You probably right."

"You've done a great job," I said. "Best playground in the Leeward Islands."

He nodded his thank you. "Billie come by earlier and say you tell her she can have mahogany she need. That right?"

"Give her whatever she wants of the pile that doesn't belong to you."

We watched Aubrey approach in his front-end loader. A single public works vehicle tailed him. Almida tailed the public works vehicle—another parade, but shorter than yesterday's.

When all the players climbed out of their vehicles, Aubrey—with assistance from Almida—staged the players so that I could get a photo of the historic occasion. With Aubrey's camera, I snapped a picture of the public works honcho handing the court order to Aubrey, the playground equipment visible in the background.

Aubrey told the public works honcho the project was complete and suggested he take a careful look at the site because Aubrey had his evidence—he held up his camera—and several witnesses that the project was completed before it was stopped.

The honcho pointed to Rolly. "What he be building?"

"A bench," Aubrey answered.

"Court order say no more building," the honcho responded.

Almida got into the act. "You doesn't need a building permit to build a bench."

"Go home," Aubrey said to the honcho. "You be trespassing."

The honcho wasn't eager to leave, and the conversation became heated, which meant I couldn't follow it. The gist of it: the honcho threatened to demolish the structures. Rolly quit work on his bench and suggested that if the honcho had any expectation of keeping his job with the Virgin Islands' government that he re-examine his stand. The honcho initially scoffed at the threat, seriously pissing off Almida when he suggested the senator and island administrator were only temporary obstacles to him and temporary allies to us. The honcho argued that next year's election could put both out of office. Rolly agreed with the man's reasoning. Then he fired a verbal salvo, and the honcho couldn't get off the site fast enough.

I said, "Let me in on the secret, Mister Rolly. It could help me in my business."

"I doesn't think so. It be *my* cousin that be that mon's boss."

"Good work," I said.

"Maybe, but I doesn't think cousin like me anymore than I like he."

Rolly had other business with the island administrator—business that wasn't mine—so I said goodbye. Before I left, Rolly pulled me aside to confirm for a second time that it was okay to give Billie the mahogany she needed. I asked him what the big deal was. He just shook his head.

I headed back to my boat, collected the Easy Rider Rally T-shirts, and packed them into two cardboard boxes. Then I set about assembling gear for our Norman Island excursion. I tossed a beer cooler and snorkeling gear for two into the dinghy. I thought for a minute or so about bringing along equipment for three and inviting the Shirt to participate, but to make the event memorable and worthwhile necessitated quickly creating something that could attract sharks. I had in mind a one-way ride.

All I could come up with was filling a plastic sunscreen-bottle with my own blood. It could prove to be effective if there were a man-eater in the vicinity, but I couldn't figure how to induce the Shirt to smear it on his limbs and dive into the sea—the color would be a dead giveaway. After wasting several minutes struggling with my quandary, I rescinded the untendered invitation. For future study, I filed away the question whether blood plasma or only whole blood attracts sharks. I finished loading the dinghy and motored ashore.

I carried the cooler to the Congo Club, ordered a beer from the bartender, and waited for Billie. I found myself studying the names carved into the mahogany bar. I stopped when I found CAPTAIN LUCKY. It reminded me that life is full of mysteries. It also reminded me that not all mysteries are solvable, though I felt Billie and I were getting close to the end of our investigation. I believed we'd solve every important riddle that surrounded Leif's death, but I couldn't be sure the last piece of the puzzle—the final moments of his life—would ever fall into place. Because the two suspects I liked for the crime both wore badges, I was pretty certain that nobody would be punished.

A few years ago, I'd watched Captain Lucky scratch his name into the mahogany countertop. His name stood out, not because of the size or the depth of the lettering but because he was left-handed and drunk at the time. It'd taken a few months, but I pretty much accepted I'd never again touch the hand that created the uneven letters.

Captain Lucky and his stateside buddies planned to pursue lobster and hang out on Anegada in the British Virgin Islands—the only atoll in the Caribbean that I'm aware of. Always a brutal trip, you beat into the wind the entire voyage. What made their cruise even more brutal was that they caught the season's first tropical storm. Still, they left Flamingo Bay in a sound boat that was well equipped and well provisioned—maybe too well provisioned. That was months ago, and they were never heard from again—no sign, either, of *Shamrock III*.

I looked up and my eye immediately caught Billie's poster, HAITIAN VACATION. What did happen to Mad Max? His boat ran aground in the middle of the night on Rhymer's Reef with forty illegal Haitians aboard, but no trace of Max. Max would never sail onto Rhymer's Reef, and he would never bring illegal Haitians to St. Judas. He knew they'd be rounded up within an hour, and he'd be thrown in jail.

A tourist couple came in and sat at the bar, taking seats two stools away. Too close. One glance told me that I'd met their sort several times before while running day-sails in Marathon. Sure enough, as soon as they ordered beers, they pronounced themselves world travelers and began to pepper the bartender with questions.

They suffered from what I termed Sojourner's Syndrome. The affliction infects only tourists, though it affects only their guide. During the short incubation period, the tourists, often dumber than dirt and as sensitive to their environment as an oil slick, attempt to pick your brain clean. And maybe they really believe they've picked it clean, because the next time you see them, they know a lot more than you. Weather, water, coral, fish, history, your personal history—they have it all figured out.

I tuned out the conversation, as the tourists raved to the bartender about the beaches and sugar mill ruins of St. Judas and a dozen other things, but I pricked up my ears when they announced that there were only two places in the world they could possibly live: New York and St. Judas. I found it an odd statement, but I listened to their chatter until I learned that they lived in Detroit.

No explanation could satisfy that riddle, so I picked up my beer and escaped before they attempted one. I planned to take a seat on the Congo Club's steps when I spotted Billie, in her jeep, and Pirate Dan, on foot, at the side of the road engaged in conversation. Billie looked more beautiful today than she ever had.

I waited a minute until it became apparent they exchanged more than greetings—Detective Billie prying information from the Pirate. Then I hiked down to the beach, lit a cigarette, and took a seat at the end of the dinghy dock.

As quickly as my mind carried me out of the present moment—where I was the center of the universe—to the place where the significance of my moment and my self were miniscule, my lightheartedness disappeared.

I couldn't help thinking that if I were the man Billie thought I was, I'd fire up *Island Trader*'s diesel and motor out of Flamingo Bay one last time—and I'd do it today. I tried to construct a voluptuous future for Billie and me. I crafted it with every bit of skill I could muster, but it was like attempting to square up a piece of lumber with hand tools—not my forte—it got no squarer, only smaller.

Despite her proclamation, Billie wasn't just a girl. But I was just a man, and arguably not the best man. I field-stripped my cigarette, but I didn't climb into my dinghy and motor to *Island Trader*.

Did I love her too much or too little?

I returned to the Congo Club, returned to where I again became lighthearted and the center of my universe.

Billie helped me pack the cooler with ice and beverages. A tiny gold cutlass—a new accessory—pierced Pirate Dan's left earlobe. I suspected that one day he'd pluck out an eye just so he could wear a patch over the empty socket.

Billie slipped into her backpack. After grabbing the two loaves of bread she'd purchased at the bakery in Sugar Harbor, she followed me out of the joint. We trudged together through the sand. To get my attention she bumped me with her hip.

"Because it's my birthday, I think you should let me skipper the dinghy."

"Be my guest."

"By the way," Billie said, "Pirate Dan told me he talked to Sarah, and Sarah admitted she stole his doubloon. She said she like gave it to Leif to buy cocaine—the day he was killed—but he never delivered. If that's true, it means the coin simply fell out of Leif's pocket after he was in the cistern."

"It works for me. Here's where we are, and correct me if I'm wrong. I think you were right when you concluded that Jason set up Vaughn to send him to jail, so Jason could rip him off. You were right, also, that Leif stole Vaughn's cocaine and cash. Because Leif made a career of stealing, I assumed that his thievery was what got him killed. In a way it was, but not in the manner I thought."

"Yeah?"

"Stealing Vaughn's cocaine was really incidental to Leif's death, a red herring—"

"Is there such a thing?" Billie asked.

"Get a canvas and some red paint, and there will be such a thing."

"Piscatorially, I mean."

"That's a question for some ologist I can't remember the prefix to—"

"Ichthyologist."

"I'm suitably impressed," I said.

"I'm a lot smarter than you think."

"I don't think you could be. I think you're brilliant—except for your taste in men."

Billie cocked her head and gave me the stare.

"I'm not complaining."

"You better not be," she said.

I set the cooler on the dock, grabbed my dinghy's painter, and pulled it up to the dock. Billie climbed aboard and organized the snorkeling gear to make room for the cooler.

"Anyway. How being a thief worked against Leif was that after he robbed the bank in California, ostensibly taping an independent film, he fled to Brazil. Flush with success, he brazenly mailed a copy of the robbery tape to the FBI. Because the U.S. has no extradition treaty with Brazil, the Feds sent a man there posing as a bounty hunter to kidnap Leif and bring him back to stand trial."

"Leif told me that story," Billie said. "He blamed his capture on some guy named Meyer Lansky."

"Billie, you *are* brilliant. You may have just provided the key to the solution."

"Apparently not brilliant enough to know what you're talking about."

"You've never heard of Meyer Lansky?"

"No," she said, grabbing the cooler I handed her.

"He was born Maier Suchowljansky, in Russia around the turn of the century. Parents settled in New York when he was a boy. A kingpin of organized crime, he hung out with guys like Lucky Luciano and Bugsy Siegel. Allegedly, he had Siegel killed for cooking the books at the Flamingo in Vegas."

"So? And how do you know so much about gangsters?"

"I've always been fascinated with Americans' love affair with gangsters. I think it's because of the old newsreels. You have Al Capone, or someone of his ilk, walking out of a courthouse to a cheering mob of civilians. I suppose it's human nature to admire someone who has enough guts to pull off successfully something that you yourself don't have enough guts to tackle, especially if it's illegal, especially if it's sordid, especially if serious money is involved."

"I get the picture."

"Okay. Now what if Leif really was abducted by a man named Meyer? What if the man's real name was Meyer Lofgrin? What if surnames didn't matter to Leif, any more than they matter to anyone in Flamingo Bay? What if the Shirt abducted Leif? Then they meet up again years later. I suspect Leif would be looking to exact some measure of revenge for his vacation to Kansas —"

"Huh?"

"Leavenworth. Prison."

I'd seen the prison once as a child, but I couldn't visualize it as it was. My memory was colored by remarks made by the man who was married to my mother. I couldn't clearly remember his words, either,

but they were more barbed than the usual bogeyman warnings of
childhood, and my remembrance of the prison was cluttered with perceived images of the Black Hole of Calcutta, various leper colonies, and Andersonville.

"I didn't know the prison was in Kansas."

Billie started the Yamaha.

"The Shirt had an agenda and a timetable — my best guess is the Shirt determined to quit his day job when he heard rumors of Diver Vaughn's big catch. Not fear of Leif exacting revenge, but fear of Leif messing up his agenda may have induced the Shirt to pull the same trick on Leif that Jason pulled on Vaughn — get him locked up and out of the way. In all fairness to the Shirt, he could've planted a kilo of cocaine on Leif. A kilo would get Leif locked up for life. But I don't think the Shirt felt any animosity toward Leif. He just wanted him out of the way. All he needed was Leif to be arrested for a minor offense. The Shirt has no jurisdiction to lock up anyone here for a minor offense, but Officer Richards does."

"Oh-my-god!" Billie shut down the Yamaha. "You're saying the Shirt bribed Richards to arrest Leif, and Richards killed Leif instead?"

"That's the general thrust of my theory, but I don't think we'll ever know exactly what happened after Richards attempted to arrest Leif. I don't think Richards intended to kill Leif, either. He obviously got him handcuffed. Then what? I suspect that something went terribly wrong."

"Maybe Richards didn't intend to kill Leif, but it wouldn't have happened if those two assholes hadn't fucked with him."

"True."

"So how are we going to bring Richards to justice?" Billie asked.

"'Vengeance is mine, sayeth the Lord' or something like that."

"That doesn't seem fair," Billie frowned. "Anyway, I'm talking about justice, not revenge."

"Starting out, I said that finding his killer likely wouldn't make me feel any better. It doesn't, though I didn't expect our investigation would become merely an intellectual exercise. I don't think justice is an option. The police aren't going to arrest Richards. They might consider arresting the Shirt, but he has connections, and he'll walk."

"What are we going to do?" Billie asked.

"We still have to prove the theory or come up with a better one."

"How do we do that?"

"Get the Shirt to talk."

"Brian, he's not going to incriminate himself."

"He will, if he wants Vaughn's cocaine."

"I'm not so sure."

"Relax," I said. "Let's go have fun."

I untied the painter, and when Billie fired up the Yamaha, I climbed aboard. Because my dinghy has no seats, we sat on the inflated tube— Billie on the starboard side in the stern and I on the port side toward the bow. We buzzed into the harbor. The intensely blue sea, saturated with color like an immense vat of dye, shimmered in the sunlight. I dragged my left hand in it. When I pulled it out, it surprised me to learn my skin hadn't turned blue.

Billie steered close to *Argo*, Jason's boat. Once in tip-top shape, the Cheoy Lee had been neglected a bit lately. Still, she was the prettiest boat in the harbor. With her white hull, teak deck, and mahogany trim, *Argo* looked like a sailboat. She looked like a boat that'd seen her share of the seven seas. We motored by the moored boats and left *Island Trader* in our wake. I watched Billie scan Rhymer's Reef. She was look- ing for a sign of *Mango Mama*, Mad Max's boat, but sea and scavengers had picked the reef clean.

Viewed from the sea, Flamingo Bay looked different. There didn't appear to be any beaches. Fat green hills rose straight up from the blue water. Of course, what you see depends upon where you are and how fast you're moving relative to the object you're viewing. Mr. Ein- stein's formulation of relativity made his career and changed the phys- ical world. As an anachronism, I've been happy just to understand Newtonian physics and Galileo's less elegant and less comprehensive theory of relativity. I'm not a flat-earther, but, except for terrestrial navigation, I have trouble with the concept that the shortest distance between two points is a curved line—I can't do that math.

"Hold on," Billie said.

I grabbed the painter for balance, and she twisted the throttle to its stop. The prop dug in and propelled us forward like a catapult. We bounced and skimmed over the waves.

Above the engine's roar, she shouted, "How's that?"

I gave her the thumbs up.

Billie enjoyed the exhilaration, though the ride was rough enough that it forced her to brace her breasts with her right forearm. We continued our bounce-and-skim progress until Billie's discomfort defeated her exuberance. She cut way back on the throttle, and we came almost to a stop. Then the wake caught up with us and gave the dinghy a big push, dropping us into a trough.

"We're going to make a detour," Billie said. "But first, I have a big question."

"Fire away."

"How can you trust the Shirt? He already lied to you about Leif being killed by a shotgun. How do you know he won't arrest you as soon as you turn over the cocaine to him?"

I couldn't say I hadn't given that possibility a thought, and Billie's alert brought the problem into focus, but I refracted it.

"Billie, you have a suspicious mind."

"Girls have to be suspicious, or we'd all be barefoot and pregnant."

"No argument there."

"I want to make a suggestion. I don't want you to take it the wrong way, but you're being awfully cavalier dealing with the Shirt. He can hurt you."

Billie had a point. I supposed that once the Shirt seemed to seriously consider my terms, I figured I had an edge. Maybe it was all in my mind.

"I'll try to show him more respect the next time we meet. Does that satisfy you?"

"It's not me I'm worried about."

Billie's hand, resting on the inflatable tube, sparkled as if covered with stardust. I examined it more closely. Tiny pinpoints of perspiration peeked out from her pores. Each twinkled for an instant before it evaporated in the sunlight. I likened it to randomly blinking lights on a Christmas tree.

"Tell me about this detour business."

"We still have unfinished business at our postage-stamp paradise. A relationship works only if each partner is like on an equal footing with the other—you said so yourself. You claimed I won three Oscars last summer. This will be your opportunity to garner three Oscars for yourself. Until last night, I was a little worried I'd have to buy you an Erector Set, but you passed the audition. Besides, if a girl can't show off her birthday suit on her birthday, what's the point of celebrating it?"

Billie twisted the throttle and steered us toward a remote and uninhabited area of St. Judas. Giant boulders scattered in the shallows—formidable as the Maginot line—protected the beach from the sea. The remote patch of sand, reachable on foot only by rappelling down a rock overhang, offered complete privacy, a degree of solitude that vacationers dream of finding in the Caribbean but only sailors stumble upon.

After Billie dodged the monoliths and got us close, she shut down the motor and tilted it out of the water. I hopped out and pulled the dinghy onto the beach. Billie stepped into the water and reached back into the dinghy to grab a handle on the cooler.

"Help me with this."

I grabbed the other handle, and we hoisted it out of the dinghy and lugged it ashore. We relocated the cooler twice before Billie gave final approval of its resting place. She returned to the dingy for her backpack. Inside was a blanket. I helped her spread it on the sand.

"Get comfortable," she said.

I plopped down on the blanket and sat Indian style facing her. Billie took off her baseball cap and pulled off her T-shirt. The breeze whipped her yellow hair from her face, as she replaced the cap and gave the bill a firm tug. Then she stepped out of her shorts. No tan lines interrupted the flow of her bronze skin. She performed a slightly awkward pirouette in the unstable sand. Pleasure emanated from my groin, as I observed flesh that I'd be excited to contemplate well into my dotage.

Billie smiled at my unconcealed delight. She reached into the cooler and grabbed a beer, a simple maneuver made complex by a series of postures that stopped short of posing but tiptoed along a fine line demarking art from artifice.

She sat on the cooler and twisted off the cap. She took a sip of the beer and held the bottle over her left breast. Condensation from the bottle dripped onto her skin. Rivulets of water ran down both sides of her breast. She moved the bottle slightly, and the condensation dripped onto her nipple, making it erect.

Billie took another sip of the beer before performing the same operation on her right breast.

"You okay?" she asked.

I nodded.

"I'm not boring you?"

"Only a little. I'll give you twenty minutes to cut it out."

Billie took up the challenge. For the next twenty minutes, she entertained me with her experiments in fluid dynamics. If I'd known science could be so titillating, I'd have become a physicist.

For the finale, Billie twisted off the caps of two beers and simultaneously dumped them on each of her breasts. The beer glubbed and gurgled from the bottles. It splashed from her breasts in beads and globules, the amber liquid sparkling in sunshine. Her breasts and belly and thighs glistened. I was sorry I brought only a dozen beers along, sorry I limited my challenge to only twenty minutes.

"Thirsty?" she asked.

I nodded.

She fetched a beer from the cooler and walked to where I sat on the blanket. She stood smack in front of me, a foot planted on either side of my thighs. I reached up for the beer. Billie held the bottle out of my reach.

She smiled. "We handle communion a little differently in the Church of Billie."

She tipped her head back and poured the beer into her mouth. It overflowed and ran down her chin, between her breasts, over her belly, through her pubic hair to my lapping tongue, which tickled her clitoris.

When the bottle was empty, Billie tossed it aside and grabbed the back of my head with both hands. I held her thighs. Not more than two minutes later, I won my first Oscar of the day. I looked up to see the jaw on the face of God contort in ecstasy before it relaxed in an accelerating smile.

I earned my second Oscar in the sea, imitating a buoy. Billie wrapped her arms around my neck and locked her legs to mine. Entwined, we just held on to each other and let the sea do all the work. We bobbed and bounced and rotated with the swells.

When the final quiver of Billie's seismic convulsion rippled through her body and my heartbeat returned to double-digit territory, I asked her if she was ready to head to Norman Island.

"Not so fast, Buster. You still have one Oscar to go."

"We're not done? You're going to drive me to the monastery."

"Hey, you're the one looking for a religious experience."

I was and I had found it, and reflecting upon it made me laugh.

"What's so funny?"

I tried to explain to Billie—in comparison to her runaway success—how feeble the attempts of Reverend Richards and Diver Vaughn to gather souls now seemed. I told her I was prepared to tithe.

She suggested the missionary position for my final Oscar competition.

19

THE NAKED WEEKEND AT A SWANKY HOTEL in St. Thomas didn't go as planned. I did spend the weekend on St. Thomas, but I spent it alone in a damp cell, and the only time I got naked was when I showered. Luckily, I had my copy of *The Stranger*, though by Saturday afternoon, I wished the book had more pages. Saturday night, I dreamed I was Meursault, and I experienced shooting Officer Richards on the beach at Pirate Cove over and over, emptying pistol after pistol into him, the sunlight splintering into flakes of fire on the sand and sea.

Sunday seemed interminable. All that kept me going was reflecting upon the Friday morning with Billie at our postage-stamp paradise. Still, Billie's two-day absence occupied my brain as much as my reminiscences did.

Where in the hell was she?

I figured I was the only admittedly guilty inmate in the joint. Though a case could be made for self-defense, I didn't believe the judge would pay much heed to my argument. I didn't believe, either, that he'd pay much heed to my accusations against Richards and his complicity in Leif's death. I went back and forth on whether to bring up that subject—concluding that I'd play it by ear, then revisiting the subject and arriving at the same conclusion, *ad infinitum*.

Late Friday afternoon—after feeding two loaves of bread to the fish and eating a late lunch aboard the *William Thornton*—Billie and I returned from our Norman Island expedition. As we neared the head of the bay, I spotted flashing emergency lights at the Congo Club. Functionaries from public works and the police stood in confrontation against Pirate Dan—the same deal that had occurred at the playground the day before.

A key to maintaining good standing with my old mates in the Marathon Militia was to determine quickly which situations demanded the all-for-one and the equally convivial one-for-all solution and which situations required the less convivial every-man-for-himself response.

Veterans—even those no longer in Marathon—act instinctively. I found myself twisting the outboard's throttle without thinking about what I was getting myself into.

The number of dinghies heading ashore was almost as large as when the Coast Guard motored into the harbor. As I threaded through the flotilla, I figured most of the folk heading to shore were intent upon watching and not helping, so I opened the throttle full bore and scared the shit out of several skippers.

A gunshot sounded, as we neared shore, and I unapologetically nosed out one dinghy trying to tie up at the dock and took his place. I left Billie to tie up and deal with the angry sailor, as I scrambled across an adjacent inflatable, hopped onto the dock, and jogged toward the Congo Club, slowed only a bit by my bum knee.

The gunshot alerted me to the seriousness of the situation, so I wasn't surprised at the absence of Almida, the island administrator. Four men from public works and two cops—the same contingent that confronted us at the playground—stood in opposition to Pirate Dan, his Louisville Slugger in the hands of a cop. Officer Richards holstered his pistol, but he pulled his baton from his belt when he spotted me approach.

I stuck my finger in Richards' face, but before I could open my mouth to give him hell for discharging his revolver, he attempted to whack me in the head with his baton. I deflected the blow with my left forearm and followed with a hard right to his jaw, dropping him to the turf. Before he gained consciousness, I was cuffed and ensconced in the back seat of a squad.

The police spared me some of the indignity of arrest by hauling me to St. Thomas on the car-ferry, instead of parading me in handcuffs through the streets of Sugar Harbor, where I—not exactly a Napoleon of crime—didn't expect to encounter throngs of cheering spectators.

Since Saturday, I'd been waiting for Billie to show up with cigarettes and reading material. Now on Monday, I was more pissed at her than I was at the police. They were just doing their job.

What in the hell was Billie doing?

I didn't open my eyes when I heard the commotion—there'd been a lot of that this morning—but I did open them when I heard my cage being rattled. Shaking the bars was the Shirt. I almost didn't recognize him. Instead of wearing an Aloha shirt, he wore an Easy Rider Rally T-shirt. And not just any rally shirt, but the shirt awarded to the event's winner—the shirt I'd planned to add to my collection.

"Get off your lazy ass," the Shirt said.

I got to my feet and stuffed the Ziploc bag with the Camus book into my pocket. My stiff knee ached. When the jailer opened the gate, I limped out.

"Like my new shirt?" he asked.

"Did you mug the winner, or did you cheat?"

"Only one cheater in the rally, and he paid a heavy price."

"Who was that?"

"You'll find out, but let's talk about me. I won the rally fair and square. Then Sarah cooked up some lobsters to celebrate. I even hired an obeah man to take care of my little problem."

I tried to sort out whether I believed enough in obeah that I should be fearful of the magic. I probably did, but I quickly determined that I had bigger problems, or more immediate problems, anyway.

"Good for you," I said.

"Let me tell you, I am in the catbird's seat."

"I suppose you have to break some eggs to make an omelet."

"Huh?

I followed the Shirt to the reception area and received a manila envelope from the man on duty. He scowled, as if I were Professor Moriarty off to the beach on sabbatical.

"What's the deal?" I asked, stuffing my personal effects into my pockets. "I'm supposed to be in court in an hour."

The Shirt handed me a pack of cigarettes. I nodded my thanks.

"You're not going to court. Thanks to me, the charges have been dropped. You and I are going to finish our business. I didn't come all this way just to feed your nicotine habit."

The more I thought about my problem with the Shirt, the more I began to believe that the weight of the cocaine tipped the scales in my direction: the Shirt wanted the cocaine, I had the cocaine; the Shirt had federal connections, I had the cocaine; the Shirt had the gun, I had the cocaine.

"Been thinking about your offer," he said, stroking his chin. "Let's do the deal. Now is a good time."

"Just to make sure we're both on the same page, how much did you pay Richards?"

"Five thou'."

"And what were your instructions?"

"Lock Leif up for a few days."

"How did Leif die?"

"The two got into a tussle, and Leif hit his head on the cistern. I wasn't there. I'm only telling you what I know."

"Okay. Tomorrow morning. Eight o'clock. Easys."

"How about now?"

"Too late in the day."

He tugged on the bill of his baseball cap, adjusted his sunglasses, and checked his whiskers, as we left the building. I lit a cigarette.

"I can't wait that long," he said.

"If you're in such a big hurry, why did you wait until now to spring me? We could've wrapped up this deal on Saturday."

"You deserved to learn a lesson for breaking the law."

"You should think about permanent residence in the V.I. You've already got the cut-off-the-nose-to-spite-the-face attitude that defines the eternal suffering of West Indians."

"Look in the mirror."

I'd done that enough to know I didn't particularly like what I saw, but I knew I'd much prefer contemplating my own image if it weren't diminished by the Shirt's overwhelming shadow.

"Know how to dive?" I asked.

"You mean tanks?"

"Tanks."

"No, but I'm willing to learn."

"I think you're a little too impatient to wait for certification, so I'm the one who's going to have to dive. Your prize is in an underwater cave. Underwater caves are a bit tricky to locate. By definition, there are no landmarks. You can't just walk thirty paces north of the kapok tree that sits next to the flat stone with petroglyphs. Because I'm smart enough not to touch the cocaine or be within a mile of it when you're around, I'm going to have to draw you a map. In order to draw you a map, I'm going to have to go there alone. You can meet me at eight o'clock tomorrow morning at Easys, at which time I will give you a treasure map for the agreed-upon-price of sixty grand, or you can take a hike. Makes no difference to me."

"If you're fucking with me, you'll be a sorry son of a bitch."

The Shirt—chummy after my tirade—offered me a ride back to St. Judas, but I declined. I determined to stay on St. Thomas and shop for sails. I headed on foot the short distance to the waterfront to grab a burger. I felt better after a decent meal, but hitching a ride in my more-than-usually rumpled state proved difficult, and I finally succumbed to the appeal of a Hispanic gypsy cabbie, despite his intention to charge me nearly double the going rate. He agreed to make a couple of stops on the way to Red Hook, so I ponied up the cash.

He drove an ancient Japanese sedan—beat-up and rusted—but every time we stopped for signal lights or traffic, he couldn't resist polishing the clock face, organizing a minute portion of the ton of crap he carried in his vehicle, or pushing the stuffing back beneath the seat's upholstery.

The second marina at which we stopped stocked all the used sails I needed. When I returned to the car, the driver had the hood open. He had the wire off one spark plug and was polishing the porcelain. I was tempted to explain that cleaning the end of the plug screwed into the engine's head would be more efficacious, but I didn't bother—it's bad karma even to interrupt the bonding of man and machine.

Back on the road to Red Hook, I calculated there were still enough hours left in the day to complete the transaction with the marina and collect my merchandise, but just like you don't plan your dinner menu in the Virgin Islands without first going to the market, you don't plan time-sensitive excursions based on the ferry schedule.

Two dozen of us purchased tickets and climbed aboard the boat. The captain, trim and fit and decked out as spiffily as a U.S. naval officer—West Indians always look sharp in uniform—kissed his sweetheart goodbye and hopped aboard. Two hands stood ready at the bollards to toss the mooring lines aboard. The captain hit the starter to the small single-engine boat. The diesel refused to start.

Off came the passengers, and off came the engine cover. For the most part, the locals—West Indians and Continentals—took the delay in stride. Not many tourists did.

Two hands climbed down into the engine compartment. Both climbed back out in just a few minutes. They wiped their greasy hands on red cloths and reported to the skipper. Because they didn't return to the engine compartment, I assumed that they were unable to make the needed repair. Prospective passengers came to the same conclusion I did. A few were quite vocal. I headed to the parking lot to get away from a particularly whiny woman and buy a beer from a once-mobile snack bar—a step van sitting on blocks—pretty sure I'd be riding to Sugar Harbor on the one o'clock boat, pretty sure I'd be postponing my shopping expedition.

When I returned to the dock, the one o'clock boat—most recently the twelve o'clock boat at Sugar Harbor—a double-decked monster, was just pulling into port. It tied up alongside the dead ferry, where the crew reinstalled the engine cover to allow passengers on the big boat to traverse the deck of the small boat to reach the dock. I had another half hour to kill, so I returned to the snack bar for another beer.

A taxi pulled up next to me, and Wendy climbed out, dragging a duffle behind her. She was about the same number of years past thirty that Billie was past twenty, and she'd been Flamingo Bay's only siren until Billie arrived. I thought Wendy and I were both surprised to see each other, and I said as much.

She looked at me red-eyed and oddly. "You haven't heard?"

"What? I've been in jail all weekend."

"Jason. He was killed during the Easy Rider Rally. Went off the mountain while driving Vaughn's pickup. That's about all I know. Easy got word to me on marine radio."

The marine radio in question was likely aboard the schooner of the young skipper Wendy sailed off with following Leif's death. I was tempted to place a portion of the blame for Jason's death on Wendy's desertion, but then I thought of my culpability in any matters relevant to Sarah's addiction and decided to give Wendy a break.

"I'm sorry."

I flashed back to their wedding day. The ceremony and reception were held aboard *Island Trader*. It was the event of the season. Their marriage began with great promise, but in a short time, things went wrong. My take: they quickly straightened out each other's kinks, then each sought diversion elsewhere—Jason with fairy dust; Wendy with serial partners.

"I'm going for a refill. Can I buy you a beer?"

"Why not."

I hauled her duffle to the snack bar. We found shade, sitting on the step van's rear bumper.

"Such a waste," Wendy said.

"Pardon?"

"Scrounging is not rocket science."

"Huh?"

"Jason, he was a rocket scientist."

"Come on."

"Well, he would have been, could have been. He finished the work on his doctorate. Wrote his thesis. Came down here on vacation. Never went back. Never bothered to take his oral exams. Never bothered to submit his thesis. When we married, our plan was to sell the boat, move to California, and become respected members of society. I hoped I'd never see Flamingo Bay again. I was sick of living in a place where you know everything about everybody except their last name. I was sick of living in a place where being the biggest loser gives you the biggest bragging rights. I was sick of living in a place where everyone is immortal until they die at an age that disgusts First World statisticians."

"Now what?"

"I'm even more sick of all those things—and plenty of others. How do you keep your sanity?"

"I have a rich fantasy life I'm able to access without drugs or alcohol."

"Lucky you," she said.

"What are you going to do?"

"Figure out how to get him buried. All our money went up his nose. I have a call in to his family to see if they want his body brought back to the States. If they don't, I'm going to bury him here."

"If you need some cash, let me know."

She rolled her eyes. "You have money?"

"Don't sound so surprised."

"I'm sorry," she said. "Thanks for the offer. I may take you up on it."

The ferry horn sounded. I carried her duffle to the dock. Wendy purchased a ticket, and we followed the last bit of luggage and cargo aboard.

After I explained the specifics of my incarceration, we didn't really talk. I'm not much on handing out condolences, and Wendy wasn't much on accepting them. I didn't think, either, that it was a good time to suggest discussing Plato.

When the boat left the harbor, the captain hit the throttle. The engines growled, and a strong vibration shuddered through the hull. Despite trading our tiny ferry for a monster one, the boat pitched and rolled even in protected seas. I hadn't heard a weather report all weekend, but it appeared a late-season tropical depression churned somewhere beyond the horizon, roiling the sea.

When we reached open water, our captain initiated a zigzag course. The monster ferry pounded into bone-jarring swells and dropped weightless into deep troughs—like a bar of Ivory in a child's stormy bathwater. Waves and spray crashed into the hull and through open windows on the lower deck, soaking passengers. Most of the tourists rode up on top, but several sat below. With the windows closed, diesel fumes filled the cabin. Probably a combination of the boat's motion and the exhaust gas caused one passenger to get seasick.

One thing about seasickness: it can spread faster than a virus. And it did. Crewmembers exhorted the tourists to fix their eyes on land—starboard passengers on one cay, port passengers on another. A second tourist vomited. Ignoring a crew's shouted orders to remain in our seats, Wendy and I exited the cabin—there's no inoculation for the malady, and even experience can't always provide immunization. When the crew reached the ladder to stop us, we were halfway up it. He quickly gave up on us and turned to block a stream of people who tried to follow us.

When the boat docked, I spotted Mechanic Jim—the only man on

St. Judas, besides Elroy, whose attire was shabbier than my own—at the periphery of a small crowd. Some stood with their luggage. Others guarded parcels and crates. Of the empty-handed ones like Jim, a few waited for disembarking passengers, but most waited for the crew to unload the light cargo.

I pointed out Jim to Wendy.

"Looks like we've got ourselves a ride to Flamingo Bay."

"Anything beats spending another minute on this boat."

Anything was a reference to the quality of Jim's jeep, sounder mechanically than Billie's (it was his profession) but distinguishable from hers mostly by its green paint job, done with a brush and roller, possibly in the dark.

I sat in back with the four tires I helped Jim load into the vehicle. I wasn't particularly comfortable, but the ride would've been a lot worse bouncing around on sheet metal.

"Did you run in the rally?" Wendy asked Jim.

"I ran, but I didn't see Jason go off the mountain."

"But you know what happened?"

"Hard not to. It's about all everybody's talking about."

"Tell me."

"First off, Jason didn't enter the rally. Toward the end of the event, he drove up the mountain, past the starting point, in Vaughn's pickup. Easy believed Jason was on his way to town. He didn't go to town. He turned the truck around and waited until Zeke began his run. Then he came barreling down the mountain after Zeke and tried to run him off the road. Zeke must have seen him coming. He locked his brakes— a minor miracle without power assist. Jason blew by him, unable to brake quick enough to make the curve, and ran off the road."

"Why did Jason go after Zeke?" Wendy asked.

"No idea," Jim answered.

"I know Zeke refused to sell him cocaine—at my request," I said. "That was after Vaughn also cut him off."

Wendy turned her head for an explanation.

"You already know about Jason's run-ins with the Pirate and the Diver, but signs of Jason's goofiness were everywhere. The other day, he spent the morning doing donuts in his dinghy at full speed, looping among the moored boats. He crashed his jeep into a dumpster on the way to Sugar Harbor. He fought and argued with everyone. When Zeke cut him off, the two got into an altercation."

On the way down the mountain, Jim pulled to the side of the road, turned off the vehicle's ignition, and climbed out. Wendy and I followed him across the road. Strong skid marks ran diagonally across the asphalt to the shoulder, where two furrows had been carved in the coarse gravel. Peering over the edge, we could see a swath cut through the scrubby trees and the crumpled metal of Vaughn's red pickup a few hundred feet below us.

Wendy's eyes filled with tears. I was surprised to see genuine emotion from her. It was the first time in five years. I always figured she was more like a guy than a girl, leaning heavily toward the rational, always behaving more rationally and less emotionally than I—the only standard I knew.

I was even more surprised when Mechanic Jim—the crevices around his nails and spaces between his fingers' whorls filled with grease—handed Wendy a handkerchief. Not any handkerchief, but a pristine white folded handkerchief, the handkerchief of another generation. What a guy.

Wendy sobbed quietly into Jim's handkerchief, while a perverse bit of humor punctured my gloom when I made out Vaughn's slogan painted on the pickup's tailgate: GO DOWN WITH DIVER VAUGHN. Jason had clearly done that—at least he'd gone down with Diver Vaughn's pickup. I refrained from chuckling, but I didn't mourn his loss. I'd already mourned it months ago when I witnessed the death of the man he was.

I wondered if Jason felt any terror at all when he flew over the edge. On the one hand, his life had been so far out of control for so long, it may have seemed like just another hurtling escapade to him. On the other hand, we all have an instinct for self-preservation. I measured Jason's instinct using the thick rubbery tracks as a gauge and figured he knew exactly what was happening to him. Nevertheless, I couldn't help suspect that somewhere in his pre-consciousness he welcomed the event.

Along with Leif, Valerie, Captain Lucky, and Mad Max, Jason would miss Flamingo Bay's New Year's Eve party for the first time. I wasn't sure I'd be there either, and the attendance of my two companions was iffy at best. Mechanic Jim hinted he was close to solidifying a date for the next leg of his around-the-world excursion on *Ketch 22*, and I figured Wendy would be heading back to her lover or back to the States when she wrapped up Jason's affairs on St. Judas.

Wendy did not speak. She wiped her eyes and scanned the mountainside, as if trying to make sense of Jason's final tantrum. Jim and I stood on each side of her and remained silent for what seemed like an hour. We followed her lead when she crumpled the handkerchief in her fist and wordlessly turned and headed toward Jim's vehicle.

When we reached the fork in the road, I tapped Jim on the shoulder to pull over.

"Let me drop Wendy at Easys," he said. "Then I'll give you a hand with your truck. Been the target of vandals."

"How bad?"

"Hard to tell if the damage is bad or just thorough. You're going to need a couple new tires. Looks like they got under the hood, too."

As we cruised through the mangroves, I spotted a red streamer tied to a tree branch. It signaled the winning mark for Saturday's Easy Rider Rally. The Shirt surpassed my record run by quite a margin.

It made me want to cry.

20

I KICKED AN EMPTY EGG CARTON. It appeared all twelve eggs were splattered against my windshield. My spare tire was flat, and an ice pick dangled from the sidewall of the left front tire, though the tire still held air. Mechanic Jim believed saltwater had been added to the radiator; a taste test confirmed this. The brake's master cylinder also appeared to be contaminated. The Shirt wouldn't do something like that. People who pretended to be your friends would, though. Flamingo Bay is a pretty okay place, but only if the locals figure you're a pretty okay guy.

I bought six one-gallon jugs of drinking water from Pirate Dan, and I drained the radiator and engine block, while Jim headed to the shack he rented for his car repair business to pick up tools and supplies.

Pony Mon—still limping a bit from his attempt the other day to tame the donkey—stopped by to chat.

"Captain Brian, mon, chickens attack you truck?"

"Angry chickens."

"How was jail?"

"Dull."

"No rubber hoses? No cattle prods?"

"Nothing like that."

"Maybe I take the next swing at that asshole. Always afraid to go to jail. Maybe they doesn't let me out. And when they does let me out, maybe I find Richards be living in my house."

I asked him if he'd seen Billie, but Pony Mon hadn't seen her all weekend, nor had Easy, Mechanic Jim, Pirate Dan, or anyone else I asked. I couldn't figure what she was up to. She always seemed as present as Elroy—another person gone missing.

Pony Mon tried scraping the windshield with my lone credit card, but the sun-baked gobs of coagulated protein had become one with the safety glass. He left to find a razor blade, and I re-inspected my vehicle. Luckily, I had a locking gas cap and a sealed battery, so the introduction of malevolent fluids to the vehicle's various systems was somewhat limited. I confirmed that the spare tire also had a puncture in the sidewall and would have to be replaced. I didn't find anything else notably amiss, but I couldn't be sure no surprises lay ahead.

When Mechanic Jim returned, we bled the brakes. Pony Mon cleaned the windshield. To be on the safe side, Jim and I also changed the oil and filter. I started the engine and flushed the cooling system. When the water ran clean, I shut off the petcocks and refilled the system with water and coolant.

I still had business at Pirate Cove before tomorrow's meeting with the Shirt, and I needed a vehicle. I also needed to buy two tires. There were plenty of people around to loan me a vehicle for a short errand, but neither of my errands could be classified as short. I kept expecting Billie to show up. When she didn't, I decided I'd try to make it to town in the old Ford.

Gripping the ice pick with a pair of locking pliers, I used Jim's hacksaw to cut the wooden handle off the tool, hoping that the piece of steel left in the tire would seal well enough that I could make it to town before all the air escaped.

After thanking Pony Mon and settling up with Mechanic Jim— he refused payment, but I insisted—I headed off around the bay in first gear, not exceeding ten mph, my self-imposed speed limit. Nearly twenty shouting kids tested the playground equipment. A mother sat on one of two new benches. I wanted to believe that life was truly simple for the young, but my own memories reminded me that, while it may've been simpler, life was never simple.

I pissed off so many people on the way to town by driving the entire distance in first gear that it surprised me they weren't all waiting to pull me from my vehicle and execute me by the side of the road when I descended the hill into Sugar Harbor.

I knew before heading out that the chance of finding tires anywhere on the island to fit my truck was about zilch, so I wasn't surprised that I didn't find any. The operator of the gas station ordered two from an auto supply store on St. Thomas that promised to deliver them to the five o'clock ferry at Red Hook. I left the truck at the gas station and headed on foot to the park.

I picked up a copy of Herman Wouk's *Don't Stop the Carnival*—the only title that held any interest for me—at a gift shop and settled on a park bench to relax. Required reading for anyone who spends more than a day in the Caribbean, I'd been urged to read the book years ago. I remembered laughing all the way through it. Today, the tears I wiped from eyes did not result from mirth. Through passing decades, nothing had changed. Paperman gave it his all to build a life in the islands, but in the end, he went home to New York, a sadder but wiser man.

When the ferry docked, I stuck the book in my pocket and joined the crowd on the pier. When the last passenger disembarked, the crew quickly unloaded the cargo in the manner of a fire brigade passing buckets of water one to the next. I considered rolling the tires the few blocks to the gas station, but changed my mind by the time I stepped off the pier. In another century, I probably could've found a couple of kids adept at the art of the old hoop and stick game. Instead, I settled on a taxi.

The driver, who'd once refused to drive me to Flamingo Bay—too late, too far—told me he was going home to supper. I thought about asking him if in the forty-or-so years he'd lived on St. Judas whether he'd ever been to Flamingo Bay. Instead, I told him my destination and suggested he could drop me off on the way to supper. He couldn't have been happier—short fare, big bucks; he treated each tire as an additional passenger.

The man at the gas station told me he'd mount the new tires and bolt the wheels onto the front of the Ford before he quit work for the day, but he might need two or three hours—he had two customers to deal with first. Not keen on hanging around the gas station for hours and trading insults with the lookers-on, I paid him upfront and told him to leave the key on top of the left rear tire, so I could pick up the vehicle at my convenience.

Though my knee bothered me, I enjoyed my walk back to the waterfront. It was my favorite time of day—warm, soft, fuzzy. The chirping tree frogs set the evening's cadence. The western sky glowed red. Gusting wind teased trees and pennants. In a bit of a stretch—even for me—the warmth of the sea seemed to be as life giving as amniotic fluid.

I found a table at the Agave Grill—opposite the wharf where the car-ferry docked—and ordered dinner. I sipped a frozen daiquiri—to remind me of Billie—as my senses roamed the seating area, guessing the ingredients in a curry sauce, picking up a bit of conversation here, spying an intriguing bit of flesh there.

Two scruffy sailors took a nearby table, interrupting their discussion of the weather forecast just long enough to order beers. Men against the sea. Big strong men. I'd sailed with their sort. Every day became a battle in life's war. Not only were they prepared for the coming storm, they were prepared for the Second Coming, prepared for the nuclear holocaust, prepared for the post-apocalyptic world—prepared for everything except ordering a meal. Their waitress told them she'd give them more time.

The forecast sounded ominous, at least from their perspective. I figured that I'd have to see a real weather report before I went to all the trouble of preparing *Island Trader* for a blow.

Hurricane season was almost over—past its prime in November, certainly—but you can never tell when a tropical depression will churn up enough energy to acquire a name and a biography. I prefer tornadoes to tropical storms. I like how the sky turns ornery and the color of bile—black with gloom and yellow with fury. I like, also, a tornado's anonymity. It has a fleeting history, a transparent personality, and—like a mugging—it's over before you can ponder it.

Tropical storms allow you plenty of time to ponder, even before the sky turns dull and drizzly and the wind starts gusting. Once the storm begins breathing in fast thick pants, it gives you even more to think about. Your mind records each perceptible notch, as the wind ratchets itself until it's cranked to where it hardly pauses to catch its breath, and you instinctively ratchet the tension in your body to compete with the storm. Long after the worst of it passes, you still feel like a hostage—rigid, in a clinch with yourself.

Rigid, in a clinch with myself, was how I felt when I heard the clunk from the car-ferry's ramp drop to the wharf's pavement just across the road and turned to see the public works vehicle ease down the ramp. The driver pulled across the wharf and parked under a light standard. When he exited the vehicle, I recognized him as the honcho who tried to shut down the playground.

It seemed a bit late in the day for official business.

He walked along the road toward the park. I could conclude only that his business was unofficial. Maybe he had a girlfriend. Maybe he had pals. Assholes—though I don't know how—usually do. Still, I figured his presence might have something to do with his earlier threat to dismantle the playground equipment—there wasn't enough nightlife on St. Judas to warrant a ferry ride, and there wasn't any destination in Sugar Harbor where a vehicle was required. To get his vehicle to St. Judas, the man paid a severe tariff—instituted by the government to keep St. Thomians from clogging the few roads—suggesting to me that he was up to no good.

My waitress brought me a plate of scampi. I never met a shrimp I didn't like, and I went to work on my meal, keeping an eye on the white vehicle. Public works' presence didn't ruin my appetite, but it did ruin the meal.

The pump jockey had probably mounted the new tires by now—he wanted to get home for dinner. Still, I couldn't be sure my truck was ready. In the time it would take me to walk to the station and back, the honcho could be long gone. I decided to wait him out, or at least wait the whole three hours the pump jockey gave as the outside estimate to complete the job.

I hoped the honcho would fortify himself with liquor or do whatever he was doing for at least another hour. If not, what? Calling the police was out of the question. I could call Easys, but I couldn't be sure anyone there would make much of an effort to find Aubrey, especially on my prompting. Easy, if he could get away, seemed the best bet. Yet, I couldn't be sure. It boiled my blood that after five years, the only man in Flamingo Bay I could trust implicitly was myself.

Even before I downed the last shrimp, I found myself stuffed. I slowly smoked a cigarette to kill time. I didn't want to give up my comfortable view of the wharf. Sensing my waitress's impatience when I crushed out my cigarette but made no move to leave, I reluctantly ordered desert. I spooned the banana ice cream from the bottom of the bowl, one level teaspoon of liquid at a time.

When I could no longer ingest another calorie and could no longer ignore waiting patrons or my waitress's disapproving glare, I paid my tab and left. I strolled across the road to the wharf and hung out there smoking and pacing. I dodged kids, clustered around beat-up vehicles, bouncing to deafening rhythms from colossal sound systems worth more than their cars—the cars themselves clustered around the many delivery trucks staged for an early-morning start.

As soon as I figured the work on my truck was finished, I walked slowly in the direction of the gas station, checking out every bar and restaurant for the honcho. I cut across the park, looking for him there. After I took a final glance at his parked vehicle before losing my sight-line, I picked up my pace, reaching my destination at a jog.

When I got my truck on the road, I returned to the wharf. The honcho's vehicle still sat unattended. I waited another hour. Then I figured to hell with it and drove up the hill and out of Sugar Harbor. I wanted to find Billie, but I didn't know if I wanted to find her badly enough that anyone would mistake me for one of those needy guys who regularly made fools of themselves by seeking a woman's where-abouts when everyone else in Flamingo Bay knows who she's with and what she's doing.

I didn't know where she was or what she was doing, but I knew in my bones that she loved me. I figured I'd let her be. Billie never seemed to have trouble finding me.

Certain that after tomorrow Billie and I could put our investigation to sleep, certain that the Shirt would be permanently out of my life, certain that I'd be back in business—again an island trader—certain that I could make my own decisions about my future, certain that I'd kept all my promises and paid all my debts, I relaxed and enjoyed the quiet drive, meeting only one vehicle.

I stopped the truck at the crest of the mountain. Enough lights still glowed from the hillsides to define the harbor's boundary. Through the open window of the passenger door, I saw clearly the light that shone brightly on Peter Island. I figured it was time to defend my title as champion of the Easy Rider Rally. I turned off the ignition and released the brake. The first leg of the course was uneventful, but I had to stop myself from braking at the spot where Jason soared off the road.

After that momentary lapse in concentration, I became Jim Clark, my boyhood hero, piloting my Lotus-Ford at Monaco. I was smooth, and I straightened every bend in the road. I was fast, and I blew by the competition. Girls and champagne waited for me at the finish line. Then I discovered that I was running on empty; the truck began to slow. I looked for the checkered flag, but I couldn't find it. I urged the truck forward by rocking in my seat. The wheels barely turned.

I tried to break the bonds of melancholia, but I was trussed up so tight that I couldn't move, and the noose around my neck constricted my throat. When my truck stopped well short of victory, I found I was crying. I couldn't say for sure how long I sat with tears streaming down my face. Maybe a long time. I thought that because when I tried to start my truck, the battery was nearly dead, worn down by the headlights. The truck did start, and I wiped my eyes. I turned the vehicle around and headed toward the dinghy dock. When I cleared the mangroves, I spotted the honcho's vehicle at the playground. His headlights were off, but the open driver's door lit the interior lights. Nearing the playground, I could see him throw a rope over the top beam of the swing set.

I was prepared to charge forward with the boldness befitting a member of the Light Brigade, but a donkey stepped in front of my truck and stopped me. The few seconds it took the animal to clear the vehicle may've been a lifesaver. It gave me a chance to reflect on the honcho's firepower. I knew he carried a pistol on his belt—no jaws of death, then.

I tightened my lap belt, turned off my lights, and moved forward at an idle. The honcho finished his knot and secured the rope to the rear of his Blazer. I inched closer. He climbed into his vehicle. I eased the truck onto the playground's turf. He started his engine. I hit the headlights and accelerator. Leaving my elbows slightly bent, I braced myself for the impact. The speedometer read twenty-five mph when I collided with him head-on.

The crash messed me up. I fought for breath, expanding my lungs against what felt like cracked ribs. Blood from a gash in my forehead leaked into my eyes. Sometimes it hurts so much that you have to laugh, and I did. What set me off was the fighter's old line about how you should see the other guy. When I stopped laughing, it occurred to me that I *should* take a look at the other guy.

I limped around the back of my truck, bracing myself with a hand on the vehicle. Damn! The asshole had an airbag in his vehicle. It never occurred to me.

Luckily, he was woozy from the airbag's impact, startled by the collision, or simply drunk. I quickly got the gun out of his holster and dragged him from the vehicle. Gun barrel jammed into the back of his head, I walked him over to the monkey bars. I pulled his handcuffs from his belt and slapped them on his right wrist. After flipping the empty cuff over a dowel on the monkey bars, I cuffed his left wrist. His body sagged just long enough for him to learn that he didn't want to support his weight by his wrists.

"You go to jail for this," he spit, straightening up.

"No, you go to jail. Want to know why?" He didn't answer so I poked his crotch with the gun barrel. "Want to know why?"

"Why?"

"Because if you don't go to jail, you'll wish you were in jail. Want to know why?"

When he hesitated to answer, I made a move to prod him again. More trainable than any of Pavlov's mutts, he spoke right up.

"Why?"

"Because I'm going to keep this gun, and if I learn you dodge jail, I'm going to blow off your testicles, one at a time. Me? I'd plead guilty. Take a nice vacation."

"No yankeemuthascunt fucks with me."

I cocked the hammer and stuck the barrel in his crotch. Pretty sure nothing but the crotch of his trousers would be damaged, I pulled the trigger. I couldn't be sure which was louder: the gunshot or his scream.

"You crazy bastard!"

"Very good. Now what are you going to tell the police?"

"Tell them to arrest you for attempted murder."

"Is that blood or urine soaking your trousers? I can't tell in this light."

"Fuck you!"

"Maybe you need some quiet time to think this through. I'll check in with you later. Maybe I'll let you go. Maybe I'll take you fishing. You might want to think about screaming. Somebody might hear you and actually care. Once we get on the water, you won't mean shit to the fish."

I walked back to my truck, secure in my understanding that every man is his own worst enemy. I wondered how many pre-reflective decisions changed the course of history. Surely, I changed the course of my history. No orgiastic future now lay within my horizon, a horizon I needed to quickly expand. If I could dodge the police for several hours, I figured I still had enough time to do Vaughn a big favor, one for which he probably wouldn't thank me.

The Ford was going nowhere without surgery. The radiator was pushed into the fan, and coolant still dripped onto the turf. The new tires made perfect sense, as much as dressing a corpse in new shoes.

I cut the fan belt and tried to start the engine. It fired up, and I drove it around the bay to the dinghy dock without headlights. Like Easys, the Congo Club was closed for the day. Even in a place where cocktail hour starts before noon, Monday evening is nearly as quiet as Sunday morning. Aside from the clanging rigging on the moored boats, the only sounds came from animals. Barking dogs and neighing donkeys fed each other's discomfort. Also, a rooster—internal clock gone haywire—tried unsuccessfully to jumpstart the dawn.

I walked down to the dinghy dock. The pile of greenheart had disappeared. I wondered for a moment if the contractor had collected it or if scroungers had taken it, but it wasn't my problem. I untied the Zodiac, pushed off, and jumped in. I started the engine. It ran for about fifteen seconds before it sputtered and died, leaving me about fifty feet from the dock. I discovered the fuel tank was missing. The waves would carry me into mangroves. There was nothing to do but get wet. I deserved to get wet. I'd violated one of the basic rules of seamanship: never cast off if you're not in control of your boat.

I slipped off my shoes, slid over the side, and dragged the dinghy back to the dock. So much for plan B—no truck, now no dinghy. I needed to be at Pirate Cove by dawn. I wasn't interested in swimming all that way. I wasn't interested in walking the six miles either, but I'd about run out of options.

I checked the parked vehicles for ignition keys. None. I could get

Billie's jeep started without a key, but I'd have to find it first. I hadn't a clue where it was.

I visited my prisoner. The quiet time I allowed him hadn't sobered him up enough to change his attitude. I headed off toward Pirate Cove, certain of only one thing: the public works honcho was going to have a more unpleasant night than I.

Of course, the cops would rescue him in the morning, but who would rescue me?

21

I WOKE TO LEARN I didn't need a weather report. Sea and sky joined in a seamless bond, feeding each other like two ancient gods at a Dionysian banquet. I expected the ambrosia and nectar would sate both by dusk, and after making love, their subsequent quarrel would erupt in violent fury. If the ancient gods taught hundreds of generations of humanity anything, it was a lesson in the certainties of love and war.

I rolled over and got to my knees. Before standing, I emptied my pockets onto the sand next to the revolver. Cold, stiff, and bleary-eyed, I pulled off my shirt and limped into Pirate Cove. Except for sand instead of shingle, it felt a bit like the Arctic Ocean.

When the water reached my thighs, I dove. Once in, it wasn't so bad. I dove again—this time with my eyes open. I could see just fine—but I already knew that. Still, the salt burned my eyes, and last night's injury to my forehead was painful enough that it felt like I'd grown a third eye. I could've used a third eye. I figured I had only an hour to find Vaughn's cocaine.

It was a swim to the area where I spotted Vaughn circling in his dinghy a few days ago. My ribs felt better, but I gave up on the crawl for the less energetic sidestroke. When I got close, I switched to breaststroke—five strokes on the surface and then a long dive. The water was surprisingly shallow, which tempted me to move farther away from the rocky arm on my left, but I maintained the discipline necessary for a thorough search, though each stroke detonated a flash of pain in my chest.

If you find what you're looking for, you always find it in the last place you look. I didn't want to not find it and have to start over. I repeated the program of five strokes and a dive several times more, until I passed beyond the rocky arm. Then I swam about ten feet closer to the center of the cove and aligned myself with the butterfly tree—barren today.

Just before I resumed my search, I spotted five key deer at the far end of the cove near the ruins of a colonial building. I'd seen them once before, nearly a year ago, but I didn't think I'd ever see them again; I thought they'd be as extinct as the monk seal. The deer were similar in size to goats, but leggy. I was pretty sure that those five animals represented the entire deer population of St. Judas. I was pretty sure, also, that in order to survive, they had to be about the smartest or most cautious animals on the island.

On the fourth dive on my new heading, I got lucky. I found eleven duffle-sized bales of what I presumed to be cocaine wrapped in yellow nylon fishnet and stuffed into a small underwater cave. I popped to the surface to catch my breath. Being so close to so much potential trouble gave me pause. I had no interest in giving the criminal justice system any more ammunition. A weekend in jail was one thing. Real incarceration was another deal altogether.

I dove again to determine if I could get the bales loose from the fishnet without swimming back to shore for my pocketknife. It took me two additional dives to determine that I could free the bales with my bare hands.

I treaded water and turned off my mind to allow desires and aims, plans and outcomes to coagulate in my brain. When one notion attained critical mass, I swam to shore and scouted the low-lying arm with its scraggly vegetation. Several kitchen stove-sized boulders helped form the arm's spine, but most of the rocks were small. Aubrey's front-end loader would have been my implement of choice to create a hiding place, but I determined to make do with what was available.

I decided to leave six bales in the cave for the Shirt to find and to drag five ashore to return to Vaughn. Each of the bales—stamped by U.S. Customs, packed in buoyant material, and wrapped in poly— weighed about seventy-five pounds. Getting the bales to the surface and pushing them ashore presented no real problem, but hauling them to the hiding place I selected involved a bit more work. After I piled them behind the largest boulder, I covered the bales with a few dead tree branches and covered the branches with several rocks.

I swam back to the small cave. From my vantage—six inches above sea level—the bales looked well hidden, but they couldn't stay there long. The first nosy tourist to show up here would likely find them in about ten minutes—the few tourists that made it all the way from Sugar Harbor to Pirate Cove generally were intent upon exploration; they seemed to cling to the notion that the island was still uncharted.

I swam back to the beach to explore the accessibility of my hiding place from land. It was the sort of trek better undertaken in hiking boots and long pants—lacerations drew enough blood that I felt like a self-flagellant. After my own bushwhacking blazed a trail, the hike presented only a moderate level of difficulty. That realization gave me serious reservations about a successful outcome to my plan, but I was out of time and ideas.

I started back to Flamingo Bay in bare feet, carrying my shoes—last night's walk raised nice blisters on my heels and hadn't done my knee any good. I figured I had at least two miles to march before I could even hope to find a ride. I knew that every step farther than two miles was going to put me in a fouler mood than I was already in.

I sank into the mangroves' oozy mud. The mud soothed my aching feet, but the sucking sound of each step reminded me of how mired I was. Beyond the swamp rose the steep hill covered with sharp loose flakes of stone broken away from the solid-rock roadbed. I stepped into my shoes and started climbing. By the time I reached the summit, my eyes no longer burned, but my chest and lungs and knee and heels did. I pulled the gun from the waistband of my shorts, where it poked into my belly, and slipped it back into my shorts against my kidney. Then I kicked off my shoes to learn I'd busted the blisters. I continued on bare feet.

When I neared Doctor's, I discovered that the old corrugated-metal roofing, punctured by dozens of bullet holes, had been torn off. The wood decking had also been removed, replaced by new cypress. Somebody else had also seen the potential in Doctor's cottage and made a deal with Miss Lucinda.

Upon reaching the cottage, I found Billie's jeep parked next to a pile of construction debris that included the cottage's old roof and decking along with kitchen countertops and the termite-infested cabinets. A mound of freshly cut bush stood nearby. New red roofing material—stacked in long cardboard boxes—awaited installation.

I couldn't believe Billie had struck a deal with Miss Lucinda.

I stopped at the end of the driveway and looked for signs of life. Nothing. The windows were shuttered and the door closed. I glanced at Miss Lucinda's. Nothing going on there either. The wan and rusty-legged flamingo—about as healthy as I felt—sat cockeyed in her yard.

I slipped into my shoes and walked up the drive, passing a mound of coconut husks left there by Sweetheart—proof of her devotion, especially since no coconut palm grew within a mile of the cottage. The husks represented the deaths of hundreds of coconuts. I wondered for a moment about the size of the mound of chaff that was the detritus of my life but quickly rejected any attempt to quantify it. I knocked on the door. I waited a few moments and knocked again.

Billie—still half asleep—opened the heavy mahogany just far enough to stick her head out.

"Oh-my-god! You look terrible."

"I feel terrible."

"What happened?"

"What do you mean?"

"I've seen that I-really-screwed-up-bad look before."

"I'm sure you're just mistaking it for my just-another-ho-hum-day-in-paradise air."

"Well, I suppose you can come in and see our new house— Mine, anyway. The *our* part is up to you."

She pulled open the door, and I followed her inside. Her dry kiss ended our long hug.

Billie wore a T-shirt that reached all the way to modesty. A sleeping bag, protected by two duffle bags, a backpack, and a cooler rested in the middle of the otherwise empty but clean room. Billie stooped to dig two Cokes from the cooler, offered me one, and gestured that I take a seat on the cooler. She sat Indian style on the sleeping bag, one hand holding her T-shirt to her crotch. The distance between us seemed to span months instead of days.

"You've ruined my surprise," she said. "Didn't you get my note?"

"What note?"

"The note I left on *Island Trader*."

"I haven't set foot on her since the day we went to Norman Island."

"I tried to visit you in jail on Saturday," she said. "I even baked cookies—Pirate Dan let me use the oven at the Congo Club. I made it all the way to the jail, but they wouldn't let me see you."

"Figures."

"We have some catching up to do."

"A lot."

"Mary and I parted. That's why I'm here. No, that's why I'm like not there. I'm here because I made a deal with Miss Lucinda. I bought the place."

"Just like that?"

"No, I've been thinking about *a* place for a long time. I'm ready to settle down. You know that. I hope to close the transaction this week. I gave Miss Lucinda an earnest money check, and she gave me early possession. I worked on the assumption that you hadn't changed your mind in the last few days. You did tell me that this is where you wanted to live."

"I haven't changed my mind."

Billie cocked her head and looked me in the eye. "You don't sound excited or even happy."

"I'm just surprised. I had no idea what you were up to."

"And you thought I couldn't keep a secret."

"When we have more time, you're going to have to tell me how you talked Miss Lucinda into selling real estate to a Continental—a hot, gorgeous, intelligent, kind-hearted Continental, but a Continental just the same."

"I appealed to her maternal instinct and her desire for financial security."

"The art business has been very good to you."

"It has," Billie said. "But my grandparents have been even better to me. I inherited their farm last year."

"You've accomplished a lot here in a short time."

"Rolly and his crew are working on the roof—"

"Good choice of color. Someday, this cottage might just have the last red roof on the island."

"I thought you'd like it. After that, he's going to build kitchen cabinets—the mahogany I asked you for. Elroy's working on the landscaping. I siphoned the water from the cistern. Then I cleaned and sanitized it, destroying three pair of latex gloves in the process." Billie held up her red swollen hands. "Look."

"Nasty."

"I have plans for a deck out back and a gazebo where I can set up my easel. I know you gave Rolly permission to give me the lumber I need, but he seems to think a mahogany gazebo and deck is like beyond extravagance."

"It's not, and I'll talk to him."

"With any luck, Rolly will finish the roof today—before the big storm. I'm undecided whether to hook up the rain leaders today or wait until after the storm. I'd prefer not to get any saltwater in the cistern, but I'm equally excited over the prospect of hot water flowing from a shower head."

"Hook them up. If the storm picks up a lot of seawater, just drain it again and go buy a truckload of fresh water."

"That's an idea."

"How big is this storm?" I asked.

"Not likely a hurricane, but it could be close. The depression is still increasing in intensity."

"Are we in its path?"

"Dead on, so far. Should hit tonight. Her name will be Penny, if she earns it."

I finished the last of my Coke and decided that I couldn't generate any more small talk. "I have a confession," I said.

"I thought you might."

"I'm afraid I made a mess of everything."

"Can it be fixed?" she asked.

"I don't know if it can, and I don't know how to do it."

"Start at the beginning."

"I'll tell you on the way to Easys. I have to meet the Shirt. Give me a ride?"

Billie pulled on some shorts and flip-flops, picked up her backpack, and followed me out the door.

"What are you doing with a gun?"

I explained the gun and shifted it from back to front, as I climbed into her jeep. On the way to Easys, my explanation continued. I explained my prisoner. I explained my truck. I explained my dinghy. I explained why I was meeting the Shirt. I explained where I hid Vaughn's cocaine—in the event I wouldn't see him again. I told her I was sorry.

Billie pulled to the side of the road when we reached Easys. The place was empty so early in the morning—part of my plan. Not part of my plan were the dozens of officials milling around at the playground, including what looked like every vehicle owned by the VIPD.

"Keep the jeep," she said. "Do what you need to do. I'm going to walk over to the playground and check out the action, see what I can do to repair the damage. I'll catch up with you later. Do me a favor?"

"Anything."

"Stay out of trouble."

"Why do women always set impossibly high standards?"

"It's up to us to keep pushing the human race toward the finish line."

I found a paper and pencil in Billie's backpack and took a seat at the bar to draw a map of Pirate Cove for the Shirt. The finished product would've embarrassed a cartographer, but I figured the *X* marking the spot gave it the only touch of professionalism the Shirt needed.

I waited only a few minutes before he showed. Wearing a yellow Aloha shirt, he climbed out of his vehicle empty-handed and joined me at the bar.

"Admiral. It is still *Admiral*, isn't it?"

"*Sir*, will suffice," I said, waving the map in his face. "I don't see my money."

"Sir Admiral, I knew you were just the man to send on this mission, and now that you've achieved success, you have to be feeling quite proud of yourself. Deservedly so. Sir Admiral *Judas*. How does it feel to be selling out one of your friends for filthy lucre?"

"I don't think of it as selling out. I think of it as buying in. Don't forget, you promised to be my best friend."

It slowed him down for an instant, but only an instant.

"You really don't get it?"

"What?" I asked.

"That you're the biggest chump in Flamingo Bay. Had you pegged from the get-go. You're a big fairy. I wished and wished and wished I had bales of cocaine, and you appeared and made my wish come true."

"Your bedside manner needs improvement," I said.

I took my Bic out of my pocket and set fire to the map. The Shirt tried to grab it, but I protected it with my body. When the flame reached my fingers, I dropped it on the ground.

"What are you doing?" he asked.

"Concluding our business transaction." I got off my stool and walked to Billie's jeep. "Find somebody else to do business with."

The Shirt followed. He pushed me against the vehicle.

"Listen up, fuckhead." He breathed garlic in my face. "I'm taking no more shit from you."

He stuck the barrel of his gun against my chin.

"And I'm taking no more shit from you."

I pulled my pistol from my waistband and waved it under his nose, just to let him know the gun had been fired recently. Then I stuck the barrel against his chin.

"Should we count to three and fire?" I asked.

My weapon took a lot of starch out of the Shirt. His teeth disappeared behind tight lips, and he holstered his gun. I held onto my gun.

"Shall we forget the insults and conclude our business?" he asked.

"Sixty grand will conclude it."

"Half now, half later."

"No *later*. I'll take it all up front."

"If I find you're fucking with me, I *will* count to three and pull the trigger. Put a slug into the back of your head."

"There you go again, threatening me. Didn't they teach you manners at the University of Narcotics?"

"They taught me only to kick ass and take names."

"And that's your problem. When the carrot works better than the stick, use the carrot."

"Let's just finish our business," the Shirt said.

"Let's see the money."

He led me to his jeep where he pulled a black leather attaché case from the passenger seat and laid it on the hood. I flipped open the lid and checked a few stacks of bills. I closed the lid.

"As soon as you toss your gun into the bay, I'll draw you a new map."

The Shirt didn't hesitate. He pulled his pistol from his belt and lobbed it into the water. It splashed a few feet from shore, making its retrieval a bit less difficult than I intended. I wanted to congratulate the Shirt on the strength of his throwing arm, but I didn't bother. I quickly drew another map.

"Just follow this road until it ends. You'll be precisely where you want to be. The beach is usually deserted, but I'd recommend early morning for diving. The stuff's in a small cave in water about twelve feet deep. Look for elkhorn coral. Keep an eye out for sharks and pirates."

"How many bales?" he asked.

"I think there's six or seven. I'm not sure."

"Where's the rest?"

"Can't help you there. Maybe Vaughn took them with him. Maybe he hid them somewhere else. It was your idea to talk to me. I'm the one who suggested you talk to him."

I tossed the attaché case into Billie's jeep, turned the vehicle around, and headed to Doctor's. The Shirt sat in his jeep studying the map. He made no attempt to follow me.

At Doctor's, Rolly's crew installed the new roofing. I chatted a few minutes with Rolly before carrying Billie's backpack and my attaché case inside. I dropped her backpack onto the sleeping bag and continued through the bath and outdoor shower until I reached the cistern. Checking to make sure the workers were still on the other side of the building, I opened the cistern's hatch and hung the attaché on the hook where I'd earlier found the bit of nylon cloth.

I rifled Billie's cooler and found a fried chicken leg and thigh. I stuffed them in one pocket and a Coke in the other, before heading out. I asked Rolly if he'd seen a vehicle come by in the last few minutes. He hadn't. The walk to Pirate Cove was no shorter heading in the opposite direction, but keeping alert for evidence of an approaching vehicle somehow made the hike less painful, forcing me to pay less attention to my injuries.

I hiked over to the far end of the cove, where I spotted the key deer earlier, and set up my camp. One corner of the ruined Great House, constructed of brick and stone and coral, rose a couple of feet above grade, providing good cover and an excellent view of the cove. While snacking on the chicken, I began to feel I could pull off my plan to limit the Shirt to only half of Vaughn's cocaine—the man was buying a lot of fairy dust for fifty grand; for however tough he talked, the bargain should make the him ecstatic. On the other hand, I figured the Shirt had a lot in common with Samuel Gompers, a man whose aim focused on the key word: *more*.

It made me a bit nervous to reflect that there might not be enough cocaine in Columbia to satisfy the Shirt.

I searched the sky for breaks in the single hemispheric cloud that stretched in all directions to the horizon. I found none. Overhead, a hawk climbed a wide spiral to meet the sky. I hoped the Shirt would hurry and pick up his cocaine. I was running out of time to prepare *Island Trader* for a blow.

I smoked my fourth cigarette when I heard a vehicle approach. I didn't know what to expect, but I certainly didn't expect the Shirt would be arriving with Easy.

Easy backed his green pickup as close to the water as he could, while still keeping all four tires on solid ground. Still, he parked a good distance from shore. After climbing out of the truck, they spoke only a few words to each other, but most utterances ended in laughter.

Each time I heard laughter, I grew angrier. I couldn't believe Easy would ally himself with the Shirt; after today, he wouldn't have a single friend in Flamingo Bay.

They unloaded the Shirt's Avon inflatable from the bed of Easy's pickup, carried it to the beach, and dropped it in the water. They returned to the truck. Easy struggled with the outboard, and the Shirt carried the fuel tank. While the Shirt attached the outboard to the dinghy's transom, Easy returned to the truck. He sat on the tailgate and unlaced his boots. Then he stripped off his shirt and bib overalls and donned his scuba gear.

Within minutes, the two began their search—Easy swimming beneath the surface, breathing compressed air, the Shirt motoring in his dinghy, following Easy's air bubbles. Then the Shirt shut down his motor. It hadn't taken them long to find Vaughn's cocaine—maybe I did have a career ahead of me as a cartographer.

Easy hauled up a bale. It was about the size of a hundred-pound sack of potatoes. He pushed, while the Shirt pulled it aboard. The seas were building, and the Shirt had to start his outboard a couple of times, as his dinghy drifted toward shore. Even so, it took them only fifteen minutes to load all six bales.

The Shirt started his motor and buzzed out of the bay in his dangerously overloaded dinghy, giving Easy a final salute.

Easy swam to shore, took off his fins, and waddled onto the beach. He dropped his gear into the bed of the truck and dressed, pulling on his lace-up boots while sitting on the truck's tailgate.

I steeled myself for the walk back to Doctor's, figuring to follow Easy. I wanted to witness the Shirt's exit from Flamingo Bay on *Golden Parachute*. I wanted to see if he'd take Sarah with him, though I doubted he would. The Shirt was smart enough not to put cocaine and an addict together. I knew I could walk all the way to the dinghy dock in the time it would take the Shirt to get there by sea—he had a good distance to go before he reached the protected waters of Flamingo Bay—but I felt a sense of urgency to get moving.

Instead of climbing into his pickup and heading out, Easy decided to take a hike. Naturally, he picked the rocky arm where I'd hidden the bales. He, along with everyone else on St. Judas, knew Vaughn found twelve bales. As soon as Easy disappeared from view, I trotted to his pickup, opened the hood, popped the distributor cap, pocketed the rotor, replaced the cap, closed the hood, and hurried back to my hideout.

Sure enough, Easy returned carrying the first bale on his shoulder. Once he'd loaded all five into the back of the truck, he climbed into the cab and tried to start the vehicle. His behavior, when the truck didn't start, reminded me of how Easy got his moniker. It wasn't because of his easy manner. *Easy* was the word his friends in Alaska used to calm him when he went ballistic.

His tantrum was similar to Officer Richards' when I pulled the dead donkey trick. When he wore the battery down, Easy cursed and kicked his vehicle. After he got that out of his system, he opened the hood, stuffed his hands in his pockets, and studied the engine compartment; he didn't learn a thing. After slamming the hood, he unloaded the bales to a new location in the bush just beyond the butterfly tree. Then he headed out on foot.

I smoked a cigarette to put a little distance between us and to allow the truck's starter motor to cool down and the cylinders' excess gas to drain into the oil pan. I crossed my fingers that the battery still held enough of a charge that I could start the engine. When I figured enough time elapsed, I installed the rotor and turned the key. The engine caught. I backed it as close to the bales as I could. Then I loaded them up.

When I reached the mangroves, I stopped and dragged the bales into the swamp, a good distance from the road. Then I climbed into the truck, shifted into four-wheel drive, and chugged up the steep hill. At the top of the hill, I stopped and thought about pushing the truck off the road. I thought the better of it—two counts of vehicular homicide was enough for one week.

Instead, I turned off the road to follow an old goat trail up the mountain. I bumped along it for about thirty feet until it became impassable. I stopped the truck and tossed the keys into the bush—anything to make Easy's life a bit less convenient.

22

At Doctor's, I ran into more company—quite the welcoming committee. A government-issue white Blazer blocked Billie's jeep, which was parked in the driveway behind Rolly's pickup. Behind the Blazer sat a Water and Power Authority truck. The wapa man, strapped to a utility pole, reconnected the cottage's electrical service. New red roofing dressed the front and one side of the hip roof, and pounding hammers rang from the building's rear. Elroy, cigarette dangling from his lips, swung a machete unenthusiastically at overgrown bush. He jerked his head to greet me. I waved.

Having spent too much time dealing with the bales and Easy's truck, I needed to borrow Billie's jeep. I walked up the driveway and entered the cottage. I found Billie and Almida. He sat on the cooler, and she sat on her sleeping bag.

"We been waiting for you," Almida said.

"Can we make this quick?" I asked. "I have to get to the head of the bay. I think something bad might happen."

"Something bad already happen," Almida said.

"Brian," Billie added. "Somebody killed the public works man you stopped from tearing down the playground."

I asked, "How?"

"Executed him," Almida said. "Shot him right between the eyes."

"When?"

"Last night late or morning early."

"It wasn't me," I said.

Billie said, "I already told him that."

"But you have his gun, right?"

"One bullet has been fired." I handed the weapon to Almida. "I shot the crotch out of his pants when he became abusive. The slug's in the ground next to the monkey bars."

"Police be wanting to talk with you," Almida said.

"You mean they want to railroad me. It'll never happen."

The wapa guy knocked on the door. I opened it.

"You got juice," he said.

Billie called her thanks, and as I started to close the door behind
him, I saw Elroy toss away his cigarette. I crossed my fingers that my
own Flamingo Bay irregular had been on duty last night. I called him
inside. While Elroy slouched toward me on bare feet, Billie flipped a
switch, popping on two ceiling lights that took the edge off the cottage's gloom.

"Elroy," I said, "who shot the public works honcho at the playground last night?"

Elroy looked at me, then at Billie, and finally at Almida.

"Just tell us what you saw," I coaxed.

Elroy bobbed his head, as if trying to get the words to spill from
his mouth. Billie crossed fingers on both hands and closed her eyes. I
stopped breathing. Almida couldn't hide his impatience.

Just as Rolly's crew started hammering a new section of roofing into
place, Almida said, "We're wasting time."

Elroy's head stopped bobbing. Billie opened her eyes and relaxed
her fingers. I exhaled.

"We have plenty of time to hear what Elroy has to say," I said.

Almida shrugged his shoulders.

"Elroy," I pled, "just tell us what you saw."

My entreaty started Elroy bobbing his head again. We focused our
attention. Rolly's crew, as if on cue, suspended its hammering. Finally,
Elroy opened his mouth.

"Captain Brian shoot he in balls. Officer Richards shoot he in
head."

After that pronouncement, Elroy turned and walked out of the cottage before I could even attempt to hoist him on my shoulders for a
victory lap. As I closed the door behind Elroy, I tried to think of how
to repay his vigilance. There weren't enough cigarettes on the island.
Something else then.

"Is Brian off the hook with you?" Billie asked Almida.

"For now," he answered.

I asked, "Will Elroy's testimony stand up in court?"

Almida shrugged. "I don't know. Better if we nail Richards without Elroy."

A glimpse at the Caribbean from Billie's patio door confirmed that the sea—gray and sullen—was turning angry, but it had a long way to go before it got as angry as I was. I promised Officer Richards that I'd jam him up. I just needed to figure out how. It didn't seem likely anyone was going to do it for me.

"Look, I've got to go. I have to get my boat over to Hurricane Hole. Can we resume this conversation later?"

Almida nodded, and we all headed out. I tossed Elroy a pack of cigarettes before I climbed into Billie's jeep.

I drove and attempted to put Doctor's rapidly behind us. I gripped the steering wheel, but Billie had nothing to hold on to, so she held onto me, left arm wrapped around my neck, right hand gripping the waistband of my shorts.

When we reached the spot high up on the mountain where I almost tricked Officer Richards into rear-ending my truck, I could see that *Island Trader* was no longer sleeping like an island. Even in the protection of Flamingo Bay, the seas were heavy enough to cause her to pitch ever so slightly.

"There he is!" Billie shouted into my ear, pointing below and in front of us.

I took my eye off the road long enough to see the Shirt hugging the shoreline in his dinghy, bouncing on the rough seas toward *Golden Parachute*. He was only a hundred yards ahead of us. I knew we'd easily beat him to the head of the bay.

At Easys, Marsha served the patrons, while Mechanic Jim and Easy conferred by the side of the road. I wanted to talk to Jim, but I didn't want to talk to Easy, so I kept going. Not wanting to clutter the road with the jeep's suspension, I came almost to a stop when we reached the sign: CLAM DIP.

"Oh, I found the gas tank for your dinghy," Billie said. "It was up the beach a ways, filled with sand. Mechanic Jim had business in town. He offered to clean the tank out with kerosene and refill it. Maybe we should go back and ask him."

"I'll check my dinghy first."

I glanced toward the mouth of the bay to see if I could spot the Shirt, but mangroves blocked my view. I shifted into second gear and crushed the gas pedal.

When we reached the intersection, Billie said, "You can drop me here."

"For what?" I asked, slowing the vehicle.

"I'm not finished with Almida. I'm going to wait for him."

I stopped the jeep and frowned. I assumed Billie was going to help secure the boat, not run off with Almida.

"Brian, are you mad at me?"

"For what?"

"For telling Almida."

"I can't say I'm thrilled. But better him than the police."

"That's what I thought. He's on your side. I think he can help get this mess resolved. It's important to me and even more important to you."

Billie planted a quick kiss on my cheek and climbed out, dragging her backpack behind her. The Shirt was about five minutes away from *Golden Parachute*. His overloaded dinghy plowed through the water like a miniature garbage scow.

"Catch you later," I said, gunning the engine and releasing the clutch.

When I reached the dinghy dock, the Shirt was a just a few yards from *Golden Parachute*. I thought about stopping at the Congo Club to recruit a hand or two to assist me in preparing *Island Trader* for a blow, but I didn't trust the Shirt to leave quietly, so I hurried to my dinghy, crossing my fingers that Mechanic Jim returned the gas tank, thinking if I crossed my fingers another time this week I'd develop carpal tunnel. I relaxed my fingers when I discovered the gas tank was aboard. I connected the gas line, squeezed fuel into the carburetor, and yanked on the cord. It took a few tries to fire up the Yamaha.

I buzzed into the harbor. The gusting wind raised a bit of a chop, and the dinghy bounced like a skipping stone. As I cleared the moored boats and closed on *Island Trader*, I spotted the Shirt standing in his dinghy, pushing a bale onto the deck of *Golden Parachute* anchored on the other side of the harbor. No one stood on deck to help him. I guessed that he and Sarah had already parted ways. I didn't believe she had enough sense to walk away from that situation; likely, the Shirt made the decision for her. At least he wasn't a complete asshole.

Of course, I knew that already. I knew, also, that in another place and another time—throw in a career change—we could be friends, just as a change of venue would destabilize many of my present relationships on St. Judas.

Nearly drenched from my ride, I climbed aboard *Island Trader* and tied off the dinghy. After firing up the diesel, I jammed the transmission into gear to take the tension off the mooring chain and headed forward to drop it. Back at the helm, I shoved the throttle all the way forward. The diesel roared, sending a strong vibration though the hull and deck, and *Island Trader* started making headway, though the engine's bark was much more intimidating than its bite.

The Shirt loaded his last bale and walked his dinghy around to the stern rail where he tied it off. He evidently intended to weigh anchor. I relaxed at the prospect of getting my life back, and I watched him struggle with the bales, carrying them below, one by one.

Hurricane Hole—my destination—was about a half mile away when the Shirt weighed anchor. Instead of hoisting the sails and heading toward the open sea, the Shirt motored toward me. I had no idea of his plan. I hoped he just proposed to say goodbye, but I couldn't be sure. I tied the wheel and hurried forward to load my cannon—just in case— though with only one round of ammo, I felt less prepared than Aethelred the Unready.

The man I bought the cannon from told me its range was about fifty feet with one load of powder. An additional load would almost double that, he said. I was pretty sure I could miss the broad side of a barn even at fifty feet. Still, I stuck in the fuse, dropped in two loads of powder, tamped it, loaded the cannonball, and tamped it before returning to the helm.

When the Shirt closed to within fifty feet, he turned sharply to starboard and ran alongside, matching my speed.

"Hey, Midshipman Brian!" he called, doffing his black baseball cap. "Before I leave, I just want to alert you to the fact that I know you fucked me out of at least four bales, maybe five. I'll forget about it eventually, but you won't."

The Shirt lit a cigar, tossed me a final salute, and pushed the throttle forward. His unbuttoned yellow shirt waved in the breeze. *Golden*

Parachute easily pulled away. When she almost cleared *Island Trader*, the Shirt turned and waved what looked to be a small transistor radio. He pointed its antenna at me.

"Give my regards to Captain Nemo!" he hollered.

Suddenly a dull explosion shook *Island Trader*, and the Shirt crossed his arms in front of his face. A puff of dark smoke rose from the bow on the starboard side and disappeared like a smoke ring in the breeze. That was all. The silence that followed was so complete it seemed almost possible to believe the explosion hadn't occurred.

You can trick your mind until you inhale your final breath, and you can trick your heart until it breaks, but you can't trick your gut—the repository of immaculate perception. *Island Trader* was dying, and I knew I couldn't save her. I knew that, despite all outward appearances that her integrity remained intact.

My eyes burned so badly I could scarcely see. I tied the wheel and hurried below. Seawater—almost to my knees—poured in from a gaping hole in the bow. It took every bit of energy and determination to not give up and simply collapse. The object of my fabulous and anachronistic dream had become a drowning pool.

I climbed back on deck with the intent of firing my cannonball right between the Shirt's eyes, though I didn't figure I had a chance in hell of hitting him. Then, when I saw his position and course, I changed my mind. The Shirt provided part of the answer to my firing solution. I installed the cannon so it fired about ten degrees to starboard to clear the bowsprit. Its trajectory would align with *Golden Parachute* in a matter of seconds.

I realized my Bic was soaking wet in my pocket. I dug it out and flicked it. Nothing. I blew and flicked, blew and flicked, blew and flicked. I wiped the wheel with the sleeve of my shirt. Flick. Flick. I wiped it again. Flick. Flick. It ignited, and I lit the fuse. I looked up to see *Divertimento*, about a mile away, steaming toward the head of the bay. If Diver Vaughn had shown up a day earlier, he'd have saved me a lot of trouble. Oh, well. I figured he'd get a noisy reception.

I plugged my ears with my fingers.

Ka-boom.

If we'd been playing horseshoes instead of naval warfare, I might've gotten some points for my effort, but the cannonball splashed harmlessly into the sea, short and wide of its mark. The Shirt responded with a hearty laugh and pointed his bloody arm at me. I wondered if it was a scratch or something serious. I wondered how serious it would have to be to keep him from laughing at my misfortune.

A dry Bic might've made the difference. A shorter fuse, maybe. I'd never know. The only certainty: I couldn't do a damn thing to stop him from blowing out of Flamingo Bay.

Island Trader was traveling maybe three knots, but not for long. The seawater would reach the engine compartment in minutes. I figured to sail her until I couldn't. Her bow slowly dropped, and she barely responded to the wheel.

A hundred and fifty feet away, *Golden Parachute* seemed to have slowed considerably. The Shirt, blood streaming down his right arm, peered over the stern rail at the hull. He went below for a moment, then climbed back on deck with wet trouser legs. I suspected that shrapnel from his explosive device not only damaged his arm but *Golden Parachute*'s hull. I suspected he was hoist by his own petard.

Island Trader sank further into the sea, and her bow dropped lower still. For the first time in my life, I sailed downhill. Like the Easy Rider Rally, this voyage would be downhill all the way. Then her engine sputtered and died.

Thinking so much recently about the second law of thermodynamics, I'd crowded out of my mind the existence of Newton's first law of motion, one part of which states that a body in motion remains in motion with constant speed in a straight line unless compelled by a force to change that state. I'd nearly forgotten that principle until the momentum of *Island Trader* rapidly closed the distance to *Golden Parachute*, nearly dead in the water.

When seventy-five feet separated us, the Shirt—puzzled and pissed—tossed his cigar and pulled out his pistol. I ducked as he fired off five rounds in my direction—one round striking the mizzenmast at eye level just a few feet away—before he hurled his empty weapon at me.

Island Trader didn't respond to the helm, but I urged her toward the stern of *Golden Parachute* with willpower instead of the wheel. The

Shirt could've easily escaped in his dinghy, but he frittered away his time hoisting his mainsail. It suggested that the explosion had seriously damaged the engine, but not the hull.

Car horns blasted, and I turned to see patrons standing by the road at Easys. Arms waved. A procession of vehicles headed toward the dinghy dock. The whole harbor enjoyed the show. Big-time excitement.

Vaughn was within hailing distance and a flotilla of dinghies cast off from the dinghy dock when the Shirt dodged *Island Trader*'s bowsprit to avoid being skewered. He was holding onto his mast with both hands when *Island Trader*, in a collision of horrifying screeching and apocalyptic destruction, crunched *Golden Parachute* and split her right down the keel.

The Shirt flew over the port rail, and the mast followed him. *Golden Parachute* sank in a minute. Well, she didn't so much sink as shatter, and shards of fiberglass and teak decking floated on the waves along with the bales, buoyant cargo, and other flotsam.

The sea started coming in through *Island Trader*'s scuppers. Midship, the deck was already submerged. I untied the dinghy and fell into it. I started the Yamaha and watched *Island Trader*'s final voyage. When the canvas canopy that covered her cockpit slipped beneath the waves, only her three masts projected above the surface. She moved through the sea at periscope depth.

I shifted the Yamaha into gear and followed *Island Trader* until her masts slipped below the sea. It was impossible for me to believe she was still as steady as a submerging attack sub, as she sailed to her grave. I envisioned her resting at the bottom of the bay, properly interred, masts pointing toward the sky, compass set for eternity.

I spun my dinghy around and motored toward the wreckage. I spotted the Shirt floating fifty feet away. I twisted the handle of the outboard and accelerated to pick him up. When I reached the spot, I found it wasn't him, just his shirt. I motored aimlessly through the wreckage. The dinghy bounced like an under-inflated basketball.

I expected the asshole to leap out of the water any second—I'd seen too many bad movies. But the Shirt was gone. At least I didn't have to worry about traveling to Washington to receive an award for saving his life. I did worry a bit that I didn't have an opportunity to tie together his great toes. The Shirt would make a terrifying jumbie.

Daylight faded quickly. Even on a clear day, twilight is ephemeral in the tropics. I spotted an aluminum suitcase and dragged it aboard. Then I corralled the six square grouper before the flotilla of dinghies arrived from the head of the bay. Diver Vaughn, keeping *Divertimento* away from the wreckage and out of *Island Trader*'s path, was almost on top of me.

"Hey, Vaughn!" I yelled. "These are your bales!"

I dragged the bales to *Divertimento*, and Vaughn and Alice hauled them aboard. When all six were loaded, I climbed aboard after them. Vaughn handed me a beer and the three of us watched scavengers from Flamingo Bay sift through the wreckage for souvenirs and items of value.

"You could've charged admission," Vaughn said. "I'd thought I'd seen it all—"

"When you fired that cannon, I almost wet my pants," Alice interrupted.

"What happened?" Vaughn asked.

I told Vaughn the whole story of the Shirt and the bales, particularly the part about how the Shirt promised to get Vaughn locked up for the rest of his life. I even included the exact amount of the cash transaction involved and the fact that he wouldn't be getting any of the cash, though he would be getting all his bales. He didn't have a problem.

"Sorry about your boat," he said. "I bet you're sorry you ever ran into me at Pirate Cove."

"The thought crossed my mind."

It crossed my mind along with a million other thoughts, but the death of *Island Trader* was so overwhelming that all other thoughts seemed trivial. I'd been stripped of identity as completely as if my fingerprints had been erased, my face torn off, and the nerves to my prefrontal lobe severed.

Vaughn handed me another beer.

"You can be the first to congratulate us," Alice said, offering me her left hand, adorned with a simple gold band.

Though she'd lived in a world entirely different from her sister's,

I recognized Valerie in Alice's mannerisms. You can read into things whatever you want, but to me Alice's presence in Flamingo Bay provided a better reminder of Valerie than the playground.

"Congratulations. To life and health." I held out my beer bottle, and a single solid clink created by the three bottles sealed the toast.

"Getting back to the Shirt and the bales, I forgot one piece of information—Easy's treachery."

"I never would have thought that of Easy," Vaughn said, when I apprised him of Easy's complicity. "Do we buy him out, burn him out, or just chase him out?"

"It's your decision," I said. "Though if you decide to burn him out, I'm available this evening to assist. After that, you're on your own."

Vaughn asked, "Going somewhere?"

"Tonight."

Both wanted to know why, so I explained the result of last night's adventure at the playground.

"I saw the playground you built in Valerie's memory," Alice said, her eyes tearing up. "I even called my parents. They're coming down to—"

Alice couldn't get the words out before she broke down and hurried into the cabin sobbing. I watched Alice leave. Then I looked at Vaughn. Vaughn shook his head.

"Got a few minutes?" he asked.

"Secure the boat?"

He nodded.

While we motored to Hurricane Hole, I ran down the other key events that had occurred during his absence, specifically Jason's death and the problem Vaughn faced in removing his wrecked truck from the mountainside. We discussed doctoring the title, so the truck could belong to Jason and deteriorate in the bush, but decided that it would only screw up Wendy.

"Seems I need transportation," he said. "Is Valerie's old jeep still parked by the Congo Club?"

"It was the last time I noticed."

About two dozen boats were already tied up in Hurricane Hole, but we found a good anchorage. We tied two lines to shore and secured two anchors to the stern—the biggest risk for your boat riding out a storm in any harbor is the chance that a poorly anchored boat will catch your anchor line on its way to shore and your boat will end up on the beach as well.

When Vaughn was satisfied, we headed for the dock in separate dinghies. I hung back to allow Vaughn and Alice to reconnoiter the area. Alice checked the Congo Club, while Vaughn circumnavigated the fire station. He signaled the area was free of police before I tied up at the dock.

23

ALL I WANTED WAS BILLIE, a hot meal, and peace and quiet. Except for the hot meal, the Congo Club turned out to be the wrong destination. Raucous patrons arrived to party, and nobody had seen Billie. I fed Elroy a pack of cigarettes and posted him as a lookout. Then I took a seat at the end of the bar and set the aluminum suitcase on the floor.

Nancy asked, "What can I get you?"

"Nancy, what are my choices?"

"For not calling me 'Antsy,' you can have whatever you want, as long as it's a New York strip."

"Medium-rare, hold the anchovies."

Young faces—a few I'd seen before but most of them new to me— congregated at three tables near the railing, part of the annual influx of reinforcements that marked the advent of tourist season. I never spent much time getting to know them unless they survived the season. Next summer would be soon enough to take an interest in the few who survived, though I suspected the locals who'd already taken an interest could—with a high degree of accuracy—determine who among them had the right stuff to prosper in Flamingo Bay.

Vaughn's reemergence into Flamingo Bay society played big. His fans greeted him as if he was a rock star returning from the grave. Like me, he wanted a quiet dinner, so after he got Valerie's jeep jump-started, he banished them from his table with a loud and icily clear, "Later." He repeated the word once, and he and Alice were able to converse in peace.

I wasn't Vaughn, and I had no real fans, but I'd become a celebrity for the evening. I didn't have as much command over the situation as Vaughn, and his desire to be left alone funneled even more folk in my direction. I found cordiality difficult. Realizing that one or more of those seeking my ear possibly vandalized my vehicle when I was in jail made me even less affable.

Just when I figured I had every right to behave in a rude and mean-spirited fashion, Freddie Fellini—a young man who'd always been kind to me—stopped by to offer his condolences. Nikon around his neck and a new girl on his arm, Freddie correctly pointed out that he'd shot footage of almost every regatta and every event at sea over the past couple of years while aboard *Island Trader*. Because he was young—about Billie's age—Freddie and I didn't really hang out together, but he'd probably spent more time aboard *Island Trader* than anyone else in Flamingo Bay.

Freddie explained that he tried to capture the sinking of *Island Trader* and the ramming of *Golden Parachute* with his camcorder, and he pulled a videocassette from his pocket.

"You don't mind?"

I did mind. Watching *Island Trader* sink once was enough. I'd no desire to see it again. It would stay with me the rest of my life without a video reminder—the Shirt was right about that. Just as I couldn't keep Leif alive, I couldn't keep my boat afloat.

"Go ahead."

While Freddie warmed up the television and persuaded the bartender to turn off the music, I reflected that there'd been no shortage of new contributions to the Lore during the past week. I attempted to enumerate them, but I ran out of fingers. It wasn't my inability to do the math; it was a qualitative thing—whether to include Easy's treachery, Vaughn's marriage, my stay in jail. Of course, two events I'd rather not have had a hand in—the murder of the public works honcho and the sinking of *Golden Parachute*—were certain to become part of the permanent record, along with Jason's death.

The music died, and Freddie inserted the videocassette in the player. Many patrons sitting at tables joined the crush at the bar. The event was filmed near Easys, so the camera angle was to the starboard and stern of the boats. Though taped in color, the lack of light gave the impression of black and white. The video began with the hole already blown in *Islander Trader*'s hull. It showed two ghostly vessels, not much more distinct than shadows. Freddie recorded the firing of the cannon, but I didn't know if others could see the puff of smoke and the cannonball splash into the sea. If I hadn't known it happened, I couldn't be sure I would've seen it either. Then it was just two phantom boats, the larger one—sinking further into the sea—closing on the smaller one from the stern. Then the larger boat seemed to meld into the smaller one. It showed me—unrecognizable—abandoning ship. After that, Freddie focused on *Island Trader*'s masts, but they were difficult see. In the last frames, the sea looked empty.

Patrons cheered. They cheered even louder when the next image to appear on the screen was Marsha in full color—wearing only a mask and fins—swimming with a hawksbill turtle.

"Oops!" Freddie said, as he punched the remote and the screen went dark.

Freddie ignored the calls for an encore. He removed and pocketed the videocassette. The bartender turned up the music. People returned to their tables.

Employing the diplomacy of a state department veteran, Freddie thanked me for creating a wreck where he could film divers. I liked Freddie and didn't take offense. At least the sinking of *Island Trader* provided job security for one person. It then occurred to me that the pirates would be up early tomorrow morning to rape her. That realization started my pulse throbbing.

Before he left, Freddie introduced me to his girl—Linda. New to the island, Linda hoped to find a restaurant job for the season. I figured she'd have no problem. All she had to do was show up for work and smile. Smart restaurateurs understood that customers were less likely to have a flawed dining experience when being served by a sweet young girl who aimed to please.

"I took Linda into Sugar Harbor to apply for a job at Mimosa Café," Freddie said. "With Sarah going back to the States and all, I guessed there'd be an opening."

"Sarah really left?"

"I gave her a ride to the ferry. She said she had a ticket home."

I almost asked Freddie if he'd quizzed Sarah about her plane ticket, but I was pretty sure the Shirt had bought it for her. I wanted him to be the most evil man ever to wash up in Flamingo Bay, but I knew I wouldn't be surprised to learn that he'd become a Big Brother, funded a program for widows and orphans, or coughed up the cash to get the clinic—derelict since Hurricane Hugo—up and running.

Nancy delivered my steak, and Freddie and Linda said goodbye.

"Captain Brian, sorry about your boat. Your meal's on the house."

"I appreciate the gesture, but this is one of those days I can actually afford to buy dinner without hocking the family jewels."

"I appreciate that you've quit calling me 'Antsy' Nancy."

"You know—old dog, new tricks. But eventually I come around. You do know that I wouldn't have given you a nickname if I didn't like you. And you do know that it would've been a different name if we weren't genuinely impressed by your energy. And you do know, if another Nancy shows up, that nickname will get dusted off."

"I'll cross my fingers that another Nancy doesn't show up."

"Crossing my fingers usually works for me."

I hadn't swallowed my first bite when Helga came by and head-butted me in the thigh. I cut the tip off my steak and fed it to her. She swallowed her snack and curled up on the floor next to my stool, forcing Madison—quite chatty and looking for a shot of rum—to choose to sit two stools away.

The storm gained momentum. Gusting wind rippled the bar's Dacron awning. Now and again, the lights flickered. Because only a few couples danced and Marsha still wore her shirt, it signaled to me that the party hadn't yet reached escape velocity, though I figured I'd attained terminal velocity—the old interplay between gravity and levity. Something about the forced gaiety of the evening, coupled with the day's events, and the advent of the storm reminded me of the masque of the red death.

Pirate Dan took over for his bartender and brought me the next beer.

"Argh, what now?" he asked.

"Long term, I haven't a clue. Short term, dodge the police. They want me for the murder at the playground."

"Who did kill the guy?"

"Officer Richards. At least according to my source."

Dan directed me to the railing where a torn-up section of mahogany rested, a deck cleat screwed to it.

"What do you think?" he asked.

"*Golden Parachute?*"

Dan nodded. "I didn't find anything from *Island Trader*."

"Send Diver Vaughn down tomorrow for my cannon. That should make an interesting conversation piece and dress up your exhibit."

Dan, responding to an order from the other end of the bar, limped away. When I turned to watch his progress, I saw Easy take a stool next to Marsha. Easy was about the last virgin on the island—over two years without a woman is a long time, long enough that it's like starting over. It was Easy's big chance, though he'd better talk fast. I suspected whatever luck Easy had accrued was about to run out.

When he caught up with drink orders, Dan slipped a new tape into his machine, "Son of a Son of a Sailor." As I finished my meal, I listened to Jimmy Buffet sing about being glad not to live in a trailer.

"Listen up." Easy banged his beer bottle on the bar to get the patrons' attention. "I propose a toast. Here's to Captain Brian who, in the best tradition of the naval service and with valor above and beyond the call of duty, acted with disregard to his personal safety and the loss of his ship to single-handedly rout the enemy and preserve the felicity of Flamingo Bay. Whenever and wherever men go down to the sea in ships, they will go knowing Captain Brian has gone there before them."

I wanted to spit on the two-faced son of a bitch for riling the crowd, but my only consolation was that I messed up his day pretty good.

"Amen!"

"Here, here!"

"Coo coo ca-choo!"

"Gesundheit!"

"Speech, speech!"

I stood and bowed. "*Island Trader* lived nearly a hundred years—" Sadness as big and dark as the sky immobilized me. That place I stored my vocabulary was dark and empty, too. Somebody else's words then. None expressed the sentiment I felt. Then it was Ezra Pound's final public utterance I stole, a line he cribbed from Christopher Isherwood: "Words no good."

Partyers didn't know what to make of it, but the abruptness of my response shut them up for a few moments.

Diver Vaughn, finished with his meal, spoke a few words to Alice before getting up from his chair. He walked over to the bar, tapped Easy on the shoulder, and the two walked out of the Congo Club together. Alice left the table and joined me at the bar, maneuvering around Helga to reach the barstool.

"Sorry about my crying jag earlier," she said. "Usually it's the baby sister who looks up to her sibling, but I always looked up to Valerie. And I never got the chance to tell her how much I admired her. She lived the life I thought I couldn't have. I tried to please everyone but myself. Valerie and I grew further apart as the years passed. It bothered me, and I know it sounds corny, but I found consolation in her very existence. I felt Valerie shared her adventures with me just because she knew *I* existed. Vaughn said you were her best friend. What was she like? I mean, what did she like?"

"Sailing was probably her biggest passion. Before she got sick, we took *Island Trader* to Antigua where she won the women's laser race, a big-time event. Participants come from all over the Caribbean."

"I'm showing my ignorance, I know, but what's a laser?"

"Small racing boat, about fourteen feet in length, single mast, single sail." I finished the sentence, as tears welled in my eyes—all these weeks and I still didn't know if I cried for Valerie or myself. "I'm sorry, we'll have to do this another time."

"I hate to continue to be corny, but thank you for being her friend. Oh, God! Just ignore me."

Madison, waiting for an opportunity to join the conversation, caught Alice's attention. "Maybe you want to see petroglyphs? I know where they all be. I be a big shot in the islands. Captain Brian know me. I been to New York. I been to Washington. They calls me the cool cat."

Just as I suggested that Madison save the petroglyphs for another day, Wendy came by.

She said, "Captain Brian, can I speak to you for a minute?"

I excused myself to Alice, gave Helga a rub behind the ears, grabbed the suitcase, and followed Wendy out. I took a few bucks from my pocket and handed the bills to Elroy, suggesting that he go inside and buy himself a Ting.

"I'm sorry to hear about *Island Trader*. I know how much she meant to you. I don't know if you're in the market or in the position to buy another boat, but I'm selling *Argo*. I've decided to go back to the States. I'm willing to let it go for forty grand."

Argo was a forty-two-footer. A grand a foot worked for me. Teak deck, mahogany cabin—the Cheoy Lee was a real sailing vessel that appealed strongly to my retro sensibility. Buying her would qualify me to enter the Wooden Boat Race next Labor Day weekend at Foxy's, but it would end my run as an island trader, unless I started importing something smaller than building material—emeralds, gold, plutonium.

"I'm interested. Let's go take a look."

We motored to *Argo* in my dinghy. The air smelled like rain, but it was the bumpy ride that soaked us. Wendy tied us up, and I followed her aboard. She opened the hatch to the companionway and turned on a few lights. The main cabin was spacious. Well-appointed staterooms were situated fore and aft. The rich mahogany felt palatial compared with *Island Trader*'s steel. The sanitized galley was equipped well enough to prepare a real meal—I made do with a camp stove, no refrigeration, and rudimentary plumbing on *Island Trader*. Wendy demonstrated that the plumbing in the head functioned properly.

"The boat's low on fresh water, but everything works. We replaced the sails about a year ago, but the old ones are still aboard in case of emergency. The engine—a four-cylinder Volvo diesel—was rebuilt two years ago. We cleaned the hull this past summer. The deck needs refinishing, but that's about it, as far as I know."

Wendy gave me the ignition key and found me a flashlight, and I climbed on deck and headed toward the bow. I found one Danforth anchor and two CQR anchors. The inventor of the CQR—Sir Geoffrey Taylor—originally intended to call it "secure" but determined the homophonic initials to be catchier. It's a good anchor. On my way back to the helm, I bounced my palm on the port stanchions that held the wire guardrail. Then I tested the starboard stanchions. I found them anchored solidly as well.

The magnetic compass sat atop the binnacle under a glass dome. It looked accurate—at least within a couple degrees; the direction of the trade wind was steady enough that the moored boats in Flamingo Bay keep the same heading most of the time for most of the year. If it were late August or early September—when boats could rotate around their moorings like tetherballs—I wouldn't have been quite so casual.

I checked the engine oil and the belts and hoses. Everything appeared satisfactory. I ran the bilge pump. The pump hummed, but the bilge was dry. I closed the hatch and started the engine. It fired right up. The gauge showed a half tank of fuel. The ammeter indicated the batteries were charging. I went below and located five batteries. The electrolyte levels were okay.

I tried the stove and learned there was propane in the tank. Rummaging through the storage lockers, I found lifejackets, cleaning gear and supplies, and a few tools. I momentarily lamented the loss of my tools—a lifetime's collection—now sitting at the bottom of the bay. The next locker contained snorkeling and fishing gear and a lobster snare. I pulled a safety harness from an adjacent locker and examined it. In a drawer, I uncovered several maps and charts. They were mostly for the Virgins and a few other Leeward Islands. All were a bit regional for my inclination. Another locker held a box of paperbacks, and I thought of my sunken library. Sooner or later, I'd have to adjust to the fact that all my possessions lay at the bottom of the sea.

Wendy, looking over my shoulder, said, "You act like you've already bought the boat and you're planning a voyage."

"I plan to weigh anchor before the storm hits. You've got yourself a deal."

I needed a heading and a destination. After the storm, I'd make that decision. I felt almost the way I felt when I left Kansas twenty-five years ago. I was leaving nothing and everything. I was going nowhere and everywhere. The big difference, of course, is when you leave Kansas your fortunes are bound to improve. I had no experience in the matter, but leaving Flamingo Bay did not offer the same assurance. A strong possibility existed that I was leaving only to seek misfortune.

Though it would insinuate itself there eventually, I didn't want to find my elusive destination in my head. Nor did I want to find it in some ethereal numerical dimension, but in an actual geographic place. And not a diamond as big as the Ritz or Shangri-La, but definable by actual map coordinates. And not some fashionably holy place where the faithful gather in anticipation of the final big updraft, but a destination blessed with sacrilege.

The place I sought seemed to me to be very much like Flamingo Bay, like my home. It may be that the final destination is always Itháki—always home, a place you leave to find, though I couldn't discount the notion that the marvelous journey is the thing, the only thing.

I opened for the first time the aluminum suitcase. All along, I assumed I'd recovered the Bank of the Shirt, and I wasn't disappointed. It took me a while to count out the bills, but I reached forty grand before I ran out of Federal Reserve notes. Measuring how much money was left in the suitcase by the volume of how much I stacked on the table, I surmised the suitcase still contained about ten grand. Along with the money in the Shirt's attaché case and *Argo*, I had about the actual monetary value of *Island Trader*—her real value was incalculable: she was one of a kind.

I took the remaining cash from the suitcase, refilled it with the forty grand, then pushed the suitcase across the table to Wendy.

"I guess I should've asked more," she said, watching me stuff the remaining ten grand or so in my pockets.

Wendy was smart enough to know that nobody else in Flamingo Bay was going to buy *Argo*—Pirate Dan, Diver Vaughn, and maybe Zeke were the only men who could afford her, and they weren't in the market. Wendy had to understand, too, that if she waited until after the storm, she might have nothing to sell.

"If you're not happy, we don't have to do the deal."

"You could add a little more cash to the kitty."

"I could, but I won't. Buying *Argo* essentially puts me out of business. I can run day-sails with her, but there's not much adventure in that. I can enter her in the Wooden Boat Race over on Jost Van Dyke come Labor Day, but I'm not going to win. At this moment, I'm simply doing you a favor. Down the road, it may become a good decision for me. Who can say? The only thing that's for sure—I'm not doing the deal unless you're not just happy about it, but ecstatic."

Wendy worked her facial muscles, her lips puckered and relaxed as regularly as a metronome. With significantly less fervor than what I'd term "ecstasy," she signed the title over to me, and we shook hands.

"I've taken everything I want off the boat," she said. "Anything you don't want, just toss overboard."

I glanced around in search of anything personal. Propped in the galley was a framed photo of Jason standing next to a several-hundred-pound Atlantic blue marlin. The photo was snapped in St. Thomas some years ago. It was a good way to remember him—innocent and forever young. I grabbed the picture.

"I think you'll want this," I said, handing it to her.

She nodded and slipped it into the aluminum suitcase.

We secured the boat, climbed into my dinghy, and motored ashore. Vaughn and Alice were leaving the Congo Club, as Wendy and I arrived. Vaughn pulled me aside.

"I took your advice," he said. "I bought out Easy. He decided that a fresh start on St. Croix was his best move. I'm not sure what I'm going to do with the pop stand, but Alice thinks she might give it a try. Work it during the day. Hire someone for the evenings. Keep her from getting bored."

"Good luck."

Vaughn turned away, hesitated, and turned back.

"You didn't tell me you and Billie hooked up."

"I don't know how permanent it is."

"I sure got an earful from Easy. He blamed his bad behavior on your good luck."

"Oh, well."

"Look," Vaughn said. "Anything I can do, give me a holler. I'll be home this evening. Big day tomorrow. The judges are coming."

The four judges would surely win a popularity contest as the locals' favorite tourists. They came down twice a year. Sometimes they came alone. Sometimes they brought their wives. Sometimes they brought their girlfriends. Unlike most visitors who just got swallowed up in Flamingo Bay, the judges' visits always added a few episodes to the Lore.

Alice hooked her arm around Vaughn's, and they strolled over to Valerie's jeep, idling nearby.

The part of my brain that wasn't mourning *Island Trader* and my eponymous and fragile vocation felt expansive and rich. When I spotted Pony Mon sitting at the bar, I peeled off two grand from my roll before climbing the steps to the Congo Club. I weaved my way through gyrating couples and took a seat next to him. I handed Pony Mon the cash.

"I want you to buy a horse with this. It's not right that you're walking."

Pony Mon expressed undying gratitude and insisted upon buying me a beer. He'd already had a few before he arrived at the Congo Club, before he arrived at his maudlin state.

"You know I serve a hitch in navy. I see whole Pacific. I see Pearl Harbor. I see *Arizona*—"

That much of his pronouncement was coherent. What followed wasn't. But I got its gist. Pony Mon was most saddened that *Island Trader* was not sunk in shallow water. The monument he visualized for Flamingo Bay was very much like the monument at Pearl Harbor. Instead of the Stars and Stripes flying over *Island Trader*, Pony Mon favored the Jolly Roger.

I assured him it was a grand idea, ignoring just some of the obstacles to the monument's creation—cash, of course, and government participation being the two big ones.

While Pony Mon mumbled into his beer like it was a microphone. I glanced around the bar, hoping to find Billie, though I didn't need eyes to determine Billie's presence, and I knew she wasn't here. What I did see was Mechanic Jim dancing and laughing with Marsha.

Jim didn't hang out much. He argued it was because he was conserving his resources. When he did come around, we enjoyed his company. All along, I figured that money wasn't his only obstacle in embarking upon the next leg of his trip—the Panama Canal and the South Pacific—he was looking for a woman to accompany him. I suspected that he'd just found her.

Flashing emergency lights in the Congo Club's parking lot caused me to suspect that Officer Richards had just found me. I patted Pony Mon on the back, slipped through the deck's railing, and hit the sand running.

24

AFTER RUNNING OUT OF BEACH, I crossed the road and hiked up the hillside. I doubled back through the bush, continually losing my footing on the sharp rocks. When I reached a spot opposite the Congo Club, I sat and rested and watched. The cop car still squatted by the building's entrance, emergency lights flashing, white strobe pulsing. I didn't spot Officer Richards or any cop. I didn't spot any human being, for that matter. I hadn't a clue what was going on inside the Congo Club, except that it sounded like a carnival.

When I concluded that Richards or whichever of his cohorts that belonged to the vehicle wasn't leaving any time soon and Billie might not be arriving any time soon, I decided to start moving. I figured I'd outflank my adversary and make a dash for *Argo*. As I picked my way around loose rocks and thorny succulents and scrubby trees, I found a night-blooming cereus—not a flower you see every day, not a flower you see every year. I harvested the white bloom using my pocketknife. I cradled the volleyball-sized flower with both hands, and the gusting wind pushed me toward the cemetery.

I stooped and placed the flower on Valerie's grave. I didn't expect we'd meet up again at a lavender-sand beach, but there was a special place in my head where refracted signals between synapses created a lavender paradise where lost friends gathered.

I stood and gazed around me, committing to memory the physical details of land and sea. I studied, until it was etched in my brain, the black ridges of the mountains where they met the blue-black sky. Then the wind died and drizzle fell as gently as snowflakes. I stepped cautiously around the markers and worked my way down the hillside just as a gunshot cracked from the vicinity of the Congo Club. It ricocheted from the hillsides like light bouncing in a hall of mirrors.

I made a dash for the playground, and kept going until I reached the mangroves. After I fought my way into the woody thicket, I stopped to rest for a moment. A moment was too long. When I lifted my foot to take another step, I left my right shoe behind. My left shoe was anchored just as securely. I tried to pry them loose but ended up slipping in the ooze and falling on my butt.

Everything I ever wanted in life seemed just beyond my fingertips. I'd lost my friends and my boat and my vocation and my self-respect. In a few minutes, I expected to lose the love of my life. I sat in the muck, while rain and tears ran down my cheeks.

Wailing sirens interrupted my descent into self-pity. I got to my feet, left my shoes in the swamp and started on my way toward the dinghy dock.

My heart nearly exploded when I reached a break in the mangroves and ran bang into another human being. Elroy didn't seem startled in the least. He jerked his head in greeting. I banged two fingers against my lips, and Elroy dug from his pocket the pack of cigarettes I'd given him earlier and offered me one. We smoked in silence for a minute or two. Elroy began to bob his head. I waited patiently for his pronouncement.

"Officer Richards say he shoot you tonight, but I shoot he."

With that mind-numbing confession, Elroy produced Richards' gun from his other pocket. The rain began to fall in torrents, and the wind picked up, whipping tree branches and our wet T-shirts. Two police cars raced past us toward the Congo Club, emergency lights flashing and sirens screaming.

As Elroy calmly smoked the cigarette protected in his cupped hand, I realized that I couldn't let him take the fall. In the irony of ironies, I realized Elroy was my new best friend. Life had dealt him a rotten hand, but it was somehow important that he continue his peregrinations in Flamingo Bay, more important than anything.

"Elroy, give me the gun."

He bobbed his head and handed it over. I tucked it into the waistband of my shorts.

"Now go home. If the police or anyone ask you about where you were when Richards was shot, you tell them you were with me in the mangroves hunting whelk."

"No whelk here," he said.

"Of course not. And if anyone asks you, you say we didn't find any.

Say, it was my idea. Say, I said whelk hide in mangroves when it storms. Okay?"

He bobbed his head and followed me out of the swamp. When we reached the road, he headed in the direction of his home. I headed for the Congo Club. The ambulance that was permanently stationed at the firehouse next door to the Congo Club raced by on the way to Sugar Harbor, emergency lights on but no siren. Red, white, and blue lights from three parked squads at the Congo Club flared against sheets of rain.

I arrived at the Congo Club in time to hear Pirate Dan holding court.

"Argh! Officer Richards, drunker than shit, walks in. After he knocks Elroy to the floor, he steps up to the bar and orders a bottle of Cruzan Rum. I tell him I sell it only by the glass. He gives me a bunch of shit. Says he isn't planning on paying anyway, and if I don't give him the rum, he'll close down my joint. So while we're arguing, Elroy picks himself off the floor, walks over to Richards, pulls Richards' gun from his holster and shoots him point-blank in the back of the head."

"Hold on," I said. "You're mistaken about the identity of the assailant. Elroy was with me. We've been hunting gastropod mollusks over in the mangroves—"

"Hold on yourself," Sergeant March said. "Gastropod mollusks?"

"Whelk. Elroy and I hunted whelk. I ran over here as soon as I heard the shot. I even lost my shoes in the swamp."

"Where Elroy be?" March asked.

"It was getting late, so I sent him home."

"Forty people place Elroy in bar."

"They're all too drunk to have a clue," I said. "Pirate Dan, can you swear on a stack of Bibles that the man you saw shoot Richards was Elroy?"

"Argh, it looked like Elroy, but it all happened so fast. I suppose I could've been mistaken."

"Mechanic Jim?"

"No way it was Elroy. Looked like some guy from down island."

"Zeke?"

"Zeke doesn't see shooter before tonight. Dude doesn't speak English. Maybe he be a Haitian."

Gusting wind carried the rain further into the Congo Club. People near the railing abandoned their tables.

Zeke, warming to the sound of his own voice, paused to concoct what I presumed would be an even taller tale when Billie and Almida strolled in. Sergeant March brought Almida up to speed. Billie separated me from the crowd.

"I'm surprised you're still here," she said. "I thought you might pull a Shane on me."

"I can't say the thought hadn't crossed my mind."

Billie gave me the cocked-head stare.

"Okay, I've been trying all afternoon to get off this rock."

"That's what I thought."

"Where have you been?"

"Taking tea with Almida and the governor. You're off the hook for the murder of the public works guy."

"Just like that?"

"Not just like that, or it wouldn't have taken us so long. You owe Almida big time."

"But you're the one who persuaded Almida. Thank you. Ever think about going to law school? You could become my attorney."

"No thanks. I'll stick to being your lover. Now tell me what's going on."

"Richards caught a bullet in the back of the head. Looks like the assassin isn't local."

We listened, as Sergeant March asked the patrons if anyone present could identify the assailant. No one could.

The wind gained momentum, pushing folk farther from the railing toward the landward and leeward side of the building. Wind-born objects of real mass sailed by, distinguishable only by the exotic sounds produced by the objects' specific aerodynamic deficiencies.

People wanted to get to their houses and their boats. Functionaries wanted to get back to Sugar Harbor. The police cleared out first. Almida wanted to talk, but getting home was a higher priority.

"Captain Brian, we talk tomorrow."

"I'll plan on it." I shook his hand. "Thanks for your help."

Almida sprinted for his vehicle. A mass exodus of patrons followed. Billie and I gave them a few minutes start.

When Pirate Dan and his crew secured the Congo Club and doused the lights, Billie sprinted for her jeep. I darted into the wall of water after her. Before she could climb in, I grabbed her hand and led her to the dinghy dock.

"Where are we going?" she asked.

"To secure my boat."

"I never figured you for a procrastinator."

"I have a surprise."

My night vision required another fifteen minutes before it functioned optimally, though I wasn't sure I'd be able to see much until after the storm. Even in daylight, visibility is about nil during a tropical storm.

Only one dinghy was tied to the dock. I didn't waste time learning if it was mine. We climbed aboard. As I groped the outboard, I felt a sense of comfort when I touched my familiar Yamaha. I started the engine, and Billie untied the painter. We motored slowly into the harbor.

"Where're we going?" Billie shouted and pointed. "*Island Trader* is over there."

"That's my surprise," I hollered.

I found *Argo*, and Billie climbed aboard with the painter when I bumped the hull. I followed her and tied off the inflatable to the rail. I opened the hatch to the companionway, and she followed me below.

"Brian, what's going on?"

"You missed the event of the season when you left for Sugar Harbor with Almida. Two events, actually. You got the justice you were looking for, or at least a close approximation—Richards is dead, and so is the Shirt. The scenario I laid out for you the other day was on the money. The Shirt did pay Richards to arrest Leif—five grand. The arrest turned bad, and Leif died. I don't know why Richards shot the public works honcho. I suspect it was to frame me, though there might have been something else going on as well. Richards evidently heard that I was off the hook for the honcho's murder, and he came looking for me. According to Elroy, Richards announced that he was going to shoot me. Elroy used Richards' gun to shoot him. That was the fuss you walked into at the Congo Club. Witnesses were quickly losing their memories of the incident. They didn't want Elroy to take the fall. Of course, this all occurred after the Shirt blew a hole in the hull of *Island Trader* and I rammed *Golden Parachute*. Both boats and the Shirt are at the bottom of the bay."

Billie punctuated each new revelation with an "Oh-my-god!" Then she demanded to hear each excruciating detail of *Island Trader*'s death and the sinking of *Golden Parachute*. When I finished, Billie asked about my purchase of *Argo*.

"I was trying to solve both our problems. When I agreed to give Wendy her asking price for the boat, I was buying transportation from St. Judas. I was also trying to solve her financial crisis—she's broke and wants to return to the States—and I was offering to take responsibility for *Argo* in light of the approaching storm."

I turned on the radio to hear the weather report. It put Flamingo Bay in the path of a tropical depression that now seemed close to acquiring a name and biography—the barometer was still falling.

"What now?" Billie asked.

"I need to get *Argo* out of Flamingo Bay—there's no time to secure her. I may also need to stay away until the dust settles."

"It'll settle quickly in this downpour— Forgive me. I'm sorry, I didn't mean that. I'm sorry about *Island Trader*. I'm sorry about everything."

Billie hugged me. The embrace was complete and ended with a kiss that lasted about two weeks.

"How does a cruise suit you? I can't leave the boat here."

"I don't think so."

"No?"

"I'm pretty busy with the house."

"That reminds me. There's an attaché case stuffed with money hanging on a hook in your cistern."

"What am I supposed to do with it?"

"Build your gazebo and deck, get some furniture and appliances, put in some landscaping, get yourself a decent vehicle."

"You're not coming back, are you?"

"I'm talking in the event I get torpedoed by a U-boat—"

"I'm sure they've all run out of fuel by now."

"Or a Los Angeles-class attack sub."

"I'll leave the light on for you. You need a little time with yourself."

"I do?"

"I've been doing some thinking."

"And?"

"I decided it was time for me to grow up. No more excessive alcohol consumption, no more public nudity—except at the beach—no more living out of a backpack. I decided— Don't get me wrong, but I decided that you need to grow up as well."

"Don't you think I'm a little old to grow up?" I asked.

"No, but I do think you're like a little old not to have already grown up."

25

After I delivered Billie to the dinghy dock and got *Argo* underway, I strapped myself into the safety harness and motored out of Flamingo Bay, blindfolded by the storm.

Recalling all the boats from Flamingo Bay that fled Hurricane Hugo only to sink at Culebra, I decided I'd sail right into the storm. I figured that sailing into the weather offered as much of a chance of eluding it as trying to flee it. If I didn't miss the worst of it, that was okay, too. I'd learn how my boat handled weather, and I'd learn how I handled my boat.

As a throwback to another century, I usually depended on dead reckoning to get me to where I was going and back home again. I did have a compass and a wristwatch—the two key tools—and I did have a radio. Hell, Cook sailed the globe without a chronometer. Many others did, also, but for most of them, a chronometer wasn't an option: it simply didn't exist.

I like to think of a tropical storm as a bagel—a big donut with a small hole in the center, the storm's eye, where nothing happens. The eye is usually about fifteen miles in diameter. Because the storm rotates counterclockwise, the easterly trade wind boosts the wind on the polar side of the storm, while it has the opposite effect on the equatorial side of the storm. Therefore, the most navigable wind is always on the equatorial side of the storm. Unfortunately, that course wasn't an option.

When encountering a tropical storm, the first order of business is to get a general fix on the location of the storm's eye. From the middle of the nineteenth century until the advent of modern technology, sailors relied on Buys Ballot Law—face the true wind, and in the northern hemisphere the center of the depression will be between ninety and a hundred and thirty degrees on your right. I knew the depression's location from the weather service, and I knew its heading—the second order of business.

Taking care of the first two orders of business leads you automatically to the third: put as much distance as you can between your boat and any leeward obstructions to navigation—continents, islands, and reefs, specifically. I had a natural predilection for that behavior: so far, I'd navigated my life to steer clear of human impedimenta.

I couldn't see that I'd cleared Flamingo Bay, but the wind and seas pounded home the fact. I maintained my heading for another half hour. It took great discipline. The waves caught *Argo* nearly broadside, causing her to roll from rail to rail, nearly capsizing her. For every increment of forward progress, I sensed that *Argo* lost twice that in drift. I felt a small victory and a great sense of relief when I brought her full into the wind.

From certain vantages, the Sir Francis Drake Channel appears more of a lake than a channel. A map, however, reveals that the dozens of islands, cays, and rocks that define the channel's boundaries create anything but a continuous border. Still, betting your boat—and maybe your life—that you will hit a safe passage if you wander off course is not a sound wager.

Over the years, I'd talked to several sailors who'd struck their sails, tied their wheels, and rode out Hurricane Hugo below deck. One ended up forty miles from his last charted position, and when he learned where he was, he blanched to realize his boat passed through a channel so tight he'd have been cautious attempting it in broad daylight in good weather. Me, I figured to remain at the helm, be as vigilant as a blind man walking the median of an interstate highway.

One disadvantage: I'd never sailed *Argo* before, so I had only a general idea of her speed and no experience of her handling characteristics. One advantage: I'd sailed the length of the Sir Francis Drake Channel dozens of times. The challenge: could I navigate the channel in an unfamiliar boat while blindfolded?

Argo pitched and rolled and yawed. Every time I sensed a certain rhythm to her movement, an abrupt change occurred and a bucket of cold seawater splashed in my face. I tipped my head up to allow the driving rain to wash the salt from my eyes, sometimes with success, sometimes just successfully catching another bucket of seawater in my face.

I stared at the compass and fought to keep my heading. Every half hour, I switched on the bilge pump and ran it for several minutes. I couldn't hear if the pump worked or tell if the bilge was filling with seawater. Most of the time, I couldn't even hear the diesel. The sea's ferocity—perhaps because I couldn't perceive the full range of its sound or observe it at all—only disconcerted me, but the all-too-audible wind became more and more terrifying. It kept building and screaming in violent rage.

Early exhilaration gradually gave way to interminable tedium. By three A.M., neither the sea nor the wind seemed as big an adversary as exhaustion; I reached the point where I was too tired to be afraid, something I hadn't felt since Vietnam—a dangerous position, a vulnerable position.

All alone on an empty sea in the middle of what felt like a hurricane, I found it necessary to create an artificial stimulant to keep my mind engaged—I'd already examined from every angle the final words Billie uttered at the dinghy dock. I could no longer be sure whether I heard a suggestion or an ultimatum. As I didn't respond well to either, I wanted to believe the distinction didn't matter. I focused instead on the immediacy of my situation. I visualized *Argo* in the midst of a wolf pack of U-boats. She was safe and undetectable, as long as she maintained her present course relative to the U-boats. Any deviation from that course and her position would be revealed, unleashing a subsequent barrage of torpedoes.

I stayed with the wolf pack over an hour before I recognized it was a trap. I sensed the U-boats led me on a course of certain destruction. I had to break out. I turned the wheel ten degrees to port and slipped out of the noose undetected. I stayed on the new heading until dawn.

Dawn only made visible the invisibility of land, sea, and sky. Rain still swept almost horizontally. I couldn't see the mainmast, a boom's length away. A milky shield encapsulated me. The wind may have lost velocity. It could've happened hours ago, but I hadn't noticed it. It was only a matter of degree and not to a degree where relief felt imminent. The waves still bashed *Argo*, but they may have lost momentum, also. All my observations seemed favorable, though ten hours at the wheel had deadened my senses.

An hour passed before I could say for sure the storm was nearly over. Another hour and the rain stopped falling and the wind stopped blowing. The calm was absolute, except for the roiling but comparatively peaceful sea. The sky turned blue. Visibility extended several miles. Dead ahead lay Virgin Gorda, the fat virgin. I felt pretty damn proud of my navigational sense, especially the ten-degree change in course.

I unstrapped the safety harness, tied the wheel, and went below to find a cigarette. It took a bit of doing to get my legs limbered. Exhaustion was complete but magnificent. Back on deck, I decided to continue on to anchor the boat and grab a meal at the Baths—a mural-sized version of the postage-stamp paradise on St. Judas. The rocks scattered on the beach and in the shallows were worthy of Stonehenge. A snaking path led up the steep hillside to a tourist trap, but vendors and restaurateurs offered hot food and cold beer.

I misjudged by an hour the distance to the anchorage—a miscalculation of one hundred percent. I wanted to believe it was my hunger and not my faulty perception. Still, motoring in a dead calm in bright sunshine offered me a lot of time to think, and Billie had given me plenty to think about.

When I left Billie at the dinghy dock, she made it clear she was no day-tripper. What she wanted from me was confirmation I was no day-tripper either. I could prove that by marrying her and becoming the father of her children. "All or nothing," she demanded.

Most of my life I'd scoffed at marriage. I'd scoffed at couples that believed they were going to mix their genes with such success that their children would spring to life fully formed like Athena from the head of Zeus. I'd scoffed at their presumption of their ability to impart to their children the wisdom of the ages—the summation of five hundred generations of humanity—by adolescence. I'd scoffed at their notion that in a world of nearly six billion people a single birth was a miracle. I'd scoffed at the lengths to which they'd go to satisfy their need for a child's unwavering love. I'd scoffed at it all. Now here I was thinking seriously about it—damn seriously.

"It's up to you," Billie said in parting. "But I don't think you'll be happy living in Flamingo Bay if you decline my proposal. You may as well just keep going."

It wasn't a threat, and Billie was right—I needed to be with her or a thousand miles away from her. The orgiastic future always lay somewhere beyond the horizon, and it always seemed to recede just as I felt myself approaching it. Now it seemed I'd run smack into it. Like hitting a brick wall, it left me stunned. Giving up my intangible dream for the tangible object of that dream seemed like a no-brainer. Still, it scared me to death.

To accept Billie's challenge, I had to convince myself that not only was I the best man in Flamingo Bay; I would become the best husband and father. Of all the women in my life, I lived longest with Sarah. That a legitimate argument could be made that I drove her to drug addiction wasn't much of a testimonial for my domestic aptitude. I had experience and at least an idea of how to behave in a relationship with a woman; I had no experience and not much of an idea of how to proceed with a child in the mix.

I lied to Billie a few days earlier when I told her I was more afraid of hurting myself than hurting her. I could continue to sail to the end of the world, to the end of my life, wounded and crippled; I couldn't live with myself if I hurt her.

At the Baths, I dropped anchor. I didn't detect any storm damage ashore. Everything was as I remembered it—rocks, sand, and sea. Only a small number of people were on the beach. I dinghied to shore and asked a man—building an elaborate sandcastle with his family— whether the businesses up the hill were operating

"Limping along," he said. "But you can get a meal."

"How bad was the storm?"

"I've seen worse. The roofs installed with hurricane clips stayed on. Some without clips didn't. We try to bury our electrical and phone cables here, so it's never as big a mess as in the U.S. islands."

"Penny-wise and pound-foolish. We'd be better off if we followed your practices instead of your aphorisms."

"Go grab something to eat," he said.

"Good idea."

"Something to tell your children about," he called after me, as I started up the sandy trail that threaded among gigantic rocks.

I waved.

When I reached the end of the trail, the storm damage became apparent. Trees and branches were down. Succulents looked as though they'd exploded, and their fleshy chunks lay scattered on a thick wet carpet of green leaves. A blue tarp covered a section of the restaurant's roof. I entered the building and learned that the electricity still functioned.

The waitress brought me a cold beer. Several minutes later, she brought me another cold beer and a hot cheeseburger. I wolfed down the burger.

"You look like you could use another," she said.

"I'll wait a few minutes. It's too soon to tell."

"You must have had a rough night."

"Big wind. Big seas. Big appetite. Maybe I should take another look at your menu."

She brought me a menu. After I looked it over, I raised my eyes to the diamond-dusted swells of the blue sea. There it was: the promise of adventure, the gateway to everywhere, a new beginning.

I didn't know if it was just my exhaustion, but the challenge did nothing to energize me. Again, I recognized that I was no longer the young eager man of my youth. Still, I understood I had one last chance to become the man I wanted to be. I closed the menu. The waitress approached.

"Have you decided yet?"

"I'll have two chicken sandwiches, two Cokes, and two bottles of water."

"You're going to eat all that?"

"Make it to go," I said. "I have to get back to St. Judas. I'm getting married tomorrow."